ULTIMATE REVENGE

At the bottom of the darkened stairway, Marsh spoke behind Lubov's back. "The light switch is that string in front of you. Pull it."

Lubov did and found himself standing in shock before Marsh's electronic arsenal. It was an overwhelming array of computers and their related hardware—the equal of a mini war room, submarine control room, or missile launch room.

What the hell does Marsh need with all this?

Then, with a stunning flash of insight, Lubov moved to the very edge of understanding . . . of comprehending who and what Marsh really was. But just as the thought was forming . . . a split second before he could complete it . . . Marsh's heavy glass Coke bottle exploded against the back of his head.

The insight was lost—forever.

QUANTITY SALES

INDIVIDUAL SALES

MISMATCH

□ □ □ □ □ □ □ □ □ □ □ □ □ □ □

Lloyd Pye

A DELL BOOK

Published by
Dell Publishing
a division of
Bantam Doubleday Dell Publishing Group, Inc.
666 Fifth Avenue
New York, New York 10103

The trademark Dell ® is registered in the U.S. Patent and
Trademark Office.

ISBN: 0-440-20221-3

Printed in the United States of America
Published simultaneously in Canada

January 1989

10 9 8 7 6 5 4 3 2 1

KRI

To my parents,
for their incredible faith in me.
And to Susan and Carolyn,
for seeing me through the worst of it.

Acknowledgments

With any writing project of this scope and duration, it's inevitable that the author will become indebted to many people; some for technical information, some for creative advice, and some for other support they were called upon to provide. Because of that fact, I'd like to publicly thank the following people for the tremendous debt of gratitude I owe them.

For technical expertise:

        Milton D. "Buddy" Bel (U.S.M.C. Ret.)
        Claire Anderson Bel (U.S.N. Ret.)
        John "Cap'n Crunch" Draper
        Bobby A. McDaniel, Jr. (U.S.N.)

For creative input:

Thomas Congdon	Richard Pine
Brian DeFiore	Thomas W. Pye
Russell Galen	Holly Roberts
Robert Mecoy	Genevieve Young

For steadfast loyalty and friendship:

Bob Dawson	Carolyn Mistoler
Jerry Johnson	Marnie Purciel
Mike MacNees	Susan Purciel
Rosalie Mars	Jim Spring

FOREWORD

One of this century's most bizarre, apparently pointless governmental decrees broke the Ma Bell communications monolith into several factious parts. At a time of otherwise rapid technological advance, our most fundamental system of information transferral was forced to replace its world-famous efficiency with massive confusion and heavy-handed ineptitude.

Why did that *really* happen? Why did Washington suddenly order Ma Bell to dismantle herself?

To those on the outside, those dealing with the endless problems it has created, the breakup of Ma Bell seems the absolute height of moronic governmental bungling. Irrational. Inexcusable. But to those on the inside, those aware of the desperate need for change and responsible for its implementation, it was an act of saving grace for the entire country.

This is the story of why Ma Bell had to go.

PART ONE

Sam Brandt closed the file on his desk with an angry *whap*!

Across the office, his assistant, Charles Doppler, looked up from the file he was working on. "What's wrong, Chief?"

Their office in the San Jose FBI building was straight government issue, filled with the drab colors and furniture some long-ago committee had decided would minimize costs and promote serious attitudes. There were gray-metal desks, chairs, filing cabinets—even a coatrack—surrounded by faded beige walls.

Brandt lifted himself from his squeaky chair and eased toward the window. He was a big, blunt-featured man who still moved with the casual grace of a onetime athlete. He'd made a point of staying in top condition since the day, years ago, when J. Edgar took him aside and poked his beginnings of a paunch.

"Take care of that, Brandt," the Director had said. "Blacks in the Bureau have to set an example." So he'd thrashed himself back into shape and later learned Hoover responded by saying, "Brandt's the only nigger I'd piss on if he was on fire." From an unrepentant racist like Hoover, that was high praise indeed.

"I'm sick of it, Charles," he said in reply to Doppler's question. "Sick to death of the whole damn thing. I want out."

"Awww, come on, Chief. It's not that bad."

Doppler lit a cigarette, then rose from his own desk and moved to the window alongside his boss. The two men gazed out over their third-floor view of a litter-strewn side street in downtown San Jose. Paper trash swirled in gusting winds. An overcast sky intensified their dismal environment.

But it wasn't the atmosphere making Brandt glum.

"It could happen any day," Doppler went on.

"Shhhiiittt . . ." The word peeled off like a patch from a worn-out inner tube. "People been saying that for—what?—better than fifteen years! 'It could happen any day.' I'm sick of it!"

"We'll get him," Doppler insisted. "And if we don't, the ones who come after us will. That's how the system works; that's why it works. Eventually we get them all."

Brandt's heavy shoulders sagged as he leaned forward against the windowsill. "I got this job because I had the attitude for it. I was a hard-nosed, ass-kicking s.o.b. who got things done. But this Ghost Glitch character . . . He's something else! How can I kick his ass when I can't get my hands on him?"

"Listen, Sam, in our two years in this office we've tagged and bagged twelve—count 'em, twelve!—major computer hackers, along with every kind of little fish you can name. And not one of those big fish has gone back to it once we got through with them. Granted, we haven't nailed the Glitch yet. But six other teams were in this room before us, and they didn't do half as well. So give yourself—hell, give *us*—some credit."

Brandt smiled as his young assistant took a deep drag from his cigarette. Doppler was a short, stocky, blond version of himself at that age, which was why they got along so well.

"Six more months," Doppler went on, as smoke swirled from his mouth and nostrils. "Six and we can request rotation without hurting our careers. We can go that long standing on our heads."

Just then the phone on Brandt's desk rang. Doppler glanced up at him with eyebrows raised.

"You get it," Brandt said. "It might be Rainer wanting to chew on me about that last tag's broken ribs. Tell him I'm out."

Doppler went to the desk, saying, "What if it's not Rainer?"

"Then I'm in."

He lifted the receiver after the third ring. "Doppler . . ."

There was a pause as he listened to the message. At first his expression revealed nothing, but then it became animated as he leaned over and picked up a pen. "You got his Hancock?"

He listened again and made a note on a pad on the desk. "We'll be right down!" He recradled the receiver, tore the note off its pad, then looked at Brandt with a wide-eyed, slack-jawed expression the older man had never seen before.

"What? Trouble? Good news?"

"The best!" he rasped. "The Clue Crew thinks they have him!" He glanced at the note. "A guy named Percy Marsh!"

□ ‖ □

Dr. Viktor Lubov stood at a conference table in the western-region FBI's San Francisco headquarters. He was there to instruct the five agents responsible for monitoring Soviet communication-intercept facilities located atop their nearby embassy. All five agents had engineering degrees and understood microwave technology, the subject he was there to discuss.

"In order to end your agony as quickly as possible," he began, "I'll skip my opening joke and get right to the point."

Only two men at the table reacted to that remark's subtle humor. The others were all business. But Lubov didn't mind. He was a polished communicator who spoke in a rich German accent that nearly twenty years in America hadn't been able to erase. Not that he'd ever tried to change his distinctive vocal style.

It was important—even essential—to his real work that people remember who he was and where he came from.

"Five years ago Paxtron Industries developed this," he said, holding up an enlarged photograph of what looked like a car battery without sides. "The PQR-4000 microwave enhancer. Some of you might recall my lecture about it at that time."

One of the men at the table spoke up. "Doesn't it amplify transmission outputs while shortening wavelengths?"

Lubov smiled at the man's recall. "By a third, yes. It was a significant breakthrough in microwave communication because it made our long-line relays highly resistant to interference."

"How long before the Russians stole it from us?" another agent quipped. Everyone in the room laughed, including Lubov.

"I was getting to that. Despite our best efforts to keep it from them, they had a working model within two years. By then we had only a dozen in place at key relay units across the country, so the loss wasn't devastating. In fact, we just kept installing them, and today they're an integral part of the system."

"What's the point here, Dr. Lubov?" Jerome Rainer asked.

Senior Technical Agent Jerome Rainer was in charge of the group clustered at the table. He was responsible for Bureau technical affairs in northern California, Oregon, and Nevada, with special emphasis on all aspects of communication. He took that assignment as seriously as he took himself.

"The Russians didn't stop at simply stealing a PQR-4000," Lubov replied. "They took it apart, figured out how it worked, then reverse-engineered an effective jamming device. Two weeks ago the first of those jammers was installed at their embassy."

"So what?" Rainer pressed. "I mean, they won't be clogging our long-lines just to prove they can do it, will they? That would be insane. And as long as the damn thing just sits there taking up space, where's the threat?"

Lubov stood gazing calmly at his antagonist. Rainer was a lean, tightly strung man in his mid-fifties, with slicked-back gray hair framing a baggy-eyed, basset-hound face. He seemed to have a special dislike for handsome, urbane Dr. Viktor Lubov, and consistently baited him at briefings. Lubov was often annoyed by his harassment but always met it with polite tolerance.

People familiar with Rainer's treatment of Lubov attributed it to the fact that, as a young man, he'd been brutally tortured in a German POW camp. But from a moment several years earlier, when they'd first laid eyes on each other, Lubov had suspected another deeper—and much darker—reason. In his thirty-eight years he'd often seen that same fleeting look of inquiry.

"Significance and meaning are not my concern," he said in response to the senior agent's challenge. "My job as a consultant is to make you and my other clients aware of the latest developments in microwave technology. It's your job to decide how to use what I tell you."

The four earnest faces surrounding Rainer at the table glanced at one another with varying degrees of discomfort. Then they focused on their boss, who was showing the strain of being sparred with. The heavy bags under his eyes twitched.

"Go ahead and speculate," he said evenly.

The men at the table looked back to the tall, elegant man addressing them from the front wall's chart board.

"You might try giving the Russians a dose of their own medicine," he replied. "Steal the blueprints or a working model of their new device. Give them something to think about in terms of your counterespionage capacities, while giving our scientists a starting point for neutralizing their current disadvantage."

Lubov knew there was no chance his proposal would be acted upon, because the Soviet Union held the reins on its scientists so tightly. Anything they happened to develop on their own was usually theirs to keep for as long as it took the U.S. to invent something similar. And because American agents had so little capacity to take hardware or data "through the Curtain," as they occasionally managed with political information, it was easy for Lubov to prick Rainer's ego by pointing out that weakness.

"Thank you for that brilliant suggestion, Dr. Lubov," he said dryly. "It'll definitely be taken under advisement. Now, can we get to the specifics of why you scheduled this meeting?"

Lubov nodded and picked up his lecture notes. He was just about to begin his analysis of the PQR jammer and how it seemed to work when a loud knock came on the conference-room door. Lubov looked first at the door, then questioningly at Rainer.

"Come in!" Rainer shouted.

An agitated young agent burst into the room and made straight for Rainer. He leaned across the table and cupped his hand against his mouth to whisper in the older man's ear.

Rainer listened impassively for a moment, but then his expression transformed and he whipped his head around to shout, "My God! When?"

"Just minutes ago, sir."

Rainer vaulted out of his chair and leaned over the center of the table, whispering to his four associates as they rose and leaned forward to hear him. By focusing all his powers of concentration, Lubov was just able to hear the message:

"There's been a breakthrough in the Ghost Glitch case!"

Rainer then straightened himself to address Lubov in a normal tone. "I'm sorry, Dr. Lubov, but we have to reschedule your presentation for a week or two down the line. We're going to be busy as hell during the next several days."

Lubov began gathering his notes and diagrams as his audience gathered theirs to hurry from the room. "I understand," he said without rancor, disguising the emotions surging within him.

If there was one thing Viktor Lubov did understand, it was the importance of any breakthrough in the FBI's relentless hunt for the Ghost Glitch. But there was no way his listeners could possibly know that—and no way he'd ever want them to know.

He left the conference room behind everyone else, wondering how he might best determine what had been discovered. One thing was certain: He'd do whatever was necessary. This was a golden opportunity to simultaneously serve both his higher purposes.

□ III □

The Clue Room was a small, windowless cubbyhole tucked away in a basement corner of the San Jose FBI building. The three-member Clue Crew occupied an area half the size of upstairs offices, and most of that was taken up by the computers, screens, printers, and charts necessary to do their work. That work was tagging, which was identifying computer thieves and hackers.

The original Clue Crew had been assigned to that inadequate space after the hunt for the Ghost Glitch spilled out of the hands and offices of the field operatives trying to manage it. Experts were hired from outside the Bureau, and as invariably happened to such individuals, they were banished to an in-house Siberia so they wouldn't get in the way of "normal" personnel.

Sam Brandt had never felt comfortable in the close quarters where the hired wizards operated because his bulk added so much to the oppressive atmosphere. Also, despite what he'd managed to learn while pursuing the Ghost Glitch, he was seldom able to grasp the arcane matters discussed and evaluated there.

After an exchange of greetings with the Crew members, he motioned to the main clue board covering the room's front wall. It contained a pastel color-coding of the nearly three hundred clues the Ghost Glitch had left during his career.

"Sure makes sense once you know his name, doesn't it?"

Carl Twigget was so deliriously happy about having finally tagged the Ghost Glitch, he responded with less than the usual delicacy he employed when dealing with "superiors."

"Of course it makes sense! That was the whole point!"

Regular FBI people considered Twigget and his two young assistants, Kramer and Duncan, FBI in name only. They were viewed as number-crunching drones whose only redeeming feature was intellectual firepower, enough to deal with the computer scoundrels making a shambles out of the country's most vital electronic systems. Nevertheless, in the time he'd worked with them Sam Brandt had come to genuinely respect their efforts, so he took no offense at Twigget's condescending tone.

Doppler put in his two cents' worth while reaching for a cigarette. "It's the swamp stuff that really jumps out at me."

"Please don't smoke in here," Twigget said as he moved to the multistriped, multihued clue board. "The air is already foul enough, don't you think?"

Though pudgy and gnomish, Carl Twigget could be assertive enough to make even a hard-nose like Doppler obey a request.

"The swamp clues were always easiest to decipher," he said, passing his hand over dozens of pale green paper strips pinned to the bottom of the board. "References to moss, cypress, alligators—anything like that was a cinch to categorize. So were the fire clues, which correlate perfectly with his address on Ash Street." His hand moved to the center of the board, where many pink strips were clustered under a category headed "Fire."

"What about the nut clues?" Doppler asked, indicating the tan strips bunched in the board's upper left-hand corner.

Twigget grinned. "As you know, nut clues never coexisted with fire clues. First came the nuts, then eight years ago they were replaced by the fires. We never knew what to make of that until we found he'd lived on Pecan Street before moving to Ash."

"And the British parts?" Brandt asked, feeling impelled to join in the discussion.

"Always the hardest to interpret," Twigget admitted, turning to the pale blue strips along the right side of the board. "We never had much of a handle on those until the last clue, the one that said, 'Look to the cinema for a stuttering pool shark.'"

"At first we thought it belonged in the miscellaneous group," Kramer suddenly put in. "The ones we couldn't figure a way to categorize. Then we went to work on it and—bingo!"

"Kramer's a movie buff," Twigget explained, nodding at him.

He stood with Duncan, off to one side. Both men displayed huge grins, clearly as ecstatic as they had every right to be.

"We first looked for literal sharks in films," Kramer went on. "That research covered everything from *Jaws* and *Blue Water, White Death,* down to the most obscure tripe."

Doppler forced a nod while Brandt glanced at the ceiling.

"Then we turned to pool players," Duncan added, "figuring he might have switched connotations on us. You know, substituting card shark for pool hustler. He does that now and then."

"So what did you find?" Doppler asked.

"We went through all pool-related films," Twigget resumed, "from *The Hustler* right on down until we hit an obscure British comedy called *Frazzled.* Kramer had seen it and remembered it had a hysterical scene where two men play billiards—which was yet another switched connotation—and one of them stutters to the point of just being able to get his words out."

"So?" Doppler repeated.

"So we got a copy of that sucker," Duncan gloated, "and found out the stuttering pool shark was named Sir Percy!"

Brandt and Doppler exchanged baffled expressions.

Twigget understood their difficulty. "When we realized Percy is a quintessential British first name, we decided to lump all the British clues under a first-name category. Then we went back and collected all the last names we could find with connections to fire, swamps, and—secondarily—nuts."

"Sounds like a hell of a lot of work," Doppler said.

"It was," Twigget acknowledged. "But then that's what we're here for, isn't it?" He cast a satisfied glance at his youthful assistants, who playfully elbowed each other in the ribs.

"Anyway," Twigget resumed, "once we had a list of all the Percy Swamps and Fires our computers could come up with, we compared them with Bay Area phone records to see if we could find matches with real people. Turned out to be three hundred and sixteen within a hundred-mile radius."

Brandt let out a low whistle.

"When Percy *Marsh* proved to be a top computer debugger," Twigget went on, "that told us he had the Glitch's technical capacity. Then we found out he lives here in San Jose on Ash Street, and previously lived on Pecan Street, so we were sure—"

"Sonofabitch!" Doppler cut in, gazing in awe at the board that had for so many years confounded the best brains in the FBI. Now it all made such logical, perfect sense—like a crossword puzzle's printed solution. "If it hadn't been for those switched connotations, you might've tagged him a long time ago."

Twigget shrugged. "Maybe . . . But even with the switches, there's a consistency in everything he did. He always played fair with us—he was just smarter than we were."

"Yeah?" Brandt said challengingly, turning to lead Doppler from the room. "Well, it's gonna be damn interesting to see how smart that prick feels once we're done with him!"

For several seconds after the two agents were gone, the Clue Crew stood there in silence, realizing their jam-packed cubbyhole would soon be minus all traces of its principal inhabitant.

That thought made the place seem much larger and emptier.

Each member knew that—as with the Glitch himself—their lives and their work would never again be quite the same. Nothing they could hope to do in the future would ever equal matching wits with the greatest computer hacker of them all.

An era was definitely ending.

☐ IV ☐

During the next week the FBI conducted a comprehensive inquiry designed to find out everything there was to know about Percy Marsh. But because classic hackers like the Ghost Glitch seldom committed actual property crimes, their prosecution by usual means was all but impossible. So the responsible field agents had to find means of negotiating over, under, around, and through the spirit and letter of the law.

Marsh's background investigation was spearheaded by Jerome Rainer's group in the San Francisco main office because they had more and better-equipped manpower for doing the tedious legwork and records research a standard BI entailed. Their efforts were rewarded by a six-inch pile of reports that confirmed what everyone chasing the Ghost Glitch had always assumed:

The individual behind it all was a truly extraordinary man.

While Rainer's group gathered personal data, Brandt and Doppler did hands-on fieldwork. They surveilled Marsh and his home to answer two vital questions about him: How and where did he spend his time? After learning that, they were able to determine when he would and would not be home.

Once certain of his daily movement pattern, they obtained a search warrant to break into his house. And because they were in such need of hard evidence linking Marsh to hacking activity, they took Twigget along to make sure they missed nothing their own computer ignorance might cause them to overlook.

All Twigget found was the expected group of unincriminating terminals and modems, although they were connected to a hi-tech amperage meter that protected them and the house phones from eavesdropping devices. Twigget assured the agents that the sensitive nature of Marsh's work required such a setup.

Stymied, they left the place exactly as they'd found it.

Their disappointment was genuine but no real surprise because the Glitch operated in an electronic medium where evidence could be erased by the push of a button. It simply meant they had to take their investigation one step further, up into the mountains above Silicon Valley. They'd discovered Marsh owned a large cabin there, a place where he spent a great deal of time.

As with the house, they waited until certain he'd be gone for several hours, then they broke in and scoured the place.

After searching every drawer, cabinet, and closet in it, they found no trace of computers, or even a telephone to bug. So they left the cabin convinced it was nothing more than a personal getaway utilized for the quiet, peaceful serenity it provided.

Once all their information was collected, they felt prepared to execute Marsh's bagging. They scheduled it for the early morning hours of a busy Monday because it was important to keep his arrest as low-profile as possible. And that was important because media exposure was the last thing they wanted or needed whenever the ethereal nature of a perpetrator's "crimes" meant he had to be prosecuted by illegal means.

Though none of Marsh's pursuers had the slightest moral qualm about their intention to find a way to convict him, they did face one giant, nerve-rattling problem: Any major screw-up could send the area's crime-beat reporters into a feeding frenzy.

While the FBI was busy building the best case against Marsh it could manage, Viktor Lubov was just as busy trying to find out what was going on. But the lid had been screwed down extra-tight on such an important proceeding, so nothing was leaking through the channels he usually employed to monitor developments within the Bureau's San Francisco office.

Those channels were two key secretaries he occasionally slept with, one on each of the building's top two floors. They had access to nearly everything of significance, and neither was reluctant to share what she knew with her casually interested lover. But after consecutive nights in the arms and between the legs of each, Lubov realized everyone lacking a need-to-know was being cut off from access to information about the Glitch.

Once aware of that, he knew it was time to find out if his long-held suspicion about Jerome Rainer was right or wrong. He wished there was some other way because what he had to do would seriously jeopardize his hard-won access to Bureau business. But he couldn't avoid pursuing this case flat out. The Glitch was the only way he could ever get closer to the King, and getting closer to the King was worth almost any risk.

His first task was to tail Rainer for a couple of evenings after work. Both times he went more or less straight home to an unattractive wife and two large dogs in the suburbs. The third night he stopped off at the bar in the lobby of the Exchequer Hotel.

Lubov decided to make his move right then and there.

☐ v ☐

Ivan Gretchko was performing his favorite chore: baby-sitting his three young grandchildren while his divorced daughter was out. If there was a way to combine baby-sitting them with tending his prizewinning rosebushes, the slight, bald, withered old man could seriously compete for the title of World's Happiest Senior Citizen. His grandchildren and his roses were all Ivan Gretchko needed to be content, and his pleasures were only more enjoyable for their simplicity.

At that moment he was amusing Skipper, the youngest, with the classic shell game, an elemental entertainment the five-year-old was still young enough to appreciate. Nine-year-old Mary was watching some mindless drivel on television, while seven-year-old Tommy was absorbed in his collection of superhero comic books.

"Do you *have* to use nalnut shells, Paw-Paw?" Skipper asked, committing one of the few pronunciation mistakes he still made. "Won't bottle caps work?"

Gretchko loved to hear such questions because they showed analytical perception and collateral thinking, manifestations of intelligence not often seen at Skipper's age. Besides, he always enjoyed opportunities to explain life's mysteries to his charges.

"The shells have more to do with tradition than function," he replied, momentarily forgetting the level of his audience.

Skipper's smile vanished and Gretchko immediately knew why. Children never appreciate being reminded of their overwhelming lack of knowledge, even though they're expected to know very little. So the offending statement was quickly amended.

"In other words, you're right: A bottle cap would work if it was big enough for the pea to fit under. For example, a regular pry-it-off cap wouldn't work because that kind is flat and low. But a twist-off cap would definitely—"

"Wait!" Skipper blurted, leaping to his feet and running from the coffee table where Gretchko was working his magic with three walnut hulls and a dried pea. "I'll be right back!"

He returned in moments with a pry-off cap from a bottle of 7-Up. "Can we check and make sure?" His small hand reached out for the pea. Gretchko's bony fingers dropped it into his palm. Wordlessly, with sternly knitted brow, Skipper carefully placed the bottle cap over the pea.

It was almost a fit, but not quite.

"See?" Gretchko said. "It's too low."

Skipper lifted the cap and started twisting and turning it in his

stubby fingers, his fawnlike eyes taking in every detail. He stopped
turning while gazing at the plastic inner lining.

"Can you take that out, Paw-Paw? Will it come out?"

Gretchko pulled a penknife from his pocket and in seconds pried
out the lining. Skipper took back the cap to place it over the pea. It
seemed to fit. He moved it slightly. It slid with ease. He looked up
at his Paw-Paw, beaming. "It works!"

The boy's determination to find out for himself filled Gretchko
with inexpressible joy. Beaming as happily as his grandson, a mist
filled his tired old eyes.

Yes, he thought, *my blood flows in a mind that won't recognize
limits. I'm leaving the finest piece of myself to posterity.*

"And so what have you learned from this little experiment?" he
asked as he let the bottle cap join the shuffle.

Skipper was absorbed in the three-way movement and shook his
head absently. "I don't know."

Gretchko stopped but kept his hands on the shells and cap.
Skipper's wide eyes looked up from the coffee table's surface.

"Things are not always what they seem. You must try to remember that. It's an important lesson about life."

Skipper smiled and shrugged his small shoulders. "Okay, Paw-
Paw, I'll try."

You don't have to, Gretchko thought. *The ones like us always
know—and we never forget.*

☐ VI ☐

Viktor Lubov was a truly handsome man. His tanned, flawless
skin, curly blond hair, and square-cut features turned the heads of
most women, and some men, wherever he went. And not only was
he good-looking, he clothed his tall, athletic body in expensive,
stylish apparel—usually pearl-gray three-piece suits he chose to
highlight his bluish-gray eyes.

In short, he entered the Exchequer's classy barroom with everything going for him in his current endeavor.

Rainer wasn't at the bar itself, which was centrally located to
leave its patrons visible to hotel guests poking their heads in to

check out the action. Lubov expected his aging prey to be exactly where he was, tucked away in a rear booth where he could see everything beyond while being seen only by individuals like himself: those who were looking.

Because Lubov knew the routine, he headed for another rear booth on the opposite side of the bar. He gave no sign of recognition as he felt several pairs of eyes follow him across the room. He took his seat and calmly perused the wine list, waiting to see how Rainer would respond to his unexpected appearance and even more unexpected choice of seating.

Lubov knew if he was right about Rainer, the man would either get up and leave or come over and begin a conversation. If he was wrong, Rainer would simply finish his drink, maybe nod in greeting if their eyes met, then leave when he was damn good and ready. That would put Lubov back on the street and fresh out of ideas about where to turn for the information he needed.

He didn't have to wait long for an answer. Within a minute of his sitting down, a waitress appeared to take his drink order. Within a minute of that she had the glass on his table. Within a minute of her departure Rainer stood, crossed the room, and slid into the booth seat opposite.

"Fancy meeting you here," he said without preamble, his thin lips spreading into a faint smile across his repellent face.

Lubov looked up with as much surprise as he could muster. "Well, hello, Jerome. How are you this evening?"

Rainer offered a noncommittal shrug. "Hoping I'm in the same shape as you, sport."

"And what might that be?" Lubov countered in carefully measured tones. This was a routine he'd been through a few times before, whenever it was necessary to get information available in no other way. He wasn't expert at it—and hoped he never would be—but he understood how the game was played.

"Alone and looking for action," Rainer said, his wary eyes boring holes in Lubov's from below his oily, slicked-back hair.

Lubov took a sip from his drink. "What do you mean by 'action,' Jerome? I mean, you're a married man, aren't you?"

This was it. He'd either decide Lubov was safe and would commit himself now, or he'd back off and pretend he meant something else entirely. Lubov held his gaze without wavering, hoping he wasn't being too direct.

Rainer returned his gaze, thinking, assessing. He had to be ever so careful about who he let into his private little world, which was why he patronized the Exchequer bar. In it he was more likely to meet men in his same situation—those living double lives who couldn't afford to have their own secrets exposed.

"My marriage is a necessity for my work," he finally said, making clear his decision that Lubov was a kindred spirit. "You must know how that goes. It's almost a tradition in the FBI."

Lubov had indeed heard that, often, although the first time had been years before when he was being trained for his defection. America's FBI, he'd been told, was a haven for men with sexual identity problems, especially those with homosexual tendencies who lacked the courage or ability to live openly. That was a result of the tolerance wrought within the Bureau by J. Edgar Hoover's apparent homosexuality.

"What I don't understand," Rainer went on, "is why you never let me know about yourself before now. I've been ready for you since the first time I saw you. Surely you knew that."

Lubov recalled the moment, visualizing the intense yet furtive look of a man searching for his own reflection in another man's eyes. At that time he'd had no particular use for Rainer, which was hardly something he could admit now.

"You never seemed to like me," he replied, letting just a hint of petulance shade his voice. This part, too, was critical, and he wanted to get it exactly right.

Rainer's expression softened, just as Lubov hoped. "I *had* to act that way toward you," he said plaintively. "I have to act that way toward everybody. Otherwise, someone might suspect I'm . . . what I am. You understand that, don't you?"

Lubov looked away, as an offended woman might. He wanted Rainer to take the leading role in their encounter because the dominant partner was more obligated to speak. Later, in bed, that would be vital when Lubov started asking about his work.

"Why don't we leave now?" Rainer suggested, unable to keep the welling urgency out of his voice. "I just can't wait to get started showing you how sorry I am for how I've treated you. I've been terrible to you, I know, and I should be punished."

That statement told Lubov he'd made a blunder regarding Rainer's POW experience. He should have considered that everyone reacts differently to torture, with some developing a perverse kind of love for their oppressors while becoming addicted to the process itself. Rainer was clearly one of those types.

That meant their encounter wouldn't involve sex—at least, not "normal" sex. Rainer was a masochist seeking physical abuse, nothing more or less. Which was fine by Lubov. Beating what he wanted to know out of the man would be infinitely more tolerable than the sexual alternatives.

He did have that to be grateful for.

□ VII □

Men like Rainer stay in a state of semi-arousal because they never know when their next encounter might occur. So they keep close at hand whatever paraphernalia is necessary to satisfy their fetish, which in Rainer's case was a gym bag filled with black-leather bondage gear locked and hidden in his car trunk. They also keep a place where they won't be disturbed, and Rainer leased an isolated, run-down farmhouse thirty miles away.

It was a bare, Spartan extension of a man with a highly developed taste for pain.

Like most people who are sexually manipulated by someone trained to do it properly, Rainer had no inkling he was being used. He was so absorbed with gratifying his perverse urges, he never thought to question why or how Lubov so easily fell into the role of a demanding "master." He chose to assume he'd simply stumbled across an ideal partner, and he thanked his lucky stars for finally bringing him into his life in that way.

The thoroughness of Lubov's training showed in his use of Rainer's black-leather bondage gear and his braided quirt. With judicious application of the quirt's frayed tip, he forced his "slave" to undress. Then, using the complicated straps and their attached chains, he trussed Rainer into a painfully contorted backward bow.

After that, it seemed perfectly natural to force the slave to disclose "secrets" about himself.

Because Lubov was careful never to ask anything specific, and because he administered the quirt in a totally random fashion, Rainer wound up spilling his guts about a wide variety of subjects. And, predictably, included in those "confessions" were some pertinent details of the Percy Marsh investigation.

It was midnight before they took leave of each other, both promising to repeat the experience soon. As much as Lubov hated to think about maintaining a sadomasochistic relationship with Rainer, he knew he had no choice. Based on what he'd learned in that first encounter, the Ghost Glitch case was shaping up as a drawn-out, complex affair he'd *have* to stay abreast of.

For now the best he could do was take what he'd just learned and make the wisest, most efficient use of it. There were several competing factors to consider, some of which he had strong personal feelings about. But it was most important that he consider and serve his life's highest purpose.

That made this one of the few times in his career when he felt a need for advice from someone less emotionally involved. And there was only one individual in all the world he'd consider bringing such a problem to: his "grandfather."

When he was safely away from Rainer, Lubov called an airline reservation service. He found the next available flight to San Luis Obispo was at nine the following morning, and he booked himself on it. Time was tight but not critical, so he could afford to wait the extra few hours. Besides, he'd make a much better presentation of the situation if he slept beforehand.

His alarm went off at seven.

He stuck his head under an ice-cold shower to clear the cobwebs, then used his phreaking rig to call his grandfather to arrange their rendezvous. As expected, the old man needed several rings to answer his phone because he normally spent early mornings out in his rose garden.

"Grandfather, this is Cousin Albert," Lubov said. That was to announce this as a business rather than a social call.

"Yes, Cousin Albert," the old man replied matter-of-factly. "How may I help you?"

Lubov indicated that the situation wasn't an emergency by saying, "I have a problem I'd like to discuss." The word *accident* was used to denote a crisis. "I can be there at eleven."

"I've made plans to take my grandchildren to the beach later this morning. Would that inconvenience you too much?"

"Not at all. Is there a way I can find you?"

"We usually stay near lifeguard tower number three."

"Tower number three. I'll see you there."

"Good-bye, Cousin Albert. And good luck."

"Thank you, Grandfather. Good luck to you too."

Lubov hung up smiling, thinking of what a genuine pleasure it was going to be to meet once again with his old friend and mentor, the legendary Ivan Gretchko.

□ VIII □

Soviet "sleepers" seldom know about one another's existence because compartmentalization is so essential to their long-term success. The fewer people who know of a sleeper's activities, the fewer are the chances of eventual exposure. Consequently, it's almost unthinkable that one should know about and contribute to furthering another's nonspying career.

Ivan Gretchko and Viktor Lubov were exceptions to that rule.

Once Lubov had undergone the rigors of his defection, his assimilation into the American scientific community was overseen by Gretchko. They'd maintained close personal contact during the first decade of Lubov's ongoing penetration, and had shared occasional visits and regular phone conversations since Gretchko's retirement. This would be their first face-to-face meeting in a year, and Lubov wondered if the old man had changed.

One thing he knew would never change was his own high regard for the man he considered the most effective Soviet agent ever to have achieved deep cover in the United States.

* * *

Ivan Gretchko was a man worthy of Lubov's respect.

In the years preceding World War II, Stalin himself had conceived the idea of planting long-term sleepers in the Allied camps. Even then he suspected the Allies might one day become his enemies, just as Churchill and Roosevelt had believed Stalin might become the world's next Hitler. All three leaders were eventually proved correct.

Before the outbreak of hostilities, Gretchko was a rising young physics student and then a physics teacher at Leningrad University. Fluent in German and French, he and six others like himself were recruited for the sleeper program early in 1937. Those idealistic young men went to Moscow to undergo various plastic surgeries and a rigorous two-year training program.

In 1939 they were assigned countries to infiltrate as refugees from the German anti-Jew campaign. For security reasons none was told where the others were going, but obvious target countries were America, Great Britain, and Canada. Gretchko was assigned to the U.S. With a superb background in physics and a convincing cover story, he became a member in good standing within the expanding ranks of German scientists, technicians, and intellectuals fleeing Nazi persecution.

When the U.S. began its push to develop the atomic bomb, Ivan Gretchko—by then known as Wolfgang Wollenstein—was fully accredited among his peers as a man capable of working on the ultrasecret Manhattan Project. And though others tried, with varying degrees of success, to steal America's atomic secrets for the Soviets, it was Gretchko, working within the Project itself, who almost single-handedly brought his homeland nuclear parity.

Gretchko/Wollenstein stayed at the forefront of American nuclear research until his forced retirement at the age of sixty-eight. There was no question of his returning to Mother Russia because he'd married an American woman and raised a family of two sons and a daughter. So despite being one of the USSR's greatest heroes, fully deserving of an honored place among the Soviet elite, he chose to live in obscurity with his prized rosebushes and his three grandchildren who lived nearby.

Then, when he was seventy-two, his wife died, and within months he became a grandfather of a very different sort.

By then the Soviets had planted many dozens of sleepers throughout the complete fabric of American science and technology, choosing to concentrate there instead of the political arena, where intense media scrutiny made it impossible to conceal or alter backgrounds convincingly.

One such sleeper was Viktor Lubov.

Lubov's main responsibility was keeping track of, and passing along, all U.S. developments in microwave technology. In addition, he was expected to keep his eyes and ears open at the government agencies that used his services as a microwave expert. All of which he did, and did well. But on his own initiative he'd become deeply involved in an illegal activity called "phone phreaking."

Because no one in Moscow understood the intricacies or the potential value of phreaking, that endeavor wasn't officially approved. But the information he gained from his consulting practice kept his KGB handlers quiet about the phreaking.

Sleepers like Lubov had an assigned channel for relaying stolen information: the unbreakable codes of one-time-pads. One-time-pad codes were delivered to secure dead-drops, then passed hand to hand from their point of origin to Washington. From there they were taken by diplomatic courier to Moscow.

Although such cumbersome relays required several days to complete, their security was virtually foolproof. So they were always the preferred system. However, when an emergency developed . . . when a situation or breakthrough had to be relayed immediately . . . then the grandfather network came into play.

Grandfathers were old ex-agents, like Gretchko, who no longer had primary access in their fields of expertise, and who, by circumstance or choice, were able to live alone. Such men were then given control of a top-secret VLF, or Very Low Frequency, radio—the ones used to make emergency contacts with the Soviet monitor submarines that continually prowled America's East and West Coast waters.

In ways that younger agents simply couldn't match, grandfathers had proven their fitness for handling such a critically important job. Which was why Lubov needed to talk to Gretchko about what he'd learned from Rainer. He couldn't decide whether or not it warranted an emergency relay, but he knew the old man could.

If Gretchko felt it was advisable to transmit, then they'd transmit; if not, they wouldn't. It was a toss-up situation that could work out well in either of two directions, but not both.

□ IX □

Lifeguard tower number three wasn't hard to find because of the huge green number painted on the back of each one. And the withered little wisp of Gretchko's body was just as easy to spot beneath a large red-and-black striped beach umbrella.

He sat in a low canvas half-chair, his spindly legs sprawled toward the water, wearing a faded Dodgers cap, tattered sneakers, baggy green bathing trunks, and a white T-shirt with PEACE NOW emblazoned across the chest in big letters.

Lubov was squatting at the old man's side before he realized he had company. "You look like a teenager out here, Ivan," he said, removing his sunglasses while extending his right hand.

"Viktor!" Gretchko exclaimed, removing his own dark glasses to reveal narrow crescents of wrinkles under delighted brown eyes. "It's so good to see you again!" He pushed himself more upright in his chair as he shook Lubov's hand. "Are you well?"

"I'm in good health, if that's what you mean. And you?"

Gretchko gave a brief wave of dismissal. "The usual old-man's infirmities doing what they can to slow me down." Then a sly wink. "Ten years from now I might have real problems."

Lubov smiled, then squinted against the glare reflected off the sand and water. "What are your grandchildren doing?"

Gretchko spread his arms in both directions. "What children always do at the beach—playing! But don't worry. They return here only for food, soda, or money, and they never stay long."

Lubov was dressed casually to fit in at the beach, so he didn't mind using his chino-clad rump to wriggle a comfortable depression into the sand. Then he locked his arms around his tucked-up knees and began. "Remember the Ghost Glitch?"

"The computer fellow? The one who breaks into top-secret data banks just to leave clues behind?"

Lubov nodded. "He's been identified as one Percy Marsh, a debugger from San Jose. Supposed to be the best in the world."

Gretchko returned his nod. "Makes sense. Only a man like that could be the Ghost Glitch."

Lubov swirled a finger in the sand, tracing an infinity symbol. "He'll be arrested at dawn the day after tomorrow."

"You say that as if it's the problem you spoke of."

"It is. . . ."

Gretchko shifted in his chair so he could look at Lubov without turning his head so sharply. "I don't understand."

Lubov smoothed over the infinity symbol, replacing it with a question mark. "The Glitch has helped the Network on several occasions, which proves the King's claim of close friendship."

A frown creased Gretchko's wrinkled face. "I'll never understand your fascination with the King and his damn phone phreaking! It's a pointless waste of your time and talents."

"No, it isn't!" Lubov countered. "Phreaking can provide a key to disrupting many of America's communication systems. If our forces should ever invade, any disruption could be vital."

"But be practical, Viktor. An invasion will never come."

"Neither you nor I, nor anyone like us, can afford to make that assumption. So we can never cut corners. Never!"

That same difference of opinion had led them into arguments on several past occasions. Both men knew it and wanted to avoid moving any farther down that path. So they said nothing for several seconds, then Gretchko changed the subject.

"Let's concentrate on the problem you see in all this."

Lubov nodded. "I must decide whether to turn the Glitch over to Moscow for subversion by our specialists, or . . ."

He paused before expressing his other option.

"Or . . . ?" Gretchko urged.

"Tell no one—and subvert him myself."

To do that would be a serious breach of Lubov's mandate as a sleeper, not to mention a dangerous risk to his cover. Gretchko could only assume he had extraordinary reasons for suggesting such a thing. "To what purpose?" he asked.

"So I can use him to become acquainted with the King. It's been twelve years, Ivan—twelve long, frustrating years."

Gretchko considered only for a moment. "To me, there is no choice and no problem. The computer knowledge this man has is far more important than a possible introduction to the King."

"But over time I might get the information both possess."

"Not the kind of detailed analyses our specialists can get."

"If I learn as much about computers as I've learned about telephone systems, I can get it all—every bit."

"Listen, if it's just a matter of learning the King's name, then I'm sure our specialists will find out—"

"It's not just his name!" Lubov cut in. "You could give me that right now, this minute, and it wouldn't do any good. I've worked with him for years; I know him. He's the most intelligent, cautious, paranoid man I've ever known, and any meeting I might arrange would only scare him away."

He paused, gathered up a fistful of sand, then flung it toward the water. That simple physical action drained off much of the anxiety he was feeling. When he resumed speaking, it was in his normal, controlled tone of voice.

"The only way I can get close enough to the King to find out what I want to know is to gain his trust. And the best way to do that is to first gain the trust of the only friend I'm aware of him having—the Ghost Glitch."

"What about your duty to the Motherland? And to the Party?" Gretchko didn't spy for patriotic reasons, but he knew Lubov did. Mentioning the Motherland and the Party to a man like him was like recalling Mom and apple pie to a patriotic American.

Lubov sighed wistfully as he smoothed over the series of question marks he'd dug all around himself. "That's why I'm here talking to you, Ivan. I can't ignore my personal feelings about the King, so any decision I make is tainted by that."

Gretchko gazed at the younger man he respected and admired in so many ways. He knew that discovering the King's identity had been an obsession with Lubov since his university days. He also knew how fervently Lubov believed in the potential value of phone phreaking. He also had to admit that he himself didn't know enough about phreaking to assess its importance fairly.

In contrast, he felt Lubov was being exceptionally fair by coming to him for advice. So could he afford to do less? Could he unilaterally make a decision with such far-reaching ramifications? What if Lubov *could* get the Glitch to introduce him to the King? What if he *did* find out what both men knew? What if he passed that gold mine of information back to Moscow?

Wasn't such a windfall worth any kind of risk or delay?

He turned his eyes from Lubov to gaze at the expanse of Pacific Ocean spread beyond his feet. Out there somewhere, he knew, approximately two hundred miles from where he sat, a monitor submarine was cruising south-to-north, waiting to relay his emergency message to send computer specialists and a subversion team to begin picking Percy Marsh's brain apart.

The question was . . . should he send for them?

If the answer was yes, then Lubov was right about time being short. The subversion team needed to start right after Marsh was arrested because that was the ideal time to introduce new people into his life. He'd be emotionally devastated, his world turned upside down, and as ripe for being subverted as he'd ever be.

Whatever he liked—males or females; young or old; blondes, brunettes, or redheads—his favorites would be discovered and provided. Then would come the surreptitiously supplied drugs that would eventually have him telling those agents everything he knew about how to access top-secret government computers.

On the other hand, Lubov might be able to gain that same essential information by himself. But he'd have to take his time and move carefully, avoiding any risk to his relationship with the King. Not only that, he'd have to be certain he never let his emotional attachments—to phreaking *and* the King—get in the way of what he had to find out from Marsh about computers.

Could he do it? Could any man walk such a fine line?

So many doubts, so many variables, and only one best solution. Gretchko could see why Lubov wanted help making this decision. He felt himself wishing he could find some way to ease the burden of it.

"How strongly do you feel about this, Viktor?" he finally asked. "Do you really believe you can get to both of them?"

Lubov paused before nodding. "It may take months—perhaps as

much as a year—but yes, I can do it. Every man has his own weaknesses to be exploited, including Marsh and whoever the King turns out to be. I'll find those weaknesses, whatever they are."

Gretchko gave one last consideration, then made up his mind. "You have my full support, Viktor, for as long as you need it."

Lubov slapped his palms into the sand, delighted. "Thank you, Ivan! I appreciate that vote of confidence."

"What's your first step?"

Glowing with anticipation, Lubov replied, "Exactly what a subversion team would do. A day or two after his arrest, I'll find a way to introduce myself to him. From that point on, I'll simply take whatever opportunities come my way."

"Will there be surveillance to worry about?"

Lubov shook his head. "They wouldn't be arresting him if they didn't already have enough to make a case. And they'll assume he won't hack again while waiting to come to trial."

At that, Skipper appeared in the distance, running up the beach toward his home-base landmark, his Paw-Paw's distinctive umbrella. Gretchko noticed him and pointed him out, so Lubov quickly said good-bye and left to go catch his return flight.

Now it was just a matter of time—something Percy Marsh was rapidly running out of.

☐ X ☐

Faint gray fingers of light smudged the eastern sky. Dawn. Brandt's favorite time to bag hackers. He enjoyed watching the poor bastards struggle to fight off sleep while trying to cope with the colossal shithammer he and Doppler dropped on them.

He was gliding a nondescript FBI sedan through an exclusive neighborhood's still, silent, empty streets, tracking along their predetermined route. With his foot off the accelerator and the car coasting in gear, he drove easily without headlights.

He glanced at Doppler peering out over the dashboard, one of his ever-present cigarettes wiggling fitfully just beyond his thin, pale lips. The wiggling stopped as he took a deep drag, then it resumed as fitfully as before. Brandt almost smiled.

Doppler was at his best when nervous, and he was definitely nervous about bagging a legend. That cigarette was the last in a pack he'd steadily gone through since they'd met at four A.M.

Although each street corner in the area was illuminated by a mercury-vapor lamp, Marsh's house wasn't clearly visible. It was the middle one of three set well back from the curb, which gave good cover for entries—legal or otherwise. They expected this time to be as easy as when he'd gone to his mountain retreat.

Brandt eased the car against the curb opposite the familiar red-brick, gray-tile-roofed bungalow to their left. He cut the engine as Doppler's grim blue eyes flicked up and down the street. As both men expected, not a creature was stirring.

Doppler pulled a final drag from his last butt and stubbed it in the ashtray. "Let's go kick some ass. . . ."

They moved across the street and along the cement walkway, heads steady but eyes moving in all directions. At the front portico Brandt turned his back to the door, watching the street for paperboys or crack-of-dawn joggers.

Doppler reached into his coat to remove a well-worn leather packet the size of a nail-clipper kit. Hidden behind Brandt's huge physique, he unzipped it, squatted in front of the lock, pulled out a tumbler pick and a tension tool, then went to work.

Two minutes later the dead bolt released. The door moved until it was stopped by an inner chain. Doppler reached into his kit for a hinged angle-iron. The chain was bypassed in another twenty seconds, and both men were quickly inside.

While Doppler repacked his kit, Brandt eased the door shut with the back of his hand. He knew there'd be no sign of forced entry because Doppler never left tracks. He was already one of the best lock men in the Bureau.

Brandt turned to find his partner scanning the living room with a pencil flashlight's narrow, laserlike beam. They followed the dancing ray as it played over chairs, couches, and tables, into a hallway. Nothing had been moved since they were there before, so they moved ahead confidently.

They tiptoed to Marsh's bedroom at the end of the hallway. Doppler moved the beam through the open door, over to a big mound centered on the bed. Satisfied that everything was in order, he put the flashlight back in his pocket and exchanged it for a handkerchief. He used the handkerchief both to close the door's inner lock, and then to ease it shut until its bolt clicked.

He and Brandt drew .38s from holsters under their arms.

"Make it good," he muttered as he stood aside, "but not like that last guy. Broken ribs are too obvious."

Brandt's huge white teeth flashed in his black face. "Don't worry, partner, I'll be gentle." With that he lifted his size-fourteen foot and kicked alongside the doorknob.

A reverberating crash rattled the silent house as the doorjamb split and the door itself slammed against the bedroom wall. As it swung open, Doppler moved through to flick on the light; then he hopped to the foot of the bed and planted his feet, extending his .38 down at Marsh.

"Freeze, motherfucker!"

Brandt, meanwhile, regained his balance and rushed in behind Doppler. He found Marsh blinking in confusion at the sudden sound and light, unable to rouse himself to his peril.

Despite Doppler's warning, Marsh reached for a pair of glasses on the bedside table. Brandt stopped that movement with a sharp backhand slap, grabbed a handful of dark hair, pinned a knee to his quarry's chest, then deliberately jammed the .38's barrel into the mound of flesh that was his cheek.

The gun barrel's well-aimed gouge dug into Marsh's trigeminus nerve, sending a bolt of crackling pain searing across his face. He winced and twisted beneath the hazy black blob holding him down, barely realizing this nightmare was real.

Then he heard a booming, resonant voice. "Easy, shithead! One more move and you're dead!"

Suddenly, everything connected in his sleep-fuzzed brain. The whole sequence fell into place as he realized his dire predicament and cut loose with a shriek of absolute terror:

"Eeeeeeeeiiiiiiil"

Brandt lifted his knee and brought the butt of his .38 down in a vicious arc. It struck Marsh in the solar plexus, driving the air from his lungs while paralyzing his diaphragm. That left him curled in a fetal position, desperately trying to suck back any molecule of the wind he'd just lost.

Brandt and Doppler holstered their weapons, grabbed Marsh under the arms, then yanked his pajama-clad body onto the floor. In so doing, Doppler lost his grip, which caused Brandt to lose his. Marsh crumpled into a wheezing heap at their feet.

"Christ!" Brandt snapped. "Hold on to him!"

"He weighs a ton!"

They both reached down to get secure holds, then dragged Marsh across the bedroom floor to the bathroom. They put him near the toilet, where he lay gurgling and sputtering as air seeped back into his spasming lungs.

While Doppler turned on the overhead light, Brandt cuffed Marsh's hands behind his back. Then he lifted him to his knees, grabbed another handful of hair, and yanked it. That left Marsh staring up bug-eyed at the sinister faces of his captors.

"Think you're a wise guy, huh?" Brandt shouted. "Like to play funny games? Well, I've got some news for you, pal! This fucking game is *over,* and you just crapped out!"

He lifted the toilet seat and plunged Marsh's face into the bowl. Marsh's mouth slammed into the porcelain, splitting his lips top and bottom. Blinding pain shot into his nose and eyes as his top two front teeth broke in half and slid to the bottom.

After about a half minute underwater, his face was lifted. He came up spewing bloody water through his split lips.

"He's making a mess!" Doppler howled, knowing it would be his job to clean it up later.

Brandt slapped Marsh hard on the ear. "Don't get blood everywhere, asshole!" Then he snapped his head back again and was delighted to see the pain, fear, and wounds etched across his victim's face, along with the missing front teeth.

"Now listen, and listen good! You been damn lucky for a long time; you ran us pretty ragged. But now we know who you are and where you live, and you won't ever be able to hide from us again. So don't even dream about hacking anymore, or we'll find out about it and hunt you down. And the next time we come after your fat ass, we'll be coming to kill you!"

Doppler then added his own threat. "And don't think it's not easy for us to croak a scumball like you and get away with it. Nothing will happen to us for busting in here and roughing you up

—it's our word against yours. And it'll be just the same if we come after you for keeps. So think about that long and hard if you ever get another urge to hack. Understand?"

Marsh tried to nod and say yes—anything to save himself from those maniacs. But before he could respond, Brandt jammed his head back into the toilet and shoved it all the way to the bottom, as if trying to squeeze it into the sewage system. Then he looked over at Doppler and winked.

"Flush it."

Doppler complied and Marsh's body started heaving as the water rose to cover his ears. When the level got near the rim, Brandt lifted his head enough so there'd be no spillover, but shoved it back down when the water started dropping.

Finally, after more than a minute, Marsh's thrashing body began to sag. Brandt waited a few more seconds, then lifted his victim's head. Marsh came up spewing bloody water again as he coughed up several drafts. Brandt waited for the coughing to subside, then once again cuffed him on the ear.

"You see? That's how easy it is for us to kill someone. I keep you down a few more seconds, you're a past tense. So don't miss the message I'm sending here. Unless your hacking career is history, *you're* history! You got my word on it."

He released his grip on Marsh's hair, allowing him to slide onto the floor, where he lay stunned and bleeding and gasping for air. Grinning with satisfaction, Brandt then turned to Doppler for a technical assessment. "Think we made our point?"

Doppler looked down at the blubbery pile of flesh quivering with shock at Brandt's feet. He always suffered a pang of deflation when the best part of the job was over. But this time was especially acute because he'd anticipated it so intensely.

"I'll go call," he said without emotion.

"Tell them not to rush. We need time to clean the mess."

Doppler smirked, knowing who'd be required to do the lion's share of the cleaning. But what could he do? He was the junior partner. So he turned to go call the San Jose city police, while Brandt began the tedious enumeration of Marsh's legal rights.

* * *

When they'd searched the house earlier, they'd found a gray cordless phone in the top drawer of the nightstand beside the bed. They'd noticed that odd location because most people kept theirs *on* the nightstand. Now Doppler sought it with no concern for its location. He was fresh out of smokes and only cared about the pack of Marlboros he remembered lying beside it.

He sat on the edge of the bed, opened the drawer, and lifted the crushproof box. As he did so, a faint alarm started ringing in his brain: not an ashtray in sight for a man who apparently smoked in bed. But the warning was drowned out by his need for a nicotine fix. He flipped the pack's top and found it full.

He removed a cigarette from the first row, lit up, then gagged on the stalest smoke he'd ever inhaled. He stubbed that one out and removed another, which produced a similar result. More alarms told him any pack that old should have been discarded long ago.

Again he ignored the warning.

Instead, in an understandable act of frustration, he threw the pack on the bed. From there it bounced off onto the floor, where the remaining cigarettes in the front row spilled out, along with the top inch of each cigarette in the back two rows. They were affixed to a thin piece of cardboard that concealed something now jutting from the pack.

He lifted it out.

It was a black, feather-light plastic oblong that exactly fit the space left inside the Marlboro pack. On its face were fifteen red, recessed buttons, each about the size of a grape seed. Despite having no clue to its purpose, Doppler knew anything hidden so cleverly had to be illegal.

He moved back into the bathroom to gaze down at Marsh.

Brandt had lifted him to a sitting position so he could drip blood into the toilet. Brandt himself was blow-drying the toilet water from his shirt and jacket sleeves. He noticed Doppler and shut the dryer off. "Mind cleaning up now?"

Doppler felt a small rush of pleasure at being able—just once—to refuse doing the shit work. "I haven't called yet." He then extended the small black box toward Marsh.

"Hey, assface! What the fuck is this?"

Brandt frowned as Marsh tried to focus his nearsighted eyes. Doppler stepped closer. When Marsh could finally make it out, an anguished groan escaped his battered mouth. This was now a total catastrophe, light-years worse than he'd ever dreamed possible.

How could he have miscalculated so badly?

☐ **XI** ☐

Guiding submarines through the world's oceans is often as dangerous as handling a jet fighter. But there are no ejection seats in subs, no way to recover from a serious mistake. It's just climb in, say your prayers, and hope for the best.

The main hazards any submariners face are the towering underwater mountains that rise from the bottoms of oceans and seas to reach half as high as Everest in some places. Those that reach within 2,000 feet of the surface are problems for all submarines, and more than 3,500 have been catalogued worldwide.

Along America's western 200-mile territorial limits lie three groups of such hazards, which Soviet emergency monitors must negotiate. The first is the Tatyana Massif, a chain of six peaks located south of San Diego, opposite the Mexican border. Any kind of detour would take Soviet subs well clear of those obstacles, but their captains are under strict orders to maintain courses through them as close to direct as possible.

Farther up the coast, north of Santa Barbara, is the Out Island Group, an extensive chain of nineteen peaks that break the surface to form rocky islands at several points. Fortunately, the Out Islands lie on an east-west axis, so the monitors' northern route requires that they weave through only four.

Off the coast of central Oregon is the Fromholtz Ridge, a final obstacle course whose nine north-south peaks are by far the most difficult to negotiate. Forty precise rudder corrections must be flawlessly executed within the thirty minutes necessary to traverse the Ridge. After passing through it, Soviet submariners always throw themselves a Fromholtz party.

Some in Russia's Naval Presidium argue that it's courting disaster to continually force crews through the tricky Tatyanas, the deceptive Out Islands, and the downright dangerous Fromholtz. But field commanders uniformly insist that such tests sharpen navigating skills in ways no other peacetime maneuvers could.

Every sailor knows he's risking death on each pass through those jagged underwater bluffs, and that knowledge produces a consciousness and a skill level that could be crucial to their survival in the event of all-out war with America.

Captain Nikolai Barzlin was a long-term veteran of Soviet submarine service, starting as an ensign on one of the few Russian boats to function throughout World War II. He'd seen the entire sweep of modern submarine technology, from those primitive buckets of leaky bolts to the sleek, incomparably sophisticated leviathans then prowling the world's oceans.

Like Barzlin, Communication Chief Josef Popov had survived World War II, though they hadn't known each other then. And like the captain, Popov was a short, compact man, the only kind chosen for submarine service when small stature and lung capacity were basic requirements. Now they served on the SSN *Mikhail Potkin* as the oldest members of the officer and noncom staffs.

Both men were sitting in the *Potkin* captain's quarters, playing chess at a small table. It was a ritual they tried to observe every day at sea, although Popov's duty schedule alternated six-hour quarter watches at his radio consoles, while Barzlin worked the odd hours his various responsibilities dictated. Those disparate schedules made each rendezvous difficult, which added value to the time they spent together.

Barzlin had an unusual triangular face, with a broad, white-thatched forehead sloping into a long, thin nose, down to an almost-pointed chin. It was a face built to express the melancholy that had been his basic mood during the six weeks they'd been at sea. Popov wondered if it would ever end.

In the middle of pondering his next move, the captain lifted his sea-green eyes from the chessboard to gaze across his desk at his opponent. "How long have we served together, Josef?"

The slight, frail-looking radioman closed his own dark eyes to consider. "Ten years next month. The second tour after the conference at Minsk. I couldn't transfer before then."

It was true. They'd met at a Naval Presidium conference held, of all places, at Minsk, a city five hundred miles from the sea. Since that location could only have been chosen to line the pockets of certain Presidium bureaucrats, both men considered it a classic example of the Soviet military's moral rot.

Both considered boycotting the conference in protest, but each knew it would be a dangerous, futile gesture. So they went, stumbled into each other, soon became friends, and decided to try serving together as shipmates. But, as with all things in their country's navy, arranging the transfer took time and trouble.

Popov smiled at his memory of how they'd met. "I'd heard so much about the great Captain Nikolai Barzlin . . . the man revolutionizing all theories of underwater navigation. I was afraid to introduce myself—a lowly radioman—to you."

Barzlin, too, smiled at that memory. "But you did. And we talked through the night about the old days, the war days."

Popov nodded his shiny bald head. "And played chess."

"Yes, and played chess," Barzlin said as he put Popov's king into checkmate. "You were much better then. Check and mate."

Popov didn't mind losing the game. In fact, for the entire cruise he'd been working harder to lose convincingly than he'd ever tried to win. It was his only means of trying to boost the sagging spirits of his captain and best friend. And because this was going to be their last tour of duty together, he was determined to do all he could to make it as pleasant and memorable as possible.

"My ego can't keep taking these drubbings," the radioman said with a wink. "Maybe it's a good thing you're retiring."

Barzlin's pale skin went livid with anger. "Never suggest that my 'retirement' is in any way a good thing! Not even to joke! I should be stepping down at a time of my own choosing, not at the whim of a stooge like Kronski!"

There was nothing Popov could say to ease his friend's deep sense of hurt and betrayal. The Presidium was removing him from command without his consent, turning him out to pasture before he felt ready to go. And though it was happening only one or two tours early, it was still being done without the dignity or honor due a man of Barzlin's stature and contributions to the State.

For lack of anything constructive to say, Popov changed the subject as he cleared the chessboard. "Where are we now?"

Barzlin's roiling emotions were still primed for an ongoing argument, but he made an effort to accommodate his friend's noncombative nature. "Twenty hours from the Massif," he said.

"And how are the new men doing? Are they ready for it?"

The captain sighed, getting himself back under control. "I assume so. We won't know until we get there, but I'm confident."

"What will you do in the meantime?"

"What I always do," he said as he stood up. "Make them think I'm aware of every move they make."

Popov rose, straightening his bright orange submariner's jumpsuit. "That is your greatest asset, Nikolai," he said with a faint grin. "You have a wonderful knack for seeming omnipotent."

The captain finished straightening his own jumpsuit, then slipped an arm around his friend's shoulders as they headed for the door. "What do you mean, 'seeming'? I *am* omnipotent!"

They left the cabin laughing at that boastful joke. But in their hearts, each was wishing somehow it might be true.

□ XII □

Nat Perkins was surprised by the call from Brandt and Doppler's secretary. Not only did it come to his condo, where he was just waking up, it was more of an order than a request for him to stop by their office on his way to work. And the secretary wouldn't tell him a thing about what they wanted.

He took his time showering and shaving, wondering as he did every morning lately about how much longer he could stave off the ravages of thirty years on the face and body that had once been voted Cutest One-year-old in Broward County, Texas. He sensed it was a losing battle. There was curly brown hair on the shower drain every morning, gray in his temples and chin whiskers, and over the past year he'd moved out a hole in each of his belts.

Where will it all end?

Only speculations like that could supersede his anxieties about meeting with Brandt and Doppler. In his capacity as Pacific Bell's chief of security throughout Silicon Valley, he was occasionally asked to take part in the FBI's phone-related cases. And he'd worked enough with those two to be appalled by their thuggery. Unfortunately, all branches of law enforcement that he knew about —including the FBI—maintained a core of hardened scum equal to dealing with like-minded opponents.

Despite misgivings about Brandt and Doppler's methods, Nat sympathized with their objectives. Computer theft was rapidly becoming the world's most lucrative method of stealing money, short of starting a new government or religion, so strong and unusual measures were needed to combat it. What bothered him about the Bruise Brothers was their lumping hackers in with thieves.

To his mind, hacking didn't warrant violent repression.

Nat equated hacking with his own bailiwick, phone phreaking. Like phreaking, hacking definitely needed to be stopped. But not at any cost. Hackers and phreaks were little more than sophisticated pranksters addicted to electronic trespass instead of drugs or loud music or ugly motorcycles or whatever.

Nat felt that hackers and phreaks should be battled on their own turf and on their own terms. Brandt and Doppler strongly disagreed, mostly because they couldn't play in the game if Nat's rules prevailed. And because of that deep philosophical difference, the three of them merely tolerated one another out of professional necessity. So Nat wasn't in his best mood as he approached their office in San Jose's FBI building.

He knocked on the door. Brandt's gruff voice called out, "Come in!" Nat did so and was reminded of his feeling that those two looked as much like government-issue items as everything else in their shabby office. Except that this time they were leaning against the front edges of their desks, apparently posed that way to indicate impatience with him. And sure enough . . .

"It's about time you showed up!" Doppler growled through the haze of cigarette smoke hovering around his head.

Nat checked his watch. "Was it a race? Nobody told me."

"We don't have time for smartass, Perkins," Brandt snapped.

Nat sauntered over to the chair beside Brandt's desk and sat down. "All right, then, what *do* you have time for? What's this all about? Or do I have to play Twenty Questions?"

Brandt moved around to the chair behind his desk as Doppler came over to sidesaddle the edge nearest Nat. "This morning we bagged a guy named Percy Marsh," Brandt said as he moved.

"Ever heard of him?" Doppler asked.

Nat shook his head.

Brandt reached into his shirt pocket and removed the device they'd taken from Marsh. "Ever see one of these before?"

Since it wasn't offered for close inspection, Nat couldn't make much of it. He shook his head again. Brandt then lifted a pencil to place its point against one of the dimpled grape-seed buttons. He pressed. A high-pitched *shreeeeeeeep!* pierced the room's bristling silence. Nat recognized it at once: the 2600 disconnect. He hunched forward in his chair.

"It's a blue box," he muttered as he reached out to receive it from Brandt. But obviously not just *a* blue box. This was as far as their miniaturization had ever been taken. In fact, were he not seeing it with his own eyes, he wouldn't have believed it was possible. He couldn't wait to get it into the lab to take it apart and see how it was constructed.

He took it in his hand, hefted it, then held it up for a close inspection. He saw it was perfect, absolutely perfect; an astounding piece of work. No, make that Art, with a capital *A* . . . Rodin's *Thinker* in a black plastic shell. Just being in its presence filled him with reverence.

"He hid it in a cigarette pack," Brandt explained.

"Damn clever job of it too," Doppler added.

"I've seen them disguised as all kinds of things," Nat replied. "Beer cans, tape measures, alarm clocks—you name it. But this has a . . . a linear simplicity I've never seen before."

"It's a little early for intellectual bullshit, don't you think?" Brandt said, scoring a solid point. "What do you say we just stick to why you're here?"

Nat tore his eyes away from the tiny marvel in his hand, realizing there was simply no way clods like Brandt and Doppler could ever appreciate the sheer, fantastic genius of it.

"Believe it or not," Brandt went on, "this Marsh character is the Ghost Glitch."

"Have you heard of *him*?" Doppler asked sarcastically.

Nat nodded. Every serious technophile had heard of the Ghost Glitch. He was a legend among American computer hackers, the one man they all believed would never—could never—be caught. So awesome was his expertise that in order to keep his game interesting, he left valid clues to his identity whenever he cracked secure access codes.

As far as Nat knew, the Glitch had never done actual harm in all the years he'd been active. But his reputation made him Target #1 on the FBI's most-wanted-hacker list. Bringing him in was a huge coup for Brandt and Doppler, which tempted Nat to offer congratulations. But temptation was as far as it went.

Meanwhile, Doppler lit a fresh cigarette from the butt of his last one, then resumed talking. "Now that we finally have him, we want to make damn sure we put him on ice for a while."

"We want to make a shining example of him for all those other assholes out there," Brandt added.

A chill of unease crawled down Nat's spine. Time in jail for harmless in-and-out hacking could never be legally justified, regardless of any need to set an example. Still, he knew better than to put anything—legal or illegal—past the FBI, especially two renegades like Brandt and Doppler.

"What kind of case do you have?" he asked, knowing the problems created by prosecuting a nebulous crime like hacking. It wasn't a lot different from his own pursuit of phreaks.

"Not as solid as we'd like," Brandt admitted.

Then Doppler added, "But we'll be pulling a few strings."

There was no point in asking what that bit of skulduggery might entail, so Nat hit them with the most obvious question he could think of. "Why not just publicize the hell out of it? Wouldn't that get you the same effect as putting him away?"

Doppler almost strangled on a drag of smoke as Brandt bolted upright in his chair. "Are you out of your mind?" he shouted.

Ask a stupid question . . .

Nat knew perfectly well that every media leech in San Jose—if not the whole Bay Area—would gladly sign an open-ended deal with Satan to be first to report on how Marsh performed his magic. And that would open a can of worms nobody could handle, not Brandt or Doppler or the whole damn FBI.

"All right," Nat conceded. "Point taken. But let's look at it from another direction. What if you pull your strings and put him on ice, then he goes public with his story to get revenge?"

Brandt cast an amused expression at Doppler, who was beginning to resume normal breathing. "Let's just say he's got more important things to think about than trying to mess with us."

"Why not say you threatened to blow his head off if he gives you any more trouble?" Nat countered.

Brandt's amused expression turned cold as Doppler jumped to his partner's defense. "Listen, Perkins, you Ma Bell guys pull the same number on the media. Whenever you bust a phreak, you don't crow about it. You keep it under wraps so nobody spreads around what a big problem they are for you. You let the phreak grapevine pass the word, which hits your target audience better than any media ever could. That's all we're doing!"

"We don't threaten to kill people!"

"Yeah," Doppler said behind a mocking smile. "Pussies like you never get to have any fun."

Nat turned from Doppler to concentrate on Brandt. "You got anything more for me besides Junior's macho insults?"

Doppler's smile froze. He slid off the desk edge and stood upright as Nat braced himself.

Brandt put out a restraining hand and spoke to Nat matter-of-factly. "We want you to build a phreaking case against Marsh—if you can."

Nat glared at Doppler's crimson face for several long, bristling seconds, then turned his attention back to Brandt. "Didn't you say your hacking case was being rigged?"

"Yeah, but we want phreaking charges hung on him too."

"Oh, I get it. He does his time for hacking, then you keep him in line by threatening him with a follow-up phreaking bust."

Brandt smiled again, this time all the way, flashing those big white teeth in that tar-skinned face. "Smart fella . . ."

Nat was getting fed up. His stomach was starting to knot. "Is there more to go on besides this?" he asked, placing the blue box back on top of Brandt's desk. "Alone, it's not enough."

"Would we be handling it if it was?" Doppler snapped, still trying to keep things stirred up.

"Knock it off, Charles," Brandt said, making it clear that the sparring was over. Then to Nat he added, "What do you need?"

Nat shrugged. "The same as you—proof."

Both FBI agents struggled to keep from laughing in his face. But not hard enough to keep from flaunting their ability to skirt the law. Nat hated their arrogance.

"We'll give you everything we have," Brandt said with a supercilious smirk. "Will that be enough to get you started?"

Nat was disgusted with the whole situation and couldn't bring himself to accept their offer. "No, thanks," he said as he stood up. "I can handle my end of it on my own."

Doppler broke into a high falsetto. "Oh, my goodness! I think we hurt her feelings!"

"In your dreams, Chuckie," Nat countered, turning to leave.

"Wait!" Brandt called out. He held up the tiny blue box and said, "Don't you at least want to check this out?"

Nat paused at the door, wishing there were some way to seize that golden opportunity. But his pride wouldn't let him give those two even a whiff of satisfaction.

"You seen one, you seen 'em all," he said with a casual shrug. Then he turned and left his antagonists behind, closing their door only a trifle too hard.

□ XIII □

As it happened, Percy Marsh wasn't totally unprepared for his encounter with Brandt and Doppler, though he'd never expected it to be so violent. All along he'd known that someday the clues would be solved and people would come to arrest him. That was an accepted part of his game plan, the part that made it exciting to leave legitimate clues behind. Which would be the final one they needed? When would that fateful knock come on his door?

Those questions added special zest to every day of his life.

He also knew Brandt and Doppler were in charge of computer fraud in the Bay Area. And, like all hackers, he knew their reputation for brutality. But he expected the Ghost Glitch to be spared dishonor because he'd always played straight with his opponents and assumed they'd grant him the same consideration.

Being handled so routinely was a seismic jolt for him.

Once the worst of it was over, however, his shock changed to anger, which quickly evolved into pure, blinding rage. If his captors wanted to play hardball, there was no one on earth capable of playing a tougher game than Percy Marsh. He could hoist their ruthless asses into the biggest, most god-awful sling anybody'd ever heard of, and have them pleading for the mercy he'd have begged for if only they'd given him the chance.

His original postarrest plan had been straightforward and simple: The King would tap into the Hot Line, inform the President of what would happen if the Ghost Glitch wasn't allowed to continue business as usual, then let the President see to it the threat was heeded. But now that plan would be modified.

Instead of threatening, he was going to *show* them what would happen if they ever laid another hand on him. And that would be a lesson none of them would ever forget—*ever!*

By the time the San Jose police arrived to take him into custody, Marsh was dressed in cuffed khaki slacks and an untucked plaid sport shirt. The arresting officers first took him to a hospital, where his split lips were stitched back together, then on to a dental clinic where his broken front teeth were fitted with temporary caps. That took four hours of typical emergency-room ineptitude, which—to a man as precise and time-oriented as Marsh—was almost as rigorous as the ordeal that put him there.

He was then taken to the San Jose city jail booking area to be processed. A rap sheet was filled out, he was fingerprinted and photographed, then allowed to make a phone call. According to his original scenario for dealing with this event, he called an old friend of his father's, an attorney named Stan Riley.

From there it was a matter of waiting for the wheels of justice to grind him up and spit him back out onto the street. Then he'd go right to work on his plan to get even with those bastards.

"You look like bloody hell, Percy Junior," Stan Riley said as he stared at the wreckage of his client's mouth.

The two were seated opposite each other in the city jail's lawyer-client room, a small bare cubicle with a battered metal card table and four metal folding chairs. Marsh's recently stitched lips had swollen badly during the past few hours. They were pushing up the rounded tip of his broad, flat nose, giving his normally owlish features a strongly porcine cast.

"And I do mean bloody," Riley repeated.

Marsh dabbed his wounded lips with a Kleenex, then looked at the pink smear on it. "That's not blood, Stan, it's just ooze."

He could speak and be understood through his tooth caps, but it was a far cry from his usual rapid-fire delivery. He had to form each word carefully, then push it past his protruding lips.

"And please stop calling me Percy Junior," he added. "I'm thirty-four years old and my father's been dead for years."

Riley wasn't too surprised at being rebuked by someone whose diapers he used to change on occasion. Percy Junior had always been a cold, calculating, warped extension of his reserved, analytical, but essentially considerate parents.

Riley turned his attention to the rap-sheet copy he'd been given when he arrived at the downstairs booking desk. He shook his wizened old head as he read. " 'Unlawful access . . . illegal tampering . . . malicious mischief . . .' The list goes on and on!"

"Look, what do you want me to say? It's all true. I *have* been playing around with computers."

"This is a damn sight more than playing around!" Riley snapped, veins bulging like mole tunnels across his liver-spotted scalp. "I'm just glad your parents aren't alive to see you here!"

Marsh became instantly enraged. "Leave them out of this!" he shouted, slamming both palms down onto the tabletop.

This time Riley couldn't help being surprised. Although the Percy Junior he'd known had never possessed the slightest tolerance for frustration, it was still unnerving to see such incandescent fury boil out of him with so little provocation.

"I thought your parents were the reason I'm here," he countered, scoring a solid point.

Marsh settled back into his chair, adjusted his thick horn-rims, and spoke with gathering calm. "That's true. I called you because your long association with my family has proved the quality of your work. But if you can't separate your personal feelings from your professional responsibilities, then recommend another attorney and we'll leave it at that."

Riley could see his client was in no mood to be lectured about the nature of what he'd done. And he also realized Percy Junior was right; he *was* being unprofessional. So he stepped off his soapbox and got down to business.

"Here's what I know so far. At the booking desk they told me you left valid clues to your identity everywhere you broke in. Now, I know you; I know how brilliant you are. You must have known that if you left clues behind, someday it would come to this."

Marsh looked at the old man who'd been the closest thing to an uncle he'd had while growing up. He spoke as if addressing a child. "Of course I knew. But don't you see? Without those clues the game would have been pointless and boring."

"Weren't you worried about getting caught?"

Marsh shook his head. "Not really. Based on what happened to other bagged hackers, I knew what to expect." Then suddenly his tone and expression soured. "The only thing I didn't count on was being treated like those others!"

Riley stood to pace the cramped room. Like every lawyer in San Jose, he knew about Brandt and Doppler's tactics of intimidation. He also knew those tactics were used to offset the leniency of judges and juries toward white-collar criminals the FBI was responsible for catching. But knowing that courthouse gossip was a long way from proving it at trial.

"To be honest, Percy, I don't really understand what you've been doing. Matter of fact, I'll need a crash course on it before I can represent you adequately. But I can tell you this much right now: You've gotten yourself into serious trouble."

"What makes you say that?"

"First of all, they've turned you over to our city-court system rather than handling it themselves."

"What's the difference?"

"They have a much better chance of . . . let's say 'influencing' a city-court judge and jury than a federal judge and jury. Of course, you can always go to the media with your story and—"

"No!" Marsh cut in. "No media! That's definitely out."

Riley mistakenly assumed Marsh's reluctance to go public was a result of Brandt and Doppler's threats. So he said nothing to mitigate those threats, hoping their message would be taken to heart. It's what the boy's parents would have wanted.

"Just get me out of here as soon as you can," Marsh went on, offering the faint smile his swollen lips would permit. "Everything else will take care of itself, believe me."

There was something eerily convincing in the way that assurance was offered, but Riley dismissed it as the kind of hopeful bluster he'd heard many times from clients in similar straits. What he had difficulty dismissing was the fire burning in Marsh's dark, myopic eyes. That, too, was something he'd seen before—in the eyes of a madman who'd slaughtered his entire family because God told him to and assured him he wouldn't be punished.

"So, what time frame are we talking about?" Marsh asked.

Riley shook off his somber musings and returned to his seat at the battered card table. His arthritis-gnarled hands shuffled through the sheaf of papers he'd been given at the booking desk. "Let's see. . . . Your arraignment is set for right after lunch."

"What happens at the arraignment?"

"You're formally charged, we offer up your pleas, you get a trial date, bond is set, and you're free as soon as you post it."

"What's the quickest way to get that done? Bank draft?"

Riley nodded. "That's certainly less time-consuming than going through a bail bondsman. But with all these charges filed against you, you'll be looking at a bond of about $50,000."

Marsh took a pen and a slip of paper from Riley's briefcase. He wrote a name and number on the paper as he spoke. "Here, this is my banker. Tell him to open a line of credit up to $100,000. No, make that $150,000—just to be on the safe side."

Riley wasn't surprised by those orders. He knew Marsh had inherited a small fortune when his parents died, not to mention a genuine fortune he made on his own, creating computer software.

"Now," Marsh went on, "assuming everything goes according to schedule, how soon will I be out and away from here?"

"An hour after the arraignment," Riley replied as he pocketed the slip of paper. "If nothing goes wrong."

Marsh shook his head. "That's not good enough. You can't let anything go wrong."

Riley's thin, parchment-dry lips stretched into a smile over his perfect dentures. "Still the same little boy who couldn't stand to be off his schedules. Thirty years without a change."

"Spare me the trip down memory lane, Stan. There's no time for it. Now, I'm serious—what can go wrong?"

"Nothing, really. They've already thrown the book at you. I can't imagine anything else being sprung at the last minute."

"What about phone phreaking? Did anyone mention that?"

"Oh, for crying out loud!" Riley wailed. "You're not into *that,* too, are you?"

"Goddammit, Stan! Yes or no?"

Riley was having difficulty adjusting to this aggressive, combative Percy Marsh, a fellow he never would have suspected might be growing up inside the intense, quiet loner he used to know three decades ago.

He rechecked the rap sheet. "Nothing in here about phone phreaking. It all relates to hacking, in one way or another."

Marsh considered, then changed his orders. "Tell the bank to have a quarter million on hand—just in case."

☐ XIV ☐

By midmorning Viktor Lubov was preparing to deliver the keynote speech at a technical symposium being held near his home in San Francisco. Unfortunately, his preparation for that speech had prevented him from developing a plan to "accidentally" meet Percy Marsh after his arrest. But he knew the arrest would take place on schedule and Marsh would be free sometime after lunch, which was also when his obligation to the symposium would end.

At that point he could and would focus his attention on arranging his first step down what he expected to be a long, treacherous road leading—if all went well—to the King.

The symposium Lubov planned to address was being sponsored by the California Committee on Ultrasonics and Microfrequency Transmission, known less formally as the Ultramike Committee.

The symposium itself was a bi-yearly meeting where many of the state's top technocrats got together to mingle socially while charting the flow of one another's research. It was at gatherings like this one that Lubov obtained the bulk of his inside information regarding cutting-edge microwave developments.

After a profitable stint of glad-handing in the lobby, he made his way into the auditorium where he'd be giving his speech. The subject was "Remedial Synthesis of Interrupted Microwave Deployment," which was an analysis of alternate flow paths during breaks in transmission. It wasn't one of his specialty areas, or even of particular interest or importance. Which was why he'd been chosen to discuss it. He was the most entertaining speaker within the ranks of microwave physicists, and if anyone could liven up such a mummified subject, Viktor Lubov was that man.

Once in the auditorium, he worked his way past friends and well-wishers, ending up backstage just as the meeting was called to order. Then the moderator, Howard Cranston, a second-rank plodder he didn't know well, came forward to introduce him.

What followed was exceptionally florid, as speeches go, full of dramatic pauses and gestures. But Lubov had endured effusive introductions since his "defection" fifteen years earlier.

Americans, it seemed, never forgot a hero.

"Ladies and gentlemen, friends and colleagues," a beaming Cranston began. "It gives me great pleasure to introduce a close personal friend, a man whose work we're all familiar with. And though most of us already know how he came to be here this morning, I see some young people out there who may never have heard the story. So if you'll indulge me, I'll fill them in.

"It began in a small town in East Germany, where our speaker was born just before World War II. He lost his family during that conflict, yet he managed to survive and grow up under the repressive Communist regime that came to dominate his homeland. And what sustained him throughout that ordeal was a dream . . . a dream called America.

"Yes, friends, he was determined to reach the shore of our country, and he cared nothing for the sacrifice it would take. He worked hard, saving what he could. Then, just when he had enough money to emigrate, the Berlin Wall went up. That was the end of such dreams for most East Germans . . . but not for our colleague.

"He began secretly training on a bicycle, and when he could sustain a speed of forty miles an hour for five minutes, he made his move. Early one morning, as the sun began glaring into the eyes of the guards at a certain checkpoint, he started barreling toward its gate. By sheer chance, a West German tourist was there with a camera and recorded his daring break for freedom.

"Those photographs were in magazines and newspapers around the world. They show a grim young man, head down, cap turned backward, with nothing but the clothes on his back as he goes whizzing past the checkpoint gatebox. They also show the two gatebox guards recovering and starting to raise their rifles.

"Next, there's a puff of smoke from a nearby machine-gun tower! Small puffs of smoke from the rifles! Bullets kick up tarmac all around the bicyclist! The cap is torn from his head by a well-aimed shot! Weaving desperately, he never falters as he pedals beyond the range of those murderous guns.

"At last he falls sideways, gasping, as the West German hurries over to take the picture everyone remembers. It shows a young man lying on his side, kissing the ground of freedom he'd dreamed of for so long—and then risked his very life to reach.

"After that he was proclaimed a free-world hero and warmly received by heads of state all over Europe. Then, when our President asked what his future plans were, he expressed a desire to continue his education in electronics. So he was soon enrolled at UCLA, where he proved to be a brilliant student. He went on to get his doctorate in microwave physics, and since that time he's been one of the shining lights in our field.

"Ladies and gentlemen, I give you a great physicist, a great man, and a truly great American . . . Dr. Viktor Lubov!"

There was sustained applause as Lubov stepped from the wings to shake hands with a trembling, sweating Cranston. Lubov guessed that introduction might have been the crowning effort of the man's public life. And it *had* been a stirring speech, one of the best renditions of that worn-out sham he'd ever heard.

He turned to the audience and found most of them on their feet, taking great pride in the fact that one of their number had per-

formed such an astonishingly brave act. And even if they'd known
the truth of it, that would only have altered their appreciation from
high drama to low farce.

When the tumult finally died down, Lubov began speaking in his
rich German accent. "I'd like to begin by thanking my good friend,
Dr. Cranston, for those overly kind words of introduction." He
turned and winked at Cranston, who had taken his place in the
wings and was now mopping his flushed brow.

"Your check is in the mail. . . ."

When the laughter subsided, he wiped the smile from his face
and got down to the serious business at hand.

□ XV □

Although Percy Marsh maintained an unlisted telephone number, Nat Perkins had no trouble obtaining his home address. Nat
worked for Ma Bell, the biggest "Big Brother" of them all.

When he arrived at Marsh's residence, he wasn't surprised to
find a city-police house-sweep team just finishing their job. Working under the supervision of an FBI agent, they were helping to
screw the hacking case-lid on as tight as it would go.

Nat presented his credentials to a police officer at the front door,
then began a calculated stroll through the house to get a feel for
the man he, too, was supposed to help nail.

He found every room well maintained—neat and orderly—but
haphazardly furnished, with no overall theme. That indicated the
occupant put emphasis on function rather than form, which was
typical of hackers—not to mention phone phreaks.

There was a large framed photograph of Marsh and his parents
hanging above the living-room mantel. Nat guessed its age was at
least a decade because it portrayed a young man in his mid-twen-
ties with long, thick, dark hair swept back behind his ears in that
period's style. He wore dark horn-rimmed glasses set on a broad
nose, like his father's, which centered above an incongruously
small mouth that strongly resembled his mother's.

Altogether, the picture didn't reveal a man even approaching
Nat's conception of the amazing Ghost Glitch. The round face and

glasses gave Marsh a look of owl-eyed stoicism, but otherwise he was difficult to categorize. There was nothing to hang on to in his face, no angles or planes to hook your eyes and hold them. It was just a smooth, round ball that revealed next to nothing about whatever lurked behind the facade.

According to Marsh's telephone records, he was a self-employed computer-systems analyst. Nat knew hacker ranks were filled with such people. He also knew hacking at the Ghost Glitch's level had to be an all-consuming passion, which was the main problem with what Brandt and Doppler wanted him to do.

It would be all but impossible to hang a serious phreaking charge on a dedicated hacker; everyone knew there weren't enough hours in the day to become truly proficient at both activities.

Nat saved the computer room for last because it was the main focus of police attention and had been crowded when he first arrived. Now it contained only a man in a dark business suit and a uniformed cop lifting fingerprints.

He stepped up to the man in the suit, extending a hand. "Nat Perkins, phone-company fraud."

The man took his hand, saying, "You damn sure *do* sound like a cowboy. Brandt said you would. Bill Keller, FBI."

Keller was older, taller, and heavier than Doppler, but nowhere near as imposing as Brandt. His bleary brown eyes and hangdog expression made it easy to see why he was on the mop-up detail. He looked and sounded sorry to be alive.

"How's it going on your end?" Nat asked.

Keller shrugged. "Not too bad. Got all the circumstantial evidence we need. Still tryin' to dig up some hard stuff."

"You haven't found anything? Notes? Files? Nothing?"

"Just business-related papers. Guy must have some kind of super memory to keep it all in his head like that."

Nat knew it was possible to store large amounts of phreaking data in your head. But no one could memorize all of it. There was simply too much, and it was highly complex. Unfortunately, he didn't know enough about hacking to make the same assertion. It didn't seem possible, but . . .

Hell, maybe it is.

The two men stood gazing at the cop lifting prints, getting comfortable with each other's presence. Then Nat broke the silence. "They found a top-of-the-line blue box when they bagged him. That's why I'm here."

"Yeah, I heard," Keller replied. "I don't believe he's a phreak, though. Just a user."

"Why's that?"

Keller gestured around what had once been a bedroom. "He's got three main console units here: screens, terminals, modems, printers—the works—plus normal phone tie-ins. And each piece has been verified as unaltered and legitimately related to the kind of work he does. Nothin' even resemblin' a phreakin' rig."

"Then how in hell can I file charges against him?"

Keller smiled sardonically. "Is that what they want you to do? Tell 'em they ought to be satisfied to have him at all. We've only been after his ass about fifteen fuckin' years."

Keller turned his attention to the cop lifting prints. "Hey, can you speed it up, Mac? I ain't got all day."

The cop gave a sour look over his shoulder and slowed down even more. Keller resumed railing against Brandt and Doppler.

"People in the Bureau been bustin' their humps tryin' to figure those clues he left behind. So what happens? B. and D. waltz in, spend a couple years in the trenches, and *wham*! The Clue Crew finally figures out who he is; B. and D. get to make the bust; they get every shred of credit; and the rest of us get a measly thanks for nothin'!" He paused to gnaw at a fingernail, then concluded, "It's a gully-washin' pisser, let me tell you."

Keller was clearly in a foul mood, but Nat had to press him for more information. "Can you tell me anything about Marsh himself? All I've got is the basics."

"He's a top debugger . . . supposed to be the best there is."

Nat knew how debuggers worked. When any company undertook a really large or complex software project, they usually had to parcel out different sections of it to different groups with specialty expertise. But that system left none of those groups seeing the overall picture, so errors invariably crept in.

Once any large-scale program was in place and functioning, errors could cause millions in losses before being detected. So it made sense to hire someone to debug them before they went on-line.

What intrigued Nat was that only a handful of people were qualified to undertake such a mentally demanding task.

If Marsh truly was the best of that breed, then there was even less chance he was a phreak. Top-notch debugging *and* hacking had to maximize anyone's intellectual capacities, along with consuming most of their time.

"Who says he's the best?" Nat asked.

"Everybody we talk to! They say he gets first shot at every important government or military job, which probably explains how he knows enough to get in where he gets in. And the rumors!"

He lowered his voice so the cop lifting prints couldn't hear. "They say he can access anything, anywhere, anytime. Matter of fact, based on what we're hearin' about him, that fat fuck is probably the top computer man in the world right now."

His sardonic smile creased his dour face. "At least, he *was*. I'd say his career arc is about to flatten way, way out."

Nat tried to match Keller's mocking disdain. "It sure as hell ought to!"

The print man finished lifting and began packing his kit. Keller was obviously anxious to follow him out and away.

"One more thing," Nat said. "What about his personal life?"

Keller gave him a piercing look that met his eyes for the first time. It was as if he were trying to think of a way that being helpful might cause him problems somewhere down the line.

"Why didn't Brandt and Doppler tell you any of this?"

"They were just about to get started when something came up," he lied. "We never got back to it."

Nat held his gaze firmly, knowing that second-raters loved to exploit their own weaknesses in others. Keller didn't find the crack he was looking for.

"He's a major-league loner, eccentric as they come, no family or friends, no known vices, secretive as hell about his life apart from work. Your typical oddball genius."

The print man left the room and Keller turned to follow him out. All Nat could do was say, "Thanks, Bill . . . I owe you."

He gazed around the tidy horseshoe of computer equipment semicircling the room. It was amazing that one man could sit in the center of it all and inject himself into the heart of the most secure data banks on earth.

Almost as amazing, in fact, as what could theoretically be done through phreaking.

Nat left Marsh's house and went back to his car, an immaculate black-on-black Corvette. As he drew near to it, he noticed someone sitting in the passenger seat. Nearer still, he was able to distinguish a female's profile. Almost on top of her, he could make out the bright red curls of the last person in the world he wanted to see or deal with at that moment.

Karen Glass was sitting in his car.

□ XVI □

On the way to the lawyer-client room, Marsh had said nothing to the bodybuilder jail guard who escorted him from the holding cell. However, once the meeting with Stan Riley was over and he was returned to the guard's custody for the trip back to the holding cell, there was good reason to talk to him. His name tag read BANDINI, so Marsh politely addressed him that way.

"Mr. Bandini, I need a favor. Would you be willing or able to help me with something like that?"

Bandini's impressive physique was enough to intimidate all but the most belligerent, brain-fried junkies, which was why he escorted prisoners around the jail. It was a job he'd secured four years earlier, just after attaining his citizenship. And during that time he'd heard every kind of plea from his charges. He could handle them in his sleep.

"A favor I don't got. Rules is what I got. *Capische?*"

"I need to make another call."

"One call," Bandini countered. "One call is rule."

"I'd like to have a friend pick me up after my arraignment. Couldn't I call him, please?"

"One call is rule," he insisted. "Lawyer make others."

This wasn't going at all the way Marsh had planned. He might have asked Riley to arrange the extra call, *if* he could have anticipated it would be thwarted by a muscle-bound rulemonger. But now he couldn't let Riley get any closer to what was going to happen, so he went back at Bandini with renewed determination.

"I'd be willing to pay," he said earnestly.

Bandini looked at him with eyes narrowing slightly. "Is this bribe you offer?"

It hadn't been. He'd only meant to show how eager he was to make the call. But something in the young Italian's tone said a bribe might not be a bad idea. "How about fifty dollars?"

Bandini's eyes narrowed even more. "A lot of money for one call. I think maybe you joke with me, yes?"

They rounded a corner and found themselves in an empty hallway. Marsh stopped and waited until Bandini looked him in the face. Then he spoke with all the conviction he could muster.

"They took my wallet when they booked me, so I can't give you any money right now. But if you tell me a way to make the exchange so you won't get in trouble, I swear the fifty's yours."

Bandini saw no need to feel him out further, but he couldn't understand fifty dollars for a phone call. Ten or twenty would make sense, but fifty? Either Marsh was some kind of agent sent into the system to root out corruption, or he was simply a rich fool to whom money meant nothing. Since the odds on any kind of anticorruption campaign were minuscule, and since money was always money, Bandini decided to go with the rich-fool angle.

"One hundred," he said, hoping he wasn't pushing too hard. It was always embarrassing to retrench in a bribe negotiation.

Ready to pay any amount, Marsh gladly said, "Deal!"

Bandini pulled out his wallet and removed a card. "Send cash to here, in birthday greeting from Uncle Vito."

Marsh glanced at the card, seeing nothing more than the fact that his plan was once again back on track. "No problem—a birthday card from Uncle Vito. You'll have it in a day or two."

Bandini smiled. Gold flashed in several of his teeth. "I can trust a man like you? A man of honor, yes?"

Marsh smiled back as best he could. "Absolutely! I always pay my debts." Then, as they moved forward again, he muttered harshly under his breath, "Always!"

* * *

Just down the hall and around a corner from the holding cell was the small empty room where Marsh had made his original call to Stan Riley. There was nothing in it but a dirty old wall phone hanging near the door—no chair or table or any other comfort to aid the difficult conversations that took place there.

With Bandini standing at his back, Marsh picked up the phone and—as before—subtly hit the disconnect button. His well-tuned ear again detected no difference in amperage flow during the reconnect, which meant the line was still clean. He then got his revenge ball rolling by dialing a special nine-digit number.

There was no ring after a caller finished dialing one of those special numbers, just the rapid click-clicking of a tandem being seized, followed by the crystal, static-free connection of a virgin trunk line. As usual, a conversation was in progress.

Spurning standard procedure, Marsh interrupted it. "King on-line. Is the Kraut on?"

There was momentary silence, then a voice spoke up. "Sorry, pal. You don't sound like the King."

It was Snowbird. As was the custom, he took charge because he was the highest-ranking phreak in the orbit at that moment. That meant the Kraut wasn't on-line. "Snowbird, it *is* me. My mouth got hurt in an accident. Now, what about the Kraut?"

Snowbird hesitated another moment, then replied, "Far as I know, he hasn't checked in yet today."

"Anyone else heard from him?" Marsh asked. There was no response from anyone else in the orbit.

"Okay, then, here's the deal: Tell him there'll be an important personal message for him at the San Jose Public Library at three o'clock this afternoon. Tell him I know it's short notice, but it can't be helped. Tell him to just go there and wait for it, if he can. The messenger will know him."

"What if he doesn't check in between now and then?"

"One reason he's Number Two," Marsh said testily, "is that he's dependable. You know he always checks in around noon."

"Yeah, okay," Snowbird countered. "But just for the sake of argument, suppose he doesn't." Snowbird was Number Five and nobody's fool. "You want somebody else on standby?"

The truth was that Marsh barely trusted the Kraut enough to do what he had in mind. He'd be playing it by ear the whole way, looking for the slightest excuse to abort. But for now, he was willing to give his long-time chief lieutenant the benefit of the doubt, in the interest of saving precious time.

More than anything else at that moment—even more than maintaining his ironclad rule against revealing his identity to anyone— he wanted to clear up this whole nasty Glitch business as soon as was humanly possible. So the risk of including the Kraut seemed worth the potential time gain he represented. Besides, if he couldn't trust the Kraut, who in hell *could* he trust?

"No, it's personal, just for him. If he doesn't check in, it's only a missed opportunity. But if he does, tell him to try to be there. He'll be glad he made the effort. Off-line."

Several voices rang out as he hung up. "King off-line!"

Marsh turned to face Bandini, who was scowling as he said, "You tell me you call someone come pick you up. You lie to me."

Again Marsh smiled as best he could. "I didn't want to explain to my other friends about where I am. You can understand that, can't you? It's embarrassing. So the one who picks me up will be in for a little surprise, that's all."

Bandini was far from being mollified. "What is all King and Snowbear and Kratt business? You not fooling me!"

"Nicknames, that's all—nicknames."

Bandini started to waver. Something about the situation just wasn't right; he could smell it, feel it. But his grasp of English wasn't good enough to clearly express his doubts.

"Library is far from here" was all he could think to say.

"You're right—it is," Marsh agreed. "But I can take a taxi from here to there."

"Then why not take taxi home?"

"I'd like to talk things over with my friend. You know, try to give it some outside perspective."

Bandini was folding. "You be at library much before three. Arraignment don't take long."

"My friend lives in Frisco. He'll need time to get here."

Bandini stood there feeling awkward, unable to come up with another objection. Besides, Marsh was showing no sign of stress.

Maybe he is tell truth, Bandini thought.

"Will that be all?" Marsh asked.

What the hell? No break in my bones. "Yeah, sure . . . we go." He turned to escort his prisoner back to the holding cell.

Marsh went along feeling much better than when he was first brought to it and thrown in with five surly-looking black men. Visions of being sodomized had knotted his stomach until he realized sex was impossible in the holding cell. There was too much intermittent activity as arrestees were taken to and from attorney meetings. By the time Bandini returned him to the cell, the black men seemed to consider him just one of the guys.

"You missed lunch, man," said the biggest one from his seat along the left-side wall.

"That's okay," Marsh replied, as he returned to where he'd been sitting along the back wall. "I'm not hungry."

And he wasn't. He was too preoccupied with the hundreds of details he'd have to pull together as soon as he got to his cabin up in the mountains. As he gathered them in his mind, organizing them into a mental flow chart, he became so absorbed that he didn't hear one of the other black men's muttered comeback.

"Mouth's too fucked up to eat, anyway."

And then another: "Dude tried to suck a firecracker!"

Marsh did hear their bursts of laughter, but only barely, from somewhere at the very edge of his awareness.

He was simply too deep in thought to be bothered.

□ XVII □

Standing quietly at the center of the SSN *Mikhail Potkin's* control room, Captain Nikolai Barzlin was a short, powerful mote in the eye of a storm of precise activity. From a small open spot near the periscope column, he could observe his men standing at their workstations or seated at consoles across arcs of 150°, left and right. Only the fore and aft passageways were clear of men or the equipment necessary to move their intricate vessel along its course beneath the sea.

Barzlin spent much of his duty time standing in that spot because every life on the *Potkin,* or on any modern submarine, depended on every action in the control room being executed flawlessly—first time, every time. There was simply no room for error, so he wanted all his men—especially the new ones—to feel the weight of that responsibility hovering at their backs. He'd always believed he could ingrain good habits that way, habits to endure long after he stopped standing those diligent watches.

When he was younger, his last day in the control room was an abstract concept he could barely bring himself to consider. But, inevitably, time and circumstance finally scissored him in their relentless pincer. The job he loved and had performed so well for so long was being taken from him; taken by someone with absolutely *no* understanding of what it took for men to live and work hundreds of feet underwater, sealed in fragile metal tubes.

And to add a frustrating insult to that humiliating indignity, on this last cruise he was being forced to break in his replacement, a young upstart hand-picked by his nemesis.

Suddenly, Barzlin's wandering thoughts were scattered by the voice of that upstart, Commander Valeri Damovitch, standing at one of his operational positions behind Sonar Chief Andrus Kim.

"Captain, we have first contact with C/S/T sensors."

There was nothing unusual about that report, since the *Potkin* was heading right into the teeth of America's western listening array. All the contact really meant was that they were on course and on schedule. "Thank you, Commander."

America's many C/S/T arrays were at the heart of Barzlin's problems with the man making this his last tour of duty. They were a network of supersophisticated electronic listening devices planted in the world's oceans and seas to keep track of every motorized vessel within thousands of cubic miles of water.

The C/S/T's transponders recorded sounds with a sensitivity roughly equal to detecting a standard belch at five miles. That allowed cataloguing of detected vessels according to individual soundprints, which were as distinctive as fingerprints.

Now, like cows with bells around their necks, all naval vessels—particularly those from the Soviet Union—were monitored by the unique sounds their engines and prop blades made in water. Those sounds—whether of surface or submerged craft—were stamped forever in the electronic circuitry of U.S. Navy computers, which could identify a ship as soon as it moved near any one of the hundreds of listening arrays scattered around the globe.

Barzlin himself—not to mention the entire Soviet Naval Presidium—had carefully monitored America's C/S/T deployment, starting with the first CAESAR transponders laid on the Pacific bottom in the late 1950s. Since then, technological gains had given America the capacity to monitor all vessel movement within several hundred miles of its coastline, as well as at certain strategic chokepoints where Soviet vessels were forced to enter and exit their own limited port facilities.

Now CAESAR transponders littered the bottom of wherever the C/S/T network was arrayed; SASS transponders were suspended in the water; and TASS arrays were towed by vessels on the surface. Those three sonar systems combined to provide three-dimensional graphic representations that could be displayed with startling clarity on cathode-ray screens. Those screens transformed the inky ocean depths into pale green, grid-filled "air" that could be monitored with the ease of tuning in a television set.

Three months earlier, High Commissioner Byiotin Kronski had called for a gathering of the Soviet Naval Presidium's Internal Policy Council, to discuss means of dealing with the vexatious C/S/T network. He considered it the foremost enemy of his country's submarine fleet because it cost even the missile carriers the one thing all submarines required for maximum effectiveness: total camouflage from any means of detection.

Captain Barzlin accepted those C/S/T arrays as a matter of course because he'd long ago ceased marveling at the miracles of modern technology. If Americans could develop cameras that read lips from 100 miles in space, how difficult could it be to construct listening devices that hear a man stub his toe 2,000 feet under the sea? Unfortunately, Kronski didn't share Barzlin's stoic acceptance of America's superior technology.

Kronski was the Supreme Soviet's representative to the Presidium's Internal Policy Council, and he strongly promoted the idea of increased countertechnology as the best way to achieve naval parity with the United States. He believed it was better to use scarce operating funds to develop means of confounding those infernal machines, rather than trying to overwhelm their more clever and efficient rival with sheer numbers.

When called before the assembled gathering, Barzlin had said, "I simply cannot agree with the Comrade Commissioner."

Backed by charts and graphs supporting his position, he addressed deskbound admirals and hidebound bureaucrats sitting at a large oval table. He was there to represent submarine field commanders, the people who would have to actually live with whatever policies the Council dictated. As such, his views were listened to with the least regard of all who spoke.

"Employing advanced countertechnology is the very worst method of dealing with the Americans," he went on. "That's the game they play best, a game they cannot and will not lose. Competing with them at it will be what it has always been for us: an exercise in gross futility. They're superior in every way."

The white-haired, broad-shouldered captain then directed his chest full of medals and ribbons toward the Council chairman.

"Americans are not resolute people until forced to be. And since creating technology doesn't require getting one's hands dirty, so to speak, they perform wonders. But to risk lives and expensive equipment routinely, as we do in our monitoring program along their coastlines—*that* they will never attempt. So it's my belief, Comrade Commissioner, that superior training on our part can and will counterbalance their superior technology."

High Commissioner Kronski was a rising star in the Supreme Soviet. He was still in his forties but already wielded awesome power. And, like most in his lofty position, he was a product of the Soviet Union's ruling elite. His father had been a Commissar under Stalin but was executed in one of that mad dog's endless purges. Now his thin mustache twitched slightly as his theory was challenged by the old codger who'd risen from the ranks.

"Tell me, then, Captain Barzlin," he said in a flat, quiet monotone, "how would you allocate the funds in question?"

"As we all know, Commissioner, submarine service is the key element of our naval force, so I would upgrade pay scales before anything else. Then I would upgrade our facility at Novgorod, particularly in the areas of berthing and tending. Otherwise, I'm pleased with our level of competence. You might consider turning back any unused funds to the Central Committee."

Kronski's round, well-fed face reddened with outrage. "Do you realize what I went through to obtain these funds?"

Barzlin didn't care. He was an uncompromisingly honest, straightforward man who always spoke the truth as he saw it. Which explained why he'd never risen above the rank of captain.

"Let the Americans have their expensive toys," he concluded. "Superior seamanship will always be of greater value in a crisis."

"That will be all, Captain," Kronski said with a gesture of dismissal. "We thank you for your comments."

Barzlin bowed slightly and left the room. Then, in the next day's mail, he received notice of his impending "retirement."

☐ XVIII ☐

Nat Perkins had good reason to be dismayed at finding Karen Glass sitting in his black Corvette. She was one of the Bay Area's most capable media leeches: an investigative reporter for the San Jose *Union-Ledger*. Keeping her off a case not meant to be publicized was like trying to keep a hound off a bloody trail. Fortunately, like all reporters, she could be stopped. But there was always a price to pay in future favors or sacrifice leaks.

To protest her illegal entry, Nat slid into the driver's seat without looking at her. That was difficult because he never much minded looking at Karen Glass. Her oval face held full, sensuous lips; a long, finely sculpted nose; and without question the biggest, greenest eyes he'd ever seen. Occasionally, when trying to dodge her on phreaking cases, he found himself wishing they could be something other than wary adversaries.

"Hi, Nat. How've you been?" she asked, sounding as if he were one of her best friends and this a routine encounter.

"Fine—till now," he had to reply. It was part of the game.

"Don't be like that," she cooed, pushing a few red curls up off her forehead. "I'm just doing my job."

"Why don't you go do your 'job' to Brandt and Doppler? This is their baby. I'm only along for the ride."

"I already tried that," she replied matter-of-factly. "As soon as my sources at the jail told me who Marsh is."

He looked over at her. He'd heard she was in her late twenties, and it was clear she'd never been married. Her face was still fresh and alive, unlined by the worries that come with a husband and/or children. "So what are you doing in my car?"

Still matter-of-fact, she said, "You didn't lock the door."

"Awww, come off it, Karen!" he chided. "Brandt and Doppler got you short-leashed, so you can't afford to be seen lurking."

She threw her hands up in despair. "Okay, okay! So my boss called me in for a heart-to-heart." She dropped her voice into an approximation of Carl Brocton's booming baritone. " 'This is just one of those stories, Karen, where we have to respect a higher priority than the public's right to know.' "

She ended her mimicry with a finger-in-throat gesture.

It amused Nat to see her so frustrated by that tactic because he always used it against her whenever she—or for that matter, when any other media leech—was breathing down his neck on a phreaking case. He'd go to his own boss, Art Wellington, and tell him the problem. Wellington would get on the horn to Brocton or whoever, plead the equivalent of national security, and some horse-trading would get done. Favors would be exchanged or logged, and the leech would be shunted onto another story.

"Their position really is valid," he said, trying to ease the sting if he could. "If you, or anyone else, were to print what that guy's been up to for the past fifteen years, you'd be guilty of the worst kind of treason. I swear to God you would."

She forced a smile that revealed her only facial flaw: uneven teeth. In a world of braces for almost everyone, she was a pleasant —and obviously self-assured—anachronism. Best of all, in Nat's mind that balanced out his own thinning hairline.

"Listen," she said, "I've had a bellyful of lectures about how printing the details of hacking and phreaking could endanger national security. I think it's all just a self-serving crock you and the two Bruise Brothers have cooked up to keep me and my crowd from embarrassing you in public. But since you keep the lid down so tight, I'm only guessing. I could be wrong."

Karen Glass owned a hard-won reputation as a pragmatic leech who always operated within those shifting journalistic boundaries outlined by the demands and influences of conflicting interests. In other words, she was a tough, aggressive competitor who knew how to give ground when she couldn't have things her own way.

Friends and foes—including Nat—respected her for that.

"Why *are* you here?" he demanded.

She reached out a hand to place on his. He had a sudden urge to pull back from her because he didn't think he was going to like what came next. But he managed to overcome it.

"I want to make a confession," she said. "And of all the characters I've come to know in this hacker-phreaking business, you're the only one I think I might be able to trust."

Nat's instincts screamed at him to be careful because part of her job entailed sticking it to people like him, just as a part of his job entailed shafting people like her. But then he recalled that she'd never been known to break a confidence or a bargain. And his heart sealed his fate by reminding him of how much he admired her and wanted to get to know her better.

"What kind of confession?"

She squeezed his hand. "I've come to the end of my rope, Nat. I'm just sick and tired of guessing, so now I want to know all of it . . . every last detail . . . for my own satisfaction."

Nat felt as if he'd just been presented with a package that could turn out to be one of the best gifts he'd ever received—or a ticking bomb. "Could you elaborate on that a little?"

She leveled those emerald-green eyes at him and he couldn't help believing she meant business. "I've got a disease called 'wannaknowitis.' Had it since I was a kid. Five years old, they tell me, I was listening at doors with a glass. Nobody could hide anything from me. I'd dig and dig until I knew it all."

"I bet you were fun to play doctor with," he quipped.

She cut loose with a wonderfully free, unselfconscious laugh that rattled the Corvette's tiny passenger compartment. Such an open, honest laugh made him decide to take the first few steps with her, just to see where they'd lead. After all, he reasoned, if the going got tricky he could always bail out.

"Let me make sure I have it straight," he said. "Are you saying that if I tell you the inside skinny on phreaking, along with whatever I know about hacking, you won't write about it?"

She nodded vigorously. "I won't take a single note. Just let me tag along on this Marsh thing and fill me in as we go."

There was such an ease of manner about her—not a tremor in her voice or a word out of place—that Nat couldn't make himself believe she was telling him anything but the truth. Even more surprising, he found himself *wanting* it to be the truth.

"Why don't we start with lunch?" she suggested. "I missed breakfast after my jail source called, so now I'm starving."

Nat ran one more mental scan to look for potential potholes, then decided to trust the instincts that had served him so well in the past. "How about the Mystic Vegetable?"

She wrinkled her long, straight nose, which skewed freckles all over her face. "What on earth is a mystic vegetable?"

"Don't let the name fool you," he replied as he turned the Corvette's ignition key. "It's new, but I think you'll like it."

She gave a hopeful shrug. "We'll see. . . ."

□ XIX □

As Nat and Karen were leaving for the Mystic Vegetable, Viktor Lubov was pressing the switch of a secret panel in a bedroom wall of his Nob Hill town house. A hidden door slid back to reveal a six-by-six-foot cubicle. In it were a swivel chair, a desk supporting a computer terminal, and what looked like a monitor-sized telephone-operator unit.

That unit was a highly sophisticated, computer-operated phone terminal. It had an acoustical coupling for receiving outputs, and a switchboard with multiple-tie-line capability. Its frequency tolerance was less than .08 percent; its amplitude tolerance, less than .05 decibel. It produced high-precision op-amps that were faster and more efficient than Ma Bell's. Those op-amps provided ultrastable amplification, superlow distortion, and frequency response from $-50°$ C to $+120°$ C.

In essence, it went about as far as phreaking technology could go at present. The only unit more widely regarded was the King's, which probably compared to this like the space shuttle to a hang glider. That was everyone's assumption, anyway, and Lubov had no reason to believe otherwise.

Lubov's purpose in becoming a phreak, the reason he'd been such a good soldier for so long, was his burning desire to one day see the King's unit and find out what it could do. He had suspicions, of course . . . suspicions he started forming as soon as he understood phreaking's full potential. But the King's rampant paranoia had prevented any personal relationship from developing.

During the twelve frustrating years he'd spent working his way up the Network hierarchy, Lubov had always believed that someday his efforts would pay off. It was a quintessential American attitude he didn't mind sharing: the belief that reward eventually flowed from effort like interest from principle. He regarded it as a capitalism of the spirit in which he was heavily leveraged. And now, if he invested wisely on the Ghost Glitch deal, he had a legitimate chance to achieve his payoff.

An important part of success would be maintaining his normal phreaking routine, which included a daily orbit call around noon. He did that for two very sound reasons: to keep abreast of any Network progress against Ma Bell; and to maintain a consistent presence in everyone's mind. Both contributed heavily to his ranking as Number Two, the top phreak behind the King.

In addition to those reasons, he'd long since learned that the character traits most valued by the King were efficiency and dependability. So he unfailingly gave the man what he wanted.

Because his consulting business usually kept him away from home at noon, he normally checked in with his pocket blue box from wherever he happened to be. But because that day's Ultramike Conference was being held so near his home, he was able to slip away during his lunch hour to use his main phreaking rig.

Feeling the surge of satisfaction he always experienced when settling down to play with his favorite toy, he tapped out the current secret orbit number on the unit's flush-button panel. The instantaneous connection that followed always reminded him of plunging a knife into a fresh, fluffy cake.

He paused for a moment to allow the verbal exchange in progress to be completed, then announced himself as was the custom: "Kraut on-line."

"Hey, Kraut! Snowbird here. The King checked in a little while ago and left a message for you, if you can believe that."

Lubov *was* doubtful because the King never left personal messages in the orbit. He had every phreak's real name, home address, and private phone number, so he could communicate with anyone directly. There had to be a very special, extraordinary reason for contacting him this way. "What did he say?"

Snowbird related their exchange. Lubov checked his watch. He'd make it with ease if he skipped the rest of the Conference.

"So how about it?" Snowbird concluded. "Can you go?"

"No," Lubov lied. "I'm totally tied up this afternoon. Whatever it is will just have to wait."

The truth was that he didn't want to risk any other phreak showing up just to get a glimpse of him. It was bad enough having the King know who he was. In his own way and for obvious reasons, he was equally paranoid about revealing his identity.

"No big deal," Snowbird said. "Just a missed opportunity of some kind. Probably a woman . . . part of his overflow!"

Everyone in the orbit laughed at that inside joke. To hear the King tell it, he had more adventures than Sherlock Holmes and a better sex life than James Bond. So behind his back they all suspected he was a real loser with women—or gay—because nobody normal felt a need to brag that much or that wildly.

When the laughter subsided Lubov said, "Kraut off-line."

He hung up to the standard chorus of "Kraut off-line!"

And then he started wondering what the hell was going on.

☐ **XX** ☐

Nat and Karen rode in uneasy silence for the first leg of their trip to the Mystic Vegetable. He needed time to get accustomed to the new situation between them, which she seemed to understand and was allowing for. But then the quiet was broken when a grumbling roar came welling up from her insides.

"Oh, excuse me!" she said to Nat as she thumped her abdomen a few times. And then: "Hey! You people down there! Knock it off or I'll call the manager and have you thrown out!"

Nat looked over at her, grinning, and saw her cheeks were flushed apple-red. "You *are* starved, aren't you?" he said.

He accelerated the Corvette through the heavier traffic outside Marsh's sedate neighborhood, knifing it along like a sleek black shark through a school of lumbering sea bass.

"How much longer?" she asked uneasily.

"Over on Burnside, near the mall." That meant ten more minutes, so he started talking to keep her mind off food. "I don't mean to doubt you, Karen, but are you sure you won't be tempted someday to use what I tell you in a story?"

"Using it isn't the same as writing about it," she replied. "I can promise I won't write about it without your specific permission. But when I investigate other matters, I might use what I learn. There's no way to separate the two. I'm sorry."

He had to admit she was saying the right things. Another answer might have made him reconsider. He reached over to his glove compartment, saying, "Okay, then—let's get started."

He opened the compartment and removed a silver-metal pocket calculator with a typical three-column, five-row spread of black plastic buttons on its face. He handed it to her.

"If this is to figure a lunch split," she said dryly, "let's just make it my treat."

He grinned at her wit. "Push a button on it, any button."

She chose #8. Instantly a high-pitched *cheeeeep!* filled the Corvette's inner space. "Hey!" she exclaimed. "This is a blue box! I've seen a few of these out on the street."

"I'm not surprised," he said. "They're fairly common."

She shook her head. "Not like this. This is quality."

"I thought it was the absolute top of the line until I saw the one Marsh had. His makes mine look like a phone booth."

She shrugged. "Why are they called blue boxes? I've never seen a blue one, and they sure don't look like boxes."

"The earliest ones were shoebox-sized and made out of blue plastic molding that was easy to buy. The name just stuck."

She hefted the device in her hand. "As I understand it, these things give complete access to the telephone systems of the entire world, free of charge. Right or wrong?"

He nodded. "Satellites, cables, microwaves—the works. Learn how to use one of those babies, and it's all yours."

"I'm impressed," she said, in no way being facetious.

"Most people use blue boxes just to rip off free long-distance calls. They're known as users, and they cost us several million dollars a year in line-time charges. We prosecute every one we catch, but what they steal is only a drop in the bucket. The people who really cause us trouble are the phreaks."

"Like the rock star you nabbed down in L.A.?"

Nat shook his head. "Because of that guy's high media profile, we weren't able to sweep his case under the rug the way we prefer to do. So we did the next best thing, which was to feed reporters down there a lot of false information to confuse them and obscure the fact that he was only a big-name user."

He fell silent as they entered a tricky intersection, then resumed when they were past. "Rock stars aren't the only ones we catch. Bookies, agents, brokerage people—anyone who makes a lot of long-distance calls." He glanced over at her with a wry grin. "Even a few reporters, so don't get too attached to that thing."

She hefted it one last time, then passed it back to him. "Don't worry, I haven't stolen a nickel since my best friend and I got caught shoplifting lipstick in sixth grade."

"Put the fear of God in you, huh?" he said as he tucked the blue box into his jacket pocket.

"Not fear—humiliation! My parents had to come to the store to pay for what we took, and I've never felt so dirty and disgusting in my entire life. I never will again, either."

Nat couldn't avoid connecting that withering experience with her reputation for integrity. And the passion in her voice was so unmistakable, it resolved his last doubts about trusting her.

"As I was saying," he resumed, "phone phreaks use blue boxes in ways far beyond simple rip-offs. They use them to explore Ma Bell's inner workings; to see what she's made of, inside and out. Their goal is to learn all they possibly can about her."

"And where, exactly, do you fit into all that?"

"It's my job to try to stop them."

She smiled. "Sounds like nice work, if you can get it."

He returned her smile, but not as wholeheartedly as he would have liked. "It's got its downside."

□ XXI □

Admiral Vince Tarnaby strode through a beautiful Hawaiian morning on his way to the gym at Pacific Command Headquarters. He was a robust man with the barrel-chested, stout-legged body of a lifetime athlete. His round, pampered-looking face belied the strenuous workouts he enjoyed before beginning his grueling workdays at HQ. He'd meet Fleet Admiral Lucius Horton, PAC-COM's commander, for a spirited game of racquetball.

Tarnaby commanded the Oahu Long-Distance Receiving post, as well as all other LDR bases throughout PACCOM. It was an assignment outside his Transportation designator, but one he'd found immensely rewarding over the six months he'd been at it.

The LDR's mission was to intercept and interpret every airwave message the Soviets sent anywhere on earth; and the men who did that were some of the Naval Security Group Agency's most valued and unique technicians. Tarnaby felt privileged to be a part of NSGA, if only until his two-year tour expired.

Tarnaby's opponent, Fleet Admiral Horton, was a man much like himself, only slimmer, older, and a slightly inferior racquetball player. Horton was one of the Navy's seven Fleet Commanders, and its first black to line himself up for a seat at the Joint Chiefs' table in Washington. If he was lucky, that assignment would come after his current tour guiding PACCOM.

Tarnaby entered their reserved court to find Horton already inside, warming up with stretching exercises. They exchanged greetings and then, as usual, Horton started talking shop while Tarnaby began his own loosening-up routine.

"What's the disposition of yesterday's intercept?"

He was referring to an emergency message relayed by a Soviet agent in Japan to a looper sub cruising near the Japanese coast. As sometimes happened, PACCOM's radio monitors at the Shinto LDR base had missed the initial transmit. That was because emergency messages were always sent on Very Low Frequency "bastard" transmitters, and VLF bastards were difficult to recognize.

Fortunately, Soviet submarines and satellites were always targeted for special scrutiny, so the LDR station there at Oahu had picked up the sub's relay to the overhead satellite, and the San Francisco LDR had gotten the satellite relay to New York.

"Purely . . . business . . ." Tarnaby replied between grunts. "Their man in Japan had to instruct their people in New York to tender a sealed bid on some hi-tech equipment he missed buying in Tokyo. If they'd blown it in New York, they'd have hung out to dry for several months. It was a close call for them."

Horton mulled that over. He knew the Soviets never sent emergency messages unless time was more critical than security, and the time factor was certainly present in this instance. But was it worth tipping off the U.S. to a major buying campaign?

"What kind of equipment are they after?" he asked.

"Decoding says it's components for some kind of acoustical jamming hardware. Looks like they might be trying to launch a counterprogram against some of our audio-scanner systems. Hell, maybe even taking a shot at the C/S/T arrays. You never know."

Horton barked a derisive laugh. "Ha! Those poor shit-for-brains are at least ten years behind us on that."

"True enough," Tarnaby agreed, then added, "for now. But they know how to play catch-up. I was in light cruisers a few years back, and I saw what they did there. It was amazing."

Sweat glistened on Horton's dark forehead as he picked up his racquet and a ball and started lacing random ricochet patterns around all six of the court's playing surfaces.

Soon both men were settled into the serious business of determining who'd be buying breakfast after the game.

☐ XXII ☐

The Mystic Vegetable was an art-deco masterpiece that served vegetarian dishes in which the "meats" were made of reconstituted gluten, a wheat flour by-product. That bizarre-sounding process was illustrated with a display of photographs and drawings set up near the restaurant's entrance. They showed how gluten was chemically extracted from its wheat-flour base, then mechanically restructured to resemble chicken, beef, and pork.

Karen reacted like most first-timers. "It's amazing how real this stuff looks!" she exclaimed. "The pork even has that reddish edge it has everywhere else! I can't wait to tell our restaurant critic about this place."

"Don't bother," Nat said. "It's already been written up. Got four stars too. You must have missed it."

While Karen examined the display in detail, Nat arranged for them to be seated at a tucked-away booth with a phone jack. Then he rejoined her and they were escorted to that booth.

Moments after being seated, they were brought small samples of each meat entrée. Karen would have wolfed hers down no matter how they tasted, but those bites proved gluten's flavor could be manipulated as effectively as its shape. Nat then gave her his share of the sample, after which they ordered their lunches.

"I love art deco *and* trying new things," she said as their waiter moved away. "Thanks so much for bringing me here, Nat."

It was obvious she meant every word, which was the response he'd been hoping for. "It's my pleasure, believe me."

She paused to gaze around one last time, giving him a lingering view of her handsome profile framed by its corona of red curls. Then she got down to business. "Okay, enough. I'm supposed to be learning about phone phreaking, so let's do it."

He smiled, appreciating her discipline. "Phreaking is a kind of electronic chess game, only a lot more interesting and demanding. In fact, it's the most taxing challenge of its type in the world, well beyond the mental reach of everyone except a very rare breed of cat. But even so, there are phreaks in at least ten countries, which is why we hate to publicize it. It's a slow-growing cancer we can't afford to speed up."

She nodded as if she understood; he felt she actually might.

"Like I said earlier, phreaks spend their time mastering the world's telephone systems . . . exploiting weaknesses and staying on top of every new wrinkle that comes along. And, as I also said, we at Ma Bell keep trying to stop them. So there's this huge electronic battle of wits always going on between us and them."

This time she leaned forward to steeple her fingers under her chin, clearly absorbed by what he was saying.

"Now, imagine our two groups—us and the phreaks—competing within this huge, infinitely complex system." His eyes glazed over as he began to visualize what he was talking about. "Ma Bell is a totally incredible, practically unbelievable system. You'd have to know her internal configurations the way we do to fully appreciate the beauty of how she works, warts and all."

He shook his head to dispel that vision of Ma's insides. "What makes phreaks special—besides their intellects—is their leader, the guy who started it all fifteen years ago. Nobody knows anything about him beyond the fact that he's the driving force behind the game. But everything revolves around him."

"Must be an interesting guy," she concluded.

It was a legitimate observation, but Nat couldn't stop a flicker of anger from rippling across the dark pools of his eyes.

"He's all of that, plus a helluva lot more: He's the King."

"King?" she repeated. "King of what?"

"Of all he surveys, part of which is giving every phreak a relevant code name. 'King' is the one he chose for himself."

"Sounds like a runaway ego to me."

"He has that too. But he's also such a bona fide genius, he deserves a grand title like King. He's far and away the greatest phone phreak in the world—a simon-pure, solid-gold phenom."

She leaned back in the booth to absorb what he'd just said.

"If you have the inclination and the brainpower it takes to be a main-line phone phreak," he went on, "you can get seriously hooked on the challenge of it. Take my word."

"Sounds like you're speaking from personal experience."

He hesitated only a moment. "I am."

As she sat there scrutinizing him across the booth's table, he couldn't help wondering what was going on in her mind . . . and how she might respond to the rest of his story.

"Would you mind elaborating on that?" she finally asked.

"I used to be a phreak," he said as offhandedly as he could manage. "That's how I ended up with this job."

Her green eyes widened for an instant, then her strawberry eyebrows knitted slightly. He viewed that subtle reaction as an illustration of how practiced she was at disguising her emotions in an interview situation. That, in turn, made him wonder how good she was at disguising emotions in other areas of her life.

Then a waiter delivered the first of their food.

☐ XXIII ☐

The Padre Island C/S/T Naval Facility was responsible for keeping track of every motorized vessel on or below the surface of 1,200,000 square miles of the Pacific Ocean. Padre Island itself was one of the Channel Island chain located off the coast of Los Angeles. It had been the Navy's western listening post since the first CAESAR, SASS, and TASS transponders were arrayed in 1950.

All subsequent C/S/T NAVFACs were patterned after the original at Padre Island. They were uniformly isolated, but varied in size from 125 personnel to 250 attached, including support staffs. All C/S/Ts were extremely secure, with high fences and secure gates protecting ever-decreasing perimeters.

At the core of the security net was the Terminal—or T-Building —a large, one-story cinderblock square with a flat roof and no windows. Inside the T-Building were a number of rooms containing key and peripheral staff.

There were offices for the commanding officer, the executive officer, the operations officer, the security officer, and the research officer. There were electronics experts on duty to repair malfunctioning sensors; cooks who prepared meals; guards who manned the gates and patrolled the perimeters; and various other maintenance personnel scattered throughout.

The heart of any C/S/T facility was its Display Room, which contained ten to twenty line-graph sensors, one or two pictograph display screens, and a four- to six-member post analysis team. All but one of those PAT members were oceanographic technicians, called O-Ts, who manned the line-graph sensors. Those sensors were connected to the C/S/T transponder arrays, which did the facility's real work.

In the case of Padre Island, that work was "listening" to the Pacific in hundred-mile-wide bands from San Diego to Seattle. As soon as any vessel entered the West Coast listening grid, Padre Island's O-Ts began tracking it with their sensors.

All O-Ts reported to the last PAT member, the operations watch officer, called the O-WO. The O-WO's main job was to utilize the pictograph screens, which provided visual representations of data transmitted to the sensors by the transponders. Thus, O-WOs kept a literal "watch" over the entire listening grid they were responsible for, and forwarded significant deviations from the norm to command headquarters.

In the case of Padre Island, that was Pacific Command Headquarters—PACCOM HQ—at Oahu, Hawaii.

Whenever a particularly attractive male or female had the O-WO job, O-Ts of the opposite sex playfully referred to them as O-WOWs. Eight months earlier, Lieutenant (Junior Grade) Hanna Buckley had been a cheerful, happily married, blond bombshell of an O-WOW.

Now she was a grumpy, self-described "Pillsbury Doughgirl," counting days until she reached the ninth month of her first pregnancy. Then she could go on maternity leave and try to figure out how she'd ever let her husband convince her that having a baby would be her "life's greatest adventure."

So far, it had been a pain everywhere but her eyelashes.

Hanna spent that day's lunch hour where she spent nearly all of them lately: sitting on a couch in the lounge of the T-Building's ladies' room. For reasons she couldn't explain, if she ate where she could throw up conveniently, she wouldn't. But if she took a single bite of food anywhere far from a toilet, it was all she could do to keep it down. And since a voracious appetite went along with her quirky stomach, she'd found that having her lunch in the ladies' room was an ideal solution.

She was just finishing off two cheeseburgers, fries, and a giant chocolate milk shake, when the rest-room door opened and Petty Officer Sally Merkle, one of her shift's O-Ts, walked in.

Sally was a twenty-year-old black woman who'd already been through a pregnancy of her own. She glanced at Hanna as she moved through the lounge into the stall area. After her time inside, she returned and stopped to touch up her appearance.

"You know, Lieutenant," she said as she picked at her hair, "you makin' a mountain out of that molehill you carryin' around."

"C'mon, Sally," Hanna said as she slurped the last of her milk shake, "I'm not in any mood for one of your lectures."

"I'm serious, Lieutenant. You lettin' *it* get on top of you 'stead of you gettin' on top of *it.*"

"Don't call it an *it.* It's not an *it.*"

"Then what *is* it?"

"It's a . . . a thing."

Sally was incredulous. "You call your baby a *thing?*"

"*It* sounds like some kind of creature from the Black Lagoon or someplace. I prefer *thing.*"

"You wouldn't if you saw a movie I seen one time. Called *The Thing* . . . Most godawful-lookin' ugly you ever did see."

There was a pause as Sally dabbed on lipstick and gave her hair one last primp. Then she turned around to face her "boss."

"What do other people call theirs?" Hanna asked.

"I called mine 'dumplin'.' That's what Momma called me and all my brothers and sisters. I figured it was good enough."

Hanna smiled. "It sure is. Thanks for the suggestion."

Sally grinned big, flashing wide white teeth. Then her expression folded back into a serious gaze. "For true, now—how you makin' it? Gonna get through the afternoon okay?"

Hanna leaned back and rested her head against the rear wall. "If I keep a barf bag near me, I can get through most anything. Besides, it's only two more weeks till I go on leave."

Sally reached out a hand and patted the top of Hanna's blond head. Anyone watching might have considered it strange to see a twenty-year-old black noncom being so familiar with a twenty-eight-year-old white officer. But the purpose behind her gesture transcended age, race, and rank.

It was necessary to convey heartfelt encouragement from one of Nature's vassals to another when compassion was sorely needed.

☐ XXIV ☐

Once the waiter was gone and Karen had settled into the task of satisfying her hunger, Nat resumed his explanation. "I used to be the top phreak in the Network, behind the King."

"What's the Network?" she asked between bites.

"I'll get to that later. For now just leave it at me being Number Two, I got bagged, then was forced to go to work for Ma."

That seemed to surprise her. "They made you turn traitor?"

His eyes narrowed. "That's what happens to all phreaks who get caught. Ma could prosecute us for grand theft and win it hands down, so she gives us a choice of jail or working for her."

"Wait a minute. You help give Ma the hassle of her life, and for that she lets you off the hook and gives you a job?"

"She has to handle it that way because her regular employees can't touch phreaks for overall knowledge of her systems. So she pits us against ourselves." He smiled with self-satisfied amusement. "Actually, neither side is complaining. Since the first phreak got bagged several years back, the game has escalated to a much higher level. We keep each other sharp."

She shook her head in amazement but made no comment.

For the remainder of the meal they kept their conversation on typical man-and-woman-getting-to-know-each-other topics. Nat began by telling her about his early life in Texas, where he won an academic scholarship to Cal Tech. At Cal Tech he became both an electrical engineer and one of the original group of phone phreaks. Later on, he promised, he'd tell her how it happened.

He next told her about his years spent working at the Hughes Research Lab in Los Angeles, up until he got caught phreaking and was eventually put in charge of Ma Bell's antifraud division in San Jose. He didn't go into the details of how he got caught, either, which she let pass for the moment. They left it at him saying his current work was immensely challenging and rewarding, and he couldn't imagine doing anything else for a living.

When her turn came, she told him about deciding on a career in journalism during the Watergate hearings. "Like a million other lemmings" was how she put it. But, echoing what he'd said, she told him how much she loved her work, and that she wouldn't trade jobs or life-styles with anyone anywhere.

Finding even that much common ground between them went a long way toward making them more comfortable with each other.

Earlier, when Karen was examining the gluten-as-meat display at the Mystic Vegetable's front counter, she'd been too absorbed to notice Nat arrange for their rear-corner booth to be provided with a phone. It was delivered and hooked into a wall jack as soon as the meal was finished and their plates were cleared away.

Nat waited until coffee had been served before he picked up the phone receiver while casually removing the blue box from his jacket pocket. He placed the thin silver oblong against the mouthpiece, using actions so smooth and subtle, it was nearly impossible to tell he was holding more than the receiver. While pretending to punch numbers on the phone's base with his free hand, he used his receiver/blue-box hand to punch buttons on *its* face.

Karen sat there slack-jawed as Nat, holding the blue box in position with his index and little fingers, used the middle two like a master musician playing a beloved instrument. And as with any classical performer, his expression while working was a mixture of supreme concentration and utter delight.

"It's not usually done in public like this," he said after punching out an erratic string of eleven *cheep*s. But like a naughty boy sampling delicious forbidden fruit, he clearly enjoyed making an exception for her benefit.

There was a short pause after the first eleven *cheep*s; then he punched a single sharp tone, paused another moment, and finally tapped out a series of fifteen more. Had there been people near enough to hear the resulting high-pitched bursts of sound, they'd have instantly known something unusual was going on in the back booth. But because the nearest diners were several feet away, and because the room's noise level had risen as the lunch crowd gathered, nobody realized what was happening.

Suddenly the performance ended. He handed the receiver across to her, minus the blue box. "Here, check this out."

He watched her cautiously take the receiver, then put it to her ear. A soft purr-purr ring replaced the usual buzz-buzz. He got a tremendous kick out of watching the change of emotion streak across her face: from bemused anticipation until it was answered, to genuine shock when she heard what she heard.

She whipped her hand over the mouthpiece. "Mayfair Hotel, London! You called *London*?"

He grinned. "Ask how the weather is."

She obeyed, but hesitantly. "Ummmm, hello? How's the weather over there?"

There was a pause as she listened to the response.

"No!" she blurted. "Well, I mean, yes . . . it *is* a kind of trick, but I . . ." Her mind seemed to go blank.

"That's enough. You can hang up now."

She did so like a zombie. " 'Bye . . . nice talking to you."

"Let's take it up a notch," he said, without trying to hide his enthusiasm. He took the receiver back, tapped out two more long, broken series of *cheep*s, then returned it to her.

As he tapped, Karen breathed deeply in an effort to regain her composure. By the time she had the receiver again, she was more or less under control. "Where's this one to?"

Her eager confusion was a typical first response, so Nat just grinned at her. "Let it be a surprise."

A moment later she reacted to the pickup, listened, then said, "Ummm, which American embassy, please?" There was the predictable pause, followed by an expression of utter shock. Again her hand whipped to the mouthpiece as she rasped, "Moscow!" He grinned even more as she reacted to what she was hearing. "No, it's *not* a crank call! It's a wrong number! Good-bye!"

She sat there exhibiting that familiar, lost-in-space gaze Nat had seen on many other "virgins." Then she shook off her reverie and spoke excitedly. "It's like riding on a magic carpet, isn't it? Punch a few buttons and *presto*! It takes you anywhere in the world you want to go!"

"Couldn't have put it better myself," he said as he laid the blue box down in front of her. "And now that you've seen what can be done, are you ready to find out how it's done?"

"You bet! This is fabulous!"

"Then look at the blue box."

She locked her eyes onto its three columns of five buttons each. No matter what he called it, to her it was a calculator.

"It works exactly like a telephone, so forget the minus, times, divide, and equal signs. Those are for going overseas or inside Ma herself. To just use it, you need only the ten digits and the plus sign, which is the 2600 disconnect. Push it."

She glanced around to make sure they were still operating unnoticed, then she pressed it. There came a high, clear tone reminiscent of a bat's screech.

"That's the only single tone in the system," he explained, "2600 cycles per second. Whenever you hang up a phone, that sound alerts the computers that control the calling process."

She nodded. "Got it . . ."

"All the other buttons produce twin-tones. Push one."

He gazed down as she pushed the #1 button. A *cheep* sounded.

"Okay," he said, "that was number one. It's a combination of 900 cycles per second and 500 cycles per second. Again."

He gazed back down as she sounded another *cheep*. He looked up with a wry grin. "How creative. Number two is a combination of 1100 and 700 cycles per second. It goes on like that through every number on every phone in the world. When you dial, those twin-tones are what the computers deal with. It's very basic technology, which is why the system is vulnerable to phreaking."

"I'm losing you," she confessed.

"Don't worry," he said reassuringly, "I'll keep it simple. Now, let's say we want to call Washington, D.C., from right here. We pick up a telephone receiver and punch in any 800 number . . . say a Holiday Inn's in Memphis. We punch it in and get hooked by an available tandem into the master computer system. Now, before I go any further, let me tell you how tandems work.

"Tandem lines blanket the world in millions of interlocking webs attached to computers at thousands of switching stations. Each tandem in the web can connect with any other tandem through those computers, which can coordinate millions of impulses in a second. I know that's hard to imagine, but take my word for it.

"Now, obviously, not all tandems are in use at any given moment. When they're not, they send out the 2600 tone you heard earlier. It's best to think of it as a disconnect button, but it's actually saying to the computers: I'm here if you need me.

"Pick up your phone and one of dozens of tandems connected to it is 'seized' and stops sending the 2600 tone. That tells the computers your tandem is ready to send your message. Then you dial and it carries your twin-tones to the computers, which direct your call to a tandem connected to the phone you want.

"Try to remember all that while we go back to our call from here to D.C. We pick up our phone and seize a tandem connected to it. That tandem stops sending its 2600 tone and waits for further instructions. We punch in our Holiday Inn's toll-free number, which our tandem relays through the computers to Memphis.

"At Memphis an available tandem is seized and stops sending out its own 2600 signal. It receives the twin-tone codes sent to it by the computer and rings the Holiday Inn phone. A note is made on the accounting tape at Ma's local office, showing a call was attempted and the code numbers to be used if it's completed.

"So far that's the normal sequence of events, but from here on it gets tricky. Before the Holiday Inn can answer and complete the call, we place our blue box near the telephone's mouthpiece and push our plus button. The Memphis tandem receives that 2600 message, stops ringing the Holiday Inn's number, and starts generating its own 2600 tone.

"Meanwhile, we release our plus button to reestablish our link with the Memphis tandem, but now there's a difference: The new connection is a *sending* one instead of the receiving one of before. The Memphis tandem thinks someone there wants to make a call, so it stops sending its 2600 message and waits to send a toll-free call anywhere we ask it to.

"All we do then is use our blue box to punch in our D.C. number. Ma's computers can't tell the difference between electronic impulses, so they relay the call as if it's legit. The billing system shows an attempted call from our local number to the Memphis toll-free number, and a toll-free call from Memphis to Washington. But there's no way to connect the two.

"That's all there is to it—simple and effective."

"Effective, maybe"—Karen laughed—"but simple? No way!"

☐ XXV ☐

Viktor Lubov got on the road well ahead of schedule for his three P.M. rendezvous with the King's mysterious messenger.

It was a ninety-minute trip from his home to San Jose, so he decided to take a break at a point near Palo Alto. He stopped at a coffee shop just off the freeway south, his pearl-gray Porsche cutting as fine a figure as he did as it entered the parking lot.

By then the lunch crowd was gone and business was slow, so the four waitresses on duty had little to keep them occupied. Seeing the quality of the car rolling to a halt outside, they were able to signal one another that a live one was coming in.

As he parked and got out, each waitress began to hope he'd choose her section to sit in. His tall, lean, blond good looks were coolly handsome, and he was richly attired. Even in casual clothes —gray tweed jacket over burgundy turtleneck—he radiated an air of immaculate elegance. He *had* to be somebody famous.

He strolled in and removed his sunglasses, then took a seat at the counter. The best-looking waitress in the place began to glow; he'd chosen her area. She moved over with a menu, glancing down to make sure her top button was undone. She offered the menu to him with as much forward lean as propriety allowed.

"Need to see a menu?" she inquired cheerfully.

"No, thank you," he replied, his resonant baritone and crisp German accent lending another indication of celebrity status. "But I would like a cup of tea—bag in water, please."

She nodded. "Coming right up."

As she turned to do her work, Lubov rose and went to the men's room. While he was gone, the other waitresses huddled together to discuss who he might be. The oldest—a foreign-film fan—felt certain he was a European movie star. And even if he wasn't, any man who looked that good *should* be a star.

Lubov returned to his seat, expertly wound the tea bag into the bowl of his spoon, then took a sip. As always, the uniform consistency of American tea amazed him. There was no variety or subtlety or integrity—only the same bland flavor, cup after cup, week after week, year after year. He hated it.

As a child, tea had been his favorite beverage. He could easily remember the great care and attention that went into every pot or cup. To his parents and their friends, tea was far more than something to drink before, during, or after a hard day's labor. Tea was an elixir of life itself, to be treated with all the respect due something so essential.

That's what he really hated about American tea—the fact that it brought back memories of a past life he'd enjoyed so much and then lost. The pain of those memories was often so intense, it was almost enough to make him take up drinking coffee. But that would have been a coward's way out. Besides, his espionage training had taught him to turn the pain of his memories—both good and bad—to his own advantage.

During his training, he'd been imbued with an unswerving conviction that his good memories were why he had to spy against the Americans. Preservation of the way of life he'd be leaving behind, the way of life that had produced those memories, was absolutely paramount. Not for himself, of course, but so that future generations might know and experience the many kinds of pleasures he'd known as a boy.

That had to be reason enough for any sleeper because memories were all they had.

As Lubov sat drinking and reflecting on the convoluted past that had taken him from a childhood in war-torn Berlin, to his youth spent in the mountains of southern Russia, he realized the waitresses in that California coffee shop were gawking at him.

As always, he remained impassive to their covetous looks, seeing all women, and men, as little more than means to his ultimate ends. As with Rainer, he exploited his gifts only when necessary, and in this instance it definitely wasn't necessary.

He stood, left a dollar beside his teacup, then walked away. As he passed his waitress, she made an obvious point of giving him a dazzling smile. He only nodded politely in return.

Leaving the coffee shop, he wondered for the first time in a long time where along the line of his life he'd lost his burning interest in sex. He'd certainly had it in his youth, back in Russia. But many things from his past were now lost forever.

Good tea and sex were just two of them.

□ XXVI □

After leaving the Mystic Vegetable, Nat brought Karen to what he called a double-bubble, which was two phones hung back-to-back from a convenience store's front wall. Each was protected from the elements by a blue metal egg.

As he killed the Corvette's engine in front of the store, he glanced over at her and noticed her worried expression.

"Hey, come on," he chided. "Lighten up! I've got great connections. If we get busted we'll be out in five years, tops."

She grinned at her own anxiety, then got out with him and went to the phones. He checked both, then decided to use the one that allowed him to face the store's entrance. "Don't want anyone slipping up on us while we're beeping," he muttered.

He went over the routine once more, then asked for someone to call. She gave him her mother's number in Sacramento. He punched it out deliberately, showing her the correct sequence of pauses to insure a proper 2600 disconnect. At the end of it she was checking in with her mother for a brief chat.

When she hung up, Nat asked for someone else. She gave him her brother Bob's number in Georgia. They got his answering service, which said he was at work. The third call was to her sister Margaret in San Diego. That one Karen did by herself.

"This is amazing!" she blurted after the short call to Margaret. "And so easy!"

"Yeah," he agreed, "anyone can handle a blue box. That's why they're such a problem for us."

He didn't add that the problem with phreaking was far more insidious, providing a huge emotional kick Karen was already experiencing. The ease and adventure of it were narcotic in their own right, but the real rush came from gaining a sense of mastery over something impenetrably complicated.

"Will you teach me the hard parts too?" she asked with innocent eagerness. "Like going overseas and inside Ma Bell?"

He shook his head. "Sorry, those are off-limits."

"Awww, come on!" she wailed, bursting with a desire she didn't even attempt to disguise.

"Just look at you!" he countered, holding firm. "I give you a taste and you're already a junkie."

That made her pause to think. She placed her palm on her chest, above her heart, then nodded matter-of-factly. "You could be right; my heart's beating a mile a minute. Then again, maybe it's just my wannaknowitis kicking in."

"No way!" he insisted. "That's phreaking, plain and simple. It's addictive as sin."

A crinkle of doubt swept across her forehead as she thought that over, then she said, "I'm just not the addictive type."

He knew better—the bug could bite anyone. "All right, I'll give you a demonstration, *if* you promise to leave it at that."

"Agreed!" she said, handing the blue box back to him.

He took it, paused to organize his thoughts, then lifted the receiver of the phone on his side and went to work. His fingers danced in a blur over the blue box's buttons, their high-pitched beeps sounding remarkably musical as all fifteen came into play.

He tapped and tapped and tapped, what seemed like a hundred times. Finally he stopped, and all she could say was "How on earth did you ever learn so many numbers by heart?"

He grinned. "With practice it's easier than you think."

Just then the opposite phone, the one beside her shoulder, rang. She jumped as if she'd been hit by a cattle prod.

"Better answer it," he said dryly. "Might be for you."

With a shaking hand she lifted the receiver to hear the last of his instructions fade into crackling static: ". . . be for you."

He handed over his own receiver. "Here, say something."

She took it and said, "Hello?" Two seconds later her voice came in weakly through the other receiver: "Hello?"

She stood between the two metal eggs like some high-powered stock trader, a receiver against each ear. And though the two instruments were linked by who-knew-how-many miles of telephone relays and a technological sophistication she couldn't begin to comprehend, she delighted in playing like a child between them.

"Hello . . . *hello* . . . HELLO!"

After a while he said, "That's enough for now. Let me beep you off." He took his receiver back and put the blue box near the mouthpiece. "When I hit it, don't hang up—just listen."

He pushed the 2600 disconnect and there was a burst of loud static on her end, followed by a short whistling sound. That was followed by a shrill screech, then a long flutelike series of tones mixed with the staccato popping of rapid pulses. The line then made a *kachunk* sound followed by a whistling *cheep,* followed by more *kachunk/cheep*s. After ten of those sounds had faded into nothingness, the line returned to its familiar white-noise hum.

The show was over.

"That was great!" she exclaimed. "What was it?"

"I stacked up some tandems, then took you around the world. That's why the connection was so fuzzy."

"You *what*?"

"I called you by first stacking up ten tandems, meaning the connection was going back and forth from here to New York five times. Then I sent it around the world: from me to Japan, Japan to India, India to Kenya, Kenya to Italy, Italy to France, France to Brazil, Brazil to Mexico, Mexico to you. Quite a trip, huh?"

"You're not kidding!"

"When you were speaking, you were hearing your voice about two seconds after you'd said the words. And those sounds you heard at the end were the country connections breaking off and the tandems unstacking. It's just a game phreaks like to play."

Karen was bowled over. "A game? Give me a break! That was the most fantastic thing I've ever heard!"

"I could just as easily have played a melody like that," he replied. "Any serious phreak can. So don't be too impressed."

Her twin emeralds were lit with passion and humor as she started working on him. "Oh, pul-eeeze! Won't you reconsider teaching me the hard parts? I *swear* I won't get hooked and become a phreak. I just want to know how it's done—honest!"

Karen's willingness to be silly about her desires was enormously attractive to Nat. It reminded him of a lovestruck teenager frantically wishing for a prom date with a movie star; knowing it was a hopelessly fanciful dream, but wishing all the more fervently for that precise reason. He couldn't help being charmed.

"Let's talk about it later," he said, deciding that was the best way to put her off without stalling their forward progress. "Right now I've got to get to work on the Marsh case."

She adjusted in an eyeblink. "Okay, whatever you say."

But they both knew the battle had only begun.

□ XXVII □

Riley and Bandini had been right about the San Jose city court's arraignment proceedings: They didn't take long.

The charges against Marsh were presented by the presiding judge; Riley submitted a not-guilty plea to each; a trial date was set for three months from that date; and bail was set at an extraordinarily high $75,000, which to everyone's surprise, except Riley's, Marsh covered with a verified cash bank draft.

Twenty minutes after the process began, he was given the routine warning to stay in the San Jose area and make himself available for subsequent court dates. Then he was released, and from that point on it would simply be a matter of executing Mismatch, his plan to make sure he never faced another court proceeding, not to mention any other government hassle.

His first step in that direction, as he saw it, was to shake the tail he was sure the FBI would put on him for the next few days. Because he hadn't yet learned about the extensive surveillance done on him prior to his arrest, he was under the impression no one knew about his cabin up in the mountains.

The next step would be carrying out his rendezvous with the Kraut, which was the only part of his plan where he had serious doubts. Would the Kraut turn out to be what he'd always claimed and appeared to be? Or would he prove to be something entirely different . . . something dangerous to Marsh himself, and even more dangerous to Mismatch? Only time would tell. But every angle had been considered, every precaution taken.

The problem with the Kraut was that he'd always been an odd

duck among phreaks. Most were young kids who'd gotten into the orbit in high school or college, then stayed with it until they worked their way into the Network. But the Kraut was completing his doctorate when he first came into the orbit, and he went at phreaking with a vengeance from day one. He had an incredible sense of purpose that impressed everyone, an insatiable drive to learn all there was to know about Ma Bell and her systems. He'd earned the Number Two position by sheer determination rather than the technical brilliance other Number Twos had shown.

Other negatives about him were his bizarre background and his obvious ambition to become personally acquainted with the King. The latter had always made Marsh uneasy because personal relationships among phreaks were neither necessary nor wise. But he couldn't attribute the Kraut's desire to anything other than devout loyalty. The guy was never crass or pushy; he just made it clear that if the King ever needed to make personal contact with a phreak, he considered himself the best man for the job.

Despite those negatives, the Kraut was exactly the right man for what Marsh needed done, so today he was finally going to meet the King. But not without close scrutiny right up to the last second. And if anything—even the slightest tremor of hands or voice—indicated he might be other than what he claimed, Marsh had every intention of switching over to Ram-Jam, a modification of Mismatch that should protect him if worse came to worst.

The biggest problem with revealing the King's identity to anyone, phreak or otherwise, was that they might already be—or might one day become—an agent for Ma Bell. It would be an unmitigated disaster if that occurred in this instance, and Marsh's recent encounter with the wheels of justice made him even more leery. But Ram-Jam was a comprehensive backup plan with excellent provisions for damage control. He was sure of that.

With those issues settled in his mind, that left only the nonexistent FBI tail to deal with. He moved from the jail's entrance to a taxi waiting on the street in front. He casually glanced around as he walked, trying to spot the surveillance team. He couldn't, but didn't really expect to. If they were good they should remain all but invisible, and he expected the Ghost Glitch to be assigned nothing but the best.

He got into the taxi and instructed its driver to head into the heart of downtown. He'd once read a spy novel that explained how to evade the three-car triangle favored by U.S. intelligence agencies, which he assumed the FBI would employ in his case. So he did everything the novel's hero had done: ordered unexpected turns; slowed down and speeded up; got out of one taxi, hurried through a large department store, then got into another taxi.

After repeating that routine twice, he found an empty taxi waiting at a red light. He knocked on its window and the cabbie invited him in. He peeled off two twenties from the wad in his pocket, handing them over with instructions to keep the change. Then he told the cabbie to drive out of town to a place several miles away. The cabbie took the money and said nothing else until they arrived where Marsh had asked to be delivered.

It was an isolated recreation area with wide-open venues all around. The cabbie sat quietly as Marsh stepped out and wandered around, looking overhead for helicopters, convincing himself he'd shaken the FBI's vaunted tail. Then he felt confident enough to give instructions to go to his penultimate destination.

"Take me to the San Jose bus station."

The cabbie nodded, started the taxi's engine, and drove away.

If they made good time, Marsh realized, they'd be at the bus station in fifteen minutes. Then a short walk to the library to watch the Kraut arrive so *he* could be checked for tails.

Mismatch seemed right on track.

□ XXVIII □

As Nat backed the Corvette away from the double-bubble they'd been using, Karen asked, "Where are we going now?"

"Back to my office. I have to do some research into who Marsh is before I can try to build a case against him."

"What kind of research?"

"Whatever I can find. We're hooked into all kinds of data banks. Something will turn up."

"I know about those," she replied. "Good for financial records, but not much else."

He glanced over at her, wondering what she was getting at. "Financial records can tell you a hell of a lot about someone."

She flashed a mischievous grin. "So can a newspaper morgue. Want to check ours on the way to your office?"

That was a good idea and an excellent sign of good faith on her part. He smiled back at her. "If it's no trouble . . ."

"No trouble at all," she assured him. "I'd love doing it for you, to pay back a little of what you're doing for me."

The word *love* caught his attention. *What the hell?* Maybe now would be a good time to try to escalate things a notch. "No payback can equal just getting to spend time with you."

That caught her off guard and she couldn't—or just didn't try—to conceal her surprise. "I . . . uh . . . don't know what to say!"

He drove in hopeful silence while she pulled herself back together. Then she reached out to touch his hand as she'd done earlier, when she was soft-soaping him about helping her.

"You're a sweet guy, Nat. I've known that since the first time we met. But we're not here to trade compliments, are we?"

He silently cursed his impatience, then tried to recover. "No, of course not. That's not what I meant to imply. Sorry."

He hastily returned to his explanation of phreaking.

"The way the King tells it—and only he knows—it all began fifteen years ago, when he was a sophomore in college. Says he was bored by school, so he'd read old technical journals to check out the evolution of things he was interested in. That's how he stumbled across an obscure article with a schematic drawing of Ma Bell's twin-tone system. That article was the key to the magic kingdom because—as you've seen—twin tones were the basis for Ma's dialing procedures. When he found out how they worked, there was no stopping him. He'd uncovered her Achilles' heel.

"Now, before you ask . . . the reason twin-tones are Ma's Achilles' heel is this: About forty years ago her executives recognized that computers were the future. That meant Ma needed a new dialing and switching system that could take advantage of the oncoming technology. So those executives chose the twin-tone concept because it was simple, it maxed the period's electronic capacities, and—most important in such decisions—it was cheap.

"As a result, twin-tones became the foundation on which Ma's entire physical plant was constructed. Unfortunately for her, nobody looked very far ahead. Nowadays her superstructure's technology is light-years beyond that primitive foundation. She's like a skyscraper built on logs. And we can't rip out the groundwork and start over because everything else would come down with it. So we're stuck with trying to patch whatever cracks we find, while phreaks make it their business to find them first.

"But I'm getting ahead of myself. Let's go back to the King in college, when he discovered that twin-tone schematic. He says up until then he'd never thought much about the phone system, but that article really cranked him up. So he went home, built the first blue box, and started using it.

"At first he only played around, getting a feel for Ma's systems. That's how it is for everyone in the beginning: You just phreak for the sake of phreaking. Eventually, though, you get tired of that, and so did the King. He wanted to bring other people in on it. But he didn't know how to do that without risking Ma finding out. And he knew her people would go stark raving berserk if they found someone using her equipment without paying. So he had to find a way that would be ultrasafe.

"He started researching Ma's systems, looking for a weak spot. He read book after book, article after article, chasing flimsy hints of relevant information. Then one day he found an article about switching orbits, which were built into the original equipment when Ma converted to control by computers.

"That looked promising because by then he was a whiz with computers, and Ma had evolved into one big unit. But she hadn't always been that way. She'd been a simple hand-to-wire relay system until computers came along, and many mistakes were made during the changeover. Two big ones involved switching orbits.

"Orbits were toll-free trunk lines set up for Ma's own switching verification and internal communication. Two hundred were in place when a technology advance made them obsolete. But instead of taking the trouble to disconnect them, Ma made her first mistake: She left them in place and forgot about them.

"The King's next project was to find out where they were. Easier said than done, because the information was stored in top-secret data banks. Which meant he had to crack secure access codes.

Nobody knows how long that took or how he managed it, but there's no doubt he eventually accessed Ma's internal files.

"Once inside, he learned all outdated material was stored in a warehouse in Waltham, Massachusetts. That was Ma's second big mistake: storing copies in only one place. The King figured no warehouse full of old forgotten papers was likely to be guarded, so he flew to Massachusetts to steal them.

"When he got there, he discovered the warehouse was a parking lot! It had burned down two years before, and the records he'd come to steal were gone with it. But even though that meant neither he nor Ma had direct access to the orbits, there was still a possibility of ferreting them out one by one.

"If not for his incredible ability with computers, he'd never have come close. But somehow, some way—and to this day nobody knows how—he finally designed a program to locate them. Then it took him nearly a year to catalogue all two hundred numbers. But when he'd finished, it was safe to bring others in.

"To start the ball rolling, he made a five-day cross-country car trip, leaving 'Want-to-hear-something-interesting?' leaflets in college frat houses and dorms. Kids like me saw them, dialed into the orbit number he provided, and found ourselves connected to an open free line. At first everyone was uncomfortable using code names and talking to faceless strangers, but before long it turned into one endless party. Anytime, day or night, there'd be people on the line, swapping stories and trading gossip.

"Naturally, Ma heard about the leaflets and had her people call into the orbit. Then she put a tap on it and went looking for its terminals to shut it down. But when she went to check her records —surprise! No warehouse and no records. She did have the orbit number, so she knew where to start; but she had to take it out the same way the King found it, piece by piece.

"Again, easier said than done. One orbit might go from Denver to Milwaukee to Atlanta to New Orleans to Amarillo and back up to Denver, with stops at all switching stations in between. And at each station, in some unknown place in the wire banks, there's a double set of terminals that have to be found by hand and disconnected. It took Ma eight weeks to track that first one down, and even now we still need about a month.

"Anyway, back to that first orbit. As soon as it started fading away . . . Did I mention that's how they go out? They don't just end—*boom*! They sort of faaaaaade away over the last few days as the last few terminals are disconnected. And there's no mistaking it when one starts to go. You can actually hear the last two terminals get disconnected.

"Okay, so it started fading and everybody flipped out. But the King just said, 'Relax, here's another number.' Everyone was on that second orbit line before the first one was completely gone, and all Ma's people could do was take the new number and go to work shutting it down. The transition was just that smooth.

"Of course, the big difference was that Ma's people couldn't match the King's skill with computers. They just couldn't design programs with enough access to do the job. He knew more about her systems than they did, so they had to be satisfied with taking away each new orbit as soon as they found out about it.

"Meanwhile, the King was forming what he called the Network. After several weeks of orbiting, the novelty wore off and most people lost interest. But a few like me started spending more and more time at it. We wanted to do more, go more places in the system; we were hooked on it. When that cream started rising to the top, the King started skimming us off.

"His first step was to safely contact us outside the orbit. We'd call into it from a pay phone and give him that phone's number, then he'd call us right back to get our real name and a safe private number. Ma's tracers just couldn't keep up. And after he'd identified and contacted his chosen few, he gave us another orbit number, but this one we had to keep secret.

"That small group became the charter members of the Network. Using the secret orbit, he told us everything he'd learned about blue boxes: what could be done with them, what they were made of, how to build them, how to use them. We went absolutely crazy and were phreaking full bore within a few days.

"When the novelty of that wore off, we started mapping Ma's systems to a degree her own people had never dreamed of. See, Ma's crowd worked for money and specialized in one or two areas, while we phreaked because we loved exploring her systems. And since the secret orbits were a perfect way for us to exchange information, we could work together to see the whole forest, while Ma's people were isolated and could see only the trees.

"Anyway, soon there wasn't anything about Ma—not the tiniest detail—that the Network couldn't find out. There wasn't a move she could make or a change she could consider that the King wouldn't know about in a matter of hours—sometimes minutes! And our security was so tight, Ma never suspected a thing.

"It went on like that until several years ago, when one of the original phreaks tried to do favors for some of his friends by making blue-box calls for them. The next thing he knew, Ma's agents were all over him like a pack of hungry wolves. They used heavy-handed Gestapo tactics to scare the hell out of him, and he crumpled under the pressure. He handed over his blue box and told them everything, including the secret orbit number.

"Fortunately for the phreaks, the King's code-name system kept everyone safe from betrayal. Only he knew real identities and nobody knew his, so Ma could only shut down the secret orbit. Meanwhile, the King called everyone privately and gave out a new secret number that stayed active till the next phreak got busted, which has only happened a half dozen times since the first one.

"Anyway, like I told you, Ma gives bagged phreaks a choice: face a jail-time prosecution, or agree to be a consultant against the Network. Like I also said, those of us on her side now have escalated the game to a whole new level. But there's still a lot more phreaks than ex-phreaks, so they stay pretty far ahead."

He paused to glance over at Karen. She was staring at him with a look of pure pity. "Didn't it just *kill* you to get caught?"

His jaw muscles rippled. "More than you could ever know."

□ XXIX □

The main branch of the San Jose Public Library was an adobe-style building whose architectural influence was the old California Missions. It had an ornate facade fronting a large courtyard replete with stone benches and a small fountain. From one of the benches just inside the facade, Marsh commanded a clear view of comings and goings in the outside parking area.

Soon after he sat down, he saw the expected gray Porsche arrive. *Typical,* he thought. *Fifteen minutes early.* Nothing of consequence followed, which indicated there was no backup group of Ma Bell's agents tagging along. A good sign. It still left the possibility of a stakeout already in place, but Marsh had thought of a way to reveal that later—if it was there.

Lubov sat in his car to await the appointed meeting hour. Marsh liked that about the Kraut: He always exhibited a healthy respect for time and timing. They at least had that in common, along with their zeal for phreaking. But not much else.

Marsh knew the kind of car Lubov drove because he'd made a religion of learning all he could about individuals he brought into the Network. He felt that was essential to keep Ma Bell's spies from infiltrating it. In Lubov's case, he even went to the trouble of attending a couple of scientific conferences where the physicist was a featured speaker. Those prior encounters caused Marsh no concern now, however, because not even the Kraut could possibly recall one specific face from such large audiences.

Actually, those conferences had given Marsh solid reasons to respect—and even admire—Lubov as a man . . . to the point of honest envy. Not only did the Kraut know his business as well as anyone anywhere, he spoke about it in a razor-sharp style that left even jaded technical audiences calling for more.

And then there was how damn good he looked.

Far more than the remote threat of Lubov being a Ma Bell agent, Marsh was concerned about the vast difference in their physical appearance. If he found that everything about the Kraut checked out, and if he felt safe admitting he was the King, he was going to have one hell of a time explaining all the lies he'd told about himself over the years. The problem was that Lubov actually looked like the romantic rogue the King claimed to be.

As always, Marsh had a scheme for dealing with that dilemma. He was going to say that the endless stories about his adventures and his love life were all part of an elaborate smoke screen to obscure his true identity. He knew it was a weak leg to stand on, but anything was better than the truth, which was that he simply loved to imagine himself starring in the lies he told.

Creating those fantasies was an important part of how he coped with the dismal reality of his barren private life.

At 2:55 Lubov left his Porsche to approach the library building. He walked slowly, trying to make eye contact with everyone he encountered. He lingered on the steps outside the facade until exactly 3:00, then stepped into the inner courtyard.

He seemed relaxed, confident, and eager to get under way.

Marsh pretended to be absorbed in a newspaper as Lubov checked him out, along with several people who entered and left the building during the next few minutes. Lubov stayed in the courtyard to remain visible, glancing at his watch a half dozen times, until he finally moved inside. Marsh knew he'd be back.

Five minutes later he reentered the courtyard looking substantially more on edge. It was now 3:15, and Marsh knew that to a man like himself, fifteen minutes was an eternity. The Kraut had to be nearing his breaking point. A few more minutes was all it would take to reveal a stakeout in place.

Lubov kept his attention focused between his watch and the faces of people moving in and out of the library. Only a few women gave him more than a casual glance, and their reaction was understandable. But he never indicated a connection to others in the area: no high signs or low signs or signals of any kind.

That made it a virtual certainty he was flying solo.

He stepped back in front of the facade, stood there one final minute, then gave up in frustration and moved down the steps toward the parking area, muttering curses as he went.

Marsh got up to follow, feeling everything was on schedule and falling into place as it should. At least to the extent that if the Kraut *was* a Ma Bell agent, he was acting alone on this.

Lubov got in the Porsche, started the engine, and was about to back out when Marsh stepped beside the passenger door to tap on the window. A soft electronic *whirrrr* lowered it as Lubov leaned over to look out. "Yes? May I help you?"

"I'm here to help you," Marsh said, as pleasantly as his handicapped mouth would allow. "The King sent me."

"Did he, indeed?" Lubov replied, holding his ground while giving nothing away. "Assuming I know what you're talking about,

I'm sure this King fellow might guess I'd be suspicious of you. He might have told you some tidbit of information only he and I know about. Were you supplied with something like that?"

Marsh's surging optimism was suddenly clouded by serious apprehension. This was the Kraut, all right—no doubt about it. But it wasn't the fawning pushover he'd imagined in his fantasy of how this was going to happen. *This* Kraut was so smooth he was oily, and he'd require careful handling every step of the way.

"He mentioned something about a faulty access link in the number-four Atlantic cable. Something about using it to backwash relay tandems once the wrinkles get ironed out."

Lubov's frustrations and anxieties were clearly eased by that arcane reply. His frown of doubt relaxed as he pressed a button that unlocked the passenger door. "Please . . . get in."

Marsh did so feeling heartened by Lubov's turnaround. They still had a long way to go together, but at least they were off on the right foot. And Mismatch was still solidly on track.

□ XXX □

Karen worked for the San Jose *Union-Ledger,* the largest of the Bay Area dailies circulating outside San Francisco's main market. It served a population of 500,000, which put it on an equal footing with all but the biggest American newspapers.

Its morgue was nothing like the old-fashioned rooms filled with dusty stacks of back issues and shelf after shelf of file folders stuffed with clippings. It was a small, brightly lit, rather sterile place in which everything was microfilmed and computerized. It provided access not only to the *Union-Ledger's* old materials, but also to those of every other newspaper—large or small—within the entire Bay Area.

The technophile in Nat took to that morgue like a kid to a new toy. He wanted to know everything: how all the data was collected, collated, stored, and retrieved. Karen could answer only about half his questions because she wasn't concerned with the nuts and bolts of how the system worked. All she wanted to know was how to obtain the information she needed.

After doing her best to satisfy his inquiries, she settled down to find out if anything had ever been written about Marsh. She sat at a terminal and took the first step—punching in his name. In seconds a bottom-to-top scroll appeared on her screen. It listed ten articles written by or about Percy Marsh.

Then a second scroll came crawling up.

That one was for Percy Marsh, *Senior,* with datelines running from two to twenty years preceding the first about Percy, Junior. Senior's article list filled two screen-widths and dealt mostly with early computer developments. Then came an obituary about his untimely death in a car crash, which also had killed his wife.

"Well, well, well," Nat muttered as he began to understand what it meant. "Seems our boy's a chip off a mighty big block."

Karen had to agree. "At least he comes by it honestly."

"Let's bring up all of Junior and most of Senior, okay?"

"It'll take quite a while to go through so much."

He gave her an impatient look. "I'm in no rush—are you?"

Her red curls shook as she wrote down the file numbers for Marsh's ten articles. She then chose a random selection from those written about his father. She took the two lists over to the racks of microfilm canisters and logged in with her access card. She then retrieved the dozen canisters they needed, sat down at a viewer, and began scrolling up the first article.

Three hours later, she and Nat had a well-rounded picture of who Marsh was and how he'd acquired the Ghost Glitch's remarkable capacities. The guy was a bred-in-the-bones computer genius!

Marsh's father, they discovered, had been an electrical engineer who'd played a major role in constructing the world's first vacuum-tube computers in the late forties and early fifties. Marsh's mother had been a mathematics professor at Stanford University, and she seemed to fully understand and appreciate each computer development as it occurred.

Marsh had told an interviewer that his father would always explain each day's progress as part of their family's dinner conversation. He also described himself as a precocious only child who avidly took part in those discussions. He'd told another interviewer he felt those extraordinary dinner conversations had given him a fundamental grasp of computer functions that few, if any, other people could achieve.

He simply *knew* the damn things, inside and out.

Academically, he'd also been unusual. He'd graduated as valedictorian from Palo Alto High School at the age of fifteen. At twenty he'd graduated summa cum laude from Stanford, with a master's degree in computer science. And because his father had been a research-and-development man, Marsh endured five years of that at NASA in the era leading up to the first moon missions.

But his heart had never really been in R & D.

Although his father owned several dozen patents on computer hardware, Marsh's forte turned out to be software. As that infant field began to burgeon in the early seventies, Marsh placed himself on the leading edge of it. He began to gain patents and copyrights of his own, which earned him a fortune by the age of thirty. Then he dropped out of the rat race to focus on debugging, which he'd excelled at for the past few years.

In short, Nat realized, FBI Agent Keller had been exactly right at Marsh's house that morning: At the moment, that fat fuck probably *was* the top computer man in the world—it was no exaggeration. The reasons for it were clear and obvious.

More pertinent to Nat's present task, however, was the realization that someone so endowed with technical expertise—be it in computers or anything similar—had more than enough mental capacity to use—or possibly even create!—a blue box as highly sophisticated as the one found in Marsh's possession.

That realization cast Marsh in an entirely new light for Nat, while it created a question that made him understandably anxious.

What would a guy like that be capable of as a phreak?

□ XXXI □

As Marsh prepared to climb into Lubov's Porsche, he wasn't worried about the Kraut recognizing the King's voice. His mouth injury had so radically altered his speech pattern, he doubted if he could recognize a tape recording of himself. That left only the problem of how to ease his bulk into the low-slung seat.

Once he was settled and comfortable, he said, "Sorry about the short notice, but thanks for coming." Then he noticed Lubov staring at him. "The mouth? I had an accident this morning. Hurt like hell right after it happened, but the doctor gave me a salve that numbs things pretty well."

"I see," Lubov said, still giving nothing away.

"I'm sure you're wondering what all this is about, and I can't say I blame you. But before I get started on that, would you mind taking me someplace to eat?" He pointed to his mouth. "Haven't had a bite all day."

Lubov nodded. "Do you have a preference?"

"Something soft, like soup. Let's try Lo Fat's over on Wiltern. You know where that is?"

Lubov nodded again. Lo Fat's was a soup-and-salad place he'd passed on other occasions in San Jose. From the street it looked as if it served cheap, pedestrian fare—the kind he avoided whenever possible.

Once they were under way, Marsh resumed. "I'm a friend of the King . . . a professional associate, you might say."

Lubov turned and gazed at his ugly, obese passenger with totally new regard. *Could it be true?*

In the two days since getting Gretchko's go-ahead to subvert Percy Marsh in order to gain access to the King, Lubov had been forced to concentrate on preparing for his Ultramike Conference speech. So he'd put the Marsh matter on a back burner, confident that once he could fully focus on the problem, he'd find a way to orchestrate the "chance" meeting that would begin the subversion.

Now, looking at the toad sitting beside him, he was having trouble accepting this poor fellow's injection into his life *by the King* and so close on the heels of the Percy Marsh affair. It was far too convenient and much too much to hope for. Nevertheless, he offered his companion a tight but friendly smile.

"I've never known the King to mention any friends."

"He doesn't have many," Marsh said, returning the smile as best he could. "But I'm definitely one of them."

Lubov said nothing in reply, knowing it would be foolish to reveal his surging eagerness to learn more.

"Ever hear of someone called the Ghost Glitch?" Marsh finally asked, knowing full well what the answer would be.

Lubov couldn't keep his head from ratcheting around a bit too abruptly. The unexpected nature of the question—as well as its chilling relation to his current priority—was simply too much of a coincidence to absorb with his usual calm. But he quickly gathered his reeling senses.

"Of course," he said matter-of-factly. "He's a legend."

Marsh couldn't help anticipating the reaction his next statement would generate. "I guess that makes me a legend."

That revelation slammed into Lubov's consciousness like a white-hot nail. In an instant he lost all control. He could barely remember how to drive his car, much less relate to the right hand being extended across the Porsche's center console.

"Percy Marsh" a voice was saying from somewhere far, far away. "Pleased to meet you."

Can it be possible? Can a man be so lucky?

That was all Lubov's consciousness could think of at that moment. And Marsh seemed to understand—even expect—such an obviously stunned reaction from him.

"Come on, now," he said in a chummy fashion. "Relax! It's no big secret anymore. The FBI bagged me early this morning."

Even a man with Lubov's icy self-control was capable of being dumbfounded by a surprise of such magnitude. But few others could have recovered sooner or with more aplomb than he showed when he reached out to grasp Marsh's hand.

"Viktor Lubov . . ." he managed to say.

"I know," Marsh replied, giving his hand a vigorous shake.

As Lubov regrouped his scattered wits, he started realizing that, for whatever reason, he was being given a direct shortcut toward delivering the Ghost Glitch's "head" to Moscow, *along with* an excellent chance of getting everything the King knew! All that remained was determining this colossal windfall's price.

"If you don't mind my asking," he said, with exactly the right note of deference in his tone, "why am I here?"

Marsh was pleased by the immediacy of that question and the precise way in which it was asked. Once again, he expected nothing less of a man with the Kraut's proven sensibilities.

"The mouth," he said, pointing to his stitched, protruding lips. "That's why." He expected Lubov's baffled look and wasted no time continuing. "The FBI did it to me."

"Did you resist them?"

"Of course not!" he snapped, furious at being reminded of how unfairly they'd taken advantage of him. "But that doesn't matter now. What counts is that I'm paying those bastards back, and you're here to help me—if you're willing."

It was all Lubov could do to stay still in his seat and keep from pounding the steering wheel in sheer exuberance. Not only was he being invited to assist one of America's two titans of illegal genius, he was being granted virtual access to the other!

It was good fortune beyond belief!

Only because it would be expected, he then asked, "What would you have me do?" He felt certain it would somehow involve phone phreaking, but it could have entailed murder—or worse.

He was prepared to do anything Marsh requested.

"My plan requires both hacking and phreaking," Marsh explained. "The King tells me you can handle most of the phreaking, which would save me a lot of time. But it's not something you *have* to do—I want that understood. If you don't feel right about it, say so and we'll leave things right here. I can manage alone."

Lubov was surprised by what that implied. "Then you know phreaking as well as hacking?" It was an extraordinary combination he'd never encountered at such a high level.

"Like I told you, the King's a friend. He's shown me a few things over the years, so I'll be able to pull this off by myself if I have to. Again, if you don't think it's right for you . . ."

He trailed off as Lubov sat there considering how to phrase an acceptable reply. He had to walk a fine line between being not too eager but not too reticent.

"I'm flattered to be recommended to a man of your stature and ability," he finally said. "But I can't help wondering why the King wouldn't help you himself."

"Simple," Marsh replied. "He's out of the area now, and I have to get this under way tonight. Otherwise, I'd wait for him."

There were two good reasons for those lies. First, Marsh felt emotionally driven to get things going—driven by the blinkered, narrow-focused compulsions that dominated his life.

Those compulsions were simply impossible to ignore.

But the other reason for haste was even more compelling: Now that his personal blue box had been discovered, the Cowboy would be looming out there somewhere, larger than ever.

That damn Cowboy was Marsh's *real* problem.

Meanwhile, Lubov entered the parking lot at Lo Fat's knowing he was at a critical juncture. From the moment he'd heard what Marsh had in mind, his own personal agenda had him committed to it. But it was still too early to make that apparent. Instead, he had to act as a normal person would in the same circumstance. Otherwise, he might give himself away and all would be lost.

He parked the Porsche and then turned to his companion.

"I'm sorry, Mr. Marsh, but I can't make such an important decision based on what you've told me so far. You have to give me a few more details, or I'll be forced to refuse to help you."

Marsh smiled faintly, then opened the Porsche's door to begin the laborious process of climbing out.

"You'll get all the details you need while we eat."

☐ XXXII ☐

Naval Lieutenant Norton Vent had been elated and dismayed when word of his transfer to San Diego first arrived. It was a classic case of good news and bad news in the same message.

The good news was that he'd been appointed deck officer on the USS *Gremlin,* one of the Navy's highest-rated nuclear attack submarines. Its mission was to "shadow" Russian loopers while providing practical training in all aspects of underwater seamanship for young officers with captain potential. Assignment to a top shadow was a big step up the submarine service's career ladder, and this position was exactly what he'd been hoping for.

The bad news was that the *Gremlin's* executive officer was his old Naval Academy cohort, Ken LeBlanc. LeBlanc was now a lieutenant commander, having risen above his ex-classmates by shrewd use of his good looks, courtly manners, and vicious backbiting. Vent was worried that his career wouldn't survive three months of working in close quarters with "Dandy" LeBlanc.

Their last semester at Annapolis had left him loathing everything about the man—everything.

"Norton Vent reporting for duty, sir," he said as he snapped off a salute to Jim Stickles, the *Gremlin's* sandy-haired, acne-scarred, pugnacious captain.

Forty-five-year-old Jim Stickles was known within the Navy as a "captain's captain," a term reserved for men who weren't particularly adept at the pressure-packed thinking tactical operations required, but who were gifted at teaching others the technical aspects of moving ships from point to point. Such men were invaluable as instructors of captains-to-be, and Stickles was considered one of the best in the U.S. submarine service.

He looked up at the slender young man braced at attention in front of his desk. The narrow face was pinched with intensity behind thin, rimless glasses. "At ease, Vent. Welcome aboard."

Vent assumed the parade-rest position. "Thank you, sir. It's a pleasure to be here."

Wasting no more time on formalities, Stickles arrowed to the heart of Vent's anxiety about his new assignment. "Commander LeBlanc tells me you two were classmates at the Academy."

Vent's ears began to tingle, the way they always did when he got upset. "Yes, sir, we knew each other."

Stickles gazed hard at the grim young officer with the dazzling reputation as an up-and-comer. Whatever he had, the captain decided, he didn't wear it on his sleeve. "There was some kind of trouble between you two, wasn't there?"

Vent cleared his throat and leveled his gray eyes at the captain's. "Yes, sir, but it was a personal matter unrelated to our military work. I'm sure you know the details."

Stickles nodded. "When the rotation roster came out, he asked me to have it changed . . . bump you to another boat."

There was a pregnant pause until Vent said, "Any particular reason you didn't grant that request, sir?"

There was indeed. Stickles wanted to test a theory he'd developed about Commander LeBlanc during their previous tour together. But that wasn't something he could discuss with either man. It was just another aspect of separating wheat from chaff among the Young Turks scheming to be captains.

"All you need to know," he replied, "is that I'm impressed with your record and I want to see if you have what it takes to be a boat jockey. Keep up the good work you've been doing, and your problems with Commander LeBlanc will resolve themselves."

"I hope you're right about that, sir," Vent said, although he knew there wasn't a chance in hell. What was between him and Leblanc would never be resolved—*not in a million goddamn years!*

"Good enough," Stickles said as he shuffled through some papers on his desk. "We'll be getting under way in a few hours, so take that time to stow your gear and settle in."

Sensing the impending dismissal, Vent shifted back into the brace of attention. "Can you give me any mission specifics, sir?"

"Our first looper intercept will be the *Mikhail Potkin,* three days out of Hawaii and due in our sector around midnight tonight. We'll be relieving the *Swordfish* as they swing through our end of the circuit. Any more questions?"

"No, sir!" he said.

"Then you're dismissed."

Vent did a tight about-face and was nearly out of the cabin when Stickles's voice came at his back.

"By the way, Vent . . . Whatever became of the girl?"

Vent turned and spoke matter-of-factly. "We got married."

Stickles glanced down at the file on his desk. "I thought this report said you were single."

"I am. We divorced two years ago."

Stickles nodded sympathetically. "It's hard on a woman when her husband's at sea half of each year."

"Yes, sir," Vent replied, a clear tone of regret in his voice. "Damn hard."

Stickles paused as if about to make some further comment, then brushed it away with a casual shrug. "Good luck, Vent."

Vent offered an appropriate smile, said "Thanks, sir," then turned and left to go find his berth in the *Gremlin's* bowels.

□ XXXIII □

The interior of Lo Fat's proved to be as gauche as Lubov had feared. Plastic and Formica were the dominant features, with fake flowers and cheap artwork rounding out the decor. Under the best of circumstances, it was a depressing place to dine.

"Isn't this place great?" Marsh said, moving through the serving line with a plastic tray in hand. "I love it when you just walk in, grab some chow, and start eating. I hate those wait-and-wait places with the sky-high prices and half-cooked food." He noticed Lubov's empty hands. "Aren't you eating?"

"I had lunch not long ago," he lied.

Marsh shrugged. "Okay, but if we stick together and you get hungry later, all you'll have is canned stuff."

"I'm sure that will be adequate."

Marsh chose a heavy lentil soup the color and consistency of used motor oil. Lubov wondered how anyone could consume such a disgusting mixture. It was hopelessly removed from the thin, delicious broths his mother used to make.

The soup itself was boiling hot, another hallmark of second-rate establishments. Marsh had to stir it for several minutes before daring to take his first sip. He used that time to fill Lubov in on as much as he could at that point.

"Like I said," he began, "the FBI finally put all my clues together and nailed me this morning. You knew about the clues?"

Lubov nodded. The audacity of leaving valid clues behind was a major part of the Ghost Glitch's extraordinary mystique. "No offense meant, but that always seemed so foolish to me."

"That's because you're into phreaking," Marsh replied, "where the game consists of operating in a tightly structured, heavily monitored system that *can* catch on to what you're doing. In hacking, the computer systems are so spread out, no one could possibly monitor them all. So you have to let them know you've been there, or they'll never figure out what you've done."

There was an illogical kind of logic to that explanation, which Lubov could almost appreciate. Almost, but not quite.

"I never really worried about getting caught," Marsh went on, "because I made it a point never to do any damage. I thought that would keep me safe when they finally put the clues together. At worst, I figured a fine and probation." Then his tone soured. "That's all it should have been too."

"But you must have known the authorities would do whatever they could to permanently end your career."

"Sure, but legally their hands are tied! I mean, what can they do except try to catch me in the act? And with me knowing they're on my tail, will I be extra, extra careful, or what? So in the end, all they really accomplish by tagging me is to make my part of the game more of a challenge. Which is the main reason I never worried much about getting caught. There should have been advantages along with the disadvantages."

Lubov was beginning to see the flow of this. "But they're not following the rules? Is that it?"

Marsh's battered features twisted with anger. "There *aren't* any rules for the FBI guys who bagged me! They run roughshod over anyone they see fit to take apart. I just never figured they'd be stupid enough to do that to the Ghost Glitch."

"So now you make them pay for their mistake?"

Marsh nodded while attempting his first taste of the soup. Still too hot. "The idea came to me this morning. I know where the King is staying, so I talked the jail people into letting me make a call. I ran it past him and he said it should work. Then he suggested you as someone who could help make it happen."

Lubov gladly asked the next obvious question. "Why did he contact me through the orbit rather than at my home number?"

The dark, eerily floating pools behind Marsh's thick glasses grew even larger. Lubov realized that question was more probing than he'd intended, but he couldn't imagine why.

"I have no way to know," Marsh replied, choosing his words carefully. "But maybe because time is such a factor in what I'm planning, he figured that was the surest way to contact you and get your attention. I mean, you did show up, didn't you?"

He tried another spoonful of soup and barely got it down, while Lubov responded in the cautious manner he felt would be expected. "Yes, I *am* here. But I must say, I have no intention of joining your scheme unless you tell me more about it."

Marsh laid his spoon down and braced his elbows on either side of his soup bowl. He steepled his thick fingers under his chin, then his normally intense tone filled with outright hostility.

"I'm going to shut down some communication systems to show those fatheads in Washington what I'm capable of. And if everybody in government—especially the FBI—doesn't get off my back and *stay* off, they'll be the sorriest sons of bitches who ever lived!" He went back to his soup, growling, "I mean it!"

Lubov had no doubt that he did. And just the possibility, however remote, of participating in Marsh's revenge had his emotions surging. Not only was that concept the precise core of his reasons for being a phreak, he could end up being taught how to do it by a master programmer! Probably the world's best!

That would be success on a scale he'd never dreamed of.

Struggling to maintain a normal tone of voice, he asked, "Can you be a bit more specific about what's involved?"

Marsh gingerly patted his stitched lips with a paper napkin, then shook his head. "Sorry, your decision has to be made on the basis of what I just told you. And don't misunderstand: There *is* an element of risk if you get involved. A lot of shit will hit the fan when the shutdown happens, and some of that would land on you if you ever got linked to it. I don't see that as likely, but you need to be aware of the possible consequences."

Some amused quality in Marsh's tone indicated there was more involved here than a simple job with minimal risk. Lubov decided the Glitch was probably just feeling him out, still trying to decide whether to trust him with the whole story. All he could do was play along as if he suspected nothing.

"All right," Lubov said, "I'll accept that for now. But will I be able to back out if things aren't as you say?"

Marsh shook his head. "Listen, you already know enough about what I'm planning to cause me serious problems after it happens. Since I'm trusting you that much, can't you trust me enough to take my word about what I'm telling you?"

Lubov paused for what he hoped Marsh would consider an appropriate length of time. Similarly, he put on a frown of concentration that he hoped would be convincing. Then he responded in tones he hoped would indicate a strong sense of caution being overwhelmed by an irresistible challenge.

"Very well, Mr. Marsh . . . I'll help with your revenge. But I'd like some assurance that you'll do all in your power to keep me clear of official involvement—or reprisal."

Marsh flashed that weak grin he could barely muster. "Just keep your mouth shut and they'll never know what hit 'em!"

□ XXXIV □

Karen quietly refiled the microfilm canisters she and Nat had been using. He stood nearby, grim-faced, considering what they'd learned about Marsh. It was the first time he'd shown her that side of his nature, the side that made him the best antifraud investigator Ma Bell had. And if he'd known how intently she was studying him, he'd have tried to look different.

As it was, by the time they were ready to leave the morgue, her reporter instincts were leading her to start pressing him for personal information. "You take all this pretty seriously, don't you? Your job, I mean."

He gave her a questioning look as he opened the door for her, then decided there was no harm in being honest. "There's more to it than just doing my job, which I do happen to take seriously. It's that I truly understand what's at stake with everything the phreaks are doing . . . where they're heading."

"Because you were once one yourself?"

He nodded. "That as much as anything else. But it's a helluva lot more than making free long-distance phone calls, or playing supersophisticated computer games. In its own way, it's pretty damn dangerous."

"No kidding! Dangerous? Really?"

He couldn't help noticing how smoothly she pried out information with what seemed to be honest curiosity and wide-eyed enthusiasm. He also couldn't help wondering how many people had come to grief trying to satisfy her straightforward zeal.

"Maybe that's overstated. The phreaks themselves aren't dangerous because all they do is have fun at Ma's expense. But every time they find a new weakness to exploit . . . a crack they can widen and run wild in until we find it and patch it over . . . the whole system gets shakier and more vulnerable. Understand?"

They were exiting the building by then, and she seemed enthralled by what he was saying. "Not exactly—tell me more."

They stepped into the fading afternoon light and he squinted into her innocent-looking green pools. Were treacherous currents swirling below their calm surfaces? Did he really want to know?

"The next thing I have to say is classified, in-house information, so I'd like to reconfirm that everything I'm telling you is strictly off-the-record. Okay?"

Without a second's hesitation she put three fingers to her lips, crossed her heart with them, then raised her palm as if being sworn in to testify. "Scout's honor . . ."

Now all he could see was pure fire in her eyes, a burning lust to simply hear the great secret. Terminal wannaknowitis.

"There's no way to be sure about this," he said, gripping her elbow to lead her across the parking lot to his Corvette. "But theoretically, at least, the Network is capable of paralyzing most— if not all—of our telephone system.

"Right now, as we speak, half a dozen phreaks and a few computers could busy out any major trunk line in the country. And if they didn't undo the damage on their end, we'd be weeks and probably months restoring that service."

"Damn!" she muttered.

"Damn is right," he agreed. "So now you know why we're always on you to keep information about phreaking out of your paper. And why I can get a little wound up about it at times. There really is a hell of a lot at risk."

"I don't understand something," she said as they approached the car. "If they have that kind of power, why don't they use it to get you off their backs once and for all?"

"Because we're not a major problem for them. We just follow along behind, picking up whatever crumbs they drop as they go on their merry way. Besides, the King is smart enough to know that if they ever did do something truly destructive, we'd have to declare all-out war on him and the Network."

That took her by surprise. "What could you do then that you're not doing now?"

They reached the car and he opened her door. "Well, for starters we could offer a million-dollar cash reward for the King's identity, plus a quarter million for any other phreak. That would get someone's attention, don't you think?"

She stood there flabbergasted, not bothering to get into her seat. "You're joking! A million dollars? For one guy?"

"A bargain at twice the price," he said with a wink as he went around to his side of the car. "I've been to contingency meetings where numbers like *ten* million were kicked around. If the Network ever did get out of hand, those are the kinds of tactics we'd be forced to use against them."

They climbed into the Corvette's low-slung seats in silence, then she changed the subject. "Speaking of tactics, what's next for us today? It's getting late."

He paused, then said, "That's what I was thinking about back in the morgue. What we found out about Marsh has me wondering if maybe that sucker isn't a full-blown phreak, after all. I mean, he certainly has the brainpower for it. And he had that super blue box. Let's face it: The possibilities are there."

"Any way we can check it out?"

"Sure," Nat said as he started the engine. "We can go over to his house and ask him about it."

"Just like that? Without a warrant or anything?"

"We don't need a warrant to try to talk to him."

"Well, maybe not, but I can't believe he'll just invite us in and tell you he's a phreak."

"Listen," he said as he pulled out of his parking space, "I don't expect him to admit anything. But going over to see him will serve two important purposes. First, it'll let him know I suspect him, which will give him something to think about, phreak or not. And second, it'll give me a chance to restart my investigation of him. I dogged it bad this morning."

"What do you mean?"

"Brandt and Doppler rubbed me the wrong way, so I got up on a high horse and didn't take their request seriously. But I also had trouble accepting a hacker as a phreak. Now that we know what we know about Marsh, I think I might have blown it."

She playfully elbowed his ribs. "Let's go get 'im, tiger!"

He intended to do just that.

☐ XXXV ☐

The orders came as they always did, telexed from PACCOM HQ in Hawaii: "Triangulate/search map sectors 108–115, starting 1400 hours." Those instructions meant what they always did: Somewhere within several hundred square miles of the ocean off Los Angeles lurked an old diesel submarine called a beater. It was manned by a skeleton crew to provide land-based antisubmarine-warfare patrols with a target to search out and "destroy."

The three-unit ASW team sent to deal with that day's beater was led by Lieutenant Vito Scarlatti. Scarlatti was an ex–point guard on the Naval Academy's basketball team, a scrappy Brooklyn wop, as he liked to call himself, with the eyes, coordination, and mental toughness of a fighter pilot. Unfortunately for him and the Navy, his 6'3" frame lacked compressibility, which meant he blacked out in centrifuge tests. So he ended up flying what he considered an adequate alternative to fighters: Grumman SH-3H helicopters, one of the Navy's primary ASW weapons.

Scarlatti and his two-man crew had already been out more than two hours, and frustration levels were rising. The surest sign of that came when his copilot, Casey Harper, gave his first fuel-consumption report, which he did with numbing regularity when beater missions began to drag.

"Down by half!" he announced.

Harper was a squat, bulky young man who'd flunked out of fighter pilot school with what was politely termed "attitude" problems. The actual reason was his world-class pessimism, which caused him to see everything as half empty rather than half full.

Scarlatti's sonarman was Bobby Wong, the exact opposite of Harper in both physique and temperament. Wong was a playful little optimist who enjoyed baiting Harper whenever he could.

"Better break out the life rafts, Vito," he said after Harper's fuel report. "We'll be ditching any minute now."

"Shut the fuck up, wimp-shit!" Harper snapped.

"You tell him, Casey," chimed in Grady Swenson, the pilot of the ship flying fifty yards to their left.

"Mid-mission fuel readings are too important to make fun of," added Bart Holloway from the ship on their right.

"*All* of you wimp-shits can shut the fuck up!"

"Okay," Scarlatti cut in, "enough's enough. We're over sector twelve now, so let's break pattern and go do our jobs."

"Breaking pattern," Swenson said as his ship peeled away toward the left horizon.

"Breaking pattern," Holloway echoed as his ship nosed right.

ASW choppers search the depths in twenty-square-mile sectors. They triangulate over a chosen dip area, then lower sonobuoys by cable into the water. The sonobuoys then execute audio scans for several miles around, relaying their data back to consoles on the SH-3Hs. The sonarmen then hear the sounds of, and view the oscilloscope images of, porpoises, dolphins, whales, schools of fish —and submarines. Each is unique.

Within that process are two different methods of finding submerged vessels. The favored one is passive sonar, which responds to the sounds a sub makes as it moves through the depths. But if it's dead in the water, hovering in silence, the passive mode won't show it. The active mode must be used.

Active sonar produces a loud underwater noise—the classic "ping" of movies—that travels outward from its source in all directions. When those sound waves strike an object—whether fish, rock, or metal—they bounce back to their source and light up an oscilloscope. The problem with active sonar is that it instantly tells a target an unfriendly is in the area.

ASW teams always try passive sonar first. If they get no result with it, they hit their active switches. If that reveals a hovering target, the chase is on. They drop depth charges and hope for the best, while the alerted target starts its engines and takes evasive action. In practice, the game is fun for all.

In wartime, it's a deadly form of cat and mouse.

* * *

Scarlatti's three choppers reached their dip zones at about the same time. Bobby Wong was the first to hit the levers that dropped sonobuoys into the water. He did so, feeling this might be one of those missions where they missed their target entirely.

Shutouts happened often enough because it was damn difficult to track subs in the ocean without C/S/T support, which ASW teams could count on in wartime but not in practice. To Wong's great relief, however, seconds after his sonobuoy hit the water and submerged, he knew his group wouldn't be shut out that day.

"Bingo, Delta!" he announced to his commander and the other two pilots in the Delta team.

The unmistakable whine of the old sub's diesels was coming through loud and clear in his headphones, while his pale green oscilloscope screens showed a cigar-shaped, graph-paper cutout moving through an unlined background smear.

"Where is it, Bobby?" Scarlatti asked.

Wong checked his timer and tracking charts. "Running one-quarter speed north-northeast at about three miles."

Scarlatti spoke to Swenson, ten miles to the west, and to Holloway, the same distance to the northwest. "You heard the man, Delta. Regroup on me and prepare to attack."

"Roger, Delta One," came Swenson's reply. "Buoy already up."

"Roger, One," Holloway repeated. "Buoy up and moving . . ."

It took them seven minutes to regroup and coordinate their mock attack. But when they were ready, six small "echo" depth charges dropped into the ocean slightly ahead of the beater cruising three hundred feet below.

The beater's twenty-man skeleton crew would be surprised and dismayed by those faint explosions, which in battle would be ear-splitting roars instantly sealing their doom.

☐ XXXVI ☐

The remainder of Marsh's meal at Lo Fat's passed in relative silence. Lubov could see the man was famished and in no mood to answer questions, so the only sound between them was noisy slurps created by eating soup with injured lips.

After the meal they returned to the Porsche. Lubov finally had a reason to speak. "Where do we go now?"

"I have a cabin up in the mountains, just off Highway 16, a few miles west of Lumberton. It's where I keep my main hacking units, along with my phreaking rig. But first, find someplace where I can buy a couple of legal tablets and some pens. I need to start flow-charting what we'll be doing."

Lubov soon found a stationery store, where Marsh went in and purchased his supplies. Then they were on their way to intersect with Highway 16, a main route into the San Jose Mountains that formed the western flank of Silicon Valley.

Normally, a late-afternoon drive in the mountains would cause Lubov to recall wonderful memories of his boyhood in other high country. But because his session with Rainer hadn't produced any information about Marsh's cabin, he had to spend his driving time assessing that revelation. And then, after coming to grips with it, he had to grapple with the other problems he now faced.

His main concern was Marsh's claim to own a phreaking rig sophisticated enough to shut down a communication system. If it was true, then he was far more than any "professional associate" of the King. He had to be a phreak, and a top-level one at that. The King would never, for any reason, put a high-powered rig into the hands of someone who couldn't maintain it or use it properly.

Not even someone as renowned as the Ghost Glitch.

Damn his mouth! Lubov thought. If Marsh *was* a phreak, in normal circumstances his voice would probably be recognizable. But with that sound-distorting injury there was simply no way.

Assuming he was a phreak, though, made Lubov wonder why he was bothering to bring an outsider in to help with a project he could handle alone. Could time pressures *truly* be reason enough?

And why wouldn't he confess outright that he was a phreak? If anybody could be trusted with someone else's phreaking identity, surely the Kraut could. Besides, Marsh knew *his* identity, so why be reluctant to balance the scales? It didn't make sense.

Those doubts combined with his previous ones to convince Lubov that Marsh's story was at best distorted, if not entirely fabricated. He could accept the part about giving authorities an example of what they might suffer if their harassment continued. But beyond that lurked something large and dark and mysterious.

He glanced over at Marsh, who was busy outlining on one of the tablets he'd purchased. It was headed: "Mismatch."

"What does that mean?" he asked. "Mismatch?"

"It's me and you against the government . . . and the government doesn't stand a chance." He paused to consider, as if finally absorbing the reality—and enormity—of it. Then he shook off his reverie to go back to outlining. "It really *is* a mismatch . . ."

Lubov felt that was gross hyperbole, but it pointed their conversation where he wanted it to go. "I have to confess a certain unease at the idea of assisting a man of your ability."

Marsh responded with a loud grunt but kept on working.

"I imagine your hardware might rival the King's."

That ostensibly subtle ploy to find out more about the King and his hardware netted only an amused chuckle from Marsh. Lubov had no idea where or how he'd given himself away, but he had.

As if granting one tidbit to a child hungering outside a candy-store window, Marsh said, "His rig is a lot smaller than you'd imagine. Got all the latest Jap miniaturization in it."

Lubov wanted desperately to follow up on that subject, but knew it would be a mistake to do so. Marsh was clearly keeping him at arm's length, a distance he couldn't afford to increase by coming on too strong. So he reluctantly changed the subject.

"Lumberton's about an hour from San Jose, isn't it?" He'd never been there but knew where it was. "That's quite a journey to undertake as often as your hacking activities must require."

"Yeah," Marsh admitted, "but I don't do much else with my spare time . . . no family or anything. Besides, when you do what I do at the level I do it, you *have* to operate off the beaten path. If you don't, the other side will find you."

That made sense to Lubov in a way leaving clues never could.

"Now, can we kill the small talk for a while?" Marsh asked as he went back to the task of outlining his flow chart. "I have to do some serious organizing before we get there."

Though it was clear he had no choice in the matter, Lubov was more than willing to keep quiet during the rest of their journey.

He had serious problems of his own to worry about.

Time and distance slipped past. Eventually they came to Lumberton, crossed it in minutes, and were soon well beyond it.

"Turn into that next driveway up ahead," Marsh instructed, pointing to a graveled turnoff on the right that passed beneath a crosspiece gate badly in need of paint.

Lubov did as instructed and began moving along a curved driveway dappled by fading sunlight that shimmered through densely packed trees like so many pale spotlights.

"An excellent location for your purpose," he said.

"Sure is," Marsh agreed as he flipped through the twenty pages of tablet he'd filled. "I told the real-estate agent I wanted peace and quiet, and she really came through."

A half mile from the highway, the driveway fanned out to become a semicircular parking area with room for several vehicles. Forty yards beyond, amid more trees, was a large, well-built, cabin-like structure made of creosote-treated logs and timbers.

There was a wide, open porch along its southern exposure.

"Three bedrooms, two baths . . . sits on ten acres with a stream," Marsh offered. "Bought it as is, furniture and all, from the estate of an old-style mountain man. Can't say much for his taste, but—like you said—it suits my needs."

As Lubov killed the Porsche's engine, he noticed a thick black cable extending ten feet from the side of the cabin to a small aluminum shed alongside it. The shed clearly wasn't part of the original property, so his next question was obvious.

"How did you solve the power problem in this remote area?"

Marsh noticed where he was looking and nodded.

"All mountain substations have independent generators with no centralized collators. If you tap into them illegally, they can't find you without instructions—and maybe not even then. I'm hooked in about a mile down the main road out there. Took me six weeks to lay the cable and three nights to make the connections. Hardest work I've ever done."

Lubov was deeply impressed. Such high-voltage trespass was both difficult and dangerous, which meant Marsh's technical capacity—not to mention his nerve—apparently knew no bounds.

A flagstone walkway led from the parking area to the cabin. As both men left the car to move along it, Lubov could feel the moment of truth approaching. He could tell Marsh was on edge, and he felt himself winding tighter with each step they took.

What was really inside that cabin?

Why had the Ghost Glitch brought him in on this?

Why had the King recommended him for it?

Could they possibly know his own great secret?

Was this some elaborate trap about to be sprung on him?

Despite the pressing urgency of all those questions, Lubov's only recourse was to move forward as if he had no more than reasonable concerns about what they were supposed to be doing.

He wondered what it would take to pull that off.

☐ XXXVII ☐

"Seven ball, corner pocket," Naval Ensign Milt Bremmer said as he bent over and tried a three-rail bank shot. He missed it.

His opponent's sleepy, almost dead eyes showed no flicker of interest. And why should they? Their owner had the damn run of the place! Slowly, grindingly, he pushed up off his stool, then moved to the table to survey the shape he'd been left with.

Bremmer studied him as he studied his shot. He was an ugly old coot, with wartlike growths on his cheeks and a bulbous, vein-riddled nose. He had raw patches of psoriasis on his arms, and his belly hung around his waist like a mud tire. He seemed totally out of place in the San Francisco LDR rec room, capable of little more than a still wicked game of pool. Yet he had the damn run of the place, and Ensign Milt Bremmer wanted to know why.

"Tell me, Pops," he said as the old man lined up a ten-ball combination. "What do you do around here? I been in this dump ten weeks and never once seen you in the posit room. You're always in the lounge shootin' pool. What's the story?"

Marine Master Sergeant Ode Samples didn't like being called Pops by the young twerps who manned LDRs these days. But he never let on that it bothered him. He just went ahead lining up his shot, more determined than ever to make it.

"I'm kind of semiretired," he muttered. Then, after a nerve-steadying pause, "Ten in the side."

He made it with a skim on the down lip, then began his slow shuffle to the other side of the table.

"How can you retire on active duty?" Bremmer asked, twisting his cue in fidgety hands. "I mean, you're in uniform, you're supposed to work. That's the way I figure it."

Samples shrugged. "I figure different."

"But how do you get away with it? I'm not bitchin', you understand. I might try it myself if it's a good enough plan."

Samples stopped analyzing the table and turned his bloodshot eyes directly on the ferret-faced young ensign. "It ain't like that, 'kid.' I come here, put in my hours, and the commanders stay off my case. Two more years and I'm out with a thirty-year pension. That's the only plan I know about."

"Jee-ee-sus! Twenty-eight *years* of this shit? Listening to all those dots and dashes? It's a wonder you're not crazy!"

Samples bent over his mud tire to line up his next shot.

"Hell, kid . . . maybe I am."

Marine Master Sergeant Ode Samples was actually anything but crazy. He was just what he appeared to be: a bloated, beer-soaked old war-horse put out to pasture to live his last two years in the Marines hustling pool with marks like Bremmer.

But in his prime, Ode Samples had been a wonder.

In the earliest days of communication interception, at the start of World War II, America needed people with radio expertise to form the intercept and decoding teams that would make up the first Long-Distance Receiving units. They were pulled from all branches of service to operate under the Naval Security Group Agency, and Ode Samples was among those first NSGA recruits.

In the beginning, and for several years after the war, messages were taken "clean"—coded but not scrambled or distorted. Band-blanketing interceptors and computer-driven letter-frequency decoding were in the distant future.

Those early messages were taken by people like Ode Samples, men and women who copied each dot and dash as it came off the sender's hand, then made of it what they could before passing it on to human decoders.

As time passed, Samples developed into one of NSGA's prized "idiot savant" interceptors, otherwise ordinary people with an uncanny ear for the minutiae of sound. They could analyze Morse code messages with a degree of precision that defied explanation.

Samples could pull a stream of electronic chatter out of the ether and tell if the person sending it was male or female, left- or right-handed, young or old. He could even tell whether the sender was transmitting in their native language, and in many instances what the native language might be.

He was like police specialists who perform similar wonders with such things as fingerprints, footprints, wounds, blood, and hairs.

After widespread utilization of the unbreakable codes of one-time-pads, secret radio transmits became a thing of the past. Nearly all intercepted messages became strictly routine military, such as troop-movement orders or shipping instructions. Those were valuable for gaining an overall view of what the other side was doing, but none required special analysis or interpretation.

Even on the rare occasions when a foreign agent was forced to send an emergency message, Ode Sample's skills weren't utilized. Such messages were decoded by computers and acted on immediately, with no concern for who sent it or what their background or condition might be. Interpretation was passé.

Despite his valueless skill, Samples kept working. Day in, day out, month after month, year after year, he copied code and waited for messages that no longer came. Then one day he simply quit, retiring to the rec room to spend his duty hours there.

Fortunately, his commanding officers knew his background and were tolerant of his attitude. They left him in peace, to tour the last of his hitch solving the endless mysteries of the rec-room pool table's faded baize.

For his part, Samples was grateful he had only two years left. Any more and Bremmer would be right: He *would* be crazy.

☐ XXXVIII ☐

As Lubov followed Marsh to the cabin, he noticed its front windows were protected by heavy wooden shutters. He assumed every other window was equally shuttered, which made it obvious that an inspection of what was inside, whether accidental or deliberate, was something Marsh intended to prevent.

Three wooden steps led up to the plank porch extending along the cabin's southern wall. When Marsh arrived at the front door, he reached up to the ledge above it and pulled down a large wasp nest that appeared to be stuck there. He held it out for Lubov to inspect in the fading afternoon light.

Anchored to its back by a magnet was a rust-flecked key.

"Built this baby out of liquid plastic," he said proudly. "Nobody'd reach behind *that* looking for a door key, would they?"

He removed the key, opened the door, and motioned for Lubov to precede him inside. "Go on in, check out the geezer's taste."

The window shutters so darkened the area beyond the door, it amounted to a cave. Lubov's neck hairs bristled at the thought of leading a potential opponent inside. But he couldn't balk, so he ignored his primal warning and stepped across the threshold.

Suddenly a sharp, metallic *click!* came at his back. In an eyeblink he whirled around in a honed defensive crouch: center of gravity low, arms up and cocked, feet braced against attack.

Marsh was standing in the doorway, his finger on the light switch. They stood staring at each other, each realizing the profound implications of what had just occurred. In those few moments of response to his training, Lubov had dropped his academic's mask and given Marsh a glimpse of his true nature.

Doing his best to recover gracefully, Lubov stood up again while adjusting his jacket and turtleneck. "You startled me, Mr. Marsh. Please forgive my reaction."

Marsh's halting, poorly formed response made clear how upset he was by what he'd just witnessed. "I'm, uh, sorry . . . I guess, uh . . . maybe I should have warned you that was coming."

But both knew such a warning should never be necessary.

Marsh turned, replaced the key and wasp nest, then his voice regained its control. "Tell me, why are you so jumpy?"

"This day has been quite unusual for me," Lubov replied, trying to sound offhanded. "I suppose I need time to adjust."

Marsh weighed that explanation's plausibility as he bolted the door. Then he nodded and moved into the living room.

Despite that seeming acceptance, Lubov knew his mistake had an enormous impact on his companion. The atmosphere between them had swiftly frozen, and now the best he could hope for was a chance to thaw things out to a semblance of where they'd been.

"Well?" Marsh said as they surveyed the large living room and the kitchen beyond. "What do you think?"

It was furnished throughout with rough-hewn wood and hand-tooled leather. In the living room was a heavy oak coffee table standing on a bearskin rug situated midway between two leather settees. Scattered about were four rustic leather armchairs and two old chiffoniers. Off to one side, near the kitchen, was a dining table for six. Four oil-lamp fixtures were hung beside two Western-motif canvasses on opposite walls; a moose head was on a third wall; and all of it centered around a large fireplace that covered half the east-side wall.

"Very, um, frontier-looking," Lubov said, trying to be both honest and diplomatic. "A distinctive example, I'm sure."

Marsh gave a casual shrug as he moved toward the kitchen. "Give you a full tour later. How about something to drink?"

Since Marsh was still going through the motions of cordiality, Lubov made a comparable effort. "Yes, thank you."

As Marsh went to the refrigerator to check out what was available to drink, Lubov relaxed enough to notice how musty and stifling the closed-in cabin smelled and felt. He removed his jacket and hung it over the back of one of the dining table's chairs.

Marsh looked over from the refrigerator and said, "Milk, beer, or Coke?"

"Perhaps a Coke."

"Me too." He pulled two twelve-ounce glass bottles from a door rack and handed one to Lubov. "Twist-off caps were sure a stroke of genius, weren't they?" he asked as he unscrewed his.

He turned the bottle up for a long drink that nearly emptied it, then he stood for several seconds with a pained expression before emitting a resounding belch. "Ahhhh . . . that's better."

Lubov took a swallow from his own bottle, then studied Marsh carefully as he crossed to the fireplace. There was something unnatural about his movements now, a jittery quality betraying inner agitation. So despite feeling foolish about his previous overreaction, Lubov went back on full alert.

Better safe than sorry—or worse.

Marsh put his Coke bottle up on the mantelpiece, then he turned, leaned down, and began pushing the stout old coffee table away from its position between the facing settees. The bearskin rug underneath the table slid along with it to reveal a trapdoor.

Marsh lifted the trapdoor and propped it open, retrieved his Coke bottle, then motioned for Lubov to lead the way down. "Get ready," he said behind his faint, eerie-looking smile. "My rig's down there. Might be a bit more than you expect."

His tone was vaguely menacing when he said that, as if some subtle quality of threat lurked just beneath the surface of fair warning. Nevertheless, Lubov had no choice but to follow his instructions with the same apparent confidence he'd shown when entering the front door. But he couldn't help wondering what recourse he might have if this turned out to be an empty cellar.

Or a trap to be sprung the moment he entered it!

Suddenly another scenario formed in his brain. What if Marsh was sending him to face some definitive test of intention? A litmus check wherein he could prove his sincere desire to become a trusted friend of both the Ghost Glitch and the King?

That possibility made the risk far more acceptable.

After the first two steps down the darkened wooden stairway, Lubov paused to set his half-empty Coke bottle on the floor beside the opening. As he did that, Marsh spoke from behind his back. "The light switch is that string just in front of you. Pull it."

Lubov took two more steps and pulled the string. A flood of light washed up from the room below, revealing a rough-hewn board floor. Four more steps down, and then a right-angle turn for a final two steps, left him standing in shock before the array of Marsh's hardware. It was packed into a twenty-foot-square basement that was like nothing he ever could have imagined.

"Nice, huh?" Marsh said as he came down the stairs behind.

Nice? Lubov thought. *It's incredible!*

Equipment filled the three walls opposite the staircase from floor to ceiling. There were terminals, modems, mag-cores, monitor screens, printout units, upright and horizontal storage discs, reel-to-reel recorders, panel after panel of multicolored lights, switches, and knobs . . . a truly overwhelming display.

And, in the middle, like a stone centered in the arc of a horseshoe, sat an extra-wide rolling armchair.

Lubov's head shook in disbelief as Marsh gently pushed him off the last step, down onto the floor. From there he could look to his right and see the empty space under the stairwell. At its far end stood three upright, gray-metal filing cabinets. He suddenly realized that was why no hard evidence of hacking had been found at Marsh's home. The incriminating papers were here!

"Which part is your phreaking rig?" he managed to ask.

Marsh pointed at the bright, four-foot square in the middle of the far wall, then shrugged. "Call me a traditionalist."

Lubov had noticed that huge blue panel the moment he looked at the central array, but it didn't occur to him that a phreaking unit could ever be *that* size. And even being the Kraut couldn't help him imagine what such a monster might be capable of.

He did imagine, however, that it could combine with all the computer hardware to create an overwhelming electronic arsenal: the compact equivalent of a war room, submarine control room, or missile launch room—any place where overkill was appropriate.

What the hell does Marsh need with all this?

Then, with a stunning flash of insight, his mind began to organize all those confusions and contradictions. He moved right to the edge of understanding what they meant, of comprehending who and what Marsh really was. But just as that thought was forming . . . a split second before he could complete it . . . Marsh's heavy glass Coke bottle exploded against the back of his head.

The insight was lost with his consciousness.

Lubov's first lucid thoughts were traditional and obvious:

What happened? . . . Where am I?

He struggled to crack his eyes into scanning slits but was overwhelmed by pain. His head was being hammered by an ache he'd never imagined possible; it felt ridiculously swollen. He tried raising his hands to examine it but found he couldn't lift them. His arms felt heavy and numb.

He forced his eyes open and surged through a wave of pain that came with the light. He found himself trussed into a straight-backed wooden chair from the upstairs dining table. He was sitting slumped forward in it, coatless, with his chin resting on his burgundy turtleneck. His ankles were lashed to the chair's front legs, his wrists tied behind his back.

Reflexively, he attempted to straighten up; but the instant he tried to unbend his bowed spine, daggers of pain stabbed him from his neck to his tailbone. That torment generated a cry of anguish, which was completely muffled by a sticky thickness in his mouth and throat that wouldn't allow his tongue or voice to work properly.

He had to swallow several times before he felt that condition was improved.

A far more serious problem was revealed when he tried to focus straight down on his ankle bindings. No matter how hard he worked at trying to resolve his vision into a single image, he couldn't quite manage it.

Then he remembered what had happened. *Marsh! He did this to me!*

Compelled to check his surroundings, Lubov carefully tilted his face up. But the moment he did that, everything started fading to black; his equilibrium skewed off-center; his chin lolled to the right; the pounding in his skull tripled in intensity. But he hung on until the darkness cleared and the swirling and pounding subsided.

The cramped basement was the same as he remembered it: his chair was tucked underneath the stairs near the filing cabinets; the mass of equipment still lined the walls opposite where he sat; and, most importantly, Marsh was still there, sitting in front of an instrument panel on the left, typing relentlessly. He couldn't tell if Marsh's blurred fingers were the result of extraordinary typing speed or his own double vision.

Suddenly, before turning to any more pressing detail, he realized that looking around had made him nauseous. He lowered his head back down to his chest, then managed to speak, softly and slowly.

"I'm going to be ill . . . please bring something."

Even being as careful as possible, he was agonized by the effort to speak. The facial movements and reverberating sounds ripped through his head. After several moments of silence, he decided to try again. Perhaps Marsh hadn't heard his muffled words; perhaps he only dreamed he'd spoken.

"I will be ill soon . . . I must have a receptacle!"

"Be with you in a minute" came Marsh's unhurried reply. "But if you have to puke, go ahead. You've already peed on yourself, so it won't make much difference."

Lubov couldn't smell the urine, although his nose was directly above his crotch. That meant he had a serious injury. Headache, nausea, loss of smell, double vision—all indicated he'd suffered a major concussion.

"Sorry I hit you so hard," Marsh went on conversationally. "Just wanted enough time to tie you up . . . never tried it before . . . guess I overdid it. Been out several hours . . . need stitches back there too . . . get it done first thing in the morning. Glad I didn't use one of the fire irons . . . might've killed you."

Lubov dared to look up again so he could focus on his captor. He was typing furiously while he spoke, never taking his eyes from the monitor screen above the keyboard he was using.

"Hang on a few more minutes . . . I'll bring you something. Can't stop what I'm doing . . . these codes have time sequences. Off too much either way . . . they shut me out."

Lubov didn't respond. His nausea returned when he lifted his head, so he dropped it back down to wait until Marsh finished whatever he was doing. He waited for what seemed an eternity, absorbed with the twin objectives of holding perfectly still while breathing in short, shallow drafts.

Finally Marsh said, "Here you go, Kraut—fire away."

Lubov lifted his eyes and the light began to dim. His head swam again and anvils pounded in his temples. Just before the wave of nausea spewed up out of him, his vision cleared enough to reveal the oblong maw of a green plastic wastebasket.

His first retch jolted him with blinding pain. He had to struggle to remain conscious long enough to draw a breath. He felt himself fading, fading to the edge of blackness; then one last frantic effort succeeded. Air gushed into his lungs with an icy chill, which instantly triggered another heave. New pain, new dimness, the desperate struggle to draw a breath, the final successful attempt, and again the resultant heave.

He lost track of how many times that cycle repeated itself, but finally it was over. He sat slumped, with his chin resting on his chest, his sides trembling spasmodically as he breathed shallowly. He was drenched with sweat and starting to shiver.

"Jesus!" Marsh said as he wiped his victim's mouth with a cloth. "I've never seen dry heaves before. Are you okay now?"

Lubov nodded weakly. "I'm cold. . . . Is there a blanket?"

"Sure, upstairs. Will you be okay while I get one?"

"Yes . . . but please hurry."

As Marsh left to fetch the blanket, Lubov began the tedious, painful process of straightening his bent-over spine. And the whole time he did that, he wondered about Marsh's bizarre behavior. The odd, prattling speeches; the unnecessary solicitude; the promise to get medical help—it all seemed so disjointed and out of place. What was going on?

Then came the more compelling question: *Why has he done this to me?* And most compelling of all: *Is my life in danger?*

☐ XL ☐

Nat's black Corvette stopped against the curb in front of Marsh's redbrick bungalow. Nat glanced over at Karen, who was assessing the neighborhood in the late afternoon's fading light.

"Looks nicer than it did this morning," she observed. "But still not a place you'd expect to find a millionaire, is it?"

"No, but it's perfect for somebody wanting to keep a low profile. Come on, let's go see if he's in."

They left the Corvette, crossed the cement walkway bisecting the lawn, then stopped at the front portico. Nat rang the bell. He waited a full minute, then rang again. Still no response.

"Maybe he went to a friend's house," she suggested.

Nat shook his head. "According to an FBI agent I talked to, he's a world-class loner with no friends at all."

As they stood wondering what to do next, Nat recalled what he'd seen inside that morning. His dominant impression had been how plain and ordinary it all was. Apart from the micro-sized blue box and the job-related computer array, there was nothing to indicate it might be the home of a phreak, much less of the world's best hacker. And with no apparent evidence, it would be next to impossible to build any kind of case against him.

Despite that disappointment, Nat wasn't ready to throw in the towel. "Let's go see if any neighbors are around," he suggested. "They might be able to tell us something."

He chose the house on their right for no other reason than that its ranch-style contours reminded him of his home in Texas. A wooden nameplate beside the front door said: THE FAMBROUGH FAMILY. He noted it as he stepped up and rang the bell.

With little delay the door was opened by a middle-aged, pot-bellied man who stood there looking annoyed. He'd been dressed in a suit, but now the jacket was gone, the tie loosened, the shirt collar undone, and the vest unbuttoned. A bristly fringe of white curls circled his bare scalp, while some kind of highball in his hand marked the end of a tough day at an office.

"This neighborhood has a no-solicitation ordinance," he said without preamble.

"We're not selling anything, Mr. Fambrough," Nat countered. "We're investigators looking for information about your neighbor over there." He nodded left toward Marsh's house.

Without even asking for proof of that claim, Fambrough straightened himself and assumed a cooperative tone. "Oh, yeah, right—my wife told me about that. Got caught screwing around with those damn computers, huh? Figures . . ."

"How so?" Karen asked, joining in without missing a beat.

"It's like my wife already told the cops: He's a weirdo! Keeps to himself, doesn't speak to anyone in the neighborhood, never mixes socially—a weirdo! What else can I tell you?"

"Does he ever have anyone over?" Nat pressed. "You know . . . guests? . . . friends? Anything like that?"

"Nah, nobody goes there except meter readers, repairmen, and his gardeners. Like I said, he's not social. By the way, you two want to come inside? Have a drink?"

"No, thanks," Nat replied, then added as an afterthought, "My, uh, partner and I are on duty." He flashed Karen a brief, ironic smile that Fambrough missed as he went on about Marsh.

"The guy wouldn't join Neighborhood Watch, never supported soccer or Little League, wouldn't sign petitions—nothing! A screwy weirdo. Unsocial. Sure you can't come in for a nip?"

"We can't, really. Did he spend most of his time there?"

"Nah," Fambrough answered, shaking his bristly curls. "He mostly stayed other places. Not on any kind of schedule, you understand. He'd just come and go at all hours, night or day." He leaned forward to offer a conspiratorial whisper. "Some of us think he's gay and has lover boys scattered around town."

There was no way to tell exactly what triggered the notion in Nat's mind. One instant it wasn't there and the next it was, roaring in from wherever bits and pieces of information were arranged into comprehensible form. By whatever means, though, it hit him as hard as he'd ever been hit by an idea in his life.

And it felt like a surefire winner.

Once the first rush was past and his equilibrium returned, he had nothing more to say to Fambrough. The man had served his catalytic purpose, leaving Nat the straightforward task of getting away and trying to prove what he'd surmised about Percy Marsh.

"Thank you for your time," he said, abruptly extending his hand to a startled Fambrough. "We sincerely appreciate it."

Fambrough turned his attention to Karen, who was standing there looking as confused as he felt regarding Nat's sudden turnabout. "Are, uh, you *sure* you can't come in?"

"No, thanks, sir," she replied as Nat gripped her elbow and started tugging. "Like my partner said, we really are on duty."

"So long!" Nat called out as he hustled her onto Marsh's lawn, heading for the Corvette. "And thanks again!"

Though his sudden manic behavior left her thoroughly baffled, she waited a decent interval before glancing at him.

"You're not gonna believe this," he muttered through clenched teeth, "but I think I finally found the bastard!"

□ XLI □

When Marsh returned with the blanket Lubov had requested, he also carried a large mug of steaming liquid. Unable to smell, Lubov could only hope it was tea rather than coffee. But he was more than ready to try either. Several hours of unconsciousness followed by dry heaves had left him badly dehydrated.

Marsh set the mug on the edge of a step above his prisoner's head, then pulled him and his chair out from below the stairway.

"Figured you could use a shot of hot coffee too," he said as he draped the blanket across Lubov's back and tucked it across and around his legs. "Hope you don't mind instant."

"Thank you," Lubov replied, without elaboration.

Speaking was easier for him now that he'd adjusted to how it felt, but he believed staying quiet would force Marsh to make his intentions clear. He also believed that's what the average person would do, and he was desperate to seem typical.

"It needs to cool a bit," Marsh went on as he rolled his chair from the equipment horseshoe over in front of Lubov. He sat down, leaned back, and locked his stubby fingers across his sagging belly. "Let's use that time to set you straight."

Only then did Lubov notice Marsh had swapped his sport shirt for a faded Stanford sweatshirt. From that he concluded the outside temperature had dropped, which could partially explain his chills. Maybe his head injury wasn't as bad as he thought.

"First thing I want to say," Marsh began, "is that I truly am sorry I hurt you. That was an accident. But I'll be glad to pay your medical bills, and for any work time you lose."

"You're too kind," Lubov said, as facetiously as he dared.

"Look, I didn't bring you here to knock you out!" Marsh

snapped, wasting no time demonstrating who was in charge. "I wanted your help! But that business with the light switch . . ." He shook his head. "You left me no choice."

"I explained that!" Lubov snapped back, trying to assert himself without being offensive. He knew if he was to have any hope at all of regaining Marsh's trust and confidence, it would start with establishing his own personal integrity.

"You explained it *away*," Marsh corrected, "but you didn't come close to convincing me it's normal for a physicist to be startled and react like a . . . a damn secret agent!"

Lubov's heart sank. *Could he possibly know?* "I was nervous and afraid," he insisted, determined to maintain his cover until all hope was lost. "It was an instinctive reaction."

That reply infuriated Marsh. "Who do you think you're dealing with? Some fucking dummy? You wouldn't *have* instincts like that unless you were used to hiding something—something big!" He leaned forward to emphasize his point, while Lubov held his breath. "Like being one of Ma's people, for example!"

Lubov's spirits instantly soared. *So that's what he thinks!* He'd started to believe Marsh suspected his true identity. But this? This was nothing! This could be dealt with. It was negotiable. So he began speaking, slowly and sincerely.

"There's been a misunderstanding here, Mr. Marsh. I can't blame you for being cautious—I'm sure I'd be equally so. But you've made a terrible error. I'm simply not an agent for Ma Bell, and I'll do whatever's necessary to convince you of that."

Marsh stared at his captive for several seconds before replying. "You talk a good game. But I'm in a situation where I can't afford to take any chances. There's too much at stake."

"I understand that," Lubov said in the most reasonable tone he could manage. "Take whatever time you need; give me any test you like. I'll pass it because I'm truly not a Ma Bell agent."

"Then what the hell *are* you?" Marsh hissed behind rising paranoia. "You're not a regular guy! I know it!"

"Of course I'm not," Lubov calmly replied. Now that he had some bearings in this bizarre confrontation, his old smoothness was coming back full force. "I'm the Number Two phreak in the King's Network. I have a responsibility to that position, not to mention my personal reputation and career to think of. How could I be certain you weren't part of a Ma Bell entrapment scheme?"

Without answering that, Marsh rose from his chair to fetch the coffee mug. "Here," he said, pressing it against Lubov's shriveled, cracked lips. "Shut up and drink. . . ."

Lubov tried a sip, but it was still too hot to tolerate. Shaking his head, he decided to risk beginning a campaign to get free. "Would you please untie me so I can hold it myself?"

"Sorry," Marsh said, returning the mug to the edge of the step as he sat back down. "We'll give it more time."

Lubov swallowed that disappointment and changed tack, aiming straight for the heart of the matter. "Listen, when you told me what you're planning to do here, I willingly agreed to help you. That makes me legally culpable, whether I take part in it or not. So why not untie me and let me disappear from your life? Or, if you prefer, I'm still willing to help in whatever way I can."

Marsh smiled faintly, as if admiring his captive's nerve. "You're staying just the way you are till I'm finished."

Lubov knew it would be acceptable to show some temper at that point. "Dammit, man! This can't possibly be worth nearly killing me for, much less keeping me tied up like this! Now, I insist you release me or I'll—"

He cut himself off as Marsh rose to recover the coffee mug.

"You won't do anything," Marsh said evenly, once again pressing the mug to Lubov's lips. Thirsty and discouraged by his failure to make headway, Lubov sipped at the still-hot liquid.

"Want to know why you won't do anything?" Marsh went on as his prisoner drank. "Because you're caught in the middle of my alternate plan, Ram-Jam, which ram-jams your ass between the rockiest rock and the hardest hard place you ever imagined."

Lubov leaned away from the mug to focus on the blurry double image hovering above him. It seemed to be smiling.

"It's like this, my friend: If you really aren't one of Ma's people, then you'll want this whole deal to blow over so your life can go back to the way it was. But if you are on her side, once you understand what I'm doing here you'll know you won't be able to tell a soul—ever—that you were anywhere near where it happened. Not if you want to keep breathing."

"Don't try to intimidate me," Lubov said, with the disdain he thought would be appropriate. "Shutting down a trunk line is serious business but hardly a capital offense."

Marsh smiled again, tipping the mug back up so Lubov could finish. "There's a bit more to it than what I told you earlier," he said as Lubov drank. "I'm not just shutting down *a* trunk line— I'm shutting everything down! Every trunk, every tandem, every relay circuit—all of it! Every communication system in this country is going stone-silent for five minutes."

Marsh delivered that threat with such withering finality, it hung in the air like a ticking bomb. Even a man like Lubov couldn't immediately grasp the enormity of it. He assumed instead that it was some twisted kind of joke. He finished his coffee and said, "I'm in no mood for this, Mr. Marsh."

It took Marsh a few seconds to understand what he meant. "You think I'm kidding? Not on your life! I'm shutting it all down— everything!—tight as a goddamn trap!" He leaned over to put his face close to Lubov's, the cold intensity of his expression matching the grim assurance in his voice.

"Once Mismatch runs, our lives won't be worth spit if anyone ever finds out how it happened. The government couldn't afford to leave either of us alive—me because I might tell someone else how to do it; you because you might've learned how this time. Nothing either of us could do or say would make a bit of difference. National security would force them to kill us."

Despite the hot coffee he'd just consumed, Lubov was hit by a hard chill. And it wasn't caused by his damp clothes or the shock of his injury. It was knowing that if what Marsh said was true . . . if he *was* capable of shutting down all U.S. communication systems for any appreciable time . . . then they'd both wind up dead whether or not anyone ever found out how it was done.

Even now, though, Lubov didn't believe it was possible, not even remotely. Which was not to say he didn't *want* to believe it. He wanted that as much as he'd ever wanted anything in his life. But the concept was simply too farfetched—period.

"Based on what I know about U.S. communication systems," he said, "which I can assure you is quite extensive, it's impossible for one man—or even many men—to shut all of them down. The job is too massive . . . too complex . . . even for the Ghost Glitch."

Marsh leaned back in his rolling chair and showed his partial smile. "You're right, the Glitch by himself couldn't pull it off. But with the King's help it's not only possible, it's not even all that hard. Just tedious and time-consuming."

That was the very last thing Lubov expected to hear, and it jolted him as much as anything he'd learned up to that point. *The King! Coming here!* He had to force himself to calm down before replying. "Uhmmm, when . . . will he arrive?"

For the first time since they'd gotten together, Lubov heard Marsh laugh. And because that giggling, childish laugh hadn't been distorted by the injury to his mouth, it was shockingly familiar. So he knew the truth as Marsh was speaking it.

"I can't believe you haven't caught on by now, Kraut . . . *I'm* the goddamn King!"

Lubov felt faint. It was simply too much coming at him at once. Or maybe it was his weakened condition. He tried to concentrate on keeping his head level and his breathing even. Otherwise, he'd fade to black and miss his golden opportunity—the opportunity he'd worked twelve years to create!

"I'm telling you this," Marsh went on, "because I think it's possible I did make a mistake about you. Maybe you aren't with Ma, after all. But like I said, I'm at a point where I can't take chances, so you just have to bear with me till it's over."

Lubov's senses were still reeling at the magnitude of his good fortune. *I'm with him! Right now! It's true!* But he knew that to keep this priceless gift moving his way, he had to assume the role of worshipful student at the feet of an anointed master.

"This is truly an honor without equal. Had I only known beforehand, we could have avoided my pain and your regret."

"What regret?" Marsh said as he rolled his chair back into the horseshoe. "I couldn't trust you before, and I'm still not convinced about you." Then, resuming work at his consoles, he added, "But I'm willing to give you the benefit of the doubt. You have to accept that till the dust settles from this."

Lubov was more than happy with that, but he was still having trouble believing Marsh could do what he was proposing. Even for

the Ghost Glitch *and* the King, the task remained formidable beyond imagining. Nevertheless, he—like Marsh—was ready to
grant reasonable doubt to the combination of those two geniuses.

"May I ask how it's possible to execute such a scheme?" he said
with correct deference.

Marsh replied distractedly, without looking up from his work.
"Once you understand how all communication systems interrelate,
there's really not much to it. It's just a natural extension of phreaking technology piggybacked onto hacking principles."

Incredible! Lubov thought. *Such confidence!*

"Picture a giant spiderweb. Now, imagine our communication
systems as its strands. One system connects with another . . .
those connect with others . . . until they're all linked together.
Radio, telephone, telegraph, television—emergency backup systems too—all held together by the common glue of computers.
Even military systems—missile controls, monitoring stations, satellite links—everything. Each depends on other systems to function.
So once I take out the first big relay unit, they'll all fall like a
gigantic row of dominoes. It can't miss."

Lubov experienced a surging desire to believe it might be true,
while Marsh went on working and speaking as if relating the details of a school lesson he could teach in his sleep.

"Remember the big New York blackout back in 1965? Know
what happened then? A freak power surge in *one* wire tripped a
single overload switch, and that overload switch tripped other
switches on other wires, until entire trunk lines were being shut
down. Within ten minutes, all five major trunks heading north and
all eight heading south were crunched. The system went down unit
by unit, section after section, until eighty thousand square miles
were blacked out and thirty million people were without power.

"Everything in America works the same way. It's all so logical
and orderly, it's vulnerable to logical, orderly attack. Just take the
basic principles that worked in '65, jack them around here and
there, and *bingo!* You create a communication overload and blackout instead of a power overload and blackout. Then expand that to
cover the whole country instead of eighty thousand square miles,
and *voilà!*—Mismatch."

Lubov tried to focus on the incredible horseshoe of equipment laid out before him. What he was hearing was utterly preposterous . . . yet it wasn't entirely impossible. And if such a monstrously complex task *could* be conceived and executed, he was listening to the likeliest candidate on earth to accomplish it.

"Look at the phone system," Marsh went on. "You know yourself how vulnerable that is—the Network's had total access to it for years. Well, the next step up from access is neutralization. All you need is expert-level skill with computers, enough knowledge about communication systems to know how to cripple them, and a setup like mine to carry it out."

With a mounting sense of anticipation he had to struggle to control, Lubov began to regard Mismatch as remotely possible. And if it did actually happen, any bits of information he could gather now might be vital later on. "Government systems . . . the military's systems . . . How can you bypass their safeguards?"

Marsh glanced over at him and chuckled. "Hell, I debugged half the damn things! And the ones I didn't work on are just as easy to overcome because their programming is so structured. But the major factor is that every communication system in this country was modeled after Ma. And as screwed-up as she is, she's a model of efficiency compared to everything else—*especially* the government and military. They're all basket cases!"

Lubov had always suspected that government and military communication systems might be vulnerable, which was the main reason he'd worked so hard to discover the King's identity. He knew the King could confirm his suspicions and might even reveal ways to exploit those systems. "Can it be done selectively?"

Marsh shook his head. "When you hit so many interrelated systems at once, it's impossible to exclude anything. I mean, we're talking about *every* government and military system—bar none—followed by everything in the private sector."

"How long will that take?" was a more immediate question.

"Each system clogs, stays down five minutes, then unclogs. Total time . . . two hours, start to finish." He smiled again. "Ought to tear some heads off in Washington, don't you think?"

Lubov knew it would do a hell of a lot more than that, which meant Marsh didn't understand its full implications. Of course, that wasn't a main concern right now. "If the New York blackout needed only ten minutes to create such extensive damage, why—?"

"I know what you're getting at," Marsh cut in, "but consider the scope of what we're talking about here. It'll start in the White House Situation Room, then spread over the country like a giant wave of silence. That means literally billions of computer relays have to be deadly-embraced. Even working at microsecond speeds, something like that takes a helluva lot of real time."

"What do you mean by 'deadly embrace'?"

"Computer jargon. Computers are designed to accept operating requests in a specific sequence, usually first come, first served. But whatever their operating sequence, you can desensitize them to their resource priorities. Run them up to their capacity overload points, they start trying to honor every request at once. Input and output freeze, locked in a deadly embrace, and they're stuck till the input load dips below the capacity overload point. Sounds weird, I know, but it works."

Lubov paused to analyze what he'd just heard. Despite his initial skepticism about Mismatch, he now felt ready to upgrade it from possible to likely. Like genuine crystal, its details had a special ring of truth when tapped by the hammer of doubt. And assuming it *was* happening, Lubov knew there was infinitely more at stake than the acquisition of strategic information.

This was his end of the line as a sleeper . . . the zenith of his career. His ultimate purpose could be taken to a level never dreamed of by himself or his superiors. But that would happen only if he could capitalize on this unexpected windfall, and at the moment he was in no position to act as he must.

His foremost objective was to make sure Marsh didn't carry out his intention past a certain critical point. He'd have to make his own opportunity there. And just as vital was his need to have his hands freed. If he couldn't talk his captor into that, all would be lost. And then, if those two objectives were met, he'd only be in position to *attempt* what he had to do.

It was a formidable task for someone in top shape, much less for someone in his weakened condition. But he had to succeed!

This was the opportunity of a lifetime—of *all* lifetimes.

□ XLII □

Once Nat and Karen were back in the Corvette, he was sufficiently under control to start explaining what he meant about having found the bastard. He took a deep breath and began.

"I know this is going to sound crazy . . . Hell, it's more than crazy—it's absurd! But . . . I think Marsh might be the King."

He said that with all the wonderment such technological heresy deserved, while Karen accepted it as little more than an intriguing possibility. "Really? Wouldn't that be something?"

"He's got everything it takes to fill the role," Nat went on, speaking with growing conviction. "The brain, the personality, the time frame, the living arrangement . . . Taken altogether, the evidence points right to him."

She shook her head. "I'm not seeing the connection."

"Okay, let's break it down," he suggested, as much to organize his own jumbled thoughts as to clarify the situation.

"First, does he have enough smarts to be the King? Highly likely. There has to be *plenty* between the Ghost Glitch's ears. Second, does he have enough free time to coordinate the Network's activities? Well, he's a strict loner, right? Works for himself? Sets his own hours? Sounds like a good bet there too. And third, is he eccentric enough to be the King?"

"Is the King eccentric?" she asked.

Nat practically exploded. "The guy's a wall-to-wall fruitcake! The most twisted, vicious fanatic you can imagine!"

Not expecting anything so severe, Karen drew back from the intensity of his response. "Is that really so wrong? The fanatic part, I mean. After all, isn't everyone a fanatic in one way or another, to one degree or another?"

That stalled him for a moment of consideration, then he plowed ahead. "Okay, skip that. It's not important. What is important is the key ingredient I missed this morning but managed to focus on this afternoon—Marsh's living arrangement."

He could see that caught her attention, even though all she did was shift to a more comfortable position in the bucket seat.

"To phreak the way the King does," he went on, "his main rig has to be set up in some remote area where power collators and random monitors can't pick out any surge drain."

"What are power collators and random—?"

"You don't need to know that now," he said, cutting her off. "The point is, he can't do it safely from city areas. Ordinary phreaks can, if they're careful, but the King operates on a very different level. That's what I couldn't figure before now."

"And that's what Fambrough gave you?" she said, beginning to figure it out for herself.

"Exactly! If Marsh leaves his house for long periods at all hours of the day and night, it's safe to assume he's not just in another part of town. Oh! And don't forget his skill with computers. That's something else the King has to have."

Karen mulled that over as the lowering sun bathed her red corona of curls in a pink-orange glow. That glow was particularly flattering to her, but Nat was past noticing.

"Now that you mention computers," she finally said, "can't Marsh be doing all that stuff strictly as the Ghost Glitch?"

"Sure, that's possible. But don't forget one thing: Hacking isn't monitored the way phreaking is. If he wanted to, he could hack all he wanted from right there at his house. He wouldn't need to go somewhere else, like he would to phreak."

"So he could hack when he's at home and phreak when he's away? Ghost Glitch at home, the King away? Like that?"

"Not exactly. He can do either one at either place because all he needs is a terminal to hack and a good blue box to phreak. But my guess is that he goes out of town to hack *and* phreak, on monster units he's developed to do both. And he probably uses the terminals in his house for his work as a debugger."

She thought that over for a moment, then offered her own analysis. "Everything you say makes sense except this: How could one person be both of those incredible people?"

Nat gave her a self-conscious, almost guilty, smile because the answer had come to him not through logical deduction, but from a moment of pure, blinding inspiration.

"That's where everyone who's ever chased the Glitch or the King—including me—has consistently missed the boat. But if you just stop and think about it, the odds against two people having that much brainpower must be a zillion to one."

Karen was quick on the uptake. "It might actually be easy for one person to do both, especially at such a high level!"

"I'm willing to bet on it. But until we get a full confession or catch him in the act, there's no way to be sure."

She caught the gleam in his eyes. "You plan to try that?"

He nodded resolutely. "That's my job." He then checked his watch and frowned. "Too late to do any more today. But tomorrow morning, first thing, I'll stop in to see Brandt and Doppler. They have some material on Marsh that I ought to go through before I decide what to do next."

Karen looked stricken. "You sound like I'm not invited!"

He looked equally stricken. "Sorry, I should have said 'we.' Guess having you along takes some getting used to."

She smiled with relief, then was reminded of the neat little con job he'd pulled on Fambrough.

"Boy, some partner *you* are!"

☐ XLIII ☐

Lubov knew that as long as Marsh was working at his consoles, the crisis point was still downrange. He also knew it would cause suspicion if he stopped asking questions. So he continued doing that, knowing he could worry about his two main objectives after Marsh had finished.

Asking the right kind of questions wasn't easy. He had to seem naturally concerned about prospects for success, even to the point of pessimism. But he couldn't push too far or Marsh might have second thoughts. It was a perilously fine line to walk.

"You say this demonstration is meant to force the government to leave you alone. On the other hand, you say we'll be killed if they find out how it happened. So wouldn't it be wiser—and safer—to silence a small area rather than the whole country?"

Marsh's eyes never left the bank of monitor screens he was focused on. "I already told you, it can't be done piecemeal. Besides, I don't want any room for doubt in their black little hearts and minds. I want them to know I mean business."

"Yes, but there must be some other way of making your point . . . some way that won't bring the cream of every federal agency after you. Not to mention Ma Bell's best resources."

Marsh gave him a brief but pointed glance. "My security has only one weak spot—you."

Lubov decided not to argue that point, for the moment.

"You know," Marsh went on, "I gave it a lot of thought before deciding to bring you in to handle the phreaking grunt work." He paused, then his tone assumed a harder edge. "This would already be over if we could have worked on it together."

"We could have!" Lubov protested, trying to neutralize the King's strong feelings about time. He knew nothing annoyed him more than being delayed or off schedule. "We still can!"

"It's too late for that," Marsh replied, the edge still clear in his voice. "Ram-Jam is where we are now, and like I told you, your Ram-Jam options are damn limited. You either keep your mouth shut—permanently—or we both get wiped out."

"I assure you, I will," Lubov said, with perfect honesty.

Marsh's mood lightened with an equally honest reply. "Yeah . . . I think you might." He held up a hand for silence, tapped an extra-long string of numbers into his phreaking rig, then resumed. "What'll happen is this: Just before I kick it off, I'll tap into the Hot Line and tell the President what's going on."

Tap the Hot Line? Lubov knew as well as anyone that phreaks could tap into most telephone lines on the planet, secured or unsecured. But the Hot Line had so many safeguards and backups that accessing it would be nothing short of . . . *incredible*!

"I'll tell him I'm the King, acting in support of the Ghost Glitch, a kindred spirit I don't know but have always admired. I'll tell him if anything happens to the Glitch . . . if the charges against him aren't dropped, and if everything doesn't go back to exactly the way it was for him . . . I'll shut everything down—permanently."

He paused for a gloating chuckle. "Believe me, the Prez will have it taken care of. He won't have any choice!"

Lubov tried to imagine Marsh's satisfaction at the thought of dictating terms to the President of the United States. He'd probably been the butt of endless jokes and bullying throughout his childhood, and now here he was, preparing to browbeat the ultimate authority of his country's massive power structure.

Lubov hated to bring up the next question but knew it would be expected. "Since your call will so clearly link the King and the Ghost Glitch, won't someone suspect they're the same person?"

"Sure," Marsh said. "It's an obvious connection to make. But two things work against them acting on it. First, they'll have a hard time believing one person could be both. It just goes against the grain of probability, doesn't it? And second, they can't afford to be wrong. The stakes are way too high."

"But you said they'd kill us both without question if they ever found out we were involved."

"And I'm sure they would, *if* they were absolutely certain we were the ones. But put yourself in their place. Can you afford to kill the Ghost Glitch just because you *think* he's the King? What if you're wrong and then the King retaliates by shutting everything down—for keeps? Could you live with that decision?"

"I see your point," Lubov lied, knowing it was important to bolster Marsh's mental superiority in his own mind. And it was obvious that had been done when he turned back to his consoles.

"Yeah, there's just too much at stake for them to bother me, no matter how much they suspect who I am. So in the end . . . they'll do exactly what I tell them; they'll explain away what happened as a freak accident that could never repeat itself; and they'll pray every night that no one ever pisses me off again."

Because of his espionage training, Lubov knew that scenario bore no resemblance to reality. Mismatch would launch the greatest covert manhunt in history, and the King would be found and eliminated, no matter the cost in time, manpower, or resources. That much was certain to anyone with a rudimentary grasp of how governments operate. Of course, if all went according to Lubov's own fatalistic scenario, Marsh would never know he'd been wrong.

"Why haven't you asked about how I look?" Marsh said out of the blue. "I mean, I'm a fat ugly troll instead of the superman I pretend to be on the phone. Don't you wonder about that?"

Lubov responded promptly, knowing this above all other answers would be crucial. "I assumed it was a strategy for protecting your identity. The King can never be too careful."

Even sitting across the room, Lubov could tell Marsh's lips were spreading as wide as his stitches would allow. "That's it! That's it exactly! I can't be too careful."

By that point Lubov understood the real reason behind those endless lies. They were the means by which Marsh nourished and protected his inflated alter egos, which were in turn the products of a need to be noticed and revered in ways he couldn't possibly achieve as himself. So he catered to that need by creating identities to rule magic kingdoms. The Ghost Glitch's phantom presence and the King's disembodied voice made him, in his own way, as awesome and powerful as the Wizard of Oz.

And, as far as his looks were concerned, just as much a fraud.

"You know, there's a little more to why you're sitting where you are than the fact that I can't afford to take any chances," Marsh said, once more changing the subject. "When they bagged me this morning"—he paused, then finished with a faint note of guilt in his voice—"they found my best hand-held."

Lubov didn't immediately understand what Marsh was trying to tell him because he was shifting in his chair, trying to ease the painful pressure on his bound wrists and ankles. But when he was marginally more comfortable, and Marsh's meaning finally registered, he looked up and spoke with genuine trepidation.

"The Cowboy . . . ?"

"I'd be surprised if the FBI got around to calling him today, especially since they have such a solid hacking case against me. But by tomorrow, at the latest, that hand-held will be on his desk." His voice lowered to a bleak mutter. "Hell, I worry more about the Cowboy than I do about Brandt and Doppler."

And with good reason, Lubov knew. The Cowboy was smarter than any ten FBI agents combined, which explained why Marsh was so crazed to execute Mismatch. The Cowboy was definitely capable of putting together a Glitch-King link, so he had to be sealed off from the entire case as quickly as possible.

"You shouldn't have kept treating him so shabbily after it happened," Lubov said matter-of-factly.

He knew that would anger Marsh, but he knew just as well that it would be expected. They'd debated the point often in the past, and the King was well aware of how the Kraut felt about it.

"I had to set an example!" Marsh insisted, sounding every bit as defensive as he did in the orbit. "Dammit, I had to!"

Lubov knew that was only marginally true. The real reason Marsh had done what he had to the Cowboy seemed to be outright ego gratification. He apparently enjoyed making the poor guy suffer, extending his punishment well beyond what his mistake called for.

"I'm sorry I brought it up," Lubov said, carrying out the second half of what he felt Marsh would expect from him.

"Me too," Marsh growled, clearly upset by the thought of finally having the tables turned between him and the Cowboy. "Now, just sit tight and don't ask any more questions for a while. I have to really concentrate on this next part."

He settled into his work as a smile of anticipation slowly spread across Lubov's haggard, glassy-eyed face. For whatever reasons, this was definitely shaping up as the end of the line for his sleeper status, his career—even his life.

And all he had to do to make his part of it happen was get his hands free within the proper time frame.

□ XLIV □

Once Nat and Karen were away from Marsh's house, heading back into San Jose, Nat began the process of trying to convince himself his theory about Marsh was true. That was difficult because fusing the Glitch and the King was a preposterous notion.

When faced with unlikely situations, Nat always remembered Albert Einstein's comment that the world is not only stranger than we imagine, it's stranger than we *can* imagine. If there was a fundamental truth he'd come to believe while chasing the King and the Network phreaks, that was it. So his mind was open.

Apart from the technical feasibility, which was improbable but not flatly impossible, the real motivation for Nat to make the King-Glitch link was what it would mean to him on a personal level. If, in fact, Percy Marsh *was* His Royal Highness, King of the Fucking

Phone Phreaks, then Ma Bell fraud investigator Nat Perkins was right on the edge of exacting a sweet, sweet revenge.

Nat had never confided to anyone why catching the King meant so much to him, but it went miles beyond the expected duties of his job with Ma Bell. It was something profoundly and intensely personal between him and his ex-"boss"—a stain on his heart and mind and spirit that he'd lived with for so long, it could be removed only by bringing his old cohort to bay.

Naturally, Karen had no inkling of the twisting swirl of emotions tormenting her companion as they drove along. So she eventually looked over at him and said, "Well, what now?"

Because he was still so absorbed with where his suspicions might be leading, it took him a few seconds to focus on her and her question. "Excuse me?"

"What do we do now?" she repeated cheerfully. "I mean, our workday's over and the night is young."

He completely missed her hint and responded with a meaningless shrug. That made his preoccupation obvious, so she politely lapsed back into silence. And he continued grappling with loose pieces of the Marsh-King puzzle until an unrelated tactical problem suddenly crossed his mind.

"Hey! I just realized—you've been with me since I found you in my car this morning. How'd you get there?"

She responded with uncharacteristic grimness. "After Brocton shut me down about investigating Marsh, I was really fuming. It was the same old national-security hype, only this time I'd heard it once too often. So I stormed out, got in my car, and for some crazy reason decided to drive to Marsh's house. Maybe I thought it would help how I was feeling . . . I don't know.

"Anyway, when I saw your car parked there at the curb, it occurred to me to just level with you and see if you'd give me a break. I mean, what did I have to lose? And if you went for it, I could get at least the phone-phreaking monkey off my back, and maybe some of the hacking monkey too."

"So does that mean your car is at Marsh's?" he asked.

She nodded. "Parked a couple of blocks from his house."

"Couldn't afford to have Brocton find out you'd disobeyed his orders, huh?" he said, braking to pull over and turn around.

"Awww, don't go back now," she pleaded. "Let's have dinner!"

By then the Corvette was stopped, so he turned to look at her. For the first time she seemed nervous. "I got the idea you wanted this arrangement kept strictly professional."

"That was then," she said softly, reaching out to touch his arm as she had a couple of times before. Unlike before, it turned into a tentative caress. "This is now. . . ."

He didn't know what to do except be as honest as he could. "Listen, Karen, if you said that to me at any other time . . ." He trailed off, shaking his head. "Believe me, I'd be doing cartwheels. But now is such a bad time. I'm too distracted by this Marsh business to give you my best shot."

She let her fingers slide down his arm to grasp his hand. "You're missing my point, Nat. You've already given me your best shot. And you scored a bull's-eye. Trust me."

He sat there with his jaw hanging open, wishing his hair were thicker and his waist slimmer. No woman had ever spoken to him so forthrightly, much less one of such quality.

"Now, you listen to me," she went on. "I feel I owe you at least a dinner for all you've done for me today. So let's have something really nice and I'll charge it to the *Ledger*. Okay?"

Irony overwhelmed him. Here was an absolutely smashing, top-of-the-line woman offering him a first-class dinner and who knew what else. Yet the physical desire he felt for her couldn't overcome the emotions that were fueling his pursuit of the King.

"I, uh, don't know how to say this," he said, "but I'm just not in that kind of mood." He felt her hand stiffen and start withdrawing from his, so he grabbed it and held it in place.

"It has nothing at all to do with you, Karen—nothing. It's just that the King has been a major burr under my saddle for a lot of long, frustrating years, so getting close enough to even suspect I've found him . . ." His words trailed off again.

She gazed steadily at him, trying to gauge what was really going on behind his gentle, hard-edged facade. Then her entire expression was transformed as an answer bowled her over.

"What a dummy I am!" she exclaimed, slapping her free palm to her forehead. "It never occurred to me you might have other plans for this evening. Excuse my presumption."

Shaking his head, he took both her hands in his. "Karen, listen: I don't have other plans for tonight. But I do have another priority, and that's the only thing that could keep me from having a nice, leisurely dinner with you. Understand?"

Her doubtful expression and the tension he felt in her hands were almost enough to make him change his mind. But he knew that would cost more in the long run than it might gain short-term.

Suddenly, as if a wave of understanding swept into her and washed away all her doubts, her hands relaxed in his. She flashed one of her brightest megawatt smiles before saying, "It's okay, Nat. I think I know what you're trying to tell me."

There was something vaguely alarming in her words and her tone, as if she'd shifted emphasis onto some tangent that would prove more rewarding than the one she was on. Nat couldn't imagine what it might be, but at that point he didn't care. He just wanted to get rid of her so he could be alone for the rest of the evening with his thoughts about Marsh and the King.

Without another word he leaned across the Corvette's central console and briefly pressed his lips to her left cheek. She didn't resist or make more of the gesture than was intended.

He then made a U-turn to head back toward Marsh's house.

□ XLV □

Lubov spent the next half hour marveling at Marsh's virtuosity with electronic equipment. He was a human dynamo, rolling his chair from point to point within the ten-foot area where he worked, typing into his computer terminals, punching buttons, assessing readouts, turning knobs, tapping out musical instructions on his phreaking unit—all with astonishing speed.

He seemed like a misshapen but sophisticated extension of his split-second machines, a flesh-covered android whose skill couldn't be diminished even when taxed to maximum limits.

Toward the end of the half hour, lights of many colors were winking and glowing all over the digital horseshoe: green, blue, red, amber, white. Whether shining steadily or blinking rhythmically, each seemed poised to do its part in the grand scheme it was programmed to complete, while a constant, powerful *hummmm* added auditory proof of the devastating forces held within.

Finally Marsh came to rest in front of three side-by-side toggle switches located low in the center of the left-side panel. He took a deep breath, lifted all three to the up position, then glanced around to see if anything had started inadvertently. When he determined it was all holding steady, his pent-up breath gushed out and he sagged forward with relief.

"That's it," he muttered over the soft drone of his primed machines. "Programmed, loaded, and ready to fire." He checked his watch, then looked over at Lubov trussed in his chair.

"Not bad, considering. We can shoot for a three A.M. kickoff on this end, which gives us a six A.M. East Coast start. A lot better to have the hours your help would have saved, but we're not critically beyond our optimum time slot."

Earlier, Lubov would have been delighted to hear Marsh speak as if the two of them were full-fledged partners. But now, if he was to have any hope of achieving his long-range objective, that partnership idea had to be dramatically altered. Also, it was now or never for him to get his hands free to do what he must.

Both those pressures drove him to the edge of caution.

"I don't care about any optimum time slot!" he snapped. "Untie my hands!"

As Lubov hoped, Marsh was startled by his outburst. "Sorry, Kraut. I still have to call the Prez, then throw the switches."

"No! I've had enough! Retie them in front if you have to, but release me from this position! I'm in agony!"

There was only a little exaggeration in his words, so he hoped the desperation he felt about his objective would come across as honest protest about his situation. And apparently it did. Marsh checked his watch and considered his options, absently scratching the stubble on his chin. Then he stood.

"You've been a good sport up to now," he said, moving over to Lubov's chair. "I guess I can afford to give you a break."

He unwrapped the blanket from around his prisoner, then squatted behind him to begin loosening the bonds on his wrists.

"Those toggles over there control the whole show," he said, chatting as he worked. "All three down kicks it off . . . leave 'em down five minutes . . . then lift 'em back up." He rocked back on his heels and stopped untying, as if struck for the first time by the incredible scope of his endeavor. "Hard to imagine an entire shutdown reduced to something so simple, isn't it?"

"I wouldn't believe it if I hadn't watched you do it," Lubov replied, hoping flattery would get Marsh moving again.

It did. He resumed untying as he cheerfully gloated, "Neither will they—until it happens. Poor bastards . . ."

Marsh's explanation of the purpose and function of those three toggles left Lubov with only one final unknown factor: the extent of erosion in his own physical condition. The circulation in his arms had been impaired for so long, he could barely feel them or his hands. He wondered if they'd be effective when he needed them —or would they cost him his golden opportunity?

When his wrists were finally unbound, his arms hung limply at his sides. He began shaking and flexing them as much as he could, but they felt strangely detached from his body, as if they belonged to someone else.

Marsh moved to the chair's front, which meant time was running out. If Lubov couldn't regain enough strength and flexibility to do what was necessary, the switches would be thrown and all would be lost.

"Put 'em up," Marsh said, indicating what he wanted.

"Please . . ." Lubov begged. "Give me a few more minutes. There's almost no circulation in them!"

"It'll come back soon enough," Marsh countered. "Now, come on, lift 'em up. I want to get the show on the road."

Lubov pumped out a few more rapid flexes as increased blood flow brought a warm, stinging tingle to both limbs. With sluggish deliberation, he lifted his wrists.

Marsh leaned over to begin the retying process, absently humming "Zip-a-Dee-Doo-Dah." And indeed, everything *was* going his way. Then, suddenly, Lubov's left hand snaked out to snatch the glasses from his captor's nose!

Instead of reacting to protect himself, Marsh opened his mouth and widened his eyes in startled surprise. That reflex presented a perfect target for the two forefingers on Lubov's right hand. Lubov jabbed them forward with all his strength, directly into Marsh's myopic brown orbs, compressing each to the farthest reaches of its socket.

Both eyeballs were driven back so violently that hundreds of tiny muscle fibers, along with the nerve endings attached to them, were torn loose or ripped apart. When they could no longer withstand the massive force thrust against them, they burst with the muted *urp!* of popping cellophane bubbles.

Each crushed eyeball spewed forth a sickly glob of vitreous humor that landed on the back of Lubov's hand.

Marsh bellowed out a piercing howl of indescribable pain and terror. Blinded! In an instant! In *less* than an instant! He threw both hands up to cover his empty sockets, as if that might somehow change the reality of what had just occurred.

Meanwhile, Lubov—stunned by a problem he hadn't been able to foresee—did the same. Except Lubov's hands flew past his own squinted-shut eyes to cover his ears, which had become highly sensitized as a result of his head injury. They were causing him an agony nearly the equal of Marsh's.

Horrified by the feel of his empty, oozing eye sockets, Marsh screamed again and again as he reeled back against the near end of his equipment horseshoe. At that point all he had to do was reach to his left, locate the switches, and pull them down to send his electronic juggernaut on its unstoppable way. But pure animal instinct had seized him, compelling him to try to flee.

He could only grope and lurch toward the steps on his right.

Meanwhile, Marsh's continuous howls arrowed straight to the core of Lubov's ravaged brain, each causing excruciating torment. Fortunately, each also affected him less than the previous one because his pain neurons lost capacity every time they fired.

Soon he was immune enough to the noise to open his eyes.

He was still sitting in the chair, bound at his ankles, weak and disoriented. But despite even blurrier vision created by squeezing his eyes shut, when he looked left he saw Marsh reach the bottom step. He realized he had to move—*now!* If Marsh got up the steps and locked the trapdoor, throwing the switches would be little more than large-scale sabotage. To maximize the damage, he had to first send a message. If he didn't . . .

No! Don't even think it!

He pushed to his feet and discovered another unanticipated problem. Rising abruptly after sitting many hours insures a short bout of dizziness and a brief loss of vision. Doing so after a major concussion only magnifies those problems. And so it was with Lubov the moment he stood. His head began throbbing with thunderous ferocity, while a surge of dizziness darkened his already impaired vision. But it was too late to reconsider.

He had to push to the end of his limits—and beyond.

Despite being unable to see, Lubov was able to execute two quick ninety-degree hops to his left, tracking Marsh so he ended up facing the stairwell. The chair legs scraped across the floor as they swung with his still-bound ankles.

Meanwhile, Marsh continued lumbering up the steps, consumed by his own permanent darkness, still screaming madly. But as Lubov followed those screams up each step, his own vision simply would not clear: *three . . . four . . . five . . . Clear, damn you!*

He then feared for his ability to stay upright through the dizziness. *Steady . . . steady!* Then came: *six . . . seven . . .*

Finally, he thought he saw a foot on a step, not one meter in front of his face! *Is it a vision?* Maybe. Then again, maybe not. Within his own murky darkness, it was impossible to be certain of anything. Certain or not, though, he had no choice but to act—*now!*

He lunged forward, arms outstretched, hands close together, desperately hoping his damaged senses hadn't betrayed him. He closed his hands where he believed Marsh's ankle would be . . .

They closed on themselves. *Missed!*

His chest slammed into the edge of the stairwell, which stopped his forward motion like a freeze-frame. He began a slow downward slide, thinking only of how close he'd come to success.

So close! Then, unexpectedly, something arrested his slide as he heard Marsh gasp and half exclaim, "Wha—?"

Lubov's hands suddenly jerked upward! *My fingers!* They'd hooked Marsh's left trouser cuff!

Marsh started trying to shake him off, lifting him from the floor, grunting loudly with the effort of trying to pull away.

Despite vision still all but useless, Lubov could see perfectly in his mind's eye. *I've got him!* But could he hang on?

He felt the pulling tension release as Marsh kicked downward to try to break his grip. He knew exactly where the ankle would end up when that downward kick finished, so he unlocked his fingers and regrabbed behind and just below where they'd been.

Marsh's left ankle slammed into his waiting grasp. *Got it!*

The next move was critical because Marsh had to be tumbled down the stairs. In Lubov's favor was the fact there was nothing for Marsh to grab on to in the stairwell. Against him was his own lack of leverage, caused by his feet barely touching the floor.

He could only cling tenaciously while Marsh screamed and kicked and twisted in desperate efforts to break free.

Each scream and each abrupt movement by Marsh sapped Lubov's will and strength. Slowly, though, the fat man's right knee began to sag under the combined strain of his tormentor's weight added to his own. Then, just as Lubov's vision finally began to clear a bit, Marsh generated one last tremendous upward surge.

Lubov countered with the best yank he could muster. It caused Marsh's right foot to slip down a step, while his shin slammed into the edge of the step above. Marsh shouted at that new pain as he rolled over onto his back. Lubov's feet hit the floor, which gave him enough leverage to yank with authority.

Marsh slid down another step, squealing in stark terror.

Lubov dug his heels in and jerked with all his diminished might. Only Marsh's stubby legs came off the steps, leaving his upper body still on the staircase. But that did provide a degree of vulnerability, so Lubov released the left leg he was holding and locked his fingers together to make a cudgel of his fist.

He lunged forward to slam it into Marsh's unguarded crotch.

Though not a decisive blow, it forced Marsh's torso up in a reflex action. While Marsh groaned, Lubov drew back again to unleash a powerful swat squarely onto his breastbone.

Air gushed from Marsh's lungs with a loud *whoosh,* leaving him helpless. He sat on the fifth step's edge, his arms squeezed around his empty chest, his mutilated face bulging with pain.

Lubov grabbed the front of Marsh's sweatshirt and yanked him off his perch to a standing position. His legs immediately buckled. He sagged forward onto his hands and knees, head hanging down, struggling desperately to draw a breath past bleeding lips that had long since torn through their stitches.

Gasping for his own breath, Lubov seized his opportunity.

He locked his fingers again, raised them high, then dropped down with his weight behind the blow. His knees hit the floor as his fist-cudgel smashed into the base of Marsh's neck with a loud, resounding *crack*! Instantaneously, Marsh's body crumpled into a soft, quivering heap, his limbs jerking in fitful spasms.

Lubov keeled over onto his victim in wheezing exhaustion, but remarkably he didn't pass out. He even stayed lucid enough to wonder how long it might take to recover the strength to untie himself from that damned chair. Then, as he felt the body of his great benefactor twitch one last time, he wondered if—in those final seconds—Marsh had had any inkling he was about to die.

Such speculation was meaningless by then because, one way or another, after what Marsh had done, he was as doomed as anyone —and maybe everyone—in America. But Lubov was truly sorry to have been his executioner.

After all, of the men he'd ever known or known of, Percy Marsh was the one whose intelligence he'd respected most.

PART THREE

□ □ □ □ □ □ □ □ □ □ □ □ □ □

Lubov needed half an hour to recover from his battle with Marsh. After regaining what strength he had left, he freed his ankles, then he managed to drag and shove his victim's corpse up under the basement stairwell. He tucked it into a fetal lump, covering it with the blanket he'd used to keep warm. That way he could avoid seeing Marsh's bloated remains when he returned.

At first Lubov didn't doubt that the body would lay undisturbed while he was away completing his mission. Then it occurred to him that the Cowboy might be hotter on the King's heels than Marsh had assumed. That caused him to consider rigging booby traps upstairs. Unfortunately, buying materials and constructing them would cost time he could no longer spare.

In the end he decided to leave both the corpse and the cabin undisturbed, with the hope and expectation that each would remain safe for the next several hours. Which left nothing more to do except try to complete his mission, trusting that the fate that had brought him to that point would carry him all the way.

His first stop was the kitchen, where he searched cupboards until he found what he now needed more than anything else—soup.

He was famished and dehydrated and facing an arduous round-trip, so he heated two cans of chicken noodle together, hoping he could get them down and keep them down. Surprisingly, they settled as though they would stay.

From the kitchen he made his way to a bathroom, where a hot shower did much to clear his fogged head. But his double vision, pounding headache, and impaired sense of smell remained.

His concussion wouldn't improve without medical treatment and rest, but now both were out of the question—permanently.

Using a hand-held mirror and the one above the sink, he examined the wound at the back of his head. It was as serious as he'd feared: forked like a tree limb across the crown, and slashed like a saber-thrust toward his left ear.

Even clean it was ugly, with all branches opened wide by the upward pressure of a dark swelling the size of half a grapefruit.

He obviously couldn't fly in such a state, which meant he'd have to drive to Gretchko's house. But considering the time lost on the long trips to and from the San Jose and San Luis Obispo airports, plus the flying time itself, he wouldn't lose more than an hour going in either direction. Besides, he might fall asleep on a plane and never wake up. Driving should keep him awake and alive . . . at least long enough to do what had to be done.

Now that he was washed, Lubov turned his attention to his clothes. He rinsed the urine from his dark gray trousers and the blood from the rear collar of his burgundy turtleneck. Neither garment showed stains well, so by the time he'd finished drying them with a hair dryer, both looked as good as new.

Next came a tediously careful shave, then one last cosmetic problem to overcome: the unsightly wound at the back of his head.

He searched the closets until he found something to serve his purpose—a battered old Stetson apparently left behind by the cabin's previous owner, the mountain man. It was black and a size too small, which made it inappropriate from both aesthetic and practical standpoints. But shoved back with the brim nearly vertical, it did conceal his wound. So, silly-looking or not, he'd wear it to keep his gash out of sight during the trip.

Leaving the hat in place, he put on his gray tweed sport coat and checked his watch—4:48 A.M. That would put him in San Luis Obispo around 9:30; at Gretchko's no later than 10:00; an hour to rest and recuperate while Gretchko coded and sent the message; then back to the cabin around 4:00. Eleven hours total . . . eleven excruciating hours . . . the most important eleven hours of his life.

He was confident he could endure them. He had to!

He lowered the trapdoor and shoved the table-rug combination back into place. When he'd finished, nothing gave away what lay beneath. It looked exactly as it had when he and Marsh arrived.

From there he moved out onto the porch, where he took several deep breaths in the bracing, chilly predawn. The crisp air felt great in his lungs as it turned his breath to mist and brought back memories of his life long past. Then he shook off those feelings and went back to work, retrieving the liquid-plastic wasp nest that concealed the front-door key.

Because everything was going so smoothly, and because his addled senses were impairing his logic, Lubov's wasn't thinking beyond the problem of how best to contact Gretchko. Consequently, after locking the door he didn't think to discard the wasp nest and keep the key. Operating on autopilot, he reattached the key to the wasp nest, then put both back over the door frame.

From there he walked down the flagstone path leading to his Porsche. He got in and found the Stetson wouldn't stay in place if he tried to sit normally. The upright brim was too large for the space between his head and the roof of the car.

He ended up having to cant the seat back, which he knew would only add to the difficulty of staying awake and alert. But he had no choice. Not only was wearing the hat essential to his security, he'd noticed that its inner band lent some kind of support to the lump at the back of his head. It had reduced his headache considerably.

Once adjusted and comfortable, he started the engine and was on his way. *Eleven hours,* he thought. *Only eleven more!*

Feeling certain he could make it, he couldn't help smiling.

Lubov had found no telephone at the cabin, other than Marsh's phreaking unit, which couldn't be used once the shutdown program was locked in. Also, there was no point in waking Gretchko at that hour of the morning. The old man was an early riser, but not that early. So he drove until the soup moving through his body necessitated a stop, a few minutes after 6:00.

After relieving himself, Lubov drove to an isolated phone booth. From the Porsche's glove compartment he removed a small music box with a false bottom. He opened it, took out his own hand-held blue box, and gazed at it lovingly.

An odd feeling swept over him as he prepared to make his call. Not because of its momentous nature, but simply because this was the first time he'd ever needed to send an emergency message. Such was the infrequency of situations that couldn't be accommodated by the hand-to-hand, one-time-pad system.

He tapped out the necessary musical tones and listened to several rings. It was just as he'd suspected. The old man was already out in his rose garden, laboring under the first blue-orange rays of the morning sun.

Finally, the receiver was lifted. "Hello?"

"Hello, Grandfather—this is Cousin Albert," Lubov said, using his code name. Then came the key word that would indicate this was an emergency. "There's been an accident. Your services are required. Do you understand?"

"Yes, Cousin Albert," Gretchko replied, with no emotion Lubov could discern. "An accident. When do you arrive?"

"Around ten o'clock this morning."

"I'll be prepared and waiting."

Lubov beeped off the line while marveling at the old man's steadfast commitment. A good, loyal Russian to the glorious end.

□ XLVII □

It was only a thirty-yard walk across an open wharf, but Naval Lieutenant Hanna Buckley hated moving from the enclosed waiting shed to the hydrofoil. She'd been raised in sweltering south Georgia swamps, and she'd never appreciated chilly morning gusts whipping in off the Pacific. Her main defense against them was to snuggle deep into her collar and waddle those thirty yards as fast as her ever-increasing bulk would permit.

The hydrofoil trip was a forty-five-minute chance for her and her coworkers to prepare themselves for another 8:00 A.M. to 4:00 P.M. day-watch at the Padre Island C/S/T Naval Facility. Such a psych-up was recommended because their NAVFAC served the vital strategic function of monitoring all water traffic—both surface and submerged—along the western coastline of America.

Even so, everyone making the trip tried to nap on the way over —especially Hanna. She'd suffered through yet another night of battling with her unborn child to snatch a few hours of sleep.

She logged in the same way she did most mornings lately: blond hair windblown, puffy cheeks without makeup, eyes bloodshot, mouth agape in periodic yawns. As usual, Lieutenant Ron Simms ambled over with a friendly grin to execute the Display Room's formal transfer of control.

Lieutenant Simms was a big, round-faced fellow who often tried to ease the stress of Hanna's pregnancy with good-natured teasing about it. But this morning he took one look at her and dispensed with the quips and wisecracks.

"You look like hell, Hanna," he said matter-of-factly. "You ought to turn around and go back to bed."

Even though she knew he meant well, exhaustion had driven her beyond the edge of civility. "Mind your own damn business, will you, Lieutenant?"

His soft face hardened as he handed over the clipboard containing the accumulated paperwork of his midnight-to-eight shift. "No problem, *sir*!" he said, throwing her a sharp salute.

That broke through her jangled emotions. She reached out to grab his arm as he started moving past her. "Listen, Ron . . . I'm being an ass. I'm sorry. Two more weeks. Can you find a way to put up with me for that long? Please?"

His rigid expression softened, then was cracked by a self-conscious grin. "I was a jerk to say what I did."

"You were just being honest," she countered. "Hell, if I look even half as bad as I feel . . ."

She trailed off as her eyes began to sting. Simms stepped forward to slip a huge arm around her shoulders. "Want me to stick around for a while? Help you ease into the shift?"

She shook her head adamantly. "The distraction will be good for me. You go on home to Carolyn. She'll be waiting."

It was clear she meant it, so he shrugged and said, "Okay."

She glanced at the clipboard. "Everything static?"

He grinned. "When is it ever *not* static?"

That meant all Soviet trawlers and loopers—the vessels of primary concern in the C/S/T scheme of things—were on station and performing their usual routines.

Soviet "trawlers" were renovated fishing vessels used to monitor communications to and from major U.S. military bases. Twelve such bases dotted America's western coastline, and a trawler was always stationed fifty miles at sea directly opposite each one.

"Loopers" were nuclear attack subs that cruised a giant loop around the Pacific. With strict regularity and great precision, they followed an underwater circuit from their northeast base in Petropavlosk, through the Sea of Japan, down to Hawaii, over to San

Diego, then up the West Coast to Seattle. From there they either continued along the loop, broke off for other destinations, or returned to base to change crews and be tended.

Everyone who monitored loopers was genuinely impressed with the consistency of their spacing and tracking. They divided the western U.S. coastline into three even units and held those gaps through thick and thin. And never, under any circumstances, did they ever penetrate the recognized 200-mile territorial limit.

They hugged that limit's topographical edge with a precision that was the envy of every American submarine captain.

In addition to loopers, NAVFAC personnel tracked their "shadows," which were U.S. nuclear attack subs that stayed within hailing distance of each looper, from the time they entered the C/S/T listening web until they exited the coverage area.

Both circled the loop like a team of merry-go-round horses.

Hanna and her mates had no idea what purpose the loopers served because that information was available only to those government and military personnel with a need-to-know. But it was common knowledge that the Soviet submarine fleet was kept on an exceptionally tight leash, and none of its movements were undertaken lightly. So whatever the mission of those mysterious patrols, the fact that Moscow would permit such close monitoring by the C/S/T arrays was eloquent testimony to their vital nature.

Lieutenant Simms turned from Hanna and started to walk away, then a thought struck him. "There's a looper pass coming up soon," he said. "Want me to stay and give you a hand with it?"

A "pass" meant a looper would be moving through one of the three underwater obstacle courses they regularly put themselves through—again, for reasons no NAVFAC grunt could understand. All O-WO's had to be extra alert during that time, and this was Simms's way of asking if Hanna felt prepared to deal with it.

"When and where?" she asked.

"About a half hour . . . the Massif."

The Tatyana Massif was tougher to monitor than an Out Island passage, but not nearly as tough as a transit through the Fromholtz Ridge. So Hanna said, "I can handle it."

Simms nodded, then he patted her shoulder and moved away. She called after him. "Hey, Ron . . . thanks. Seriously!"

Hanna was responsible for twenty line-graph sensors, which were arranged along three of the Display Room's walls. Each of her O-Ts was responsible for monitoring a group of four.

The sensors themselves looked and worked like polygraph machines, recording the telltale sounds of engines and prop blades instead of heartbeats and fear. And like their civilian counterparts, their wire arms traced squiggly tracks along never-ending rolls of lined paper called "grams."

In the middle of the room was a large square table covered with several neat rows of manila folders—perhaps 200 in all—containing everything known about every significant vessel currently in the C/S/T monitoring web. Color coding for each country of registry made for a bright patchwork display, but only one file group really mattered to those working in the NAVFAC.

That was the blood-red cluster lying apart from the others: the Soviet vessels now in the web.

There were four columns of those red files: commercial, commercial/military, military, and submarine. There were seldom more than three files in the submarine column—representing loopers—although other attack subs occasionally ventured inside the 400-mile range of America's listening arrays.

Russian missile-carrying subs never came within 500 miles of the coastline, preferring to cruise random patterns in the vastness of the mid-Pacific. There they remained invisible to all but airborne monitoring, awaiting orders to send their deadly payloads barreling into their great enemy's heartland.

Hanna moved to the table and noted the bottom file in the looper column: SSN *Mikhail Potkin.* That sub was just entering the lower part of the loop segment near San Diego. It would move north in the #3 position until the #1 sub moved well past Seattle and a new #3 moved in to take its place. Then the *Potkin* would become #2, and that cycle would continue perpetuating itself.

Even when groggy from lack of sleep, Hanna was good at visually monitoring loopers as they moved through the underwater mountain ranges they had to negotiate to stay on the edge of the

200-mile limit. She moved toward Seaman Dennis Stone, the O-T monitoring the four sensors that covered Southern California.

Stepping beside him, she studied the line-graph on the #1, or southernmost, sensor. The vertical slashes and horizontal lines measured hertz, time, speed, and audio signature to give readouts on position, heading, depth, and identity.

"How long before the *Potkin* enters the Massif?" she asked, feeling herself coming to life to face the upcoming challenge.

Whenever O-WO's like Hanna got together socially, they often discussed the grim fascination they felt knowing that—someday, some way—they might watch a looper fail to make it through one of those dangerous transits. That knowledge added spice to a job that in many respects was numbingly routine.

"Twenty minutes," Stone replied, "give or take."

Hanna nodded and moved over to the two thirty-inch display screens situated against the free wall near the door. She dialed the proper codes and punched the on buttons. Immediately, both screens filled with computer graphics of several ridges in the Taty-ana Massif. Those scattered pinnacles were represented by closely packed gridwork lines that looked like graph-paper cutouts in the pale green haze that represented clear water.

Such graphics always reminded Hanna of wire sculpture.

Both screens provided three-dimensional views movable in any of 360°, so she was able to focus on any part of the Massif from any position she chose—up, down, high, low, near, far—it didn't matter. Like a movie director, she was able to angle for the best shots. When she found the ones she liked—directly above, then below to one side of the first ridge to be negotiated—she pressed the hold button and turned the screens off.

That left it just a matter of waiting until the *Mikhail Potkin* moved into range. Then the show would start.

□ XLVIII □

Equally aware of the impending show was Captain Nikolai Barzlin, the *Potkin*'s commander. He entered his boat's control room and stood for several moments like the snow-topped old rock he was, preparing to oversee every element of his crew's journey through the difficult Tatyana passage.

Each looper's primary mission was to act as a continually available relay for emergency messages sent by agents on shore. But equally important was the underwater-navigation training provided by circuits in the loop. Barzlin was a conscientious man who served that latter purpose by being in the control room during every major passage, regardless of the hour it occurred.

He eased alongside Commander Valeri Damovitch, the young upstart selected by the Naval Presidium to assume the *Potkin's* command after this voyage. Damovitch was a cold, direct, uncompromising fellow, with a bodybuilder's stout physique and the heavy jawline of his Ukrainian homeland.

He was directing the Tatyana passage from behind Navigator Technician Yuri Lemnotova and Sonar Chief Andrus Kim.

Lemnotova was a wiry, intense man who, like all submarine navigators, spent his quarter-watches sitting glued in front of the four black dials whose floating white needles showed the boat's attitude through every quadrant. Beside Lemnotova sat Chief Kim, their fat, irreverent sonarman from Mongolia.

Kim, too, labored constantly before four glass-covered screens, but his were square instead of circular and were twice the size of Lemnotova's attitude dials. On each glowing green screen was a shifting parade of geographical features revealed by sending out subsonic sound waves and then making graphic representations of what bounced back.

Barzlin stepped behind the sonarman to scan his four viewing screens. Two of the Massif's peaks were already in sight at a distance of 3,000 yards. The first was well under their boat's cruising depth of 500 feet, and so presented no problem. But the second topped off at less than 300 feet below the surface. That one would have to be negotiated, along with the four others that would soon be in their way.

"All is well?" he inquired of Damovitch.

The lantern-jawed commander turned only enough to be respectful. "Yes, Captain, all is well."

What bothered Barzlin about Damovitch was his damnable similarity to himself at that age: certain of his ability and fully able to back it up. It was an unfair prejudice, one he wished he didn't feel, but there was no way to deny it or pretend it wasn't there. It was.

He nodded to his second-in-command, then crossed the control room to the radio area. His chess-playing comrade, Communications Chief Josef Popov, occupied the first radio chair, while Seaman First Class Rudi Rykoff had the second.

Because each pass along the American coastline was so important for training the sailors on board, it was easy to overlook the emergency-monitoring responsibility of the radiomen. So Barzlin always tried to pay attention to their less critical but no less important jobs.

"How is traffic on shore today, Josef?" he asked.

Popov leaned back and pulled the headphone from his shiny bald head, dropping it around his neck so the earpieces came together under his chin. Their relationship was such that he could completely relax whenever the captain stopped to chat.

"The usual, sir. Mostly rock and roll, and something new called heavy metal. But Rykoff has excellent reception of a cowboy station. Would you like it piped to your cabin?"

Barzlin smiled at his thoughtfulness. Everyone on board knew the captain had developed a quirky taste for American country-and-western music during his many voyages in the loop.

"Perhaps after we clear the Massif," he replied, "if the reception is still clear. And if you promise not to use it as an excuse for losing our next chess match."

Popov grinned big. "Excuse?—never! Explanation?—maybe."

Barzlin smiled again, then changed the subject. "How is the training of young Rykoff coming along?"

He already knew the answer to that because they'd already discussed Rykoff several times during chess games. But it would give the strict teacher a way to praise his pupil openly.

"Not bad at all, sir," Popov said with a smile. "He's an excellent student and a pleasant fellow to be around."

Even with his earphones on, the reed-thin young apprentice could hear them talking about him. He grinned sheepishly.

"Just make sure he learns to keep an eye and ear attuned to that," Barzlin said, pointing to the console divider between the two radio units. On it was a dark green, almost black bulb the size and shape of half a hen's egg. "Even more than training our sailors to navigate, that light is why we're here."

Rykoff knew that remark was solely for his benefit, so he lowered his earphones to speak. "Sir, in radio school we were taught that emergency messages are sent only under extreme circumstances. Has either of you ever seen the light come on?"

Barzlin and Popov cast knowing glances at each other, revealing the special camaraderie of a longtime common endeavor.

"Twice," Popov answered matter-of-factly. "The first time, we rescued an agent who had to parachute to the rendezvous point in his business suit!" He made a pinching motion to indicate a small space. "The Americans were that close behind!"

Rykoff glanced at the somber light with new respect.

"The other time," Barzlin added, "was when an agent and his grandfather were caught in the act of sending their message. We transcribed only their verification, then it stopped." He pursed his lips at that disturbing memory. "Their names were Simonova and Blatski. Naturally, neither man was ever heard from again."

Popov's smooth melon shook in genuine sympathy. "It's terrible work agents do, even worse than this. I wouldn't trade places for a new television, a telephone, a car—"

Rykoff cut in to quip, "Throw in a new apartment and I'll consider it!"

As the three of them enjoyed an indulgent laugh, Barzlin could see why Popov regarded this particular student so highly. He seemed perfectly at ease in a situation others his age might find thoroughly intimidating.

Quickly, though, it was back to business for all three men.

The two radio operators replaced their headphones to resume their work, while Barzlin returned to the navigating area. More than wanting to see how Damovitch and the crew would do against the Massif, he was feeling nostalgic about his last trip through.

☐ XLIX ☐

When saying good-bye the previous evening, Karen and Nat had arranged to meet for breakfast at an International House of Pancakes midway between their two apartments. From the IHOP they'd go together to the FBI building, where Nat would ask Brandt and Doppler for access to their file on Marsh.

She arrived first and was waiting when his Corvette drove up. She nearly fell over when he got out wearing a blue blazer over light brown slacks. For reasons she couldn't begin to explain, she'd chosen to wear a dark blue jacket and tan skirt.

It seemed a bizarre coincidence.

They joked about their similar outfits as he gave her a light kiss of greeting on the cheek. And she made no more of that kiss than the one of the previous night when they'd parted. As Nat suspected, she had indeed shifted her emphasis away from finding out about phreaking and hacking.

But he didn't suspect her new focus of interest was himself.

She had two good reasons for the change. First, she'd found herself strongly attracted to his country edges and steely core, which gave her a personal desire to learn all she could about him. Second, she'd become wildly curious about why he was so intent on finding the King. It was clearly more than a straightforward game of hunter-and-prey. There was some huge emotional connection between them—a link so painful to Nat, he appeared willing to sacrifice anything to break free of it.

Finding that connection was a challenge she couldn't resist.

The surest route to discovering more about him seemed to be the path she'd been following: Staying with him on the pretext of finding out about phreaking and hacking. That way she could watch him reveal himself as he conducted his investigation. And though such subtle pursuit was much slower than she preferred, it was far more likely to get her where she wanted to go.

Relaxed and feeling no pressure to make anything happen, she shared breakfast with him while discussing typical morning topics, such as the day's headline news, projected weather reports, and prospects for change in city government.

Finally, he leveled a serious gaze at her. "You know, I got to thinking last night. . . ."

"Really?" she asked, in the way she felt was expected.

He leaned forward and lowered his voice. "If Marsh is both the Ghost Glitch and the King—and I've just about convinced myself he is—do you realize that makes him potentially one of the most dangerous men on earth?"

She matched his serious tone with a firm shake of her head.

"It's true!" he insisted. "If you put those two incredible abilities together"—he locked his fingers to illustrate—"then God only knows what he might be capable of."

"What do you mean? Are you accusing him of something?"

"No! Nothing like that. But a combination of top-level hacking *and* phreaking would give him access to just about every sensitive bit of data in this country. And I do mean *every* bit. He could create all kinds of havoc if he wanted to."

"Like what, for instance?"

Nat shrugged. "Jam telephone lines . . . steal top-secret military documents . . . create a false incoming-missile alert at NORAD. . . . Hell, anything! Just let your imagination run wild, and whatever you can dream up, he could probably do it."

"Didn't you say phreaks aren't out to screw the system? Especially the King, because of how Ma Bell would go after him?"

Nat leaned forward even more and lowered his voice to barely a whisper. "Look, we both know how Brandt and Doppler treat the people they bag. And we know they wouldn't pull punches for the Glitch because they hate him. So assuming they did their usual number on Marsh, and assuming he *is* the King, I'd bet some serious cheese that he'll be out to get revenge against them."

She leaned forward to meet him, just as intense. "You mean do something like you said? Something really awful? Even if it meant putting a million-dollar price tag on his head?"

"Believe me, I know the guy!" Nat rasped. "Piss him off, he goes crazy, then he carries the grudge to lengths you can't imagine. And he doesn't give a damn about consequences."

There it is! Karen thought.

Something in the way Nat spoke . . . the tightly held rage bubbling under the surface of his words . . . convinced her she'd gotten a glimpse of what was fueling his pursuit of the King. It was related to some deep-seated animosity between them. She was as certain of that as anything she'd ever deduced as a reporter.

"What kind of grudge are you talking about?" she asked, with all the innocence she could muster.

He ignored her question. Instead, he looked at his watch and said, "It's after nine. I have to give the Bruise Brothers a call to tell them we're coming, so they can have Marsh's file ready when we get there." He was out of his seat and heading for the IHOP's pay phone before she could register any protest.

Several minutes later he returned, scowling. "Great news!" he snapped sarcastically. "Because they had such a long, hard day yesterday, they're sleeping in this morning. And they can't be disturbed unless it's an emergency. They'll be in at noon."

It never occurred to her that FBI men needed rest, much less thugs like Brandt and Doppler. But her attention stayed focused on Nat and the deep lines creasing his ruggedly handsome face. She enjoyed seeing him in such a state of simmering agitation. It made her feel the way she always wanted men to make her feel: as if there were something in them beyond all control.

But why him? she couldn't help wondering. *Why a guy with a damn white whale swimming around somewhere?*

"Got something to work on for a couple of hours?" he asked.

She laughed. "I always have things to work on!"

He covered their check while rising to his feet. "Then I'll pick you up at the *Ledger* at 11:45. It's not far out of my way."

She rose with him, asking herself if it was tactically wise to be separated for that long. Then she decided it might be best to avoid appearing too eager. "Sure, that'll be fine."

Karen followed Nat from the IHOP while mulling over the two new certainties she'd discovered inside. First, there was definitely a serious, giant-sized ax being ground between Nat and the King, whoever he was. And second, if Marsh did indeed turn out to be the King, then Karen Glass was working her way into position to write one helluva banner-headline news story.

Her promise to Nat notwithstanding, she knew if Marsh ever

actually did something truly outrageous, no amount of interference by Ma Bell or the FBI could stop the media from publicizing it. And, she realized, she'd be the only reporter anywhere with access to so much information about him.

What it all meant was that, with only the most innocent of intentions, she might well have stumbled onto the kind of story that won Pulitzers. All it would take to find out was keeping Nat on her side, which she wanted to do anyway.

When they arrived at her red BMW, she turned to face him with the warmest smile she could generate, hoping this time he'd kiss her with more feeling. But he didn't kiss her at all.

He was already lost in thought as he mumbled, "I'll see you later." Then he turned toward his Corvette and walked away.

□ L □

The day he graduated from high school in the backwoods of Kentucky, tall, skinny Obadiah "Junior" Quinlan joined the U.S. Marine Corps. He did that to achieve two long-cherished goals: to learn how to retaliate against those who made fun of his enormous jug ears; and to become a first-class diesel mechanic like an older cousin making a fortune in the oil fields of Oklahoma.

The Marines were glad to help Junior accomplish his first ambition. He returned home from boot camp twenty pounds heavier and highly skilled in self-defense, which he promptly used to kick the crap out of several ex-classmates. But then, when he reported back to the Marines for mechanic's training, he found they—and fate—had other plans for their hillbilly recruit.

While taking the usual battery of skill tests, Junior Quinlan had revealed two extraordinary but hitherto unknown abilities. First, his hearing acuity was off the chart, which led to more jokes about his ears until his flying fists silenced them. Second, he was exceptional at distinguishing tones, which made him an ideal candidate for the military's main Morse-code school in Pensacola. Good code men were hard to come by, so all four branches of service were quick to exploit any that appeared.

After graduating at the head of his Morse class, Junior pulled a plum assignment: replacement duty at San Francisco's top-secret Long Distance Receiving base. His first actual view of such a place was when he reported that morning for the first day of his new job. The bus carrying his sixteen-man group was stopped at the guarded gates of three successive perimeter fences. Each stop brought a close look at the LDR itself.

Just inside the final perimeter fence was a 100-yard-diameter circle of twelve of the largest telephone poles he'd ever seen. Each was a 100-foot-high redwood log, connected by five thick black cables, one atop another in concentric rings. That was the receiving antenna. He knew from his studies that this one in San Francisco could pick up Soviet communications halfway across the Pacific—telephone, radio, or satellite.

Such was the power of intercept technology.

Inside the antenna ring was the "shack"—a squat, windowless, cinderblock square that was the basic design of all secret military buildings. And inside the shack was the position—or posit—room where Army, Navy, and Marine specialists spent their time intercepting and cataloguing foreign radio communications.

Junior knew the intercept game was a two-way street: Russia did the same thing to America and her allies. Mobile listening posts—called trawlers—were always stationed near key American installations throughout the world, while embassy staffs handled the lion's share of domestic traffic. So he had no moral qualms about the new job he was beginning. It was hi-tech tit for tat.

As he stepped into the ready room, adjacent to the posit room, he looked around for the naval ensign he'd been told to check in with: Bremmer—Ensign Milt Bremmer. In the confusion of bodies in the cramped ready room, it was all Junior could do to keep from being swept in or out by the soldiers and sailors changing shifts at the monitoring consoles.

Suddenly there was a tap on his shoulder. "Quinlan?"

Junior whirled and snapped off a brisk salute. "Yes, sir!"

"Cut the salute business," the ferret-faced, bored-looking ensign said. "We don't do that in here. I'm Bremmer."

"Pleased ta meetcha, sir."

"Yeah, right," Bremmer said, as if it pained him to be even that polite. He scrutinized Junior for a moment, then shrugged and said, "You sure as hell got the ears for this job." He then turned and was on his way toward the posit room. "Come on . . ."

Junior decided to let that first insult go. No sense in starting off on a sour note. Besides, that might be the end of it. He'd found physical oddities were generally no big deal in the military. In fact, he'd already seen a few worse than his own.

The posit room was a drab gray, forty-foot square that contained sixteen monitoring consoles arrayed within cubicles, four cubicles per wall, with a door in the center of each wall. Each console was a superpowerful receiving unit designed to continually scan within a narrowly defined bandwidth of 12.5 cycles per second. Those sixteen machines monitored the entire 200-cycle radio band to an exceedingly fine degree.

"You start at the 50-posit," Bremmer said, pointing to a corner console. "Not much happens on it—weather reports and such—so you can polish your copying without losing anything."

Junior didn't need any practice copying Morse code. That's all he'd been doing in Pensacola for the past four months. But he wasn't about to make waves by asking for a more taxing posit.

"If you have any trouble," Bremmer went on, "don't try to gut it out to show us how good you are. Switch on the recorder. It's worse to hand in an incomplete message than a recording."

Junior nodded. Each console had an overhead reel-to-reel tape recorder. Whenever a message came in unclear or faster than it could be copied by hand, a posit man was supposed to hit the recording switch so it wouldn't be lost. Junior knew it was bad form to be forced to record, but he also knew it might take a while to get the hang of real copying. So he was prepared to hit the switch if he had to, at least for the first few days.

"That's all," Bremmer said as he turned away. "Go to it."

With that, Marine Corporal Junior Quinlan sat down to begin the most important day of his young life.

□ LI □

At 8:05 that morning Ivan Gretchko left his house atop the highest bluff overlooking the Pacific in San Luis Obispo.

He'd bought that place shortly after his wife died, claiming two legitimate-sounding reasons. First, he said he wanted and needed to remove himself from the heartbreaking memories of her that he kept recalling in their Los Angeles home. And second, his divorced daughter and her three children already lived there, which couldn't have worked out much better for his true purposes.

Those true purposes for the move to San Luis Obispo were also twofold. First, its location midway between the major population centers of Los Angeles and San Francisco made it difficult for American triangulators to pinpoint the emergency messages he occasionally sent. Second, the house's height let it stand free of nearby radio and television antennas, which allowed messages to be sent safely and clearly over a wide area of ocean.

All Soviet grandfathers needed access to such places.

Each weekday morning Gretchko drove two miles to his daughter Ursula's house. He'd take charge of her youngest son, Skipper, while she took the two older children to school on her way to the real-estate office where she worked. He'd walk Skipper to the kindergarten where he spent his days, then return home to putter with his beloved roses.

So went his usual mornings.

This, of course, was a highly *un*usual morning, which was all the more reason to keep to his normal schedule. In fact, whenever he received an emergency call from an agent, he maintained the same policy. But hearing from Lubov made it far more difficult.

Gretchko knew Viktor Lubov could deal with all but the most life-threatening situations, which meant the "accident" he'd mentioned was an extremely serious event. And coming so soon after their discussion of the Ghost Glitch's impending arrest, which had been scheduled for the previous morning, Gretchko felt safe assuming the crisis revolved around Percy Marsh.

But how? And to what extent?

* * *

"Paw-Paw?" Skipper said as they walked along hand in hand in the bright morning sunshine.

Gretchko looked down into his grandson's beatific five-year-old face, hoping with all his heart this wouldn't be their last walk together. But he was prepared to die doing his duty if it came to that. And he wasn't worried about the boy being marked for life as the grandson of a notorious Soviet spy.

That wouldn't happen because the CIA went to great lengths to hide the fact that America was saturated with sleepers. Whenever one was caught or eliminated, the circumstances were made to look as routine as possible. So Gretchko knew he'd keep his good name and honors, which provided some degree of comfort.

"Yes, Skipper? What is it?"

"Remember a long time ago when you told me about spiders? How they're really not bad 'cause they eat lotsa bugs?"

Gretchko smiled at the boy's concept of time. His lecture about the value of spiders had been given only two weeks earlier.

"Yes, I remember."

"My friend Jimmy wanted to kill one yesterday, but I didn't let him. I picked it up and held it in my hand to keep it safe."

There was a pause as they walked along a few steps farther, then Skipper continued in a somewhat smaller voice.

"But guess what happened, Paw-Paw?"

"What?"

"I think it got sick in my hand, 'cause it was all rolled up when I turned it loose and I couldn't make it unroll."

Gretchko now had much experience dealing with the trials and tribulations of being a small boy. This was Skipper's way of obliquely inquiring if or what he'd done wrong.

"The spider probably went to sleep in your hand and then woke up later after you left. Such things happen, you know."

The sag in Skipper's spirits immediately lifted. "You think so, Paw-Paw? Really?"

"Yes, I think so."

Now it was safe for Skipper to confess the truth. "Boy, I sure was worried! I thought I might've killed it!"

Soon they were close enough to hear delighted squeals coming from the kindergarten grounds, so Skipper started tugging the old man's hand to hurry him along.

That was a signal Gretchko knew well.

"You may go the rest of the way by yourself," he said. "But before you go, I must tell you one very important thing."

He stopped walking and turned Skipper to face him. He eased down onto one knee, taking the boy's tiny young hands into his bony old ones. Then he spoke in an emotion-filled voice.

"I love you very, very much—you and your mother and your brother and sister. If I'm not able to walk with you tomorrow, or any day after, you must be certain to tell them I said that. And you yourself must always, always remember it."

Naturally, Skipper missed the underlying meaning of those words. He beamed a happy smile and leaned forward to hug his wonderful grandfather's neck. "I love you, too, Paw-Paw. 'Bye!"

He then turned on his small heels and sprinted away.

Gretchko stood, blinking back tears.

Gretchko returned to his house shortly after 9:00 A.M. to complete his preparations for Lubov's arrival.

He went up into his secretly refurbished attic, where he'd already taken the powerful VLF transmitter out of its hidden case and put it on the table against the wall. He then hooked up the narrow-beam antenna, aimed it where the subcycle charts indicated, placed the current code book on the table in front of the transmitter, and put two cyanide capsules near the code book.

After double-checking his handiwork, he stepped over to a hidden wallboard niche in a far corner of the cramped room. He opened the compartment and removed a rolled-up bundle of leather straps: the shoulder holster containing his Smith & Wesson .32-caliber automatic pistol. He put it on, vowing to use it before the cyanide took effect, determined to avoid dying as pathetically as Simonova and Blatski had five years earlier.

He'd be taking someone with him if it came to that.

He looked around one last time. Everything was ready. But once Lubov's message was coded, a collapsible antenna had to be extended ten feet above the roof to maximize transmission over many miles of water. That was Gretchko's only worry. Even for the few minutes necessary to transmit, the silver, gull-winged, silicate antenna was conspicuous jutting above the roof.

From the attic Gretchko went back downstairs to the bathroom. He relieved himself, then splashed tap water onto his face. Gazing in the mirror as he toweled off, he realized that today he looked his age. The fringe of white hair looked thinner than ever; his rheumy brown eyes looked dull; his mottled skin had a grayish cast to it; and his jowls sagged lower than ever.

He stuck his hands out and saw they were shaking. He hoped that meant he was ready.

There was nothing more for him to do but take one last lingering stroll through his garden of earthly delights, trimming and pruning only those bushes most obviously in need of care.

Then he'd go back inside to await his protégé's arrival.

☐ LII ☐

Lieutenant Norton Vent's first day and night aboard the shadow sub USS *Gremlin* went without major incident. He encountered his old nemesis Ken LeBlanc only once, in the control room during Captain Jim Stickles's formal welcome to the old and new members of his officer staff. Not a word passed between them before or after Stickles's brief speech, but they couldn't help noticing the physical changes time had wrought in each other.

Vent found "Dandy" still as tall and patrician-looking as ever, but twenty or so extra pounds had smoothed the handsome angles of his face. Vent knew he himself had also gained several pounds, but that was muscle added after joining a health club for distraction from the grind of his divorce. Unfortunately, that body overhaul had done nothing for his thin, bespectacled, ordinary-looking face. He was still a Midwestern farmer's son, while LeBlanc was still a Virginia aristocrat.

During the cruise out to assume shadow duty alongside the Russian looper *Mikhail Potkin,* watch rotation had been informally assigned by veteran officers and crew deciding who should stand and who should sleep. That was done to speed the recovery of those who'd tried to cram too much into the final hours before setting off on their ninety-day voyage. So it had been easy for Vent to avoid LeBlanc after the formal welcome.

Now, however, the official watch list had been posted, and for inexplicable reasons Stickles had scheduled the two antagonists for the same shifts on deck. Lieutenant Commander LeBlanc would be executive officer in charge of the control room during first and third watches, while Lieutenant Vent would be officer of the deck, directly under him in the chain of command.

Even without the emotional barriers between them, such a schedule would be a demanding challenge for both Annapolis men.

Sitting on his bunk in his cramped, two-person quarters, Vent pondered the situation. He gazed at the empty bunk of his cabinmate, David Hawkins, who'd be performing deck-officer duties under Stickles on the second and fourth watches. Why hadn't Hawkins been paired with LeBlanc? Stickles knew the situation between them, so what was he trying to do? Stir up trouble? Force one of them to lose control because of unresolved anger?

Vent vowed to do all in his power to make certain he wasn't victimized by Stickles's apparently sadistic scheme. LeBlanc had already put one huge blot on his life; he couldn't afford to let him put on another. Just then there was a rap on his cabin door.

"Come in!" he called.

The door opened and Ken LeBlanc stepped inside. Vent's ears began tingling their danger warning as he rose to meet his unwelcome visitor. They stood eyeing each other across the cabin's ten-foot depth as Vent removed his rimless spectacles.

"Don't worry, Nort," LeBlanc said, holding both hands up with the palms turned out. "I'm not here to pick a fight."

"Then what *do* you want?" Vent said evenly.

"To see if we can reach some kind of accommodation for the rest of this tour. I mean, both our butts are on the line here, so maybe we should try to work something out."

Vent hated to accommodate LeBlanc in any way, but this instance was clearly in his own best interests. "Strictly by the book on deck . . . keep out of each other's way when we're off."

LeBlanc nodded as if that was what he expected to hear. But he wasn't foolish enough to stick a hand out to shake on it. Instead, he shifted into his usual line of smooth talk.

"You know, I read your file when we were compiling the crew lists," he said, flashing the blazingly insincere smile only he could generate. "I don't mind telling you—I was impressed. You've made quite a name for yourself as an up-and-comer."

"Obviously not as well as you have," Vent countered.

He was referring to LeBlanc's early promotion to lieutenant commander, a career boost he knew had come to Dandy the same way everything else did: He'd sucked up to someone in authority who could do him some good, and that person had made it happen.

"Little hard work, lotta luck," LeBlanc said, showing more teeth than ever. There was an uncomfortable pause, then he went on with overweening sympathy. "I, uh, also read that you and Glynda got divorced. I was sorry to hear that, Nort—truly."

Despite Vent's promise to himself to stay cool, that pushed him over the line. "You should be. It was mostly your fault."

A scowl spread across LeBlanc's straining features. "Let's not dredge that up again, shall we?"

Vent stood looking outwardly calm, but he was seething inside at the memories flooding back. Several years ago he and LeBlanc had been classmates at Annapolis. They'd never been friends because of the vast differences in their backgrounds, attitudes, and personal styles; but there was a bond of trust that was supposed to be honored among all midshipmen.

In the spring of their final year, a big formal dance was scheduled. At that point Vent had been going steady with Glynda for more than a year, and they'd recently become engaged. Then his father suffered a heart attack two days before the big dance, so he was called back to Iowa on emergency leave.

Coincidentally, Ken LeBlanc's date had been injured in an automobile accident one day earlier. Vent was aware of LeBlanc's reputation as a womanizer, but rather than allow Glynda to miss the dance, he decided it would be safe to ask LeBlanc to escort her in his place. And Glynda was attractive enough to meet LeBlanc's high standards, so he agreed to honor Vent's request.

During the dance LeBlanc was a perfect gentleman, but afterward he slipped Glynda a drug that addled her senses and badly weakened her. He took advantage of her helplessness by bringing her to a motel room he'd rented, where he raped her.

Once Glynda recovered enough to realize what had happened, she filed charges against LeBlanc. He admitted having sex with her but vehemently denied any use of force, insisting Glynda had been the aggressor. He then suggested that her charges were a trumped-up smoke screen to protect her engagement to Vent.

The case was brought before an Academy board of inquiry, which listened to the conflicting testimony and decided in LeBlanc's favor. He was exonerated, while Glynda was left emotionally shattered and with a reputation as a sleazy little townie out to snare herself a midshipman at all costs.

And she was pregnant.

Because Vent knew what a decent girl Glynda was, and because he knew what a cheap opportunist LeBlanc was, he fully accepted her version of what happened. So he did what was morally correct by going through with the marriage to her, even though she was no longer the person he'd fallen in love with.

Like many women in her circumstance, Glynda could never forgive herself for becoming a victim; nor could she forgive Vent for failing to avenge her. She also couldn't accept the reality that he had no means to avenge her. A head-on, man-to-man confrontation would only play into LeBlanc's hands because he was so physically superior in every way. And any more serious revenge would cost Vent his naval career, if not his freedom.

In the end LeBlanc suffered no negative effects, actually gaining a reputation as an irresistible charmer. Meanwhile, Vent and Glynda were left to live with their own disillusioned bitterness. And then came LeBlanc's son, born with such a severe case of Down syndrome that he had to be institutionalized at birth. So it was at great personal sacrifice that Vent managed a civil reply to LeBlanc's comment about dredging up their past.

"Would you please leave my cabin now and not speak to me ever again outside the line of official communication?"

LeBlanc stiffened to his full height, bristling with anger. "Better watch how you talk to me, Nort. I'm your superior now."

"You're *shit* now, you yellow-balled sonofabitch!" Vent snapped. "Now and for-fucking-*ever*!"

LeBlanc raised a clenched right fist. "I'm warning you!"

Vent cracked a faint, mocking smile. "Still can't take the heat, eh, Dandy? Still fly off the handle too easily."

LeBlanc stood trembling with misplaced rage.

Vent's smile faded. "Even an ass-licker like you won't make it to the top without self-control. Now get out of my cabin before I lose mine and we both end up in trouble."

LeBlanc could tell he meant it, so he reached back, opened the door, and stepped outside. But there was cold fury in his eyes and voice as he said, "You'll be sorry for this, Nort."

He slammed the door shut as Vent eased back onto his bunk feeling seriously mixed emotions. He'd won round one without working up much of a sweat, but he'd won it on his home turf. From here on they'd do their skirmishing on the control-room deck, where LeBlanc would have the overwhelming advantages of superior rank and witnesses all around.

Vent's ears started tingling their prickly alarm, telling him this was going to be the most difficult three months of his life . . . *if* he could get through them without being confined to quarters for insubordination or assault—or worse.

☐ LIII ☐

Ivan Gretchko had first met Viktor Lubov shortly after his near-disastrous "defection." But his awareness of him went back to three years earlier, when the KGB sent word that a young electronics genius had been recruited for the Service. They told of special plans for him, special training to be directed at gaining parity in the vital field of microwave communication.

Gretchko was told to explore microwave technology in order to recommend material and methods to incorporate into the prodigy's training. He applied himself to the task with typical thoroughness, and three years later Viktor Lubov was as ready to take a place in American culture as any man his age could be.

The defection scheme was hatched to take advantage of his good looks and scintillating personality, qualities Americans were known to have a weakness for. It was felt that a dramatic "escape" would give him instant credibility no amount of creative background work could match.

That part of the plan worked perfectly.

Americans took the handsome young scientist-to-be straight to their hearts, and few doors were ever closed to him. But no one on the Soviet side could ever forget the almost-fatal accident that took place during the checkpoint "crossing."

Everything had been thoroughly rehearsed and practiced several times—guards firing shots that just missed; a cameraman there to take pictures—but no one counted on a shot straying too close to the prized "escapee." His backward-turned cap was torn off his head by the misaimed bullet, yet he was untouched by it.

That one shot—caught perfectly on film by the KGB's "tourist" —gave Lubov's defection an unchallenged air of authenticity. As far as Moscow knew, the CIA never bothered to verify his fabricated background as an East German national with a long-dead Russian father. They apparently assumed that a man who risked his life for all the world to see *had* to be genuine.

Once Lubov was safely in America, Gretchko became his behind-the-scenes adviser. Using his influence as a professor emeritus at UCLA, he got him accepted into its graduate electronics program with a minimum of bother. And though they were careful never to be seen together apart from university functions, Gretchko continued to guide Lubov's academic career.

After earning his doctorate, Lubov struck off on his own to establish his reputation in microwave technology. But by then Gretchko was having doubts about his protégé, doubts that were emotional rather than intellectual. He began to realize Lubov was more of an automaton than a normal, feeling human. And though such a personality deviation wasn't without cause or precedent, Gretchko's acceptance of it in Lubov came slowly.

When Gretchko went through SINO, the Soviet Institute for Nationalist Objectives, as one of its first seven recruits, the concept of planting long-term sleepers was new. Men were chosen, trained, sent to their target countries, and expected to perform. But as it turned out, many became assimilated into their foreign culture and defected. By the mid-fifties, the rate of loss was unacceptable, particularly in the U.S., where a booming postwar economy was making every man a prince, if not a king.

As a result of advanced brainwashing techniques learned in World War II and perfected during the Korean War, the SINO spy school's leaders decided to employ those techniques on their own agents. Something drastic had to be done to cut the soaring defection rate, and brainwashing their students was the most drastic method they could employ.

Fledgling Soviet agents were soon being subjected to countless mind-bending manipulations meant to insure long-term, long-distance fealty to their Communist Party. And those manipulations worked, better than anyone had ever hoped. But Gretchko objected to the loss of morality suffered in the process, as indicated by Lubov's behavior.

Spying was the most amoral of professions, a fact nobody could deny. But within that amorality, Gretchko believed, there had to be standards to cling to, linchpins to support an agent's personal code of ethics. He was proud to be from the old school, answerable only to his own conscience for what he did.

Gretchko spied for his country because he felt it had a right— no, a duty—to counterbalance America's awesome nuclear might. Such power in the hands of only one country—even self-righteous hypocrites like the Americans—was certain to be used for world dominance somewhere down the line.

Consequently, his moral linchpin was the maxim that power corrupts and absolute power corrupts absolutely, which he'd believed since he witnessed the first atomic explosion in 1945. That horrifying demonstration of unmitigated destruction had firmly set the course of his life. He always acted with the unshakable belief that he was doing the world a tremendous service by helping to maintain its "balance of terror."

Men like Lubov, he realized, had no such moral purpose behind what they did. They were like robots, focusing on their objectives with grotesque, even frightening, single-mindedness. They'd been programmed in the most Orwellian sense to deny all instincts except propagating the Soviet State.

Gretchko's normal instincts had led him to marry and raise a family, whereas Lubov was an emotionless neuter who used sex only as a tool to further his objectives. He was married to his work, even to the extent that he'd joined those damn phone phreaks in an effort to find methods to corrupt the telephone system.

Gretchko had no idea where such extracurricular pursuits might lead, but they were symptomatic of the new sleepers' compulsions to maximize efforts. Fortunately, those like Lubov were as limited in their activities as he was. None could master more than a small part of the vast spread of American technology, so whatever influence they might develop—both official and unofficial—would always be limited to a manageable degree.

In other words, none of them would ever be able to single-handedly start World War III . . . or so Gretchko believed.

☐ LIV ☐

When the doorbell rang at 9:48, Gretchko dismissed all negative thoughts about Lubov. The man was a comrade, a patriot in trouble, and duty dictated that he be given any assistance possible. Gretchko prided himself on always doing his duty.

With shaking hands and a pounding heart, he kissed the framed picture of his wife he'd been holding. Then he set it down, pulled his pistol from its holster, and moved to answer what could be the highest call of his homeland.

From behind a safety chain he cracked the door and peered outside. He was stunned speechless by the haunting apparition he saw. In many ways it was the face of a total stranger, yet—despite the uncharacteristic, tipped-up cowboy hat—there was a strong resemblance to Lubov. And sure enough . . .

"It's me, Ivan . . ." the specter said, with a voice barely resembling Lubov's. "I'm injured. . . ."

Simple injury could never explain such an immense change in anyone's features. The tipped-up hat gave a comical cast to an otherwise tragic countenance: slack, sallow-looking chin below bluish-tinged lips struggling to stay together; hollow, ash-gray cheeks, skeletal in their lack of shape and color; and eyes sunk so deep and surrounded by such wide, blue-black circles, they hinted at a last long walk to the gallows.

That's it! Gretchko realized. Lubov's distorted face was a portrait of impending death, even though his sharp blue eyes glittered with incongruous intensity.

"Come in, come in," Gretchko said as he hurriedly unlatched the chain and swung the door wide. "I'll call a doctor at once."

"No!" Lubov growled as he crossed the threshold to enter the living room. "There's no time or need for one. I'm well enough to complete my mission. After that, my condition won't matter."

"But . . . what's wrong?" Gretchko asked, holstering his pistol and then helping his colleague to the couch.

Lubov answered by gingerly removing his hat to reveal the gaping, oozing cuts on the bulging lump at the back of his head.

"Ach!" Gretchko moaned, with the profound sympathy anyone feels at seeing a fellow being bear up under the pain and trauma of a serious injury. He reached over in a comforting gesture.

Lubov deflected his hand with a flinching motion. "You musn't touch it," he said matter-of-factly. "The skull is cracked in many places and very sensitive to pressure."

An ugly purple edema was clearly visible under his blond hair, already seeping below the skin toward his neck. There was probably some seepage working its way into his braincase, too, which made it a miracle he was conscious, much less functioning.

Gretchko sat down and took Lubov into a fond, sad embrace, the embrace of a forgiving father for a wayward son. "Ah, my Viktor . . . How did this happen? Were you discovered?"

Lubov returned the embrace and quietly said, "No, there's no danger. Your weapon isn't necessary. But now I must have something to eat. Do you have soup?"

"Yes, of course," Gretchko said, rising to lead him to the kitchen. "Come, tell me everything while I prepare it for you."

Lubov nodded dully, then stood to shuffle along behind the anxious old man. "Chicken noodle is best, if you have it."

While Gretchko found the requested can of soup, opened it, and heated it on his kitchen stove, Lubov sat at the room's small table giving him a summary of happenings to that point.

Just as Marsh was waylaying Lubov at the cabin, Gretchko reached up to an overhead cabinet to get a bowl for the soup. It slipped from his hand, fell to the floor, and shattered, causing Lubov to stiffen and squeeze his eyes shut.

"Sorry," Gretchko muttered. "It slipped."

He kicked the shards over against the floorboard, then reached up to fetch another bowl, this time using both hands.

Meanwhile, Lubov shrugged slightly and said, "Don't worry yourself. All loud sounds hurt me now. It can't be helped."

Gretchko poured the hot soup into the bowl and set it on the table in front of Lubov. He then took the seat opposite.

"Your injury," he said, "surely that wasn't the accident you spoke of?" Though serious, it clearly wasn't *that* serious.

"Of course not!" Lubov countered as he stirred the soup to cool it. Then a faint smile softened his haggard features. "I was referring to something I couldn't explain on the phone."

He leaned forward with mounting excitement. "Ivan, how this fact emerged is unimportant . . . but believe me when I tell you that Percy Marsh turned out to be the Ghost Glitch *and* the King!"

Gretchko was flabbergasted into silence. *Is it possible?*

"And because he was both, he turned out to be a hundred—no, a thousand!—times more effective than I ever imagined!"

Could one man master hacking and phreaking to that degree?

"To prevent the people who arrested him from putting him in jail, he created the means to disrupt not only American government and military communications—as I always suspected he might be able to do—but *all* communication systems. Radio, telephone, telegraph, television—everything! Think of it!"

Gretchko slumped back in his chair, muttering, "My God!"

"And not only did he create the means to do this incredible thing, he put it together! I watched him with my own eyes! Right now, in the mountains west of San Jose, his computers are poised to shut down this country's entire communication network! All it requires is the lowering of three switches!"

Lubov paused, then shook his head as if to clear it. "Even now it's difficult to believe this isn't a dream."

"Perhaps it is," Gretchko managed to reply. "Perhaps the injury to your head has made you—"

"No!" Lubov snapped. "I'm not hallucinating! The situation is exactly as I've described it. Those switches *are* there—and now I alone control them."

"Why would Marsh put such power into your hands?"

"He didn't," Lubov said coldly. "I took it."

Gretchko was confused. Surely Lubov hadn't killed Marsh, a man he'd labored so long and hard to become acquainted with. Yet that clearly seemed to be his implication.

"You took it . . . in what sense?" he asked.

Lubov shrugged, downed a spoonful of soup, then calmly said, "I killed him. He'd served his purpose."

Gretchko realized he was missing something fundamental in their exchange. He was thinking of the proposed communication breakdown as a super bargaining chip Moscow might be able to use against the U.S.—a new and possibly vital element in their never-ending struggle for dominance.

Lubov was on some radically different line of thought.

Gretchko let his companion take several more spoonfuls of soup before trying to resolve his confusion. "What's the point of all this, Viktor? Why are you here instead of a hospital?"

Lubov seemed genuinely surprised. "Isn't it obvious? We've won!" He then began ranting like a true zealot, and Gretchko subtly recoiled from him. "The long struggle is almost over! We—you and I—will soon send a message that will make this day—these very moments we're now sharing—go down in history as the day our homeland achieved liberation from the Imperialists!"

The injury has made him mad!

"Our message will notify the Kremlin that in six hours all American communication systems will begin to fail. One hour later they'll be dead—permanently. At that point this horde of warmongers can be safely conquered with little or no losses on our side! Victory is ours!"

Truly mad! "But, Viktor . . . such an attack . . . such a murderous assault . . . it's unthinkable!"

Lubov misunderstood Gretchko's complaint. "Listen to me! The only possible way to win a nuclear conflict is if one side doesn't fight. The only way that can happen is if they *can't* fight. And the only way that can happen is as basic as warfare itself: They can't communicate the orders to fight!"

"Moscow will not respond!" Gretchko shouted. Lubov winced at his volume, so the old physicist lowered his voice below his level of agitation. "How can they dare? What if you're wrong?"

Lubov's doomed eyes blazed with passion. "Of course they'll doubt me! I'll doubt it myself until I see the computers begin to work. But if they *do* work . . . and if the systems here *do* fail . . . then our leaders can attack with impunity. And they will! It's their historical imperative!"

"But think of the death . . . the destruction . . ." Because of his perfect understanding of the effects of nuclear explosions, Gretchko had no trouble grasping the enormity of what Lubov was suggesting. "The absolute horror of it! You can't be serious!"

"Ten well-placed missiles on the ten largest cities—that's all they'll need!" Lubov insisted. "And when you consider the great advantage of universal order throughout the world . . . Well, the loss of several million enemies is hardly worth mentioning."

"What about those who live? Won't they resist occupation?"

"Without communication they'll be helpless—isolated pockets that can be easily controlled. And Moscow knows that, Comrade. It's a part of their strategic thinking. They *will* act!"

With a sudden, chilling flash of insight, Gretchko realized Lubov might be right. If everything he said was true, and if he successfully carried out his threat, World War III could be over in a matter of days. And the Soviets, not the Americans, would be masters of the world. *They'd have absolute power!*

Thoughts started pouring into Gretchko's mind—a wild, cascading jumble of memories, hopes, and fears fighting to be formed in the intensity of the moment. *This must not be allowed to happen!* Out of the jumble, that thought reigned supreme.

Lubov sensed something coming because he was out of his chair and leaning across the breakfast table as Gretchko reached for the holstered pistol under his arm. The old man's reflexes had slowed enough for the younger man—despite his injury—to be able to seize the gun and push his opponent back over his chair.

Suddenly sprawled on the floor, Gretchko found himself looking up at his own weapon held by a man wild with rage.

"Don't even *think* of trying to stop me, Comrade!" Lubov

hissed. "I have great respect for you and your achievements for the Party—but I won't tolerate your interference!"

Gretchko gathered his courage. "What if I refuse to help?"

"Then I'll send the message myself. I had emergency-code training at the SINO school—you know that. And I know enough about what's changed since then to make myself understood."

Gretchko did indeed know that was true, which meant the situation was desperate. The attic ladder was down and everything was laid out upstairs, so Lubov would have little trouble finding what he needed. And even a badly coded, poorly transmitted message would reach the emergency monitor sub and be relayed to Moscow, which would await further developments.

Then, if things here went as Lubov claimed they would . . .

"You must decide *now*, Ivan!" Lubov snapped. "How will history remember you?"

That seemed to have a withering effect on Gretchko as the importance of it sank in. His features filled with remorse, and he nodded from his position on the floor. "Of course, you're right, Viktor. I don't know what came over me."

Lubov gazed hard at him, pretending to judge his sincerity. But his vision was too blurry to notice subtleties of expression. He could only hope the old loyalist had truly come to his senses.

"I, too, had trouble accepting it at first," he said with a genial smile. "I can understand and forgive your reaction."

Gretchko returned his smile while reaching up with his hand for assistance. "You're a true friend, Viktor."

Casually, and without considering possible consequences, Lubov shoved the pistol into his belt before reaching down with both hands to help the old man to his feet.

Gretchko smiled again, patted his companion on the shoulder, then stepped toward the kitchen door with resolute determination.

"Come," he said. "The transmitter is in the attic."

He stepped around the overturned chair he'd been sitting in before Lubov pushed him down. He listened carefully as Lubov also stepped around the chair to move in behind him. When he felt the positioning was correct, he heaved himself backward.

His strategy was immediately obvious: that Lubov would tumble over the chair, strike the floor with his head, and end the matter permanently. It was a good strategy, too, one that sent Lubov sprawling backward over the chair exactly as planned.

Unfortunately, a catlike instinct allowed him to twist just enough as he fell to absorb the impact with his right shoulder. Which left Gretchko sprawled on the floor beside Lubov, with no choice but to try to prevail in the mad scramble about to ensue.

His first objective was to keep the pistol in Lubov's belt, which he did by rolling over and pressing his torso tightly against his opponent's back. To enhance his grip, he slipped his right arm around Lubov's neck. Lubov was left with his face turned down, stunned from the shock of falling.

In that brief moment of calm, Gretchko glanced up and realized their heads were near the floorboard where he'd kicked the shards of broken bowl. He reached out his left hand to grab the largest piece, while at the same time using his right hand to pull down the top of Lubov's turtleneck sweater.

He slashed that jagged piece of glass across the left side of Lubov's neck. Blood spilled from the wound. But it wasn't the pumping spurt of a cut artery. He'd have to try again.

Meanwhile, Lubov was galvanized by being cut. He bowed his back and surged upward, throwing Gretchko off and onto his side on the floor. Then he quickly rolled over to face his foe.

Gretchko countered with a slash aimed at Lubov's eyes, but Lubov turned away and grabbed Gretchko's left wrist in his own left hand. Lubov then moved his right hand down to the pistol still wedged in his belt.

Gretchko countered by grabbing Lubov's right wrist with his own right hand. That left both men straining against each other, awkwardly cross-armed, gasping for breath, recognizing the stakes in their struggle and exerting maximum effort.

Utilizing experience gained in his recent battle with Marsh, Lubov grabbed the pistol butt and mustered a desperate yank that snapped his right wrist free from Gretchko's weakening grip.

The pistol came loose from his belt and slammed up into the bottom of Gretchko's chin. The blow so stunned him, his head lolled onto the floor and he dropped his piece of broken bowl.

Now able to swing the gun freely, Lubov pushed himself up

enough to generate a thudding forehand that smashed the barrel into a spot just behind Gretchko's left ear.

The old man's brittle mastoid cracked, crumpling him flat.

Beside the still body, Lubov lay gulping air, recovering strength, and checking his neck wound to discover he was only cut superficially.

Finally he struggled to his knees, then gazed down at his inert opponent. Realizing he might not be dead, Lubov changed his grip on the pistol from handle to barrel. Then gently, even delicately, he shifted Gretchko's head to a facedown position.

"Farewell, old friend," he whispered with honest feeling.

He hammered the butt down in a whistling arc that ended at the base of his mentor's skull. Gretchko's body jerked spasmodically as twin jets of blood spurted from his nostrils.

Lubov stood, gathered his reeling senses, put the pistol in the inside pocket of his jacket, and stepped around to his original side of the table.

With trembling hands, he gulped down the last of the soup. Then he left for the attic, where he knew he'd find the emergency-relay equipment.

PART FOUR

□ □ □ □ □ □ □ □ □ □ □ □ □ □

□ LV □

Seaman Rudi Rykoff sat alone at the SSN *Mikhail Potkin's* radio consoles, monitoring a Los Angeles country-and-western radio show that was being piped into Captain Barzlin's cabin.

Communications Chief Popov was away from his console, using the head.

Suddenly, on the eye-level panel situated between them, the deep green emergency light began faintly winking to life. A stab of panic shot through Rykoff as he switched off Willie Nelson.

All Soviet radiomen knew their country's worldwide spy network used "bastard" channels to transmit emergency messages. Bastards were always located in seldom-used parts of the band width and were disguised to read like ordinary traffic. That provided maximum security and minimum interference to their precisely calibrated receivers—like the one on board the *Potkin.*

Up against bastards were the extremely powerful American LDR scanners, which could easily pluck them out of the air. But because they were transmitted within the seldom-used band widths and were coded like normal traffic, LDR monitoring personnel often had difficulty recognizing them for what they were.

Though his aligned receiver couldn't miss such a message, Rykoff didn't dare mishandle it. So he hit his tape machine's record button while shouting to those in the control room.

"Get Popov and the Captain! Emergency message coming in!"

He then rechecked the calibration codes to make certain the tuning needle was aligned correctly. Both code and needle said exactly 52.172 cycles per second.

As the message came in, he was expecting to hear a crisp line of dots and dashes. Instead, he found static crackling over them as they came through weakly. Something was wrong with the transmission itself, which meant he had to compensate.

He activated his frequency equalizer, which reduced certain frequencies and boosted others. The static immediately dropped to a soft hiss, while the dots and dashes became clearly audible.

* * *

Just before Rykoff began dealing with his crisis, Marine Corporal Junior Quinlan sat at his LDR console desperately wishing he had more than eight sheets to show for his first morning at the 50-posit post. Ensign Bremmer had just entered the room and was starting another of his rounds.

Every hour LDR section supervisors went to each console to pull all message sheets from their bins. Those sheets were then taken to analysts in a back room to be checked for basic consistency. If any message seemed other than routine, it was transferred to Decoding for a full translation. Everything else went into burn bags that were destroyed every twenty-four hours.

Each day saw twenty to thirty pounds of message sheets collected and burned, while only a handful were kept and decoded.

Thus far Bremmer hadn't even bothered to pull Junior's sheets, illustrating their insignificance in both number and substance. Each time he simply glanced at the bin and moved on, leaving Junior to wonder how long it might take before he could move to a posit that mattered.

An answer of sorts came as he absentmindedly listened through his earphones to the quiet hum of his scanner covering its assigned frequencies. His supersensitive hearing detected what sounded like a remote dash blip, but it was so faint that the scanner didn't lock onto it and kept moving across the band.

He waited until it passed 52.00 again, but this time there was nothing. He'd have shrugged it off as an anomaly or a fault in his own hearing if he hadn't been so desperate for another sheet to add to his meager stack. He flipped the automatic scanner to manual, then twisted its fine-tuner back and forth across 52.00. Outside 52.10 he thought he heard another blip, fainter than the first. Back and forth across 52.10 . . . nothing.

He was just about to give up when he pushed the needle over near 52.20 and crossed a blip just inside it. Now he had a problem. There was unmistakable activity on a channel between 52.10 and 52.20, which meant he was dealing with a VLF bastard, equipment failure, or weather interference.

A bastard would normally have been his first interpretation, but this wasn't as clean a transmission as he'd been trained to expect.

The bastards he'd been told about were supposed to be damned tough to interpret as such; but *if* he ever managed to recognize one, it was supposed to be crystal-clear. A bastard with static just didn't make sense, especially in the VLF range.

Junior knew that throughout the world, routine military use accounted for ninety percent of all nonverbal radio traffic. And those messages were always relayed in Morse code because it was so easy to codify and send. No better method had ever been found. Not only that, people who used bastards always kept their equipment in top working order. So he downgraded the possibility of a malfunctioning bastard sending static-filled VLF Morse, in favor of a less likely equipment failure or weather disturbance.

In either case, he knew he'd better handle it properly because headquarters would want to be accurately apprised of any unusual situation. Then a third possibility suddenly slammed into his consciousness: This might be some kind of special test beginning code men had to pass to keep a seat in the posit room!

Christ on a wormy crutch!

He flipped his record switch on and began playing this one strictly by the book. He fine-tuned his dial with a few more twists to bring the needle to rest on 52.172. His earphones immediately filled with crackling static, underneath which he could hear a consistent pattern coming across:

----• ----• ----• *Nines? Why nines?*

Whatever the reason, they meant it was definitely a bastard because equipment or weather problems wouldn't cause patterned blips. And despite knowing that secret codes normally went out in five-unit blocks of numbers, he'd never been told to expect continuing blocks of one single number, especially not on VLF.

He hated to ask for help his first morning on the job, but he couldn't risk failing if this was some kind of secret test.

"Ensign Bremmer!"

From across the room Bremmer grimaced and shook his head. He expected the jug-eared young hick with the backwoods accent to be a slow learner, but he didn't think it would show up so soon.

When he got to Junior's position, he snapped, "Yeah?"

Junior decided to keep his report matter-of-fact and professional, avoiding the buzzword *bastard*. No sense having them think he was the kind to go goggle-eyed under pressure.

"Sir, I got somethin' odd here: a Morse stream on a narrow-width VLF frequency, comin' in bad . . . lotsa static and flutter. So far it's been only a repeatin' series of nines. I don't know what to make of it."

Neither did Bremmer, but the "nine" business rang a faint bell in the back of his mind. It meant something—or used to mean something—but he couldn't remember what.

Much as he hated to give the new shitkicker credit, this was first-rate work. "Hit your record button," he said.

"I already did," Junior replied, surprised to see the charade continuing.

"Good. Keep it rolling and I'll go tell Langdon."

Bremmer turned away and left Junior wondering if this "test" might be no test at all. If Langdon was being called in, then . . .

Shit-fire! This could be the real thing!

He buckled down to it as the nines turned into other digits.

Rear Admiral Fritz Langdon was in charge of the San Francisco LDR. A lanky, beak-nosed, thin-lipped veteran of intercept bases around the world, Langdon had been working with codes for the better part of his eighteen-year military career. Little got past him because he knew his job so thoroughly.

Bremmer stepped into the ready room and pressed the intercom button to his office. "Yeah?" Langdon answered.

"Bremmer here, sir. There's something unusual coming in on the 50-posit. Looks like a VLF bastard tapping sets of nines."

"Nines!" Langdon roared. "How many sets?"

Bremmer was taken aback by the intensity of his response. "At least three, sir, but some were probably missed tuning in."

"Holy Christ! Record it!"

"We are, sir!" Bremmer assured him.

"I'll be right there! And get Samples!"

That baffled Bremmer. "Samples, sir? *Sergeant* Samples?"

"You heard me, Ensign—get him!"

"Aye, aye, sir!"

Bremmer let up on the intercom button, wondering what the

hell was going on. He couldn't imagine what would agitate Langdon to such a degree, much less require the participation of that old rummy Samples. But whatever it was, it would be good to see the lazy slug do something besides shoot pool.

Langdon was standing over Junior Quinlan's shoulder in the posit room when the last of the garbled message clicked through the young copier's headphones. Junior waited several long, tense seconds to make sure it wouldn't be repeated, then he sagged with relief and switched off his recorder.

"Reckon that's the end of it, sir," he said, turning to look up into his commanding officer's hawk-nosed face.

"Good work, Corporal!" Langdon beamed. "Excellent work! Breakthroughs like this are what it's all about."

Junior gave a broad grin, then self-consciously scratched the top of his head. "Thank yah, sir!"

Just then a door to the posit room opened and Master Sergeant Ode Samples stood framed in the doorway. Junior noted how the bulky spare tire around his middle jiggled as he made his way across the room to the rear admiral.

"You wanted to see me, sir?" he asked behind a weak salute that perfectly paralleled the languor in his expression.

"Sergeant, we have a message here I think you should take a look at. It came in on a VLF bastard."

Samples's lifeless eyes showed a flicker of interest.

"Looks like a stutter-nine," Langdon added.

Samples took on the appearance of a man stepping into the Twilight Zone and liking what he saw. His eyes became alert; his mouth tightened; his dismal slouch straightened.

Langdon turned to Bremmer. "Ensign, run that tape through the frequency equalizer, then make two copies. Send one to Decoding and give the other to Samples. I want an oral report within the hour and a written account by noon. Understood?"

"Yes, sir!" Bremmer snapped.

"Yes, sir!" Samples followed.

"Good. I'll be in my office when you finish. Carry on."

Langdon left the posit room and went directly to the communication room. He stuck his head in the door without knocking and caught the two men there playing cards.

"I want Admiral Tarnaby on the scrambler as soon as you can get him. Make it a flash."

Both men had shot to their feet and ripped off bladelike salutes, then the Marine corporal in charge responded.

"Yes, sir! Immediate flash-code to Admiral Tarnaby!"

"And you're in the brig the next time I catch you playing cards on duty—either of you."

The corporal and his partner blurted in unison: "Yes, *sir!*"

☐ **LVI** ☐

Just as he said he would, Nat picked Karen up at 11:45.

They entered the FBI building at noon, when Brandt and Doppler were scheduled to arrive. Unfortunately, both men were late, so Nat and Karen were escorted to a small waiting room where the chairs were pea-green plastic shells with no padding. The room's walls had only government plaques, official seals, and one looming photograph of President Daniel Baxter.

Karen stared at Baxter's picture, wondering how such a homely-looking old man could get elected President. He was completely bald on top, and the white fringe below that was thin and wispy. He had dark, jutting, bushy brows overhanging sad, baggy brown eyes. Only a prominent, square-cut chin radiated the sense of rock-solid stability he was famous for.

That chin had gotten her vote; maybe it was enough.

Without taking her eyes from the picture, she spoke to Nat. "What exactly are you looking for in Marsh's file?"

He shrugged. "No idea. But I'll know it if I see it."

"Something to indicate he's the King?"

Nat laughed sardonically. "Luck like that happens only in the movies. No, if they had anything solid, they'd have said so at yesterday's meeting. Hell, they'd have screamed it at me."

She considered. "Maybe there's something in it they didn't recognize. Maybe when you tell them what you think, they'll—"

Her next words froze in her throat as she saw the radical change in his expression. She'd never imagined he could look so intense. "That's the *last* thing I'd tell those bozos," he rasped. "I don't want them tracking all over my case!"

Karen suddenly realized she and Nat were running on parallel but widely divergent tracks. "I thought your whole purpose in all this was to prove Marsh is the King."

"It is, but in my own way and on my own terms." He realized how harsh that sounded, then forced a quick make-up smile. "Present company excepted, of course."

She leaned back in the uncomfortable waiting-room chair, twisting so she could get a better look at him. His conciliatory expression made her feel this might be the moment to try to gain some ground. "What is it between you and the King? Really?"

He smoothly sidestepped that one. "Look, if I can bag the guy with his hand in the cookie jar . . . with his rig or—please, God —actually phreaking . . . then I can force him to go to work f.. Ma Bell. That's what it's all about."

She tried to fathom the depths of his dark, mysterious eyes. What was it she saw there? Hostility? Determination? Cunning? All three? And what was he trying so hard to hide? Her personal instincts and her reporter's instincts both screamed for answers.

"If what you really want is to get leverage over him," she said, "it seems the FBI could do you a lot more good than harm. I mean, it's their business!"

"It's my business too," he said evenly.

His tone warned her to back off, so she changed tack. "What if you just can't get that leverage? What if he gets so careful, you won't be able to catch him in any compromising position?"

"He's an addict. And the great thing about addicts is, you can count on them doing their thing." His eyes glazed over as he retreated to a faraway inner space. "Sooner or later I'll find a way to nail him. And he'll end up exactly where I want him."

Nat made that statement with a conviction that was downright eerie. "How can you be so sure?" she asked.

He focused on her with the same intensity of before, a look she couldn't yet decipher. "I've chased him for years. I know how his mind works." Then a wry smile. "We're a lot alike, the King and me. We just work on opposite sides of the street."

She was ready to pursue that statement when a middle-aged woman finally opened the waiting-room door. "Agents Brandt and Doppler will see you now. Would you please come with me?"

Nat and Karen rose to follow the woman's lead. And as they walked along the central hallway, he couldn't help wondering how much longer he could hold Karen off. At the same time, she was wondering what it was going to take to get him to open up.

□ LVII □

Admiral Vince Tarnaby arrived at the Pacific Command Headquarters' gym for his early-morning racquetball game with Fleet Admiral Lucius Horton. As usual, on his way inside he passed his boss's blue PACCOM staff car. Horton's extra five years of age required an early arrival for ten extra minutes of warm-up.

As Tarnaby entered the gym he found Horton's driver waiting near the door. The young man came forward and saluted sharply.

"Sir, Admiral Horton asked me to inform you of a flash scramble from the San Francisco LDR. He suggests you take the call at your office. Admiral Barton will be his partner today."

Tarnaby's initial reaction was the deflation he always felt when he had to skip his morning game, which happened regularly enough because of the time-zone difference between Hawaii and the mainland. That contest was so much a part of his routine, missing it was like starting the day without a shave. His only consolation was that often he could sneak in a make-up game at lunch.

"All right, sailor—thanks," the stocky admiral said as he turned to begin the short walk back to his car.

"This better be damn good, Fritz. You're screwing up my racquetball game again."

"I was afraid of that," Langdon replied matter-of-factly. "But it just couldn't be helped. We've got a potential problem brewing over here, something PACCOM still might have to act on. You need to open some lines and put people on standby, just in case."

"Oh?" Tarnaby said. He knew Fritz Langdon to be a thoroughly reliable, astutely cautious man, which meant this probably *was* serious. "What have you got?"

"Looks like a VLF bastard aimed at one of those Russian subs that cruise off the coast. The wire's still hot and Decoding is working on it. We'll know in another hour."

"Care to speculate?"

"I'd say it's an emergency call for help from an old-time Soviet agent. The indications are solid."

"Such as . . . ?"

"He prefaced his message with blocks of nines. Years ago that was the universal distress code for Iron Curtain agents."

"Called stutter-nines, weren't they?" Even in the Transportation Corps, he'd occasionally dealt with secret codes.

"Good memory," Langdon replied. "Now, besides sending a stutter-nine, the guy blew his transmission. Our reception was so weak, we're having to run it through a frequency equalizer."

"Frequency equalizer?"

"FBI wiretappers developed them to cut room noise behind conversation. We use 'em to clean static off garbled transmits."

"Why haven't I heard about the goddamn things before now?" Tarnaby grumbled. Because he'd spent the past six months in charge of radio intercepts throughout the entire Pacific Command, frequency equalizers sounded like something he should know about.

"We don't use them much because our reception is normally perfect. Which tells us the agent didn't know what he was doing. If he'd been on top of it, he'd have come in loud and clear."

The round-faced admiral scratched a nervous itch under his left ear. "All right, I'll have my people go on standby out here." He paused a moment, then added, "And Fritz . . . ?"

"Yeah, Vince?"

"Cover my ass on this, will you? I'm still fairly new at it, and I can't afford to get caught with my dick in my hand."

A bemused smile spread under Langdon's beak. Tarnaby made a habit of getting people to bust their butts for him, and his technique was simplicity itself: He'd just admit he needed help and let nature take its course through everyone's conscience.

"Don't worry, we'll take care of you. I'll get back to your people as soon as I'm sure we have a live one."

"They'll be ready," Tarnaby promised. "So long."

Now it was just a matter of waiting for Samples and the decoders to do their jobs.

□ LVIII □

American decoders would need a minimum of one hour to transcribe the intercepted message because millions of letter permutations had to be computer-analyzed in just microseconds. The message itself would first be digested as it was received, in units of five-block digits, starting with:

95980	39998	92063	94441	81309	72664
99841	92412	41792	09751	79252	34218
24750	62449	81011	21849	24334	01077

Once the entire list was copied and stored on magnetic tape, computers would go to work arranging and rearranging possible letter combinations until coherent patterns emerged.

It was like solving a hugely complex anagram puzzle.

Soviet decoders on the SSN *Mikhail Potkin* had the tremendous advantage of having the code key in front of them: 08-A, 27-B, 33-C, 41-D, 02-E, 85-F, etc. They had the message translated and on Captain Barzlin's desk ten minutes after the transmit ended.

He read it the first time with a sense of excitement that turned to disbelief by the time he finished. The second reading changed his feelings to urgency. The third turned them to fear.

Whether sane or not, Agent KR-72 might well have consigned the *Potkin* to its doom. So Barzlin hit his intercom to summon Commander Damovitch and Communication Chief Popov to his cabin.

He had little regard for Damovitch's judgment because of the man's damnable certainty about his opinions and abilities. But because he was the *Potkin's* second-in-command, his presence was required by Soviet military law. Popov, on the other hand, had as much undersea experience as Barzlin; and like his captain, that experience had taught him one of life's great lessons: The more you know, the more you know you don't know.

Damovitch entered first, briskly stepping into the cabin that would soon be his own. The powerfully built, square-faced young officer snapped off a salute and stepped forward.

Popov's shiny head followed him through the door, and the wiry radioman matched the first officer's smart salute.

"Please, Comrades, take seats," Barzlin said in businesslike fashion. "The emergency message we've received requires careful deliberation before we act."

Damovitch and Popov moved across the small room to squeeze into the two straight-backed chairs Barzlin and Popov used when playing chess. The captain's cabin, though the most spacious on the *Potkin,* didn't serve well for more than two people at once.

As in all submarines, space was at a premium.

"Read it twice before we begin," Barzlin said as he handed a yellow sheet across his desk. Damovitch received it and held it beside his right elbow so Popov could read it simultaneously.

KR-72 REPT. GRNDFTHR KR-3 DED. USE HIS EQUIP. UNFAM W/NU CDES. MISTK INEVTBL. BT KNO EQUIP ENUF TRNSMT.

MESAG: BY LNG, CMPLX METHD, HAV GAND POWR 2 DISRUP AMERCN COMM NETWK. INCLU TELPH, TELGR, RADO, TELVI—AL THT TRAVL BY COMPUT. INCLU AL DEFNS/MILIT COMM. DISRUP TOT, IRREVS IMD FUTR.

PROCES BGN 6 HR (1630 PST) FRM TRANS THS MESAG. 1 HR LATR DISRUP COMP. AMER HEPLES AGNST ATAK. URG U TK VANTG OPOR2NTY.

LNG LF 2 PRTY. GDBY. KR-72.

While they read, Barzlin sat stroking his pointed chin, gathering his thoughts about it. When they finished, Damovitch handed the sheet back and, with Popov, sat there grim-faced. Each man sensed the magnitude of the problem the message represented, but neither was able to put it into perspective. At least not yet.

"As you see," Barzlin began, "we can definitely question its validity. It may even be the work of a madman. But that's not for us to decide. Moscow will know if he can be trusted, and if what he describes is possible. Our duty is to relay it to the proper authorities in the most practical manner."

"We can do that as soon as it's recoded," Popov said. He knew quite well how particular his old friend was about duty, even one as terrifying as this. "Rykoff and I have already calculated the satellite relay point, and the transmit cable can be extended while the coding is finished."

All submarines could receive pinpoint VLF communications at any place and at almost any depth. But except for emergencies, they refrained from transmitting. In emergencies they had the option of surfacing to transmit directly from their sails, or remaining submerged and releasing the cable Popov referred to.

When extended from its storage drum in a sub's sail, the transmit cable floated on the water like a giant strand of hair.

"I said we must relay in the most practical manner," Barzlin repeated. "Sending right away might not serve that purpose."

Popov looked obviously puzzled, while Damovitch reacted with more subtlety. Still, there was no mistaking his confusion, or the shade of apprehension furrowing his broad brow.

"Ordinarily we would relay immediately," Barzlin went on, "because our orders are to assume the Americans intercept in every case. But this message was transmitted so poorly . . ." He shrugged, then stood. "They could easily have missed it."

He began pacing the cramped room, his own wide brow wrinkled with concern. "If they did miss it, then how we handle it will determine its effectiveness. And our first option is to relay now. But if we do that, we know the Americans will intercept it because they so closely follow everything emergency monitors do."

"And they'll spare no effort to decode it," Damovitch said.

Popov nodded in agreement. "They'd succeed within an hour."

"Exactly," Barzlin agreed. "And if Agent KR-72 can't begin his shutdown process for six hours, that leaves the Americans at least five hours to find him and stop him."

"Excuse me, Captain," Damovitch interrupted. "Are you suggesting we wait those five hours before relaying?"

As the situation was resolving itself, Damovitch's expression was progressively clouding with doubt. Now his voice revealed honest objection mixed with quiet alarm.

"That's our second option," Barzlin replied as he moved to sit back down at his desk. "If we choose it, the Americans won't have a translation until after KR-72 starts executing his plan. If his message is genuine, then he can't be stopped. If it's a hoax, we've lost nothing by waiting. And in either case, Moscow will have more than enough time to decide what to do."

"That option assumes the Americans don't have the message," Damovitch said, "which is not an assumption to make lightly!"

"That's why Chief Popov is here," Barzlin said as he calmly turned to his trusted friend. "Josef, what's your professional assessment of that possibility?"

Popov first considered the message itself.

Obviously sent under great duress—the dead grandfather, using the old codes, failing to extend the antenna fully—it was barely received while being aimed directly at the *Potkin* over open sea. Those optimum transmit conditions had produced a minimum result, so it couldn't have carried far inland.

Next he considered the American equipment. He knew it normally covered great distances, but the unraised antenna had produced an exceptionally weak signal sent over an exceptionally narrow wavelength. Perhaps their scanners passed over it, or registered it so faintly as to be unnoticed. And even if it was received, its significance might not have been recognized.

The nine-block emergency system hadn't been used in years.

"How much depends on my opinion?" he finally asked, wanting to be sure of his position before making a judgment.

Barzlin expected as much from someone old enough and shrewd enough to be tempered by the results of hasty decisions.

"Possibly all our lives," he replied, not bothering to mince words. "If the Americans have the message, and if they understand its importance, they're decoding it right now."

"If you'll please allow me, Captain," Damovitch put in. The younger man had analyzed the situation for himself and now wished to make that clear. Barzlin grudgingly gave way.

"If the Americans translate this message," Damovitch said to Popov, "the first thing they'll do is begin an intense search for KR-72. Next, they'll determine which Soviet ships were capable of receiving it. Because it was aimed at us, and because the signal was a VLF sent weakly on a narrow band, it's highly likely the *Potkin* will prove to be the only possible target. So their final concern becomes whether or not we've relayed it."

Barzlin resumed the discourse, admitting to himself that his quick-witted replacement deserved a certain degree of respect. "If they find we *have* relayed, they can only try to find KR-72 before he can complete his mission. Then, if they fail to stop him, and if their communication systems do start going out . . ."

Popov had trouble completing his captain's ominous thought. "They might . . . launch a first strike . . . against our homeland?"

"Who can say?" was the frank reply. "But if we relay now, the Cuban missile crisis might seem trivial in comparison."

As Popov absorbed that, Damovitch moved their analysis in the opposite direction. "On the other hand, if they do have it now and we wait to relay, we can be certain they'll do anything to prevent us from sending it—including sinking us."

Popov searched frantically for a handle on their dilemma. "All right, let's assume the worst—they have it. If we continue as if nothing's happened, won't they assume we missed it?"

"The weak signal would be strong evidence," Barzlin agreed. "We should be able to bluff them until the moment we transmit."

"But could they dare risk letting us continue?" Damovitch asked. "Wouldn't they have to sink us to insure our silence?"

Again Barzlin was impressed by Damovitch's uptake. He still didn't agree with his reasoning, but he admired it nonetheless.

"Not necessarily," he replied. "Moscow has the advantage of knowing precisely who KR-72 is, and if he's to be believed. The

Americans can only know they'd risk a major—and quite serious
—confrontation by sinking us without an ironclad provocation."

Damovitch leaned forward in his chair. "Then it's a gamble
however we choose. Either we relay the message now and jeopardize KR-72's security . . . or hold back and jeopardize ours."

A haunted silence permeated the room, binding them to the fate
of Agent KR-72 like the silvery strands of a deadly spider's web.
Even in the perfectly humidified atmosphere of a nuclear-powered
submarine, sweat was beading on their foreheads.

Popov finally pursed his lips and said, "I don't envy making that
decision, but I hope my opinion will help." He paused to look in
his captain's eyes. "I think it's unlikely the Americans were able to
intercept it. But I wouldn't bet even one kopek on such a guess,
much less the value of this ship and its men."

Barzlin nodded at that well-balanced assessment. It was more or
less what he'd expected his thoughtful friend to say.

"And you, Comrade Damovitch? What's your opinion?"

Damovitch spoke with his usual conviction. "Obviously there's
been serious trouble for KR-72. Maybe he was only one step ahead
of the authorities. Maybe they have him now. At any rate, a man in
such a state shouldn't be protected with our lives. Also, I have
greater respect for American technical capacities than you or Chief
Popov, and I think it's quite likely they *did* intercept our message.
So I'm for relaying now."

Barzlin stared hard at him, wondering how the Presidium could
choose such a cocky man to be his replacement. "What if KR-72
can do what he says? Can we risk giving the Americans an excuse
to launch a preemptive strike against our homeland?"

Damovitch was unfazed by that rationale. "Though I have great
respect for American technicians, I have little for their leaders.
They're basically cowards who always prefer negotiation—even in
matters as serious as this. In my opinion, there's no chance at all of
a preemptive strike."

"But earlier you said they would sink us!" Barzlin snapped.

"Sinking us is a far cry from starting nuclear war, sir!"

Barzlin knew it was bad form to be drawn into an argument with
a subordinate. He also knew there was wisdom in what his first

officer was saying. But his own doubts were causing him to take out his frustration at Damovitch's apparent certainty.

"I don't happen to agree with you, Valeri," he said to end the debate. "I think we should continue on as if we missed the message and leave the next move to the Americans. If they start closing in on us, we'll know to relay immediately."

"If we have enough time," Damovitch muttered darkly.

"We must see to it we have enough time!" Barzlin growled.

Then Popov added, "That's what we've been trained for."

□ LIX □

Radioman Lee Hayden sat at his receiving console in the control room of the USS *Gremlin,* nursing the remains of a massive hangover. He was one of those who'd partied to the last second in anticipation of ninety days without wine, women, or song—unless god-awful shower warbling counted for anything.

Now, like several others standing the new tour's first official watch, he was struggling to stay awake and focused enough to do his job. Suddenly a satellite VLF message started clattering into his headphones. He started copying it while raising his free hand to signal a watch officer.

The message was a standard code-green alert to all PACCOM vessels, advising them to assume Level-4 readiness until further notice. Not the most routine situation report, but one he'd received many times before. He tore it off his pad and handed it to Lieutenant Norton Vent, that watch's officer of the deck.

"A code-green SITREP, sir," he said.

Vent glanced at it with a sense of foreboding that caused his ears to tingle. This would require his first line-of-duty encounter with Dandy LeBlanc since their earlier confrontation, and he wondered what tone would be set in the exchange.

There was always an undercurrent of rivalry between the second- and third-in-command on training vessels like the *Gremlin* because they were competing head-to-head for a future boat of their own. That gave LeBlanc another huge advantage over Vent:

Others in the control room would write off his small breaches of naval etiquette as natural bits of one-upmanship.

Seconds-in always had an advantage in that way, which was part of the testing process for thirds-in. Vent could only wonder what the other men on the deck knew of the far deeper undercurrents swirling around this particular rivalry.

He took the SITREP to where LeBlanc was leaning over the shoulder of Sonar Technician Agamemnon Rodrigues. Both men were watching intently as the sonar screens tracked the Soviet looper cruising a mile off their port side.

"Sir?" Vent said, in the customary control-room salutation.

LeBlanc rose to his full six-two height and stood towering over Vent's standard five-nine. "Yeah, Nort?" he said with complete disregard for formality. "What is it?"

Vent's ears were driving him wild as he performed his duty according to the book. "A SITREP from PACCOM, sir . . ."

LeBlanc took the routine message and glanced at it. "You need *my* help to handle this?" he asked with dripping sarcasm.

Vent's whole body flushed hot with anger. So this was how it was going to be: small one-on-one insults until he lost his temper and verbally or physically fought back. He squelched an urge to counterpunch with sarcasm of his own, continuing to play it by the book. "No, sir! But regulations state that—"

"Forget the regs!" LeBlanc said, cutting him off with loud, disdainful insolence. "Learn to think for yourself."

He turned back to the sonar screens and left Norton Vent standing there, feeling the uneasy stares of the crew and wondering if there was any way at all he'd get through the next twelve weeks.

☐ LX ☐

Nat hadn't been able to talk with either Brandt or Doppler before their meeting, but he'd told their secretary he wanted to be briefed on what they knew about Marsh. Consequently, she escorted him and Karen to a meeting room with padded armchairs, colorful decor, and a slide projector set up and ready to go.

When they stepped into that room, before a word of greeting or apology for the delay could be exchanged among any of them, Nat was quickly made aware of an important aspect of the meeting he'd forgotten to mention to the secretary.

"What the hell's *she* doing here?" Doppler howled.

"Nice to see you again, too, Charles," Karen said sweetly.

"What are you trying to pull, Perkins?" Brandt said behind an angry scowl. "You're supposed to be on our side!"

Because of his preoccupation with other matters, Nat hadn't even considered Brandt and Doppler's reaction to finding Karen with him. Especially so soon after they'd dropped the "national-security" sandbag on her story about Marsh. But he wasn't about to be thrown off-stride by men with the combined IQ of a turnip.

"C'mon, guys!" he said jocularly. "Of course I'm on your side! Karen's just doing a profile piece on me, and she has to tag along to see how I operate. That's all."

Karen couldn't let quick thinking like that go by without a follow-up of equal magnitude. "Brocton's orders," she added offhandedly. "Go ahead, give him a call. Check it out."

That was one of the nerviest bluffs Nat had seen in a long time, and the best part of it was its effect on Brandt and Doppler. They exchanged questioning looks, then Brandt shrugged.

"What the hell?" he said behind a strained smile. "Even if you tried to double-cross us, Brocton wouldn't let you print it."

"I'm not here to double-cross you," she assured them. "You squashed the Marsh piece fair and square. And the Nat piece is just one of those luck-of-the-draw deals. If you hadn't cut me off when you did, someone else would be profiling him."

Karen's reputation for fairness and honesty settled the dispute. Brandt and Doppler exchanged nods of agreement, then Brandt said, "Okay, let's get down to it." He motioned toward the chairs he wanted them to take, while saying to Nat, "Agent Keller told us he spoke with you at Marsh's house."

"He gave me some basics," Nat replied as he and Karen took the indicated seats. "But the best information I have came from background research. And to be honest, I haven't found anything that would support a phreaking charge."

Brandt nodded. "Our stuff should help a lot. Charles . . ."

Doppler hit a switch that darkened the room and turned on the

Nat's path with an aggressive stance and a demanding whisper. "Nat Perkins, will you please tell me what's go—"

He cut her off by putting his hand over her mouth as he swept her away from the door and down the hallway.

"The cabin . . ." he muttered.

That was all he said.

□ LXI □

Rear Admiral Fritz Langdon sat at his desk in the LDR shack, stunned by what he'd just read. He read again, slowly, making sure to fill in every missing letter and word: "I have gained the power to disrupt all American communication networks. This includes all defensive and military communications. The disruption will be total and irreversible for the immediate future."

It was either some wildly sophisticated joke—or the work of a maniac. He looked across his desk at the two men sitting opposite: an obviously flustered lieutenant from Decoding; and Master Sergeant Samples, serious but not visibly upset.

"Lieutenant Baker, do you realize a practical joke of this nature will result in a court-martial?"

Baker swallowed hard past an overly large Adam's apple.

"Yes, sir, but this is no joke. There are three other men in my section, and we all saw it come from the printer. We're double-checking it through NSA computers at Fort Meade . . . but we're sure that's the translation as it was sent."

Langdon glanced at his watch. If by some horrendous twist of fate the message was genuine, they had roughly five hours to prevent it. *Where to begin?*

"All right, Baker. I want the contents of this message kept on a strict need-to-know basis when you forward it to PACCOM. We can't afford to start a panic there or here. Besides, there's no guarantee someone isn't pulling our leg."

"Yes, sir!"

The lieutenant stood, saluted, and left Langdon's office, leaving the LDR commander and Samples to try to make sense of what they were faced with. Langdon opened a pack of cigarettes and offered the Marine one. He took it and they both lit up.

"How about you, Sergeant?" Langdon finally asked, holding up the printout sheet. "What's your interpretation of this?"

"I haven't read the decode, sir, so I can only talk about the transmission itself."

"All right, then, tell me about that."

Samples shifted his bulk and got comfortable, showing the easy confidence of a has-been back on top of his game.

"It's a Russian code sent by either a German national brought to live in Russia at an early age; or a Russian with close, German-speaking family members. There's childhood fluency in both German and Russian, with English and French as secondary but well-spoken languages."

Langdon shook his head in amazement, wondering how a marvel like Samples could ever be resigned to the scrap heap. It was no wonder the poor bastard spent his time hunkered over pool tables. Pool at least made sense.

"Something wrong, sir?" Samples asked.

"No, sorry—please go on."

"The sender is male, right-handed, about forty, and hasn't sent Morse code in years. That's unusual because emergencies nowadays are handled by older men who keep their coding sharp."

"I know what grandfathers are," Langdon said.

"Then you know how strange it is for such a young man to transmit. My guess is that, for some reason, the grandfather who was supposed to send it couldn't—sick, hurt, whatever."

Awestruck, Langdon couldn't help shaking his head again. "How do you do it? How in the name of God can it be done?"

Ode Samples had been asked that hundreds of times in the past. He shrugged and said, "Key pressure and rhythm, sir—that's really all there is to it. If you have an ear for it, each dot and dash is different from all others . . . and a group of them can tell you everything."

Langdon knew no way to adequately recognize that kind of genius, so he only said, "Can you tell me any more about him?"

"Only that I think he'd been drinking."

"Drinking?" *Pot calling the kettle black!*

"His motor control wasn't nearly what it should've been. Couple that with the poor transmission quality, and I'd say it's a good bet he had a few belts before he started."

Langdon flipped the translation across his desktop. "Read that and tell me if you think he's a drunk."

Samples went through it and looked up with a perplexed expression on his vein-riddled face. "He sounds like a goddamn *nut*, sir! 'Scuse the language. . . ."

Langdon leaned across his desk to make clear the urgency he felt. "Well, which is it, Sergeant? Is he drunk or a nut? What the hell do I tell PACCOM?"

Samples was momentarily rattled, but an old pro is hard to box into a corner. "He may not be drunk or a nut, sir. He could be perfectly on the level. But something *is* wrong with him. I'd bet anything on that."

Langdon leaned back and crushed out his cigarette. "You might be betting everything on it, Sergeant. That'll be all."

Samples left the room to return to the certainty of his pool table, while Langdon rang the communication room to request a code-red flash to Admiral Tarnaby at PACCOM.

☐ LXII ☐

Fleet Admiral Lucius Horton was just finishing a hearty breakfast when Admiral Vince Tarnaby approached his table at the PACCOM officers' mess. Horton was one of those whippetlike men without visible fat, so he could eat voraciously at every meal—to the envious chagrin of heavier friends like Tarnaby.

"Vince, my good man," he said in greeting, "you're lucky you missed our game this morning. My backhand was pure death—the best it's ever been." He lifted his coffee cup. "You eat yet?"

Tarnaby nodded as he sat down. "A little while ago. Listen, finish that fast. Something messy just hit the fan in California, and it has to go to the top."

The cup of coffee froze just outside Horton's lips as he finally bothered to read his friend's tense expression. "You mean me? Or the Joint Chiefs?"

"Higher," Tarnaby said in clipped tones. "All the way up."

Horton gulped the last of his coffee and stood up smiling. "Let's go—but move leisurely. No need to get people alarmed."

Rather than take Horton's staff car and speak in front of his driver, the Fleet Commander rode in Tarnaby's vehicle. And as Tarnaby hustled them across the base, he brought his superior up-to-date on the crisis brewing on the mainland.

Horton listened in attentive silence as they reached the headquarters building and headed for his office. He was the Navy's highest-ranking black officer for reasons other than tokenism: He could do the job. So when Tarnaby had finished, Horton stood up behind his desk and pressed an intercom button.

"Has the looper relayed yet?" he demanded.

A disembodied voice crackled into the room. "No, sir!"

"Good! Tell the Situation Room that Admiral Tarnaby and I will be there in five minutes. I want all stations reporting."

"Yes, sir!"

Horton let up on his intercom while staring blankly into space. Then he focused on Tarnaby. "I want your best gut feeling on this, Vince. Is it science fiction, or what?"

Tarnaby shrugged like a man with no options. "I know Fritz Langdon from way back. We can trust his judgment."

"And I know I can trust yours," Horton said as he began moving toward the door of his office.

The PACCOM Situation Room was the largest, most complex unit of its type beyond the American mainland. Forty feet underground and protected by reinforced concrete hardening, it could only be seriously damaged by a direct hit with a nuclear missile. And even then, less than ten megatons might not do the trick.

The lesson of Pearl Harbor had been well learned.

Like all Situation Rooms scattered around the world, it was a central terminus for millions of bits of information required for swift, accurate decision-making. There were a dozen long banks of computer consoles connected to three giant screens on the walls. Those screens could show data readouts, graphics, or satellite pictures with remarkable clarity and ease.

The Situation Room's command bubble was a glass-walled cubicle where two controllers directed activities on the floor. PACCOM's was different from all others in that it was located at floor level instead of suspended ten feet in the air.

The new location was an experiment to see if a lowered perspective on the all-seeing "Big Board" video screens might produce more careful and reasoned responses in crisis situations.

Horton and Tarnaby entered the command bubble and were met by Commander Keith Rogers, the senior officer in charge. Rogers was in his early forties, a handsome man with a dark crew cut.

Horton spoke to him without preamble. "Any relay yet?"

"No, sir. Not yet."

"Could they have missed receiving it?"

Rogers shrugged. "We're hoping, but we can't be sure."

"Has the point of origin been zeroed?"

"Triangulation indicates somewhere on the coast, near San Luis Obispo. We've heard from it before, but the signal never lasts long enough to nail. And this time was even worse. It came out at about quarter-power and dropped off from there."

"How'd *that* happen?"

Rogers shrugged again. "A malfunction in the transmitter, or the antenna wasn't fully extended. I'd bet on the antenna."

"What about its direction?"

"South-southwest, straight at a looper near Los Angeles. And since trawlers leave emergency monitoring to the loopers, that one is our prime candidate."

Horton nodded, then turned to Lieutenant Glenn Kelly, a flaming redhead in his late twenties with a cauliflower left ear and the solid body of a wrestler. Kelly's job was to manage the bubble's console boards and direct its technical traffic.

"Show me the situation, Lieutenant."

Kelly punched buttons and the central screen dissolved into a computer graphic of the northern Pacific's boundary coastlines. More buttons lit the graphic with an erratic red loop snaking around the hemisphere's edges. Within the thin red loop were twelve white lights glowing at roughly equal distances apart.

Kelly pressed a final button to start the white lights blinking. One was alongside Los Angeles.

"The current looper disposition, sir."

He pressed another button and twelve green lights came on, scattered irregularly just off the American coastline. They were all between the red loop and the coast, nearer the coast. Three were south of Los Angeles; none were immediately north.

"And there's the trawler disposition," he went on. "As Commander Rogers said, we can rule them out as receivers because they don't tune into VLF and none were in the sending alley." He pressed another button and a green circle lit up around the white light near Los Angeles. "That looper's the only possible target."

Horton turned to Rogers. "Which one is it?"

"Padre Island says *Mikhail Potkin.*"

"Who's its captain?"

Rogers lifted a clipboard to read from a profile sheet. "Nikolai Barzlin . . . line officer in World War II . . . underwater navigation expert . . . retiring with honors after this tour . . ." He stopped to look up at his commanding officer with a somber expression. "In short, sir, he's one of their best."

Horton winced, then he stepped beside Kelly to lean over a microphone on the central console panel. "Show the area above the *Potkin!*" His voice echoed through the Situation Room, and within seconds a U.S. spy satellite zoomed into close-up. Another second saw the left-wall screen covered with dirty cotton balls.

Horton continued speaking into the mike. "Is that the ceiling out there, or a malfunction in here?"

A crisp female voice came into the bubble over an intercom attached to the rear wall. "The ceiling, sir. A heavy-weather front will be over them for the next few hours."

Horton permitted himself a smile of satisfaction, then he muttered to Tarnaby, "That's a big break for us. Moscow won't be able to monitor what goes on out there."

He turned to Rogers. "Order our nearest ASW chopper team to fly out and establish over the *Potkin.* If they find its transmit cable up, blow it off the second it starts to relay. If it comes up after they arrive, same thing. If nothing's up and nothing comes up, stay on top of it until further notice."

"Aye, aye, sir!" the commander snapped as he turned and left the bubble to carry out his orders.

Horton then turned to Kelly. "Let me see our shadows."

"Yes, sir!" The lieutenant punched some buttons and the red loop on the central screen pulsed with electronic life. Twelve blue lights came on adjacent to the twelve white lights.

"Who's with the *Potkin*?"

"The *Gremlin*, sir—training cruise."

This time Horton winced perceptibly, so Tarnaby leaned over to him. "What's wrong, Luke?"

Horton stepped away from Kelly and muttered so only Tarnaby could hear. "If it's a trainer, the damn thing's half full of rookies! We need our oldest hands out there in a situation like this!"

He looked over to Kelly. "Who's in charge of the *Gremlin*?"

"Captain Stickles, sir."

When Horton turned back to Tarnaby, his expression was clearly stressed. "Jim's a good man, one of the best at-sea instructors we have. But he's not our clearest thinker in a tight situation, and he doesn't have anything approaching the combat experience that old Russian has."

He paused to let the implications sink in, then he clenched his fists and teeth. "Shit!" He again looked over to Kelly. "Put the *Gremlin* on general alert with no specifics. We won't rile them up unless the ASW team can't do what needs to be done out there."

"Yes, sir," Kelly said. "But, sir? What if our choppers blow the *Potkin*'s cable, then it surfaces to transmit direct?"

Horton replied in his sternest tones yet. "Let it. That's all we can do unless and until the President gives us an emergency directive to sink it."

Kelly's freckled face filled with concern as Horton turned to Tarnaby and resumed talking while moving toward the door.

"Let's go put the ball in Washington's court."

☐ LXIII ☐

Lieutenant Commander Ken LeBlanc ducked his lanky frame through a hatchway that led to Captain Jim Stickles's cabin. He knew the "old man" would be asleep, but there was no choice about waking him. The captain was a go-by-the-book type who brooked no bending of rules aboard the *Gremlin*. Consistency was his credo.

LeBlanc rapped the metal door loudly, then stuck his head inside. "Captain?" he said into the room's cramped darkness.

"Yeah, Ken?" a groggy voice replied. "What's up?"

"We've been put on alert. Want me to handle it?"

"Come in and hit the light. . . ."

LeBlanc stepped inside the cabin and turned on the light. He found Stickles sitting up in his bunk, round face creased with sleep, regulation underwear askew, small paunch edging toward his lap, left arm raised to shield bleary eyes against the glare.

After a few seconds like that, he rubbed his gray-streaked brush cut in a determined effort to clear away the cobwebs.

"What's it about?" he asked his second-in-command.

"No specifics. Just get on the alert and wait for further orders. Could be anything."

Stickles tossed his covers aside, then swung his legs out over a pair of slippers beside his bunk. "Anytime a sub gets put on full alert, the captain should be in charge. This is a training cruise, don't forget. I have to set the right example."

LeBlanc nodded dutifully, wondering if the old man would ever give him a chance to actually take over. Then he'd show that asshole Norton Vent what a *real* up-and-comer could do.

"Yes, sir . . . you know best."

The call for President Daniel Baxter came from Air Force General Dale Weatherspoon, chairman of the Joint Chiefs of Staff at the Pentagon. Mike Gravelle, the President's chief of staff, took the call in the Oval Office.

"Hello, General, this is Mike. Listen, the President's really up against it right now, handling the embassy takeover, so he asked me to tackle your problem. What is it?"

"An extra large ball-buster just came in from Hawaii," the general replied. "No disrespect intended, Mike, but there's no way you can cover this one for him."

Gravelle paused, then said, "Rate it on a scale of ten."

"What?"

"You heard me: Rate it on a scale of ten. And for purposes of this discussion, let's call a ten the strong likelihood of Soviet nuclear aggression in, say . . . the next hour."

Weatherspoon wasn't used to being addressed so sharply, especially by a friend like Gravelle. The embassy crisis had to be at a major crux, he realized, so he felt guilty having to add fuel to the fire. But there was simply no other choice.

"Is this a secure line?" he asked.

"It's supposed to be. It damn well *better* be!"

"Okay, make that a four- to five-hour time limit, and you've just described the situation."

Gravelle knew Weatherspoon was the most sober-minded of the Joint Chiefs, which was the main reason he'd gotten the job of heading them. But his first reaction was still skepticism.

"Seriously, Dale, it's that bad?"

"No guarantees, Mike—it could be nothing at all. But the top-end possibility is as bad as it gets. And if the worst does happen, we'll need some hard decisions only the boss can make."

Crystalline silence filled the line between them, then a heavy sigh broke the spell. "How soon can you get over here?"

"I've got a chopper warming up."

"I'll meet you at the helipad in ten minutes."

As Billy Connors washed the pearl-gray Porsche's windshield, he examined its driver with carefully casual glances. What first caught his attention was that the driver put sunglasses *on* as he entered the station. It usually went the other way around.

After that, the odd tilt of the cowboy hat caught his eye, cocked way back like it was. Didn't see 'em worn that way very often, especially not in Porsches. Then he noticed a horizontal line of dark stain on the collar of the man's maroon turtleneck.

"Somethin' on your collar there, mister," the teenager said.

The driver forced himself to focus his attention through some kind of difficulty. "Excuse me?"

"There's a stain or somethin' on your sweater neck," he repeated with a friendly smile. "I'd want someone to tell me."

The driver checked himself in the rearview mirror, then nodded. "It's blood. I cut myself shaving this morning."

Billy was rightfully astonished. "Blood? Really? Gee, that must have been *some* nick!"

The driver nodded again. "That's why I wore a turtleneck."

This guy's got a problem, Billy thought.

A car rolled up to the adjacent pump station and the alert bell went *clang! clang!* The Porsche driver jerked as if he'd grabbed a live battery cable, while his knuckles went white around the steering wheel. It looked like he'd closed his eyes, too, but the dark glasses made it difficult to tell.

A real problem! "Seems that bell really bothers you," Billy offered as he squeegeed the windshield dry.

The driver answered without moving. "Yes, a little. I have a terrible headache."

Aha! A hangover! "Where you headin'?"

"North, near San Francisco."

"You in a big hurry?"

He answered with a note of suspicion. "Why do you ask?"

"Well, it's none of my business, mister," Billy said amiably, "but you look plum wore out. Frisco's still a few hours away, and we've got a cot set up in back of the shop. Would you like to take a nap or somethin'?"

The man tried to smile, but the effort of rearranging his face seemed to cause as much pain as the clanging bell. "No, thank you. All I need now is your rest room."

Billy shrugged. "Around the side. Cash or charge?"

□ LXIV □

After the abrupt end of the meeting with Brandt and Doppler, Karen's initial reaction was little more than stunned surprise. Nat hustled her out and away from their office before she had a chance to reflect on how suddenly everything had changed. But in the frosty silence of their exit from the FBI building, she started regrouping her scattered mental forces.

As they walked along corridors and out the front door, a few glances at Nat told her how thoroughly he'd drawn into himself.

His brow was knitted in intense concentration as he shuffled and reshuffled the bits and pieces of his growing case against Marsh.

"The cabin . . ." he had said, which was obviously why they were hustling across the parking lot toward the Corvette. But what were they supposed to find when they located it?

Marsh? His phreaking equipment? Or both? And even if we find what Nat wants, what happens then?

As she continued analyzing the situation she'd been swept up in, she began realizing how dramatically her parameters had changed. At first she simply wanted to learn about phreaking and hacking— no more, no less. Getting to know Nat better was little more than an afterthought. But now she felt totally committed to him and to his pursuit—intellectually and emotionally—as if she actually was the partner he'd jokingly told Fambrough she was.

She wanted to *be* his partner.

Almost as compelling as her growing personal attachment was the relentless surge of her wannaknowitis. She wanted desperately to know what there was about the King that kept disturbing Nat so profoundly. Every instinct she had, as both a woman and a reporter, told her that whatever it was would probably be a 24-karat doozy. *At the least!*

The more she thought about all the questions and contradictions swirling between her and Nat, the more she resolved to clear the air by leveling with him. So by the time they were seated in the Corvette, she was ready to begin.

"All right, Nat, this has gone far enough! I'm sick and tired of being kept in the dark about what's going on here. Now, okay, I know you're under no obligation to tell me anything. But dammit, I care now! Not just about finding out what's between you and the King—I care about *you*! Can't you see that?"

While she spoke, he sat there staring straight ahead, giving no indication at all of how he was receiving her words. But when she'd finished, he turned to her with a relaxed, almost joyful expression that warmed her to her toes.

"It's a funny thing," he said. "Whenever we'd bump into each other—every time—somewhere in the back of my mind I'd wonder what it might be like to get to know you, apart from our jobs. You know, just as the two people we are, underneath what we do for a living. I always wondered if I'd like you as much as I thought I would, or if you'd like me at all."

"I *do* like you!" she insisted. "A lot!"

"Believe me, I can see that," he said, "and I like you too. Which is why I'm going to go ahead and tell you the truth about me and the King. Not because I feel obligated to, but because I think we'll be seeing more of each other as time goes by . . . and this is something you need to know about me."

She couldn't have agreed more and nodded her head with eager anticipation. "It'll be just between you and me, I promise."

He returned her nod, then said, "Remember I told you I used to be a phreak? And that I was Number Two in the Network behind the King? Well, there's a little more to it than that." He took a deep breath, then pulled out his next words with an effort the equal of yanking teeth. "*I* was the first phreak to get bagged."

She collapsed inside like a puffed-up blowfish after danger has passed. That just didn't seem to warrant all the fuss he'd been making. She couldn't even recall what he'd told her about how the first phreak went down. Then she thought she remembered something about making blue-box calls for friends.

"Some of my family members and several of my friends had relatives in Vietnam," he went on. "Brothers and cousins and nephews and such. And calls to them meant so damn much. . . ." His words choked off for a moment. "Hell, I just started doing what I could to help out. Naturally, everyone was sworn to keep it a blood-oath secret, but you know how things like that tend to go. Sooner or later someone lets the cat out of the bag."

She said nothing, not because she felt it was the right thing to do, but because she had no idea what to say. She was feeling terribly proud of him and terribly sorry for him, both at the same time. And she knew he had to feel that same way about himself. It was like being one of those people who give their lives to save others, only he didn't die—all the way.

"I'm so sorry for you," she finally managed to say. "It must be terrible having to live with something like that."

He sighed, then got himself under control again. "Yeah, especially with what the King's put me through because of it."

Here it is! she thought, realizing she was about to learn what the big bone was between them. "What do you mean?"

He reached forward and turned on the Corvette's ignition. "I'll tell you about it on the way to Lumberton."

□ LXV □

Chief of Staff Mike Gravelle stood near the White House helipad, watching the silver Sikorski settle onto its bull's-eye. In moments he saw General Dale Weatherspoon, in his blue Air Force uniform, appear in the helicopter's opening doorway.

Gravelle was a sixty-year-old political infighter who looked the part: short, compact, coiled body, with piercing gray eyes and perfectly combed gray hair. Weatherspoon was the same age, but the exact opposite in stature and temperament: tall, lean, blond, and reassuringly casual in his approach. Yet the two men had never crossed ideological swords, sharing a common bent of mind and a devout loyalty to America and its current President.

"Sorry about this, Mike," the General said when they were far enough away from the whining rotors to be heard.

"It better be worth it," Gravelle said flatly.

"Who's on hand?" Weatherspoon went on as they entered the East Wing doorway.

"Just the President, you, and me. He put Harley in charge of the embassy takeover until he can get back to it."

Weatherspoon approved of that tactic. Harley Hudson was an excellent Vice President, but too often had to take a backseat in crisis situations. For the good of his party—and the country in general—he needed to drive the bus now and then. Besides, until they knew exactly what they were dealing with out West, it was best to keep those directly involved to an absolute minimum.

As they approached the interior elevator Weatherspoon asked, "Where are we meeting?"

Gravelle punched the button and said, "The basement. Everything relating to the embassy is going on up here."

Weatherspoon nodded as they stepped inside. "Just as well."

If the message turned out to be real, they'd wind up in the

underground Situation Room anyway. So it was far better to start down there than to have to transfer later under extreme pressure.

When Weatherspoon and Gravelle entered the main office of the White House Situation Room, the President was already sitting at his desk, telephone in hand. Like most people, Weatherspoon considered Daniel Baxter physically unremarkable. His wrinkled forehead, heavy brows, basset eyes, and wispy fringe of white hair made him appear more like a meek college professor than what he really was: a battle-scarred veteran of countless political wars.

Baxter's long years in Washington's trenches had given him an extraordinary grasp of bureaucratic realities, a grasp he utilized better than any of his contemporaries. And welded to his practical experience was the courage to act on his convictions.

Harley Hudson was getting an earful of those qualities as they walked into the President's office.

"I don't give a damn, Harley!" he shouted into the phone he was holding. "We'll be facing situations like this as long as we try to negotiate! Tell 'em to put up or shut up!"

One of many things Weatherspoon liked about Daniel Baxter was his abhorrence of repeating history's mistakes. The current embassy hostage crisis was a perfect example. Its resolution would incorporate the best aspects of previous takeover solutions to gain safe release of the hostages, while avoiding the failure of other administrations to uphold American dignity.

Now, of course, the question was how the President would handle the California nightmare, if it became reality. There was no precedent for anything like it, and a mistake could be catastrophic beyond imagining. Then his dry-parchment scalp flushed pink as he reacted to his Vice President's response.

"You tell that mealymouthed sonofabitch he's bitten off more than he can chew this time! You tell him if I have to, I'll . . ." He paused, searching for a suitable punishment. "I'll ask Israel to send some of *their* commandos in after his ass, and all they'll bring out is pieces! I mean it, Harley, tell him exactly that! And don't call me again until he answers!"

With that he slammed the receiver onto its cradle, then winked at his two companions to show the tirade had been only for effect.

"That tinhorn greaser has a middleman upstairs, sitting at Harley's elbow. Think I made the right impression on him?"

Gravelle grinned as he moved across the room to take a seat on the couch beside the President's desk. "It may not make the right impression on him, but it'll damn sure get his attention!"

The President enjoyed an indulgent laugh with his shrewdest friend and oldest political crony. Then he extended his hand toward the couch so Weatherspoon would feel free to be seated.

"Okay, General, what's up?" he asked.

That was another thing Weatherspoon liked about his Commander in Chief: There was no beating around the bush with pointless formalities. The general joined Gravelle on the couch, placing his briefcase on the coffee table in front of it.

"We're not certain what we have here," he said as he unlocked the briefcase's combination snaps and popped them open. "But we've taken some precautions, just in case. I'll elaborate on those after you read this." He handed a light blue sheet of paper to both Gravelle and the President.

"The top paragraph is the text of an intercepted message sent out on a secure-band, very-low-frequency transmitter. It was directed from a land base in California to a Soviet emergency sub cruising off the coast there. You know the ones."

"Has it been authenticated?" the President asked.

"There's a slight doubt because of a faulty transmission, and there's also a question about the sender's physical condition. But our best cryptographic analysis indicates it was sent by a bona fide, German-speaking Russian agent. All that is explained in the material following the message."

The President and Gravelle nodded, then turned their attention to the reports in their hands. When Gravelle finished reading his, he let out a low whistle, while the President's somber expression showed that he, too, understood its meaning.

A strained silence settled over all three men until Gravelle spoke up, haltingly. "A thing like this . . . shutting down our comm-systems . . . that's just not possible! . . . is it?"

Weatherspoon spread his hands in a gesture of ambivalence. "That's everyone's first reaction: It's so farfetched, it seems ludicrous. But if you stop to think, the fact that it's so hard to assess in rational terms is what's so frightening about it."

The President pulled out a pipe and began filling its bowl. "You mentioned taking some precautions?"

"We have a full alert on our sub shadowing the Russian. Also, three antisub helicopters are out with it to make sure there's no cable relay. Cloud cover in the area has allowed that."

"What about trying to find the agent?"

"Everyone in California is working on that, sir. But our chances are poor. The man's obviously a pro, and time is short."

"If they haven't relayed yet," Gravelle put in, "that means they didn't get it. They're supposed to do that right away."

Weatherspoon nodded. "That is their normal procedure, but there's room to run on this one. They could have received it, realized how badly it was transmitted, then decided we probably missed it. If I was the captain of that sub and that's what I believed, I'd wait till the very last second before relaying."

The President lit his pipe, drew a couple of puffs to get it going, then spoke to Gravelle. "If he did assume that authority, he could be confident Moscow would approve. Besides, this report says he's about to retire, so what's he risking? A demotion?"

Gravelle was stymied. "So both sides are guessing?"

The President's baggy brown eyes narrowed. "Nobody can afford to gamble on something like this, Mike. The stakes are way too high. We have to pull out all the stops until the situation comes to a head—and so do they."

He then turned to Weatherspoon with a bottom-line question. "General, what'll happen in the next few hours? Best guess."

Weatherspoon didn't hesitate. After receiving PACCOM's latest situation report, every Joint Chief had formulated possible scenarios. "Our ASW choppers will stay on top of the Russian sub to make sure they don't try to relay that message. If they don't try, we'll know they missed it. And if the cloud cover holds, Moscow will never even know we were following them.

"On the other hand . . . if they try to use their cable, our guys will blow it off. Then they'll know we know, and they'll have to surface to relay directly from their sail."

He let a heavy silence hang in the air, the kind of oppressive quiet that takes the measure of men's spirits. Then the President forged ahead by stating the obvious conclusion.

"So push comes to shove, we let them surface—or sink them."

Weatherspoon nodded stiffly. "If we let them transmit, and if their agent's on the level, we'll be vulnerable in a matter of hours. But if his message is a hoax, nothing happens, and all Moscow can do is gripe about a blown cable.

"On the other hand . . . if we sink them and the message is genuine, we've possibly saved our country. But if the message is bogus, then we've been suckered into creating a major crisis."

Gravelle shrugged his wide, heavy shoulders, as if trying to shift an invisible burden to a more comfortable position. "So what it comes down to is whether or not the message is legitimate."

"Not exactly," Weatherspoon corrected. "Our response depends on whether we choose to *believe* it's legitimate."

The President pointed his pipe stem at his copy of the report. "Let's talk to someone who can give us a better handle on this. I'm sorry, General, but I find it inconceivable that one man alone could tie up all of our communication facilities."

"I've already consulted several experts at the Pentagon, but none of them could say with any certainty that—"

Gravelle interrupted with a loud snap of his fingers. "Alan Pinkley's our man! He's as good as there is at his job."

The President glanced across at Weatherspoon. The general nodded. "He's as good as anyone we've got—maybe better."

The President pressed a buzzer atop a small green box on his desk. The outside door to the room immediately opened and a Secret Serviceman appeared.

"Have someone go to the Annex Building and pick up Alan Pinkley. He's the communications chief of staff."

"Yes, sir!" the dour plainclothesman said.

"And if he's not there," the President added, "find him."

"Yes, sir!" the agent repeated, then reclosed the door.

When they were alone again, the President spoke to Weatherspoon. "I'm still not willing to gamble on this, but I don't want to go off half-cocked, either. I'll feel a lot better about an attack order after we hear what Pinkley has to say."

"What about between now and then?" Weatherspoon asked.

"If the Russian sub got that message, they'd either send it right away or wait till the last minute. I don't think we have to worry about the middle ground, which is where we are now and where we'll be for the next few hours."

"How about a drink, General?" Gravelle said to lighten the room's heavy mood. He stood up and moved toward the portable liquor cabinet tucked in an alcove near the far wall. "We have some time to kill before Pinkley gets here."

Weatherspoon asked for a Scotch, then he leaned back on the couch wondering if time was all they'd have to kill that day.

☐ LXVI ☐

Lieutenant Vito Scarlatti's three-unit ASW team received their telexed orders from PACCOM HQ with a mixture of excitement and alarm: excitement because it was the real thing, not a boring exercise; and alarm because of what they were ordered to do:

"Intercept SSN *Mikhail Potkin,* map sectors 118–119, approx 1300 hrs. If audio transmit begins through external capacity, terminate immediately. If otherwise, stand by further notice."

Their commanding officer's verbal orders were even more stimulating—and ominous: "Get on that fucker's ass and stay there! And don't let it cable-transmit!"

Ordinarily when ASW choppers went looking for a target, they pretended they were beyond any C/S/T listening arrays. They'd locate it using sonobuoys in passive or active mode. But this time they were given coordinates that permitted a direct flight to their target. Once there, they were locked onto it within minutes.

They flew the standard triangle pattern, with Scarlatti's Grumman SH-3H out front at the apex, Grady Swenson piloting at his left rear, and Bart Holloway's bird bringing up the right.

The storm-tossed ocean lapped a hundred feet under their wheels as they paced the *Potkin,* which was cruising at 30 knots 500 feet beneath the surface. The sky above was overcast in all directions, with scudding, iron-gray clouds that rendered them invisible to the prying lenses of spy satellites.

That dreary sky matched the glum mood of the ASW team.

By then, each man in the unit had brought his excitement under control and replaced it with the harsh reality of their purpose: to initiate real hostilities if that became necessary. It was a sobering responsibility, filling them with misgivings. Nevertheless, each had a job to do and a duty to carry out.

If combat was necessary to discharge those obligations, each was trained, equipped, and willing. All, that is, with the possible exception of Casey Harper, Scarlatti's copilot.

Harper's oppressively negative attitude had him mired in the most pessimistic funk any of his crewmates had ever seen. When Scarlatti turned his helmeted head to glance at his similarly attired copilot, he found Harper checking fuel readings with the cold fury he'd exhibited since the mission briefing.

Scarlatti decided to risk speaking, which was difficult to do properly under those circumstances. It had to be loud enough to be audible above the roar of their rotor blades, but not so loud that the Soviet sub they were tracking could "hear" them.

"C'mon, Casey," he said into his helmet mike, "lighten up. Things could be a helluva lot worse, you know."

Harper fired back with a nakedly hostile tone. "I'd like to know how! We could wind up sinking those people down there. And if we do, you know what that means? We'll end up like those guys on the *Enola Gay,* the ones who dropped the big one on Hiroshima!"

"A sub's not the same as a whole city," Scarlatti replied.

Scarlatti's puckish sonarman, Bobby Wong, could never resist an opportunity to zing their moody copilot. He joined in from his seat at his sonar screens, located behind Harper's back.

"Jeez, Case, can't you look on the bright side of anything?"

"Absolutely!—we're down to about three hours of fuel. And if we have to ditch before those Russians down there try to transmit, then our shadow has to stop them all by its lonesome."

Scarlatti couldn't stifle a laugh as Wong rested his case. "See what I mean, Vito? We're flying a mission that could save the whole free world, and Mr. Optimism here wants to give someone else all the glory. We don't need him—let's ditch him now."

"Shut the fuck up, you moon-faced little—!"

"All right, knock it off!" Scarlatti cut in. "We still have to lay quiet up here so they don't tap into us and get spooked."

"Roger . . ." Harper grumbled sullenly.

"Roger, wilco, and out, sir!" came Wong's cheerful counterpoint. "And by all means, Casey—enjoy your flight."

□ LXVII □

Chief Popov and Seaman Rykoff sat at their radio consoles aboard the *Potkin,* hunched forward expectantly, pressing their headset earphones against their heads beneath cupped hands. But there was no more of the faint static they'd been picking up as Scarlatti and his crew communicated among themselves.

The intercom transmitters on the American craft operated at extremely low wattage so as to be intercept-proof. But at only 500 feet down, the supersensitive Soviet receivers could respond to even slight radio-wave disturbances in the above-water ether.

Nobody had a monopoly on hi-tech marvels.

After a sustained period of static-free monitoring, Popov relaxed and sagged a bit in his seat. Rykoff followed his lead.

The two anxious officers standing behind them didn't relax.

"What do you think, Josef?" Captain Barzlin asked, placing a hand on his shoulder. "Have they come to stop us?"

Popov turned around to face his best friend. The two aged warriors expressed volumes of concern through haggard glints in worried eyes. "I can't be certain, but there is a possibility."

Commander Damovitch had never cared for Popov's tendency toward equivocation. One of his first steps as captain would be to replace such a cautious old man.

"Your opinion, Popov!" he snapped. "What is your opinion?"

Popov refused to be intimidated by the captain-to-be's belligerence. "I have no opinion, sir. I deal with facts."

"Then what are the facts?"

"Our reception pattern indicates that the sea above us is restless. Maybe we're below a storm—maybe not. If we are, the static we heard could easily be from lightning flashes."

"Then why so few of them, eh?" Damovitch countered. "And why did they appear so suddenly, and then no more?"

Popov shrugged with the supreme indifference age could bestow on certain men. "Weather at sea is unpredictable."

Damovitch turned to Barzlin in frustration. "I believe the Americans have found us. I say send the message now"—he looked contemptuously at Popov, as if their predicament were entirely the old radioman's fault—"*if* we still can!"

Barzlin could see the strain was beginning to take its toll; even he felt it. He hadn't experienced such trapped, fish-in-a-barrel anxiety since the war. But he vividly recalled the mindless agony—the pure ache of howling panic—caused by being sealed in a metal cylinder beneath tons of deadly water.

"If the Americans are above us, they'll wait for us to start the action," he said calmly. "They can't be certain we received the message any more than we can know if they did. So if there's to be a battle, it won't begin until we try to relay."

That still wasn't good enough for Damovitch, who lowered his voice to almost plead for reassurance. "Tell me truthfully, Captain: Do you even suspect we've been discovered?"

"No," Barzlin said flatly, "I don't." Then he looked across the control room, to where Sonar Chief Andrus Kim sat monitoring his screens. "Chief Kim!" he called out. "Is there any change in the course of our escort? Any change at all?"

Kim's round Mongol face beamed across the room like a happy jack-o'-lantern. "No, Captain! They continue matching our depth perfectly—and not one whisker closer!"

Barzlin nodded, then turned back to Damovitch. "I'm satisfied we alone possess the message. But just in case, we'll relay as soon as we reach the Out Island Group." He checked his watch. "Three hours from now is close enough to the last possible moment to protect KR-72, ourselves, and the Motherland. I'm sure the Presidium—and the Kremlin—will understand."

Damovitch nodded his own grim understanding. If there was to be an engagement with helicopters above, and the submarine off their starboard side, their chances for survival would be greatly enhanced by the Out Island Group's towering underwater peaks. Despite all the sophisticated gadgetry of the American C/S/T arrays, which penetrated thousands of cubic miles of ocean, the Out Island Group was one of the few places in the listening grids where it might be possible for a submarine to hide.

☐ LXVIII ☐

Karen kept respectfully quiet as Nat drove through and out of San Jose. She assumed his silence meant he was preparing for an especially difficult explanation. And sure enough, once they'd cleared the city and were on Highway 16's two lanes into the mountains, he took a deep breath, slowly squeezed it out, then began speaking in the soberest tones she'd heard him use.

"When I was doing the Vietnam calls, a friend told a friend who told a friend who had an uncle who worked for Ma. Next thing I knew, my ass was strung up in a giant sling, and it was go to work as a security agent or—like I told you—go to jail.

"Fortunately, things turned out much better than I imagined or could have hoped for. It wasn't long before I honestly came to enjoy the challenge of heading up the antiphreak division. And I got an incredible overview of *all* communication systems by working inside Ma. It was miles beyond the nut-and-bolt mechanics I'd learned helping the King build the Network."

He paused as a sour note slipped into his voice. "But even after gaining full access to Ma's innermost secrets—even those the Network hadn't found yet, and there were a lot of those left back then —I still couldn't touch the King for overall phreaking ability. The sonofabitch stayed in a class by himself."

That left Karen looking confused. "Is that the big problem between you two? The fact that he stayed ahead of you?"

Nat shook his head vigorously. "It's because he took it so damn personally when *I* was the first phreak to get bagged."

When she maintained her confused expression, he elaborated.

"You have to understand that I was his favorite, so what happened to me was a terrible reflection on his judgment in the eyes of the other phreaks. And you can't imagine how much he cares about what the other phreaks think of him. He's always trying to come off like an infallible genius or something. So my bagging called his judgment into such question that . . . Well, it may not sound like much now, but back then it was a disaster!"

"What did he do to you for making him look bad?"

Nat stayed still for a long moment, jaw muscles rippling, then said, "He tried to make my life as miserable as possible. He'd call me at all hours, day and night; berate me for being disloyal to him and the Network; insult me about how stupid I'd been; tell me what the other phreaks were saying about me. And since I didn't have a leg to stand on to argue back or defend myself, I had to just sit there and listen to him cut me up."

"Why?" Karen countered. "I mean, why didn't you just hang up? Refuse to listen to him?"

"I tried that, but it's not easy to ignore the King. He knew who I was, where I lived, where I worked. . . . Hell, I'd even get calls at my parents' house in Texas, if you can believe that. So there was no point in hanging up on him because it only pissed him off and made things worse. It was a lot better to just take whatever ration of shit he wanted to dish out to me, then go on about my business until the next time he called."

"How long did that go on?"

"Just about every day for two years. Then he gradually began to slack off. Now I hear from him only every week or so."

She thought that over for a moment, then said, "Now I see what you mean about him carrying grudges to extremes."

"Ha! That's putting it pretty damn mildly."

The wavering sounds in his voice made it clear that the wounds he was probing were still raw and bleeding, so she reached out to once more place a comforting hand on his arm.

"He really got to you, didn't he?" she said softly.

Nat forced a bitter smile. "He sure did. So I made a sacred promise to myself to stay after him until I found a way to turn those tables and make him eat some of *my* shit. And now, after all these years, it looks as if I've finally found it. So I hope you can excuse how distant I've been since I figured out the connection with Marsh. It has nothing to do with you."

She patted his hand reassuringly, hopeful that, through nothing more than her touch, she could convey how satisfied she was to finally know the truth about him. And how relieved she was that such a devilish problem might soon be resolved.

By that point Karen had slipped well past the point of no return in her feelings for Nat. In every way she knew how to evaluate, she kept finding him to be an exceptional man acting on extraordinary motivations.

She wanted him for her own.

□ **LXIX** □

Alan Pinkley entered the Situation Room office twenty minutes after the Secret Serviceman was ordered to retrieve him. He was a slim, dolorous, stoop-shouldered man in his mid-fifties, notable for his almost complete lack of physical presence. For two decades he'd been in charge of all communication systems used within the White House complex, from the general switchboard in the Annex to the underground War Room they were now in.

It was his job to see that everything worked smoothly.

After greetings all around and a thorough recap of events up to that point, the President put it to him squarely: "So what do you think, Alan? Is what this man says even remotely possible?"

Pinkley shifted uncomfortably in his chair opposite the President's desk. He was seldom addressed on a first-name basis, though he'd been on the White House payroll longer than all but a few cooks and butlers. He glanced across the coffee table at Gravelle's open anxiety and Weatherspoon's restrained concern.

"I'm not sure anyone can answer that," he said in a voice only a few decibels above a whisper. "I don't consider it at all likely. But then again, anything's possible."

"That doesn't help us much!" Gravelle exclaimed.

The President frowned at his top associate, then went on. "Let's assume it is possible. How could it be accomplished?"

"That's easier to answer, sir," Pinkley replied with confidence. He was much better at making objective assessments than rendering speculation. "The agent's message says he'll take out all systems that use computers. That's everything we have except shortwave, which is useless for defending ourselves because launch codes are verified only through computer relays."

"And it was set up that way," Gravelle cut in, "so some maniac couldn't start World War III! Can you believe this?"

The President still refused to sidetrack his train of thought. "Can our computers be compromised as he suggests?"

Pinkley gave a barely perceptible shrug. "Any single computer is vulnerable. But our communication systems use thousands, and they're all interrelated. So the sheer numbers of them should render the overall system immune to sabotage."

Weatherspoon spoke up behind an annoyed frown. "Come off it, Alan! We all know our comm-web is vulnerable. Hell, last year alone the WMCCS system gave us five false-alarm warnings of Soviet missile attacks. Everything we have is full of holes."

It was surprising to hear defeatist talk coming from a military man, but Pinkley politely gave ground. "Murphy's Law is at work everywhere, General, especially in something as complex as our communication network. But just as human intervention prevented those false alarms from escalating into crises, human intervention can correct other breakdowns."

The President cleared his throat and began tapping out the bowl of his pipe. "We're not here to criticize your area of responsibility, Alan. What we want—what we desperately need—is a hard, bottom-line evaluation of our position. Now, given all you've heard, how seriously should we take this?"

Pinkley felt three pairs of eyes boring into his defensive perimeter. It occurred to him that maybe his job performance wasn't at issue; maybe they really *did* want the truth.

When he spoke, his voice was lower than ever.

"As I said before, this threat seems highly unlikely to me. But as I also said, we have to accept that anything is possible. So given what's at stake here, I'd advise hedging all bets. A total shutdown would be just as he describes: We'd be utterly helpless. Even a partial disruption would be a disaster."

The President waited a moment to make certain Pinkley was finished, then he stood and extended his hand. "Thanks, Alan. You can go back to the Annex now. And I'm sure I don't need to tell you—not a word about this to anyone."

Pinkley rose, offering his hand to his hosts, each of whom shook it perfunctorily. "I'm sorry I couldn't be of more help," he told them. Then, at the door, he paused for one final assessment. "It's just . . . such a thing is *truly* inconceivable."

The door closed with Weatherspoon muttering, "That's what everyone said about landing on the moon."

When they were alone again, Gravelle wasted no time expressing his disappointment. "If that guy's one of the best in the business, I sure as hell pity his business!"

Weatherspoon intervened. "He's a brilliant staff man, Mike—give him credit. But people like him have no imagination, so in a crunch like this all they can do is play cover-your-ass and hope for the best. Besides, he told us what we needed to know."

The President spoke up. "That's right. As long as there's even the slightest chance of this happening, we have to act as if it will. So, what's the first step?"

Weatherspoon assumed the initiative. "First up, we need a directive from you to sink the Russians if they try to surface."

The President nodded heavily. "I'll stay here and draft it. Meanwhile, you two go out to the command bubble and prepare some contingency plans, in case our systems do start failing. I'll meet you there as soon as I'm finished."

Weatherspoon snapped his briefcase shut, then rose with Gravelle to begin a process he'd never even bothered to imagine, much less anticipate. "Yes, sir," he said as they turned to leave. "And may God have mercy on us all."

The President looked up with a blank expression, his mind already thousands of miles away—or a few hours into the future.

"Amen . . ." he muttered.

☐ LXX ☐

Admirals Horton and Tarnaby stood in the PACCOM command bubble, quiet and still, awaiting word from President Baxter.

Sounds in the Plexiglas sphere had been muted for well over an hour, so when the secure-line teletype printer finally surged to life, it made a doubly loud clattering noise.

When the message was complete, both admirals took it aside.

Horton's smooth black forehead crinkled as he read the President's emergency directive. Tarnaby's round, intent face hung above Horton's right shoulder as he, too, scanned the order. When they finished reading, tiny beads of sweat were glistening on Tarnaby's upper lip as Horton offered a stark analysis.

"You really can't blame the man, Vince. I'm for sinking it, too, if it comes to that. The stakes are just too high."

"I know," Tarnaby replied, already considering worst-case scenarios. "But I hate to think what Moscow's reaction will be."

Dispatch of any military vessel on the high seas was an outright act of war, and the Soviet response was certain to be swift and deadly. They believed in the eye-for-an-eye plus an-arm-and-a-leg method of settling grievances.

Fully aware of that, Horton grimaced before turning to face the control panel. "Rogers!" he snapped.

Commander Rogers hustled over from his position alongside Lieutenant Kelly at the panel. "Sir?"

Horton handed over the directive. "FASTRAC this out to the *Gremlin* and the ASW team. And get verification from both."

"Aye, aye, sir!" he said as he turned and hurried away.

Horton and Tarnaby then leaned back with their rumps against the desk flange that circled the inner perimeter of the bubble.

"You know, Luke, maybe this is all for nothing," Tarnaby offered. "Maybe they didn't even receive it out there."

Horton was more than willing to play that game. "Maybe . . . And even if they did, once we blow the cable they might decide against forcing our hand. Let's face it: Even without this directive, we have those poor bastards in a hell of a bind."

Tarnaby had to agree. Once their transmit cable was blown, the Russians would be dealing with an unspecified number of ASW choppers above and the *Gremlin* on their right. And if they waited until their optimum relay time, they'd be scraping by the Out Island Group of underwater mountains on their left.

Even where they came from, that had to be known as boxed in.

"So you think they'd decide to hold what they've got?" he suggested. "Continue on the loop as if nothing happened?"

Horton shrugged. "Their orders are to relay at all costs, but coming up into the teeth of an ASW attack would be suicide."

Tarnaby considered that, then offered a hopeful thought.

"Maybe Captain Barzlin is a reasonable man."

Captain Barzlin and Commander Damovitch stood hovering over the desk in the *Potkin*'s captain's quarters. Before them was a three-foot-square, three-dimensional relief map, one of three such sea charts all loopers carried. They were the training boards Soviet submariners used while learning to negotiate the three obstacle courses along America's western coastline.

The map before them was the second in the series, the one depicting the Out Island Group. It showed what looked like an aerial view of a mountain range bisected laterally by a wide, deep canyon. It could have been a map of northern Arizona but for the whitened, eroded-flat tops of its highest mountains.

Those broke the ocean's surface as islands in the sea lanes.

Using a pointer stick, Barzlin touched a white-topped mountain at the underwater canyon's eastern terminus. All peaks in the range had white numerals on their sides, and this was #28.

"We should do it here," he said, "at Peak 28. Then, if necessary, we can slip around this way to get down safely."

He moved the pointer's tip from the northeastern flank of the peak, around its midsection in a westerly arc, then straight down its western flank into the mouth of the canyon.

Damovitch lifted a doubtful eyebrow, which caused Barzlin's hackles to rise. The past hour had seen a steady escalation of animosity between the two men, who were being forced by Soviet military protocol to work side by side through the crisis. Damovitch was seizing every opportunity to illustrate his scorn for Barzlin's decision to delay sending the message on to Moscow.

"Yes," he said from behind his frown, "the timing of that will protect KR-72 and the Motherland. But whatever safety it gains for us will be temporary, at best." Then he added with undisguised contempt, "In my opinion, it's still a poor trade."

Barzlin finally snapped at his replacement's haughty insolence. He raised the pointer as though to strike him with it, but

Damovitch stood unflinchingly to receive the blow. In his eyes was some sense of absolute righteousness that caused Barzlin to falter.

He lowered the pointer, then stalked from the room behind an angry retort. "In these circumstances, temporary safety is the most we can hope for!"

☐ LXXI ☐

Like all men on the *Gremlin,* radioman Lee Hayden was wondering if they'd be forced to yet a higher grade of alert by whatever crisis was developing. Then he heard the warning bell that preceded the garbled screech of a FASTRAC, the new coded and scrambled bursts of sound that provided remarkable message security by means of an incredibly short send-time.

FASTRACs could jam three pages of single-spaced typing into an electronic burst lasting 3.2 seconds. Thus far, no Soviet monitors could intercept any aspect of such unique text. FASTRACs would slip through their listening web until they could buy or steal the American technology to defeat them.

Hayden motioned Deck Officer Vent to his console to tell him they were receiving FLASH traffic. "FASTRAC in Decoding, sir."

Vent nodded, realizing it would probably be the explanation of why they were on full alert. "Right—thanks."

He moved toward the decoding room, which was a computer-filled cubicle just off the rear port side of the control room. The computers in that cubicle received, elongated, decoded, and printed the FASTRAC in a matter of minutes.

Would this one would be a step away from, or a giant leap toward, the doom it was their mission to insure? Either way, Vent felt ready to do his part. Then he read the text, realized its seriousness, and promptly left for Captain Stickles's cabin.

A half hour earlier Stickles had pulled Ken LeBlanc off the control-room deck to help formulate their attack options against the Soviet looper. LeBlanc hated to leave Vent in charge of the deck, but the captain and his most senior officer were expected to confer whenever a confrontation might be in the works.

"Come in!" Stickles roared in response to Vent's knock.

Vent stepped inside to face both men. Animosity poured out of LeBlanc as he asked, "Another SITREP you can't handle?"

Stickles gave LeBlanc a reproachful look, so Vent ignored Dandy's jibe to concentrate on the captain. He held up the message in his hand. "Sir, a FASTRAC from PACCOM. 'Escalate to precombat alert, with permission to engage if necessary.' "

LeBlanc's jaw dropped open, while Stickles stepped forward.

"Sounds like we play this one for keeps," the captain said, taking the FASTRAC and adjusting his half-lens reading glasses.

"Will that be all, sir?" Vent said before the captain had a chance to start reading the message for himself.

Stickles looked up over his half-shells. "No, I want you to help with our planning. We need all the help we can get."

Vent glanced at LeBlanc's outraged expression, wishing like hell he could stay and compete with him nose-to-nose, brain-to-brain, in front of the captain. But rules were rules.

"With the lieutenant commander here with you, sir, I'm the senior officer on deck. I think I should stay out there, just in case anything starts between now and when PACCOM expects it to."

"Right," the captain said, immediately seeing the wisdom of that analysis. "Good thinking. Go to it."

Stickles turned away, absorbed in the FASTRAC, as Vent gave a fuming LeBlanc the most self-satisfied grin he could muster.

He realized it wasn't much of a victory, but—like the small one earlier in his cabin—he was more than glad to have it.

Like most men in similar straits, Stickles was alarmed by even a remote possibility of engaging in mortal combat. Yet deep within the folds of his modern, civilized brain was a primitive core that relished confronting the ultimate challenge of war.

Would he be up to it? Could he stand the strain?

His second-in-command, however, held no such sentiments. LeBlanc had always considered himself as brave as any man, as long as he could choose where and how he made his stands. This kind of locked-in acid test was something he'd never anticipated.

Stickles had given him the FASTRAC to read, and he returned it with a trembling hand that Stickles noticed. "What about the

ASW team?" he managed to ask. "Can't they do the job . . . themselves?"

Stickles nodded. "If their fuel holds out long enough."

LeBlanc's voice surged to a higher note. "What if they . . . have to ditch before the looper tries to relay?"

Stickles put his glasses back on to reexamine the FASTRAC. "I read this the way Vent did. We now have the authority to engage them the second they try to transmit."

Stickles didn't use the word *sink* because sinking was what submarines did to surface vessels that were sitting ducks. Other submarines were "engaged," because only other subs stood a chance of survival against an underwater attack. In fact, computer simulations indicated that if two modern, nuclear-powered submarines tangled for keeps, it was doubtful either would escape an exchange of the sophisticated, deadly torpedoes they carried.

Simple luck would be critical to the survival of either.

Ken LeBlanc was barely able to squeeze out his next words: "Yes, sir. . . . That's the way I read it too."

Eight minutes after Captain Stickles called for battle stations, the *Gremlin* was at full readiness. Each man was at his post and charged with the adrenaline rush that came from knowing every chip was on the table. From then until the crunch came, the crew would do little more than maintain tight-lipped conversations—or pray—whichever made them feel better.

The four forward tubes were loaded with MK-48s, horrific 3600-pound marvels of destruction that tracked the sounds of their targets with the tenacity of hounds after foxes. And, as it was with foxes, the only escape from those homing torpedoes was to throw them off the scent.

Consequently, tubes five through eight, located in pairs amidships, were loaded with clusters of scuba-tank-sized and bullet-shaped electronic decoys. Each decoy would scurry away in a helter-skelter pattern, making noises exactly like its full-sized mother ship. Those decoys were any submarine's only hope of escaping a homing torpedo fired at it. And the Americans could expect Soviet counterthrusts seconds after the first shots were fired.

The four rear tubes were split: Nine and eleven were loaded with

MK-48s, while ten and twelve held decoys. Such front and rear protection was necessary because, in the lethal world of underwater warfare, volleys could come from any quadrant. If combatants were caught less than fully prepared, not a thing in the world would save them.

Accordingly, everyone on the *Gremlin* knew a clean kill was unlikely. Survival was the very best they could hope for. They also knew that their lives now depended on two things: the effectiveness of their decoys against Soviet torpedoes; and the effectiveness of the officers in charge of their control room.

They had surprising faith in both.

□ LXXII □

Nat and Karen didn't say much during the rest of the trip to Lumberton. She could see how absorbed he was with trying to get everything arranged in his mind, which left her free to do some analyzing of her own. By the time they reached Lumberton's outskirts, she'd been through the situation enough times to have formulated several questions about what seemed to be going on.

Though Lumberton's traffic was sparse, Nat appeared more focused on his driving than his thoughts, so she decided it might be a good time to speak up. "Is it okay to talk to you now?"

He glanced at her and smiled. "Fire away. . . ."

"What makes you so sure Marsh's cabin is the key?"

"It's where he has to keep his phreaking rig."

"But you heard Brandt say they checked the place out. You saw the pictures they took. How could they have missed it?"

"There's no way to know how big it is," he explained. "Or if it's cleverly disguised . . . or hidden in some brilliant way. A phreak called the Kraut taught us all how to build sophisticated wall-panel hiding places. The King might've built one of those."

"Wouldn't the FBI be sharp enough to check for that?"

Nat shrugged. "It depends. All they were looking for was enough computer hardware to hack at the Ghost Glitch's level. They found that at Marsh's house their first time through it."

Karen got his drift. "So you think they weren't really looking all that hard at the cabin?"

"Not like they would have if they'd missed at his house."

She thought it over for a moment, then said, "I guess that makes sense. So what now? How do we get his address?"

Lumberton was a five-block-long, one-stoplight town, with its combination courthouse and jail in a converted movie theater. "We go in there," Nat said as he pointed at it, "check the local property records, find his parcel, and ask how to get to it."

"Why didn't you just ask Brandt and Doppler for directions?"

He looked at her as if she'd asked him to commit suicide. "Are you kidding? There'd be no reason for me to want to check the place out unless I thought they'd overlooked something."

She couldn't help admiring the deviousness of pretending indifference to keep them from going back to double-check.

"Like I said," he went on, "I don't want those bozos tracking all over my case."

"But they've already got an airtight hacking case against Marsh. Why should they care about crowding your phreaking case?"

He answered as he parked the Corvette at an angle between two battered old pickup trucks. "Simple! They put the Glitch away for a while—it makes a statement to other hackers. But if he hires a good enough lawyer, he might get off with probation.

"Now, the truth is, a jail term isn't really warranted for what they can convict him of. But if they can get him tagged as the Glitch *and* as a phreak—never mind as the King—that should give them a lock on putting him away and setting their example."

"So why not just give him to them?" she asked as she opened her door and got out. Then, with an ironic twist, she added, "After you make him eat his ration of shit, of course."

He locked his car, scowling like a man about to even a bloodfeud score. "Because I don't want him sitting in a jail cell making Brandt and Doppler happy. I want him making *me* happy . . . working for me . . . dancing to my tune for a change."

"But if they can put him away for sure if they connect him to phreaking, won't nailing him defeat your own purpose?"

Nat's grin was demonic as they walked along the sidewalk to the courthouse. "If he's the Glitch and just a phreak, yes. But if he's the King . . . Well, that's another story.

"Ma's higher-ups will have a talk with the FBI's higher-ups, and in the best interests of national security, Mr. Percy Marsh will be coming to work for Ma, which means me. Count on it."

A shudder of unease swept up Karen's spine as she realized how much bitter vindictiveness he was carrying around because of the King. She hoped Marsh did turn out to be their man so Nat would have a way to start getting rid of all that pain.

☐ LXXIII ☐

Admirals Horton and Tarnaby were in their off-to-one-side place in the PACCOM command bubble, discussing how to handle the fuel problem Scarlatti's ASW team had reported. The fact that their main coverage unit was down to about an hour of flying time had put both men on the horns of a serious dilemma.

Since clear weather extended for 180 of the 200 miles out to the *Potkin,* Soviet Situation Rooms already knew an American ASW team had gone under cloud cover near one of their loopers. One team they could chalk up to a coincidence of training, but two in the same area would definitely arouse their suspicions.

Especially since the first team hadn't reappeared.

After bandying the pros and cons, Tarnaby staked out his bottom-line position: "I say it's a mistake to trade off keeping Moscow in the dark about what's going on out there, at the risk of leaving the *Potkin* without overhead coverage for even a few minutes. That could leave it all up to the *Gremlin,* and the *Gremlin* doesn't have the tactical advantages of the overheads."

"You're right, Vince," Horton agreed. "A coverage lag could be trouble. But I think it's just as important to protect ourselves against Moscow as it is to cover that relay. I mean, we know what Moscow will think if they see two ASW teams go out near one of their loopers; but we don't know whether that message was received—or even if it's legitimate."

Tarnaby's expression didn't give ground. "I still say this is a situation where any risk—however slight—is unacceptable."

That set Horton thinking. He gazed at the central screen's current graphic, which showed a crescent shape of heavy weather spiraled up from Mexico to cover the *Potkin*. He called out to Rogers at the control board. "How's that front holding up?"

"Dispersing over the Out Island Group, sir," Rogers said.

That wasn't what Horton wanted to hear. "Damn! Somewhere along in there is where the relay will go out—if it happens."

"That's right," Tarnaby muttered, "and if it does happen, Moscow will know the score anyway. They'll be able to see it! So, c'mon, Luke . . . what do you say? Let's protect ourselves."

Horton considered again, then shrugged. "What the hell? Maybe you're right." He raised his voice once more. "Rogers! Get a backup ASW team airborne. Send them south first, up under the front, then curl them north along its edge for the linkup."

"Aye, sir!" Rogers snapped as he hurried from the command bubble to carry out his orders.

Horton turned to Tarnaby with a strained smile. "Satisfied?"

Tarnaby tried to return his smile with genuine enthusiasm, but he'd only gotten half of the loaf he wanted. "Sending them south first will still leave time with no overhead coverage."

Horton's smile faded under the pressure of the moment and his friend's dogged persistence. "The *Gremlin* can take up any slack, but it won't come to that. If the Russians do have the message, they'll relay past the five-hour mark to protect their agent on shore. Our second team should be there by then."

Tarnaby knew the PACCOM chief was putting his career on the line, so it was time to back off. He gave his tense friend a reassuring pat on the back. "Sure, Luke . . . you're probably right."

☐ LXXIV ☐

The *Potkin*'s crew had prepared for battle an hour before the *Gremlin*'s. Both sides knew the basic fighting strategy the other would employ. What they didn't know—and couldn't know until the last second—was whether an engagement was actually looming, or if they were preparing to confront a phantom.

Despite that huge uncertainty, everyone knew an all-out clash would be decided by the proper execution of fundamentals.

Captain Barzlin sat in his cabin, doubting it would come to that. He remained convinced the Americans had missed the message, and he believed he'd relay it without incident. But he accepted the possibility that his boat was now in jeopardy.

Even if the intermittent static Popov and Rykoff kept hearing was indeed the communications of ASW aircraft hovering above them—as Commander Damovitch believed—he had fashioned a battle plan with excellent potential for success.

Soon they'd enter the Out Island Group, the range of nineteen underwater mountains that extended from the ocean's bottom to cover a surface area of nearly 500 square miles. It was there—among those submerged peaks, valleys, and ravines—where he planned to evade any American pursuit. He'd spent most of his career preaching the value of precision navigation through such fearsome obstacles, and he was certain his crew could negotiate them far better than their opponents—if it came to that.

He rose on his old legs that had been given new life by the impending crisis. Then he left for the control room to assume command of the last vessel he'd ever captain.

There were two reasons Valeri Damovitch was much less confident than his captain about the crisis point they were barreling toward at thirty knots. The first came when Barzlin tried to explain his proposed battle plan to him. He'd stalked away in protest because his own opinions weren't being properly valued. Now he had no idea what was coming next.

The second reason for his anxiety was more fundamental and intense than the first: Unlike Barzlin and Popov, he had no first-hand knowledge of combat.

To the younger generation of Soviets—which included most men on board the *Potkin*—Americans were the owners and manipulators of a technology gone berserk. They were unfeeling automatons, incapable of action outside the province of their machines. So they seemed invincible because they'd melded with their weapons to become a juggernaut of infinite power and sophistication.

Ironically, that was precisely how veterans like Barzlin and Popov had felt about the Germans and Japanese during World War II. They started out thinking of their opponents in near godlike terms because they were so unfamiliar with them at close range. But as it turned out, the Germans and Japanese had made mistakes in battle and died for them, like the Russians and everyone else.

That was the advantage the older men had over the young in the current situation: The old ones knew it would be a fair fight, if it came to that. A mistake would mean death, surely, but the decision wasn't preordained. The young men, however, were going in feeling they had nothing on their side except the possible failure of the well-oiled American war machine.

Now Damovitch stood at the center of the *Potkin's* control room, waiting for his captain to come execute the plan he'd so hastily dismissed out of hand. And he was genuinely sorry he hadn't bothered to hear the old man out. Because all their lives might be at stake, and because he himself had several important tasks to accomplish if they were to have any chance of success, the time for shipboard dissension was past.

Besides, if anyone managed to survive, the Presidium would decide whom to reward and whom to punish—and to what extent.

That being the case, he was determined to make amends, in the best interests of the boat—*My boat, dammit!*— and its crew.

□ LXXV □

While separate but similar preparations were being made on board the *Potkin* and the *Gremlin,* above them Lieutenant Vito Scarlatti and his ASW team had finalized their own battle plans.

If the *Potkin's* cable came up while they were still airborne, they'd destroy it the moment it began transmitting. Then, if the *Potkin* itself tried to rise, they'd drop a few more depth charges to make their point emphatically.

If the *Potkin* ignored that warning and continued heading up toward the surface, they'd be forced to launch MK-46s, 560-pound junior-grade versions of the MK-48s submarines carried. Under no circumstance would the Russians be allowed to surface to relay from their sail.

As he'd done several times earlier, Scarlatti broke radio silence to update PACCOM on the gradual worsening of his team's situation: They were down to a half hour of fuel and prepared as well as possible for their inevitable ditchings.

He couldn't help being reminded of the basketball games he used to captain at the Naval Academy, the ones where his team was usually overmatched and outmanned in everything but spirit. Those games always came down to a similar wait: They'd hope like hell to win, praying for last-second miracles; but they were also prepared to lose as the final minutes ticked off the clock.

PACCOM had already informed him of the backup team scheduled to arrive about fifteen minutes after they hit the water. PACCOM also told him they had two high-speed rescue choppers on standby, ready to fly out and pluck all three crews from the ocean the moment there was clear evidence Moscow knew what was going on.

By then the weather front was breaking up several miles ahead, so Scarlatti asked if the rescue birds could leave as soon as his team became visible to Soviet spy satellites. Even high-speed craft would need an hour to reach them, during which they'd be bobbing in open life rafts on a choppy sea. All of his men were concerned about that prospect—especially Casey Harper.

PACCOM agreed to consider his request, then signed off with no further comment. That wasn't a good sign.

In analyzing his team's status at PACCOM, Scarlatti had to acknowledge that the cavalier loss of three multimillion-dollar helicopters—not to mention the serious risk to their crews—was the clearest possible indication of the situation's gravity. That, plus the deadly risk to the multi*billion*- dollar *Gremlin,* which could easily be lost in a head-to-head with the *Potkin.*

It was then that Scarlatti realized the stark predicament he and his team now faced: They'd be mighty damn lucky if the worst that happened to them was an extended choppy raft ride.

☐ LXXVI ☐

Captain Barzlin's step was lively by the time he entered the *Potkin*'s control room. He went directly to his second-in-command and clapped a friendly hand on the younger man's shoulder, hoping they could lay aside the differences between them in the interest of achieving harmony at this critical time.

"Is everything prepared, Commander Damovitch?"

As he'd promised himself, Damovitch was quick to show he was ready to bury the hatchet—temporarily. He looked his captain in the eyes and spoke with typical subordinate respect.

"Yes, sir! All is in order."

Barzlin recognized that gesture for what it was and smiled his appreciation. Then he turned to Sonar Chief Andrus Kim.

"Chief Kim, where are we now and when do we reach Peak 28?"

Kim checked the ghostly green peak outlined on his two top screens. "We're approaching Peak 9 . . . parallel in two minutes." He then checked a route sheet logged to the second by countless other trips through this Group. "We reach 28 in ten minutes."

Barzlin nodded, then spoke to a technician standing in the rear of the control room. "Release the transmission cable!"

And then to Chief Popov: "Transmit when it surfaces."

The technician pressed a button that released the buoyant sail cable and would send several hundred feet of it snaking toward the surface. In two minutes the transmitter at its end would reach its destination, Popov would start relaying, and they'd know for certain what the stakes were in this potential endgame.

"Is everyone prepared?" Barzlin asked the control room in general. "Are there any questions?"

The room's tense silence was broken by the ever-cheerful sonarman, Chief Kim, who turned from his console to say, "Don't worry, Captain! The Americans can't find a beet in borscht!"

Strained chuckles swept the room for a few brief seconds, but they were quickly extinguished by the ragged breathing of men who knew they might soon be fighting for their lives.

☐ LXXVII ☐

Minutes after making his last situation and fuel reports to PAC-COM, Scarlatti was notified that the worst was indeed happening. His right-side wingman, Bart Holloway, spoke through the tiny microphone embedded in his heavy protective helmet.

"Cable up, Vito! Dead ahead!"

Within seconds, sonarman Bobby Wong spoke up from his seat behind copilot Casey Harper's back. "It's starting to transmit!"

Scarlatti didn't hesitate. "Drop surface depth-charge!"

"No!" Harper croaked. The most negative scenario he'd ever imagined was starting to play itself out. "It's too early!"

"Charge away!" Holloway called out.

A football-sized bomb dropped from his craft and plummeted through a hundred-foot descent. It entered the water, there was a fractional pause, then a column of spray erupted like the spume of a gargantuan whale.

The *Potkin's* transmitter vanished within that powerful explosion. As the ASW team watched its plume splatter back down onto the surface, they knew the battle was joined.

Now all they could do was keep to their positions and hope their fuel held out long enough to settle the issue decisively.

☐ LXXVIII ☐

Lieutenant (Junior Grade) Hanna Buckley's morning at the Padre Island NAVFAC had given way to another lunch eaten in the ladies' room, followed by a relatively comfortable afternoon. At that moment she was gazing blankly at the two side-by-side monitoring screens in the Display Room, daydreaming about what her "dumpling" might turn out to be.

In night dreams it always appeared as a girl, and she'd heard that was a reliable indicator of an unborn baby's sex.

As her thoughts drifted among those private concerns, her sub-conscious remained on the job, monitoring the *Potkin* as it navigated through the Out Island Group. There was no indication to her that it had become the target of intense speculation and pursuit until Seaman Dennis Stone, who was monitoring the #1, #2, #3, and #4 line-graph sensors, called out a discovery.

"Something just went off above the #3 looper!"

Hanna turned from her screens to look at his back as he stood facing his machines. "Went off . . . ?" she muttered.

"An explosion of some kind, on the surface!"

She yanked herself into the here and now by adjusting her left-side monitoring screen to bring in a close-up of the *Potkin*. It appeared as a cigar-shaped, graph-paper cutout moving along through the pale green haze of water, with the wire-sculpture outlines of subsurface mountains in the background.

Everything about it seemed normal.

She punched one of her console's buttons and a different cigar-shaped, graph-paper outline materialized on the right-side screen. It was cruising through clear, unobstructed haze. The *Gremlin*, too, appeared to be perfectly on track.

"The explosion," she said, "did it read like a meteor?"

Stone leaned over the #4 sensor to get a close view of its gram sheet's squiggles. He gave them a thorough read, then replied hesitantly. "Not exactly. More like a detonation than an impact. But what else could it be?"

What indeed? Hanna asked herself. Both meteor impacts and oil-exploration explosions routinely showed up on their sensors. But neither ever occurred anywhere near Soviet loopers, so this event was highly unusual. *Better safe than sorry* . . .

She opened a special drawer in the console and lifted a telephone receiver that was a direct line to PACCOM in Hawaii. It was to be used only in emergencies, but she felt confident that headquarters would want to be appraised of this. To the best of her knowledge, nothing like it had ever happened before.

What she couldn't know, but was about to learn, was that PAC-COM had been monitoring the *Potkin* for nearly four hours.

Concern there now was not for the overhead explosion, but for the next course of action it would precipitate.

☐ LXXIX ☐

Captain Barzlin stood near the periscope tube, gazing up at the
sail hatch. He could feel the eyes of the men in the control room
crawling fearfully along his spine.

Just like in the old days, he thought. Crews then always turned
to their captains to draw courage in times of crisis, and it pleased
him to see that tradition being maintained.

In his opinion it was a good one.

In this circumstance, however, the echo of the explosion above
them had reverberated to the core of his soul as profoundly as to
theirs. He'd been wrong in his assumption that the Americans
missed the message—wrong and damned for being so.

Now he was responsible not only for relaying it, but for preserv-
ing his boat and the lives of his men in the process. He turned from
the sail hatch and focused on Damovitch, whose square jaw was
set but whose expression showed no rebuke.

"You were right all along, Valeri," he conceded without rancor.
"I should have listened to you."

Damovitch started to say something in return, then thought better of it. There was simply no way to mitigate the captain's mistake. And to Barzlin, his successor's silence was eloquent proof
that he'd also been wrong about him. But, as it was with
Damovitch, expressions of regret were useless now; so he stepped
to the bridge intercom and got on with what had to be done.

"This is Captain Barzlin," he began, addressing every sailor on
board in calmly resolute tones. "The explosion you just heard was
an American antisubmarine force destroying our transmission
cable. That means they had our message all along, and now they
know we have it. That also means they'll be prepared to take any
measures necessary to stop us from surfacing to relay it.

"As I'm sure you know, trying to surface in these conditions will
be dangerous. But I've worked out a plan I believe will allow us to
rise safely, then accomplish our mission. If you each perform your
duties as you've been trained to do, we can prevail. The elements of
surprise and planning are on our side."

He paused a moment so everyone could grasp the situation, then he concluded, "That's all for now. Good luck, Comrades."

He switched off the intercom, then turned to the technician who'd released the transmitter. "Retract what's left of the cable." He then turned to Damovitch, whose stalwart intensity was strangely soothing to his own quiet fears. "Take position."

Damovitch nodded, then stepped to the torpedo fire/control station. It would be his responsibility to release the decoys and fire their torpedoes, if it came to that—although Barzlin wanted to avoid an exchange if possible.

If the message turned out to be a hoax or a mistake, he didn't want it noted on his record that he'd lost his boat without making every effort to save it. And he especially didn't want that noted on his record as a posthumous entry.

He called to his sonarman. "Chief Kim! Peak 28?"

Kim understood that abbreviated request and replied without looking up from his monitoring screens. "Three minutes, sir!"

Barzlin turned to Diving Officer Leonid Sarlov, the man who would execute his orders and "steer" the ship through the depths.

Sarlov sat in the "pilot" chair, a low-slung, cockpitlike affair. He was watching duplicates of the same four attitude needles Navigation Technician Lemnotova used to chart and track their course. In his hands was the highly movable pilot wheel.

"Lieutenant Sarlov, on my command I want a left heading of zero-one-zero degrees, and drop eighty meters in thirty seconds. At that point we'll launch our decoys, after which you must follow my instructions to the letter. Do you understand?"

Sarlov replied without hesitation. "Exactly, Captain!"

Leonid Sarlov was an exceptionally thin, freckle-covered, russet-haired young man whose thick glasses, gaunt looks, and quiet, studious habits had earned him the nickname "Professor."

Nothing could have been further from his true nature.

He was a granite-willed competitor with the cool, steady nerves of a jet-fighter pilot, which he'd always wanted to be, and very likely would have been, if not for his faulty vision.

Steering submarines was the closest he could come to "flying" combat machines, and he relished this opportunity to test his skills against the monumental challenge they now faced.

Barzlin's final preparation was to step behind Sonar Chief Kim, so he could monitor their progress underwater. As he stood waiting for just the right moment to make his move, he gazed around the room one last time, focusing on each man in turn.

"Let me repeat," he said with unwavering conviction. "If you all do exactly as I say, precisely when I say it, we can win this battle. Not just survive it—*win* it! Believe me!"

He felt everyone's confidence level begin to rise as his own resolve seeped into the younger men. Then he glanced at Popov, and the veteran radioman winked in appreciation of the old chess master's shrewd performance.

Popov understood. . . .

□ LXXX □

Widely scattered rays of light were beginning to pierce the cloud cover over Vito Scarlatti's ASW team when Sonarman Bobby Wong noticed the *Potkin*'s change of course.

"Vito! The bogie's turned about ten degrees northwest. Same speed, with a shallow angle down."

"Why would they head toward the island?" Scarlatti wondered aloud as he surveyed the seagirt oval known as Traynor Island. "That's mighty risky for a sub to get anywhere near."

Traynor Island was the official name for the exposed pinnacle of Peak 28. It's area was only one square mile, with a flattened, undulating surface of jagged, wave-scoured basalt.

It lay squatting in the water like a huge, ugly toad.

"Maybe they want to put some distance between themselves and the shadow," Wong suggested. "Maybe they figure because it's so dangerous, our guys won't follow."

Casey Harper ended a bristling sulk to put his two cents into the exchange. "Ha! Fat chance! Those Russians are up to something. You can bet your Chink ass on that."

"Whatever the reason, Mr. Optimism," Wong countered, "it won't do them any good as long as we're up here."

"Yeah, right!" Harper snapped as he checked a fuel gauge. "All twenty minutes we have left!"

"They can't possibly know that," Scarlatti said with finality as he activated the intership mode on his helmet.

"Grady? Bart?" he said to his wingmen. "You guys see where the target's heading?"

"Roger, One," Swenson replied.

"Roger . . ." Holloway repeated.

"Okay, then, let's just stay on top of it as long as we can. Nobody can expect more than that."

"Why toward the island?" Holloway asked.

"Yeah," Swenson added. "That's really asking for trouble."

"No idea" came Scarlatti's curt reply. "But as long as they keep going down, we're in good shape."

"Ha! Fat chance!" Harper groused.

□ LXXXI □

The chief concern on board the USS *Gremlin* was how best to pursue their target. A dispute arose when Sonarman Agamemnon Rodrigues called out the *Potkin*'s course change. "Sir! The bogie's turned northwest about ten degrees, dropping slightly."

Captain Stickles looked to Officer of the Deck Norton Vent, who was now in the cockpit seat performing his battle function of steering their vessel. "Zero-one-zero!" he called out.

Vent immediately made the navigational correction while calling out his verification. "Zero-one-zero, aye, sir!"

Stickles turned back to Rodrigues. "What's its drop angle?"

"About ten degrees, sir. No more than twelve."

Stickles nodded and turned to Vent. "Hold at five down!"

"Five down, aye, sir!" Vent responded.

Suddenly a voice shouted from the other side of the control room. It was Executive Officer Ken LeBlanc calling out from his position at the torpedo fire/control station. "But, sir! That leaves us above them! They'll have a clean belly-shot at us!"

Stickles turned to glare at his X-O. It was an unbelievable breach of naval etiquette to openly question a captain's orders, especially in the control room during a crisis situation.

"Commander," he said with icy formality, "our primary and

only responsibility here is to keep that boat from surfacing. And we can do that most effectively if we stay above it."

That explanation had no effect on LeBlanc, who nervously fingered the gunnery board in his agitation. "But they could be setting us up! What if they—?"

Stickles cut him off sharply. "That'll be all, Commander!" He couldn't let one man's paranoia infect everyone else.

Suddenly Sonarman Rodrigues called out again. "Sir! They just released something! One . . . two . . . three . . ."

The *Gremlin* was just as suddenly filled with the hollow, reverberating hisses of decoys and torpedoes being ejected by thousand-pound bursts of compressed air.

"Decoys!" Rodrigues concluded. "They're decoys!"

As soon as those words were out of Rodrigues's mouth, LeBlanc announced what he'd done. "One and two away!—behind decoys!"

Stickles rushed him, yelling, "Cut all engines!" He grabbed his arm and spun him around. "Goddammit! Who told you to fire?"

LeBlanc jerked his arm loose from Stickles's grip, looking fearfully at his enraged captain. "They . . . they fired at us!"

"Decoys!" Stickles roared. "They released decoys!"

LeBlanc shook his head obstinately, making clear how badly his judgment had been warped. "No! They *fired* at us!"

Stickles backed off and tried to think, but he was overwhelmed by the fact that two of his boat's torpedoes were on their way. That meant he and the Russian captain were now irrevocably locked in mortal combat. In fact, answering torpedoes should be headed their way at that very second! The Russians had had enough time to realize they were under attack.

Stickles abandoned LeBlanc in the pressure of the moment to hustle over to Rodrigues's position. "Where's the return volley?"

"No sign of it yet, sir," Rodrigues replied, "but our two are four hundred yards and closing."

Stickles settled in behind Rodrigues's back to focus his attention on the sonar screens. All he could do now was locate the Russian counterthrust as it came barreling out of the haze, then do anything possible to dodge or divert it with more decoys.

Meanwhile, Norton Vent did what everyone else in the control room was doing: He stole worried glances at rattled Ken LeBlanc, who was still in charge of the torpedo fire/control board.

☐ LXXXII ☐

There'd be no immediate return volley because Barzlin had no idea he'd been fired at by his opponents. He'd just assumed his decoys had done their job of laying out an acoustical smoke screen to blind the American sub's sound sensors, which was necessary to slow it down so the *Potkin* could increase its lead beyond a mile. In their deadly game of cat and mouse, that kind of advantage—thought slight—could be crucial.

Once out of the *Gremlin*'s "sight," the *Potkin* raced flat-out around the northwestern slope of Peak 28, rushing headlong toward the entrance to the canyon at its western base. Barzlin was moving his vessel into position to execute the daring maneuver he'd conceived, although there was no guarantee his crew could perform it. But they had no chance to relay unless they tried.

Then came a muffled roar from somewhere on the northeastern slope. That blast was quickly followed by another.

Several younger men in the control room looked around in confusion. They'd never before heard the sound of real torpedoes exploding within two miles of their position. It was surprising how well the sound carried and how sharp was the concussive jolt. Even with the mountain shielding them, it felt as if their whole submarine had been shoved forward several meters.

"Have the Americans hit the mountain trying to follow us?" Damovitch asked hopefully.

Barzlin glanced at Popov's knitted brow and shook his head. "Those were torpedoes—big ones."

Damovitch and the other young men in the control room were struck dumb by that revelation—all except the icy-nerved driver, Sarlov. "They fired at our decoys!" he exclaimed from his seat behind the pilot wheel, unawed by the prospect of engagement.

The captain nodded grimly. "Perhaps we underestimated their belief in the message. Perhaps they *know* it's genuine."

Whatever the reason, he realized, their lives were now indisputably at risk, not only from the submarine behind them but from the ASW force overhead. In fact, if sinking them outright was the American intention, why hadn't the ASW force done that immediately rather than only destroying their cable?

Maybe they were being given a chance to live, he reasoned. Maybe if they went down and stayed down, the Americans would try to avoid the worldwide scandal an unprovoked sinking would create. But if that was the case, why did the sub fire when they were so obviously heading down? None of it made sense.

A few facts were clear, however. Barzlin realized with deep regret that his desire to avoid a confrontation had gone up in a boiling mushroom of foam. And there was no denying the situation as it now stood: The American gauntlet was down. The Russians had no choice but to pick it up or die cowardly, futile deaths.

Which meant they had no choice at all.

There was nothing more for Barzlin to do except prepare for the worst, so he went to the bridge intercom to speak to the entire crew. "Comrades, the explosions you heard were torpedoes hitting our decoys. That means we're officially at war with the Americans. This in no way changes our plans to escape and relay our message. But we must double our efforts to insure success. Do your jobs well and we *will* prevail. You have my promise."

Throughout the *Potkin,* several seconds of profound silence followed that statement. Then everyone went back to their tasks with renewed vigor—and fear.

☐ LXXXIII ☐

Standing in the PACCOM command bubble, gripping a console panel hard enough to crinkle its finish, Fleet Admiral Lucius Horton tried to comprehend what he and his group had just witnessed on the Situation Room's three monitoring screens.

The Out Island Group's wire-sculpture mountains had come to life, with two graph-paper sausages moving parallel through them. Then came the overhead explosion, followed by the Soviet sausage breaking away from its American twin. Soon after, three small blips of red light emerged from the Soviet's tail, followed by four blue blips from the American's sides and two from its nose.

The three red blips began the characteristic twisting pattern of decoys, which weren't necessary at that point but were understandable considering the situation the Soviets faced.

Next came the American boat's four decoy blips, which were also unnecessary and absolutely unexpected. Then, when the final two blue blips appeared, every heart in the Situation Room froze.

Horton, Tarnaby, and the others watched in shock as the twin lights moved away in the direct routes of torpedoes. Their shock turned to horror as those deadly beelines spread apart to destroy all three of the Soviet decoys in bright, overlapping blasts.

That put the *Gremlin* in a bleak position. It was forced to cut its engines to keep away from the detonation of its own torpedoes, so the *Potkin* easily extended its mile lead. There was also a mountain between the two now, shielding the *Potkin* as it dived down into a long, wide, and deep underwater canyon that no transponders could let them "look" inside of.

No one had ever seen a reason to array such a deadly place.

"What the hell is Stickles *doing?*" Horton muttered through his shock. "The stupid bastard's lost his mind! I ought to—!"

He cut himself off, realizing there wasn't a damn thing he could do to find out what was going on inside the *Gremlin.* It couldn't transmit an explanation without extending its cable or surfacing, and it couldn't easily maneuver away from torpedoes in either state. So the best he could possibly do was radio a browbeating to a man obviously in the throes of hysteria.

Since any further overwrought responses by Stickles would only worsen the chances of his ship and crew surviving the confrontation, Horton could only watch impotently as the whole sorry fiasco played itself out. Worse yet, he knew that in the final analysis, he'd be the one held accountable for what resulted.

"What's happening, Luke?" Tarnaby asked from behind his shoulder. "Why'd our guys fire like that?"

"They're being outfoxed!" he snapped. "The Russians baited some kind of trap and Stickles fell into it!"

"But they're going down! Isn't that what we want?"

"Of course, but not after we fired at them! We come off looking like a bunch of trigger-happy warmongers!"

Tarnaby could see Horton was losing his composure, so he raised a palm and moved his friend to the area of the bubble where they could speak with a degree of privacy.

"I'm sorry, Luke, but I just don't get it. The Russians are supposed to be heading to the surface to relay a message we don't want them to send, right? But all they're doing is tucking tail and running away! So where's our problem?"

Horton's dark eyes glittered with intensity. "Look, Vince, forget the goddamn message! They showed us their decision on that as soon as they headed down. What we've got to worry about now is our media image when this mess is over!"

Tarnaby shook his head in confusion.

"All they have to do is find a safe place to hide," Horton went on, "then wait for their own people to come escort them to the surface. The weather front is already clearing, so their satellites will be able to see everything before long!"

Despite his brief failure to understand the rapidly shifting situation, Tarnaby quickly realized that the improved bottom line it presented was still harsh and unyielding. President Baxter now had a half hour, at most, to come up with a plausible explanation for what American forces were doing to a Soviet naval vessel ostensibly minding its own business in international waters.

☐ LXXXIV ☐

President Daniel Baxter, Chief of Staff Mike Gravelle, and Joint Chief Dale Weatherspoon were sitting in the White House Situation Room's command bubble. Unlike PACCOM's floor-level bubble, this one's enclosed console tables were elevated ten feet above and behind a dozen rows of consoles, and their operators, located on the floor below. Stretched across the left, right, and center walls opposite were three "Big Board" screens.

Each man sat there looking utterly baffled by what he'd just witnessed, while on the central screen a computer-enhanced graphic of the *Potkin* was gliding down Peak 28's northwest shank, toward the eastern opening of the canyon beyond.

"*Why,* Dale?" the President finally rasped. "Why in God's name would our people open fire like that?"

Weatherspoon shifted on the hot seat, uncomfortable with having to get inside the heads of men plunged deep into a boiling cauldron of pressure. But he gave it his best interpretation.

"The Russians clearly wanted to slip around that mountain to get down into the canyon on the other side of it, which is a good tactical maneuver if they've decided against surfacing to relay their message. But they didn't need to release decoys to make that work. Maybe they were paranoid about being torpedoed if they made *any* move, up or down. Or maybe they had some good reason to want the *Gremlin* to hang back for a while."

"Releasing decoys is no reason to try to torpedo them!" Gravelle snapped.

"I was getting to that," Weatherspoon countered. "As you know, decoys make the exact same sounds their mother ship makes. So by releasing them when they did—with the mountain off their flank acting as an echo source—they could have multiplied their covering noise to a point where it blinded the *Gremlin*'s sonar for a few seconds. If that happened, someone on board might've panicked and pulled the trigger."

"All right," the President cut in, "so the Russians put one over on our people out there, and now we're the bad guys. But I still don't get one part of it. If they're supposed to be heading for the surface to try to relay their message, what are they doing going down into that dead-end canyon?"

Weatherspoon shrugged. "I see two possibilities: First, they've decided to ignore their military responsibility and save themselves. And second, this whole thing has been one huge setup to make us come off as world-class heavies."

Gravelle shook his head emphatically. "I don't buy either of those. If the Russians are turning tail for real, then they should just keep on going right into the bottom. I mean, we all know suicide is preferable to what they'd face when they got back home. And as for staging a propaganda setup . . . Hell, no one in the Kremlin is stupid enough to play with this kind of fire."

The President nodded agreement, then ominously added, "This is the real thing, all right. At least, that Russian sub *thinks* it's the real thing. Why it's going down, I can't say . . . but I doubt we've heard the last of it."

□ LXXXV □

Viktor Lubov pulled his Porsche over to the side of California's Pacific Coast Highway, the famed Highway 1. He parked under a small copse of trees clinging to the base of a bluff of rock, overlooking the sparkling Pacific spread along the horizon to his left. In this unfamiliar terrain, he could no longer recognize landmarks from his trip south that morning.

He'd begun to suspect he was lost.

For hundreds of miles and several hours, all Lubov had concentrated on was keeping his car on the road and in its own lane at a steady, manageable speed. He knew Highway 1 north would junction with Highway 16, which would lead east into the San Jose Mountains and back to the entrance road to Marsh's cabin. Also, there would be road signs as he got near the junction, so he didn't have to follow a complicated, unmarked route.

Nevertheless, he felt sure he was lost.

By then his hands were trembling and shaking with a palsy he couldn't control, but he had to check his map. He reached into his glove compartment, pulled it out, and began unfolding it. Cursing the inefficiency of his hands, he grappled with the intricately folded paper until he located his general area.

Moving that area back and forth, he tried to find a focal length at which his damaged eyes could read fine print and lines. It was no use. Try as he might, he couldn't read a thing through the stinging, watery haze that kept filming over his eyes.

In anger and frustration, he wadded the map into a ball.

Why now? he wondered. *Just when I'm on the verge of fulfilling my life's great purpose? Dear God . . . why now?*

Then, as that plea passed through his mind, his anger suddenly ceased. As quickly as it had risen, it was swept away by amusement at the fact that, once again in a moment of desperation, he'd called on a deity he knew didn't exist. It was a quirk he'd never really understood about himself; something troubling yet strangely comforting at the same time.

He knew it related to his early childhood, when he and his mother had lived in Germany and she was a devout Christian. But her Catholic beliefs had disappeared from sight when they moved to Russia to live with his strictly Communist stepfather. He was only five when that had happened, so the question was whether his mother's religious practices could have rubbed off on him even as she held him in her lap? To her breasts? *Was it possible?*

Evidently. Something had put it in his mind to a point where even the SINO school's intensive indoctrination had been unable to scour out every vestige. But Lubov had never really worried about it. He knew there was no God, even if some tiny part of his brain still clung to that primitive belief.

In any event, the question was thoroughly moot. In less than an hour he'd be throwing switches that would precipitate a change in the course of history that even God Himself, if He existed, would have to stand back and admire. *He would indeed!*

That thought caused Lubov to smile as much as his head injury permitted. And then he thought of his dear, lovely mother and his stern, hardworking stepfather. What would they think if they could know he was about to become more powerful than any man on earth? Yes, even the equal of a God, if there was one.

Surely they'd be so proud!

Restored somewhat by those thoughts of his past and future, he restarted the Porsche and continued north. He couldn't help feeling certain that even without the map or road signs, he was going to know his turnoff when he came to it. He'd studied it carefully that morning as he exited it on the way south, and now that he'd been refreshed by his rest, he began to remember it.

It was not far ahead. . . . *Not far at all.* . . .

☐ LXXXVI ☐

Even though the *Potkin* didn't send a counterstrike their way,
the *Gremlin*'s crew did have to deal with the shock waves generated by their exploding torpedoes. Those waves sent them bobbing
like a cork on a windy pond, which was a terrifying illustration of
their seemingly rock-solid craft's fragility.

More than anyone else, Jim Stickles was confronted with a bliz-
zard of decisions that had to be made simultaneously. Because one
gutless dimwit had put them technically at war, he hardly knew
where to begin coping with the problems he faced.

Then a voice intruded into his whirling thoughts. "Captain?"

It was Lieutenant Norton Vent, speaking softly and calmly from
his seat in the steering cockpit. Stickles looked at him.

"Sir, may I suggest resuming the chase?"

"All ahead full!" Stickles roared without hesitation.

"May I also suggest," Vent went on, "that we have Lieutenant
Hawkins take over the fire/control board?"

In the deathly silence of the *Gremlin*'s control room, LeBlanc
could hear Vent's murmured suggestion. And so could everyone
else. A dozen pair of hostile eyes focused on LeBlanc, who stiffened
at his post, loath to admit his horrendous blunder.

"No!" he shouted. "You can't get rid of me like that!"

He started bulling his way across the twenty feet that separated
him from his Naval Academy rival, ignoring the fact that his path
would carry him right past Stickles's position.

Vent scrambled out of the cockpit to meet the attack on his feet,
but his efforts were unnecessary. The burly Stickles took a step
forward to lash out with a thumping right cross that caught Le-
Blanc flush on the chin and dropped him like a wet rag.

Stickles glanced down at him, muttering, "Never did trust that
slick sonofabitch. . . ." Then he reached up to the overhead intercom switch and flipped it on. "Lieutenant Hawkins, report to the
control room, on the double!"

Gazing at the prostrate body of his nemesis, Vent eased back into
his cockpit seat, barely able to believe what had happened. It was

finished. Just that quickly. *Finished!* He'd finally triumphed over the man who'd destroyed a full decade of his life.

More importantly, if they somehow managed to survive their battle with the *Potkin,* Dandy would never get over it. *Never!*

□ LXXXVII □

Vito Scarlatti's entire ASW team was stunned by the twin explosions at their backs. Not in any physical sense because they were more than a mile ahead of both. But the psychological shock was devastating because of what it implied.

Typically, Casey Harper was the first to react by shouting into his mike. "What the hell's going on down there? Those clowns trying to start a war or something?"

Scarlatti ignored his comment in favor of finding out who'd opened fire. "Ours or theirs?" he asked.

Bobby Wong double-checked the reverberating echoes on his sonar screens. "They read like Big Macs."

The MK-48s American submarines carried were called "Big Macs," as opposed to the ASW team's MK-46 "Little Macs." Big Macs meant Harper was right: Someone *was* trying to start a war down there. Worse yet, that someone was American!

"What got hit?" Bart Holloway asked from Scarlatti's right. He knew it wasn't the Soviet sub, which was still below them.

"Decoys," Wong replied. "The bogie released them just before it made its move."

"Our guys *fired* on them?" Grady Swenson asked from the left.

"I know it seems stupid to us," Scarlatti said, "but they might know something we don't."

"Ha!" Harper snapped. "Fat chance!"

At that moment, the team rounded enough of the underwater mountain below for Bobby Wong's screens to indicate what their target was up to. He practically jumped out of his seat when he realized the "war" being waged below was apparently over.

"Hallelujah! They're heading down into a canyon!"

Harper was quick to disparage such a fortunate turn of events. "It has to be some kind of trick!"

"Rave on, Mr. Optimism!" Wong shot back. "Those torpedoes must've convinced 'em we mean business!"

"Maybe those guys on the shadow *did* know something," Scarlatti added. Then to Wong, "How big is the canyon?"

Wong punched numbers into a keyboard, then checked the readouts. "Plenty big enough . . . Five miles long, averages a half mile wide, a quarter mile at its narrowest. Hell, they could hide a battalion of subs down in that thing."

"Must be our lucky day," Scarlatti said.

Harper wasn't letting him off that easy. "What about after we ditch, but before our backups get here? What if the Russians try to come up then? Our shadow sub can't cover five miles!"

"No problem," Scarlatti countered. "Once those guys find a hole to crawl in, we won't hear from them again until the evening news. Face it, man—it's as good as over."

"These things are never over till the shit hits the fan!"

"Rave on, Mr. Optimism," Scarlatti muttered as he pressed the intership-mode switch to talk to his wingmen.

"All right, guys, listen up! There's a five-mile-long mini-Grand Canyon stretched out in front of us, and it looks like the bogie's going down there to ride out the hassle. All we need to do now is cover it end-middle-end until we have to ditch. Bart, you and Grady move ahead and split up. Bart, take the west end; Grady, take the middle; we'll stay right here. Got it?"

"Roger!" Holloway and Swenson replied.

Both ships began pulling away as Swenson thought to add one final bit of camaraderie. "Last one in the soup buys the beer!"

"Deal!" Scarlatti called out. "And may the best man lose!"

□ LXXXVIII □

The three-dimensional relief map of the Out Island Group had been moved from Barzlin's quarters to the *Potkin*'s control room so he could follow their progress on it. And apart from the unexpected torpedo volley, everything up to that point had gone precisely as he'd anticipated. So as he stood poring over the map, he was eager to chart their next step on it.

As they entered the stone cleft that was the underwater canyon, Chief Kim justified his captain's growing confidence by reporting that their engines were starting to bounce faint echoes off its jagged rock walls. That was clear confirmation of one of the two fundamental aspects of Barzlin's plan.

The first aspect was that sound generates echoes in any canyon, above or below water. The second was that it carries much better through water than through air. Ironically, it was that very phenomenon of sound carrying so well in water that the Americans had used so successfully for so long against their Soviet foes. Now Barzlin intended to take those damnable listening devices and turn them on their masters.

"Five-hundred-meters depth, sir!" Lemnotova called out from his navigation console.

"Four-hundred-meters port clearance, two-hundred starboard!" Kim added, announcing that moment's relationship between their vessel's fragile "skin" and the convoluted canyon walls.

Barzlin glanced at Lemnotova's depth and attitude needles to gauge their precise location and orientation, then he turned to Damovitch, standing at the gunnery board. "Release decoys!"

Immediately came the soft *squish, squish, squish* of compressed-air bursts expelling decoys from opposite tubes at the front, middle, and rear of the boat. As soon as all six were clear, they began sending out sound waves that filled the entire eastern half of the canyon. They multiplied themselves ad infinitum by creating echoes as they twisted and turned through all quadrants, bouncing off whatever they encountered.

Until that thick blanket of noise faded back into silence, there was no way the Americans tracking the *Potkin* could pick out its prop or engine sounds, or "see" the shape of its hull.

That meant Barzlin and his crew had twelve minutes of escape time—the twelve it would take for their decoys to wind down.

Admirals Horton and Tarnaby were back at the PACCOM command bubble's consoles, standing alongside Rogers and Kelly. All four were staring intently at the central screen as the canyon graphic on it slowly filled with a solid block of snowy green haze.

"What's happening?" Tarnaby asked Horton.

"They released more decoys in that canyon!" Horton snapped.

"Is that bad?"

"Bad? They'll blind every tracking instrument out there until they wind down!"

Tarnaby wanted to follow that up, but Horton's agitation forced him to back off. Rogers noticed his anxiety and whispered to him, "The *Potkin's* instruments are tuned to ignore their own sounds, sir. They'll see everything perfectly."

Tarnaby whispered back, "So?"

"So when the *Gremlin* gets there, it won't be able to see torpedoes coming out of the haze. And since it fired first . . ."

He left that thought for Tarnaby to finish in his own mind.

When he did, his face revealed the anguish of his sudden understanding. "Oh, my God . . ." he muttered.

Barzlin stood near the relief map laid out on a chart table, double-checking his calculations. Suddenly Lemnotova called out from his navigating console. "Six hundred meters, sir!"

"Clearance?" he shouted in return.

"Three-zero-eight, port!" sonarman Kim called out. "Three-five-five, starboard!"

That's it! He turned to Diving Officer Leonid Sarlov. The bespectacled Professor looked eager. "Commence maneuver!"

Without hesitation Sarlov pulled back hard on the bowplane lever. The *Potkin's* nose lifted sharply. Up, up, up the great leviathan pointed, until every hand was forced to hold on to something to keep from keeling over backward.

At the same time Sarlov was aiming the boat up at such a precipitous angle, he turned the wheel sharply to put it into a tight, rolling maneuver. That created a sensation several men on board remembered from their youth: a fairground ride that twisted in a spiral as it went around on its axis arm.

Up, up, up and over, over, over—until the *Potkin* executed an underwater loop-the-loop with a twist. Then it was upright and pointed back in the direction it had just come from, totally invisible to the ASW force and the submarine stalking it.

"Good work, Lieutenant Sarlov!" Barzlin called to his ace Diving Officer. "All ahead full!"

The Professor beamed happily in return, as did everyone else in the control room. Whatever their captain was trying to engineer, they seemed to be making it happen. But despite having total faith in the crusty old warrior, they couldn't help wondering what would come next. He'd avoided telling them so they'd have no chance to dwell on it and tighten up even more.

Because Barzlin was the only man who knew what was coming after their turnaround, he was far more concerned about it than his crew. He knew that after three or four minutes of flat-out, dead-ahead sprinting, the worst would only be beginning. And since he'd come to loggerheads with Damovitch at their meeting about what he wanted to do, he felt the next few minutes of relative calm would be an opportune time to try to resolve their differences.

"Commander Damovitch, would you join me here, please?"

Damovitch was on his way to the chart table before Barzlin could reach his pointer stick.

□ LXXXIX □

As Nat predicted, he and Karen found Marsh's land parcel listed in the Lumberton courthouse records. The county clerk then gave them directions to it, and they were soon back on Highway 16, the two-laned byroad that twisted and turned from the eastern base of the San Jose Mountains, up and over to Highway 1 at the western base's coastline. Marsh's cabin was somewhere near the midpoint, on a plateau between two ridges.

Getting to it was just a matter of going a few more miles.

Since learning the real reason behind Nat's relentless pursuit of the King, Karen had been wrestling with her conscience. In fact, knowing why it wasn't simply a hunter-quarry chase was causing her to question her own role in the affair.

Even more disturbing was the shadow of doubt it cast on Nat. *Is he worth my effort? Can I trust him?* She had no choice but to try to find out. "How will things go once we get there?"

"If Marsh is around," Nat said, "I'll confront him face-to-face. Tell him I think he's the King, and I'm out to prove it."

"Wouldn't it be better to investigate behind his back?" she countered. "So he doesn't know what you're doing?"

"Maybe . . . But my way does the job too. Sure, it'll make him more careful, which will make it harder to monitor him. But it gives me the satisfaction of knowing he's always out there somewhere, sweating, just waiting for me to tighten the noose."

"You're that sure you can nail him, huh?"

He nodded vigorously. "If that bastard *is* the King, then his ass is mine! All I have to do is keep putting one foot in front of the other for as many times as it takes."

"No matter what he does to dodge you?"

He looked at her with his dark eyes blazing. "The harder he tries to get away from me, the more I'll enjoy pinning him down."

She let that ride for several seconds, hoping he'd realize he was carrying his grudge to an extreme. Then something else occurred to her. "What if he's not there?"

Nat shrugged. "No problem. We'll just have a look around . . . see what we can see."

"Outside? Or inside?"

Nat shrugged again. "He won't be keeping his rig outside."

"In other words," she pressed, "you plan to break in."

"If I can," he said with a questioning glance at her. "You sound like you have a problem with that."

She did. Though investigative reporting sometimes carried her over the line of strict legality, she always avoided flagrant abuses. The prospect of getting caught was just too distressing.

"I'm with you all the way," she said. "You know that. But maybe breaking and entering is pushing things a little too far."

His jaw muscles rippled. "Stay in the car if you have cold feet. But if he's not there, *I'm* going in."

That harsh response only increased her doubts about him.

□ xc □

Barzlin and Damovitch stood over the relief map as the tip of
the captain's pointer traced out the path he was projecting.

"We're here at this moment," he began, indicating a spot one
mile from the eastern end of the canyon.

At that eastern terminus the canyon quickly narrowed from a
quarter mile in width, to disappear completely into the western
flank of Peak 28. Also at that eastern terminus, a narrow ravine
branched to the right and circled halfway around Peak 28's southern flank. It was little more than a crack in the rock caused by an
underwater land shift in some long-ago cataclysm.

But it was the key factor in Barzlin's plan.

"In three minutes we will enter this ravine," he went on, placing
his pointer in its slender throat.

Damovitch blanched with shock. "Impossible!" he rasped. "It's
no more than . . . fifty meters wide!"

"That's wide enough! We must be extremely careful, yes. But our
training has been adequate; Sarlov has the nerves for it; and I've
checked every calculation twice. We can do it!"

Damovitch knew it was pointless to argue. Death from a rup-
tured hull was the same as death dropped from above. Death was
death. At least they'd be *trying* to fulfill their mission.

"All right," he agreed. "What next?"

Barzlin curled the pointer tip along the ravine's narrow, curved
length until it reached an area very near the end. That left the tip
centered on Peak 28's southeast flank.

"We should be here when our decoys wind down—" he said.

Suddenly, in the pressure-packed atmosphere of the *Potkin*'s
control room, Damovitch grasped his captain's shrewd intention.
Utterly transformed, he muttered, "—just as we empty our ballast
tanks, cut our engines, and start rising to the surface!"

Barzlin nodded at his replacement's typically quick uptake.

When Damovitch spoke again, it was with the hushed whisper
of someone afraid his voice might burst a beautiful bubble. "Can so
simple a plan . . . actually work?"

Barzlin shrugged. "Why not? The American instruments key on our sounds. If we're making none after the decoys wind down, they have to know *exactly* where to look to find us."

Still on the uptake, Damovitch added, "And since they'll assume we're hiding in the canyon, all their attention will be focused there!" Suddenly, his mind shifted to another, more worrisome problem. "What about the helicopters?"

"It's impossible to guess how many are above us. Perhaps three, more likely six, maybe even nine . . . It doesn't matter." He fanned his hands above the canyon's entire length. "Whatever number will be forced to spread evenly across this area."

He then moved the pointer tip about 100° around the southern half of the white-topped pinnacle called Traynor Island. It stopped at a spot very near the southeast escarpment.

"Meanwhile, our forward momentum should carry us to the surface approximately here, as close to the edge of the island as possible. That way its mass will block their view of us and they won't know we've risen until their satellites inform them. Naturally, if the weather overhead is as bad as Popov claims . . ."

Damovitch nodded, glancing over at Popov and Rykoff. Both radiomen were sitting tensely before their consoles, waiting to relay the message that had put all their lives in such jeopardy.

"What about the American radio monitors?" he asked.

"If all goes as it should," Barzlin replied, "the message will be completed before they can intercept it, inform their helicopters of what's happening, and then come to stop us."

"Captain!" Sonar Chief Kim called from across the room. "We're nearing the end of the canyon!"

"Cut speed by half!" Barzlin called out to Sarlov as he started moving from the chart table.

Damovitch stopped him by grabbing his elbow. He wanted to clear up one final point of concern. "What about the submarine?"

"We must hope its captain isn't a fool."

"Can we expect that of a man who fires torpedoes at decoys?"

Barzlin smiled faintly. "A madman isn't necessarily a fool."

The two men locked eyes for a brief moment, as regret about

past attitudes wordlessly passed between them. Then the captain turned to assume his critical duties behind Kim's sonar screens, while the captain-to-be resumed his place at the gunnery board.

□ XCI □

In the *Gremlin's* control room, LeBlanc had been roused to consciousness and hustled off to confinement in his cabin. He'd be dealt with further when and if they made it through the crisis his breakdown had precipitated. Now Lieutenant Hawkins was at the gunnery board and, like everyone else, anxious to do well.

Captain Stickles was leaning over the shoulder of sonarman Rodrigues as their boat rounded the northern flank of Peak 28. When the canyon beyond came into view on the screens, it looked like a pale green cloud hovering below them.

"Jesus H. Christ!" Stickles shouted to the room in general. "Cut all engines! They released decoys in some kind of canyon!"

"Cut all engines, aye!" came Norton Vent's confirmation.

Stickles took a last look at the shrewd tactic revealed on the sonar screens, then he turned to face the younger men in the room. Each nervously awaited his next order. Since that decision could well mean everyone's death, the burden of command bore down extra heavily on the captain's slumped shoulders.

"We're blind, men," he stated matter-of-factly. "If we go any farther before those decoys stop transmitting, we'll be a sitting duck for a point-blank belly-shot."

A blood-chilling silence permeated the control room. Then Vent cleared his throat to voice the obvious next question. "Can we afford to hang back, sir?"

Stickles faced the slight young lieutenant sitting in the steering cockpit. "Our orders are to do everything necessary to keep them off the surface. As long as they're down there releasing decoys, I'd say we're doing our job."

There was no hint of cowardice or rationalization in his tone. He simply responded with the analytical perception of a man better suited to teaching than reacting to the unexpected.

Vent glanced around to see if anyone else would press on, but he found all eyes directed his way. The ball was clearly in his court. "What if they're throwing up some kind of smoke screen? Maybe a run for it at the other end of the canyon?"

That illustrated why Vent had one of the highest efficiency ratings among the Navy's junior officers. He had intelligence *and* initiative. Stickles nodded in appreciation of his analysis.

"Rodrigues!" he suddenly snapped. "How big's that canyon?"

"Five miles, sir—give or take" came the reply.

He turned back to Vent. Even in this crucial situation, he couldn't keep the instructor in him from taking a turn. "Five miles, Vent. Impossible for us to cover end-to-end. Does that mean the ASW team has to handle it alone?"

"Negative, sir," Vent countered, getting into the spirit of the lesson. "If they have to ditch before it comes up, we'll be held accountable. And since we know they're low on fuel, we're obligated to maintain our support capacity."

Stickles smiled vaguely. "So what do you suggest we do?"

"I'd position us high over the center of the canyon. If the Russians sneak to the surface anywhere along it, we can hit them with surface-to-surface missiles, which decoys can't protect them from. We might take them out late, but we will take them out. We might even get lucky and cut off some of their relay."

"What about the belly-shot we'll be giving them if we hang up near the surface like that?" Stickles pressed.

"The farther we are from the haze, sir, the better chance we have of seeing an attack coming. And if one does come, we at least have some ability to maneuver away from it. But if we stay where we are, or move out low, we have no chance at all."

Stickles broke into a beaming grin. "Excellent, Vent! My feelings exactly!" He turned to the others in the room to express his admiration. *"That* is what a training cruise is all about, gentlemen! Learn while you earn!"

He turned back to Vent and settled into the task at hand. "All ahead flank! Depth one-zero-zero!"

Vent couldn't suppress the grin splitting his narrow face. "Depth one-zero-zero, aye, sir!"

☐ XCII ☐

Like his American counterpart, Captain Barzlin hung over his own sonarman's shoulder to see if his opposite number would decide to hover somewhere above the canyon, or simply hang there on the mountain's flank to await further developments.

When the upper-left sonar screen showed the *Gremlin* speeding away, he realized he'd guessed correctly: The American captain *wasn't* a fool. He'd chosen the safest, most viable option at his disposal—the one Barzlin had counted on him selecting.

Once that issue was settled, he turned his attention to the remaining three sonar screens, which gave their left side, right side, and bottom clearance from the jagged walls of the narrow ravine they'd slipped into only moments before. For the next six minutes he'd be taking his astonished crew through a nerve-racking sequence of rapid course adjustments.

Fortunately, each man involved in moving the boat was fully capable of negotiating in close quarters. Especially Lieutenant Sarlov, the nearsighted, would-be fighter pilot who was finally getting a chance to maximize his steering capacities. So Barzlin felt confident they could maintain the flat-out pace necessary to curl them out of sight around the mountain.

Despite that optimism, however, no one was more aware than Barzlin of what would happen if they did more than graze one of the ravine's walls. They'd slash their hull open, implode the boat, and cause the tremendous water pressure at that depth to squeeze everyone on board into ghastly caricatures of human beings.

Nevertheless, something in their perilous situation was profoundly uplifting to the captain's worn spirits. After so many years of insisting to the Presidium that a time might come when precision handling of a submarine would pay big dividends, he'd lived to see it happen. And not only had he lived to see it happen, he'd be its primary beneficiary!

That was a great personal achievement for him, something to almost mitigate his failure to relay the message promptly.

Almost, but not quite . . .

* * *

In the Padre Island NAVFAC, Hanna Buckley sat before her console monitoring screens, totally baffled. Then O-T Dennis Stone called out to her from his post at the #4 sensor, along the opposite wall's row of machines.

"Still nothing but fuzz coming from the canyon, sir!"

"Come take a look at this," she said with an edgy tone.

Stone crossed the room and took a position behind her shoulder. He was in his early thirties and one of the best O-Ts in the rotation, so Hanna felt it was prudent to consult him.

He gazed at the left screen, which was a high-angle view of the entire canyon. The right screen was a close view of the *Gremlin* leaving the northwest flank of Peak 28, rising above the snow-clogged trench in the earth below.

"Does any of this make sense to you?" Hanna asked.

Stone wasn't used to being called over to give advice to O-WOs, so he hedged to be sure of his ground. "In what way?"

"In *any* way!" she snapped.

This bizarre situation was combining with her extreme fatigue to push her beyond the edge of civility. She had to struggle to lower her voice to a respectable level.

"I mean," she went on, "PACCOM says the Russians have a critical message they're supposed to relay. Okay? But instead of making for the surface, they hide down in a canyon. Why?"

Stone shrugged noncommittally. "No guts?"

"C'mon, get serious! What could they be trying to pull?"

"Why do they have to be trying to pull something, sir? If I were in their shoes, I'd be telling myself this is a perfect instance where discretion is the better part of valor."

"Yeah, right!" Hanna said mockingly. "How would you like to try selling *that* to their Presidium?"

Stone turned away, muttering, "Bitch, bitch, bitch . . ."

☐ XCIII ☐

One of Chief Popov's duties was keeping track of the decoy life spans, which he did with characteristic precision.

"Three minutes, sir!" he called out.

"Left two degrees!" Barzlin called from his position behind Sonar Chief Kim. "Down one!"

"Left two degrees, down one!" Lieutenant Sarlov repeated from his seat in the steering cockpit.

As Barzlin kept calling out those rapid, excruciatingly precise rudder and bowplane adjustments, Sarlov kept smoothly curving the *Potkin* around the ragged southwestern and southern skirt of Peak 28. But even the Professor's icy nerves and raw courage were being pushed to their absolute limits.

Sweat beads were glistening on his pale, freckled brow.

As Damovitch surmised earlier, it was Barzlin's intention to race through the ravine at full speed until just before the decoys ran down, then blow their ballast tanks, cut the engines, and silently drift up from wherever they'd managed to reach.

If all went according to plan, they'd break the surface in the shadow of Traynor Island's southeastern escarpment, which should shield them from sighting by any ASW helicopters hovering over the canyon beyond the western escarpment.

Those helicopters wouldn't know the *Potkin* had surfaced until they were informed by satellite, if the weather was clear enough, or by radio monitoring stations once the message was being relayed. That is, unless they were hovering much higher than the island's fifty-meter crest. But since there was no way an SH-3H could go that high and still maintain sonar contact, it was a virtual certainty the *Potkin* would surface undetected.

Barzlin had factored several other considerations into his plan, even ones that defied anyone else's powers of anticipation. And though each crisis point had held serious elements of risk, up to now each had gone his way. He could only wonder if, once they were on the surface, his luck would hold through the few minutes it would take to transmit the message.

* * *

Seaman Stone was back with his sensors as Hanna Buckley sat punching up different canyon views on her monitors. Those pale green graphics continually shifted as she pushed button after button on her console, twisting and turning her view, zooming close and moving back, desperately trying to determine what was going on in the ocean area she was responsible for.

Where is it? What are they up to?

She went all the way to the eastern end of the canyon to begin a methodical, section-by-section check. She rotated the scene so that her viewpoint was directly above it. Suddenly, a faint green line became visible, snaking away to the right.

What? There shouldn't be any sound there!

She zoomed into a close-up of the faint green line and realized it was a narrow fault in the mountain's base. She punched some buttons and a readout flashed on her left-side monitor: "AV WID —48 meters, AV DEP—62 meters." *Big enough!*

She tracked the fault around the southwestern and southern flanks of Peak 28. Its whole length was filled with the same green snow as was in the main canyon. That told her something was *in the crack,* bouncing echoes like the ones in the gorge!

It was possible a decoy had miraculously wandered into the fault's narrow opening. But there was absolutely no way one of those twisting, turning machines could move very far along it. So Hanna felt certain she'd figured out what the Russians were trying to do. And it was chillingly, frighteningly brilliant.

Her next step was to wait until the decoys died down and the green haze faded. Then she'd have to monitor the south-southeast rim of the fault. If she was right, somewhere along it she'd find the *Potkin,* sliding up like a checkered ghost. If she was wrong, no one would ever know what she'd suspected.

Either way, she felt she couldn't lose.

□ XCIV □

The black Corvette rolled to a halt at the far right side of the empty parking area in front of Marsh's cabin. Nat parked there to take advantage of the shade cast by a drooping old elm. He killed the engine and quietly studied the bucolic scene spread beyond the car's windshield. The rustic cabin seemed to melt into and become a part of the forested property surrounding it.

"Looks like nobody's home," he said, referring to the empty parking area and the tightly shuttered windows.

"Is this the kind of place he needs to phreak?" Karen asked.

"Absolutely," Nat said, opening his door and stepping out onto the parking area's gravel drive. "Maximum safety from all forms of technical monitoring, with a minimal chance of being accidentally discovered by people. Couldn't be better."

He pulled on his blue blazer, then pointed to the aluminum shed Lubov had noticed when he first arrived, the one connecting the thick black electrical cable to the cabin. "See that?"

She nodded as she opened her door and got out. "Yes . . ."

"The cable's linked to his power source, and inside the shed there's an emergency generator connected to a surge-suppressor."

"What's that?" she asked as she pulled her own jacket on.

"Out here in the country, power's not as reliable as it is in the cities. So he'd have to protect his equipment from flow inconsistencies. Bet that sucker's a monster."

"Why?"

"Look at the size of the cable! No telling what one that big can accommodate."

She considered for a moment, then said, "Why didn't Brandt or Doppler or any of their people figure that out?"

"Wouldn't occur to them. Only a serious phreak or hacker would understand the need for something like that way out here."

They both stood there scrutinizing the cabin itself, until Nat said, "Care to join me for a small reconnoiter?"

She took a deep breath, squeezed it out, then resolutely nodded her head. "Of the outside, okay . . ."

He returned her nod, then led her along the flagstone walkway. When they reached the three board steps that led up to the rough-hewn porch, he stopped and turned to her.

"Just to be on the safe side," he whispered, "let's keep our voices low and move around quietly. You never know . . . maybe some-one dropped him off and he's in there after all."

They tiptoed up onto and across the porch, then edged over to one of the heavily shuttered front windows. Nat pressed his ear to the wood and listened intently. He couldn't hear a thing.

"Sounds empty," he muttered.

From the window he led her back to the front door, where he knocked loudly. No answer. He then tried its handle to see if it would open. No such luck. He then returned to the shutter and tried opening it. He could have guessed it wouldn't budge.

He then led her down off the porch and around the cabin's right side, where they found every other window shuttered against out-side viewing. Then they came to a smaller back porch and its door, which was also locked tight.

"Guy knows how to keep intruders out, doesn't he?" Nat said.

"Like Santa knows Christmas," she replied. "So what now?"

He looked at her without the least sign of frustration. "We figure out where he hid the key, then we walk in."

He was already on his way back to the front when she said, "Wait! What are you saying? The place is sealed up like Fort Knox, and he's got a key under the doormat? Give me a break!"

"Nothing as simple as that," he agreed, "but there *is* a key around here somewhere. Has to be. Nobody in their right mind would have a place this far from their main residence and not keep a spare hidden somewhere. You know, in case their pocket key got lost or stolen or whatever."

By then they were back at the front porch, and Nat leapt up the three steps in one energetic bound. The excitement of his pursuit had him practically dancing.

"What if he comes back while we're inside?" Karen said as she took the more traditional way up. "I mean, he could have us ar-rested for trespassing!"

"Naaaah!" Nat insisted as he began looking all around the front door's floor area. "We'll just say we stopped by to have a friendly little chat, found the front door open, assumed that meant *mi casa, su casa;* so we came in to take a load off our feet. An honest mistake anyone might make."

Hearing that, there was no way for Karen to avoid drawing the obvious conclusion: Given half a chance, Nat Perkins could be one crafty, ruthless sonofabitch. Which meant her doubts about him were more valid—and pressing—than she'd thought.

"Besides," he went on, his eyes moving from the floor up to the recessed ledge above the doorframe, "the cable and that shed are strong indications he's got a major-league phreaking rig hidden inside. So technically I'm just doing my job."

"Your job isn't to break the law," she reminded him.

"But it *is* to get results!" he suddenly snapped at her. "Now back off and start acting like a partner, or go sit in the car. I don't care which way you choose, but dammit, choose!"

His harsh tone blasted her into reflective silence.

Placing aside her personal doubts about him, she knew she was on solid ethical ground with her complaint. He had a right—even a duty—to pursue his objective with any legitimate means at his disposal. But the emphasis was on *legitimate,* and he was heading off into some shadowland of moral and legal quicksand.

Her thoughts were suddenly interrupted by a gleeful shout from Nat: "Ah-*ha!*" She watched as he reached up to gingerly pull down something affixed to the cabin's upper doorframe.

He held it out to her so she could see it up close. When she saw what it was, she promptly skittered away, mobilized by an ageless childhood fear of stinging insects. *"Aiiieeeee!"*

Nat just gazed at it, muttering, "You clever bastard . . ."

☐ XCV ☐

The green haze in the Out Island canyon began to fade as Hanna Buckley programmed a continuous scan of the last half of the fault at the base of Peak 28. She'd figured out that if the *Potkin* was in fact using that fault as an escape hatch, the hatch cover would probably be somewhere in the southeast quadrant, as far away as possible from the western, canyon-side quadrant.

After programming the scan, Hanna watched as the C/S/T transponders ratcheted through their monitoring grids like underwater cameras. Then she felt her restless dumpling kick—hard. Placing both hands over her distended belly, she took a deep breath and pressed. She'd found that sometimes soothed it, and she couldn't afford to be distracted now.

Suddenly, she thought she saw something moving on the right-side monitor. She expelled her held breath with a *whoosh* of excitement, then stopped that monitor's ratcheting in mid-scan. She clicked it back—*click, click, click*—then focused on a spot about one hundred meters from the end of the fault.

Zooming in for a close-up, she called out to O-T Dennis Stone. "Number four! Any reading on the southeast flank of Traynor Island, about four hundred meters down?"

Stone bent over the #4 sensor and called on all his skill as a gram-sheet interpreter. "Hard to say, sir," he concluded. "There *is* something here. Maybe a blip from a ballast blowout. But there's too much covering noise to be sure."

Blowing out their ballast tanks made sense if they were . . .

And then she saw it. *Gotcha!*

It was a checked-sausage outline canted at a 45° angle, gliding upward and curling around the stationary wire-sculpture background of Peak 28. It looked to be spiraling up as close to the mountain's natural slope-angle as it could maintain with reasonable safety.

Infused now with the energy of accomplishment, Hanna once more opened the special console drawer that contained her direct phone link to PACCOM in Hawaii. As she lifted the receiver, she felt her baby kicking again. She paused to give it a reassuring pat while wondering what effect her discovery was going to have.

Then she punched in the proper code and number.

☐ XCVI ☐

When the *Potkin*'s decoys finally faded into silence, massive relief swept the PACCOM Situation Room. It looked as if the Russians had decided to, in effect, hoist a white flag, knowing the U.S.

wouldn't risk exacerbating its image problems by sinking them when they were down. They could simply stay in the canyon and wait for their own vessels to come and escort them to safety.

Despite the Situation Room's relief, Horton and Tarnaby knew they were only past the worst of it. There would still be much hell to pay as a consequence of the *Gremlin's* actions. So they were locked in a private discussion about possible approaches to take with Moscow and the media, when the command bubble's interfloor buzzer sounded. That meant someone at the main-floor instrument deck was calling for help from a higher authority.

Horton and Tarnaby glanced at Rogers as he lifted the console receiver. Though tension in the bubble had greatly diminished, he still spoke in a muted whisper. "Yes . . . ?"

A shrill female voice from out on the floor came ripping into his ear. "Sir! Padre Island just reported the *Potkin* rising, engines off, on the southeast side of Traynor Island!"

"Jesus!" Rogers gasped into the bubble's quiet. "Depth?"

"Three hundred meters, rising fast! P-I says they might've blown their ballast tanks just before the decoys went dead!"

"Punch it up on the big screen—over and under view!"

"Already ordered, sir!"

Rogers cradled the receiver while staring transfixed at the big central viewing screen. It changed into the fractured lines and squiggles that meant a new perspective was being called up from the millions it was capable of delivering.

"What is it?" Horton asked as he and Tarnaby moved beside Rogers and Kelly at the console.

"Padre Island found the *Potkin* surfacing on the southeast side of Traynor Island," Rogers replied in a lifeless tone that indicated the degree of his shock and disbelief. "It's coming up silent, like a cork . . . tanks blown, engines off."

That same sense of shocked disbelief riveted the other three men in the bubble as all four waited for the picture on the central screen to clear. They could only wonder what fluke of luck had tipped off Padre Island to the Russian captain's grand strategy, because grand it most definitely was.

Each man felt in his heart of hearts that he could never have been as resourceful, especially in such desperate circumstances.

How in hell did they get themselves around—?

That thought was interrupted as the central monitor's left half filled with a split-screen image of the graph-paper *Potkin*, gliding up in front of Peak 28's wire-sculpture shoals. Blinking red meter marks followed beside it: 250 . . . 245 . . . 240 . . . 235 . . ."

The screen's right half was a satellite shot of Traynor's southeast side and the choppy sea around it. Despite scattered clouds left by the departing weather front, visibility was decent. A light-beam dot marked where the *Potkin* was expected to surface, 200 yards from the island's southeast escarpment.

Peak 28's jagged basalt cap had one square mile of bare surface rising only 150 feet above the water. In bad storms its sinuous top got washed by spray from giant swells crashing into it. At that moment, for those watching its unfolding role in the impending conflict, it was the ugliest hunk of rock in the world.

"Get me Scarlatti!" Horton bellowed.

Kelly was already on it, punching in the necessary radio codes to contact the hovering ASW team. "Right away, sir!"

Horton moved to the console microphone and bent his taut frame into a bow above it. Then Lieutenant Vito Scarlatti's static-laced voice filled the command bubble. "Delta One, over!"

"Scarlatti, this is Admiral Horton! What's your team's position and status?"

"I'm about a mile west of Traynor Island, sir! Holding at a hundred feet and waiting for relief! My wingmen are already down, and I'm almost out of fuel!"

"Listen carefully, son!" Horton went on, speaking with barely controlled urgency. "Your target is surfacing on the southeast side of the island—*right now*! It's almost up, but there's still time to get over and complete your mission!"

"Aye, sir!"

Static filled the command bubble as the SH-3H's rotor speed accelerated, and the big bird leapt up and away heading south-southeast. Then Scarlatti came back on in a worried tone to ask his final question. "And, sir . . . ? Use Little Macs?"

The choice was that or depth charges, which might not be destructive enough to do what needed to be done. But to use Little Macs at point-blank range would mean the *Potkin*'s total destruction, the cold-blooded murder of many—if not most—of its seamen, and a diplomatic embarrassment of monumental proportions. In short, a full-blown political disaster.

Lucius Horton understood those consequences, but what else could he do? The lag before he answered Scarlatti's question was so he could take a last deep breath before the plunge.

"Right, use Little Macs! That message *must* be stopped!"

"Aye, sir!" Scarlatti repeated and clicked off his radio.

As the eerie silence of impending doom filled the command bubble, Horton's dark eyes left the screens to gaze at Tarnaby. "You know whose neck's going on the block for this, don't you?"

"You're only following orders!" Tarnaby rasped. "They can't do anything to you for that!"

"Every disaster needs a scapegoat," Horton said wearily, knowing he'd be it and feeling a perverse relief in that certainty. "Hell, Washington will be damn lucky if all the Kremlin wants is my head on a platter."

Horton turned back to the main screen, which had filled with a wide-angle shot that included Scarlatti's SH-3H and the spot where the nearly surfaced *Potkin* would appear. He'd done all he could as effectively as he knew how to do it, yet that was going to mean the end of his career . . . and possibly even his freedom.

He felt like throwing up.

Meanwhile, Tarnaby watched the SH-3H lift up to clear the western escarpment, heading for its rendezvous with destiny. He knew Soviet satellites would be transmitting the same scene back to Moscow, and it sickened him to think that in about two minutes the *Potkin* would be blown to pieces.

He also knew there was no way anyone in Moscow would settle for any kind of apology or compensation for a seemingly unprovoked loss of that magnitude. They'd want revenge and lots of it, and retribution would certainly include the man who'd given the direct order to fire. So Tarnaby reached over to place a comforting hand on his friend's slumped shoulder.

There was nothing else he could do or say—at least, nothing Horton didn't already know.

□ XCVII □

Karen watched, fascinated, as Nat figured out and then explained to her the brilliance of Marsh's hiding place for the key to his cabin. *Who'd have ever thought . . . ?*

When he finished explaining, he put the key in the lock and turned it, gleefully muttering, "Momma said there'd be days like this, but she never said how much I'd enjoy them!"

"Quit gloating," she chided, still reluctant to go inside.

"Gloating?" he said as he cracked the door open. "Who's gloating? This is *way* beyond gloating. This is ecstasy!"

He cautiously poked his head inside, looked around, then shouted, "Helloooo! Hey! Anybody home?"

He waited several moments, then tried again, this time opening the door all the way. "Here we come, ready or not!"

Still no reply.

He grinned confidently as he replaced the key and wasp nest exactly like he'd found them. Then he stepped into the dimness beyond the doorframe, found the light switch, flicked it on, and turned to face Karen. "After you." He bowed low and made a sweeping gesture with his arm. *"Madame, s'il vous plaît."*

Here it was: her moment of truth. She considered everything one last time, then decided she had more to gain by going along willingly than she stood to lose by hanging back. After all, she might miss something important. So she took a deep breath, forced a brittle smile, then moved past him with a mocking quip.

"Right—send *me* in first to face Custer's last stand."

He stepped in and eased the door almost shut, saying, "Huh?"

"Didn't you see the same slides I saw? Look at this place! If General Custer didn't decorate it, I want to know who did."

He gazed at the Wild West motif. "I see what you mean."

"All that's missing is a cigar-store Indian."

Despite the jovial bantering, both were uptight about what they were doing. She could see it in his darting eyes, while he could hear it in her cracking voice. But both were the type to see commitments through to the end; and despite going along reluctantly, she'd committed herself to checking the place out.

Nat cautiously moved past the living room's wood-and-leather furniture, heading for the hallway that went to the bedrooms and baths. Karen crept along behind him, feeling guilty yet excited, realizing this kind of malfeasance was a lot easier to go along with from behind someone's back.

He led her on a quick tour, starting with the two smallest bedrooms. They were served by one bathroom, and none of the three looked as if anyone had been in them for years.

A thin but obvious layer of dust was on everything.

The third bedroom was much larger and contained a mass of typical bachelor clutter around an unmade bed. That could only mean it was the room Marsh used whenever he stayed there.

"What a mess!" Nat muttered when they entered it.

"That's not a mess—that's a Dumpster with a door!"

He smirked, then headed for that bedroom's bathroom. It revealed that someone had used it to take a shower that morning. A bath towel and a washcloth were still slightly damp. The towel also had some faint pink stains on it, which they couldn't figure out and so dismissed as unimportant.

Once they understood the cabin's layout, Nat showed her how to participate in a detailed wall-thump, banging away every few feet to make sure no secret spaces were hidden from plain view.

When he'd satisfied himself that he could account for every square foot of the single-floor living area, his eyes drifted upward to the rough-hewn timbers used for the ceiling.

"Maybe the attic," he said, heading back out the front door.

It was late afternoon, and the sun was near the treeline. The temperature had dropped with it. Nat buttoned his blazer and jammed his hands in its pockets. Karen stood in the doorway, holding her jacket lapels across her chest to keep the chill off.

He backpedaled out into the front yard so he could look up at the roofline, moving left, then right, eyes taking in every detail, judging angles and distances. Finally he shook his head.

"Nope, not in the attic. Not even headroom up there." Then he moved forward to the edge of the porch. "Maybe a basement."

He squatted down to try looking under the cabin, but found his view blocked by small logs and chinking all around the base, obviously added on after the original timbers were laid on stump blocks. He had to poke and search, but eventually found a piece of board jammed against the base to cover a fist-sized hole.

The hole looked fresh and allowed a view up under the cabin. But when he looked in it he couldn't see a thing. "Wait a sec," he said as he got up and jogged to the Corvette. He returned moments later, puffing slightly, with a flashlight in hand.

"There's a hole here," he explained. "Looks recently made."

"You need to get in shape," she said as he scanned around through the hole. "You're wheezing through your bay window."

"Hold that thought!" he suddenly exclaimed, eyes riveted on something in the darkness.

She stayed silent as he tracked the light left and right, then up and down. Then he did it again. Then he rocked back on his heels and gazed up at her, looking supremely satisfied.

"There's about twenty feet I can't account for," he said. "I can barely see through around both sides of it, but that central part is pitch-black. It's as if it's been painted over or covered with a black tarp, or something like that, to hide the whole area if anyone ever looked up under here."

"Maybe somebody did," she suggested, thinking of the hole.

"It has to be camouflage for basement walls," he said as he got to his feet and put the flashlight inside his jacket.

"But we didn't find any kind of basement door," she countered as he moved back up onto the porch.

"I know," he replied, "which means it's probably accessed by a trapdoor of some kind. That's the way a lot of backcountry basements are built—with flat, storm-cellar type doors."

"How would you know something like that?" she asked as he brushed past her, back into the living room.

"That's how it's done in Texas. Protects us from tornadoes that can rip houses apart like stacks of kindling."

After he explained that to her, he started stomping his heels all around the living room's leather armchairs and couch. Soon he stopped to focus his attention on the stout oak coffee table resting on the bearskin rug.

After a moment's thought about it, he snapped his fingers, then bent over and shoved the coffee table aside. A big grin split his strained features as the trapdoor's edge appeared.

"Bingo!" he quipped. "Chalk up one for the Cowboy."

"What?" she asked as she bent over to help him push.

"Chalk one for the Cowboy. That was my phreak code name."

By then the table and rug were off the trapdoor, and it was visible to them as they stood over it. Karen glanced at Nat and saw that a sublime expression of relief had transformed his face. She couldn't help leaning over to give him a small kiss on the cheek.

"Congratulations, Cowboy," she murmured. "I'm impressed."

He turned to face her, beaming with satisfaction. "Thanks for the help." Then he leaned down, gripped the trapdoor's handle, and lifted it to see what lay beneath.

A gush of warm, almost hot, air wafted up to greet them. It carried a faintly rank odor, too; something they'd both smelled often enough throughout their lives, but which they had trouble placing when it first reached their nostrils.

They stood staring into the lighted stairwell for several seconds, feeling the machine-generated warmth and smelling the smell. Then Karen voiced what Nat had realized only seconds before.

"Smells like something's dead down there, doesn't it?"

□ XCVIII □

As soon as Scarlatti received Horton's affirmation to use Little Macs against the *Potkin,* he switched off his radio mike to intercom with copilot Casey Harper and sonarman Bobby Wong.

"Well, guys, you heard the man," he said, speaking with the calm assurance of the star basketball player he'd once been, as if at a foul line with one last chance to win a game. "We're arming one and four . . . releasing at optimum target range."

He hit a pair of lever switches, which activated two of the four MK-46s carried like oblong seed pods under their craft's belly. Suddenly, their engine coughed and sputtered, followed by a brief sag in their rotor-blade speed.

That could only mean one thing, which Harper was quick to express. "Shit! We're out of fuel and going down on that rock!"

"Jesus Christ, Casey!" Wong snapped, knowing this time their pessimistic copilot could well be right. "For once in your miserable life, *try* to think positive!"

"Amen!" Scarlatti added forcefully as they crested a low ridge near the center of Traynor Island.

They were startled but not surprised by the view on the other side of the ridge. The *Potkin*'s nose was breaking the surface about a half mile away, less than 200 yards from the jagged cliff face eroded by eons of pounding surf. It lay sideways to them as its sail rose up like a fat black shark fin.

A perfect kill shot. . . .

"Dead ahead!" Scarlatti announced as he moved the SH-3H lower to line up for its torpedo run. "Preparing to release!"

Harper shouted in alarm. "Wait, Vito! Pull up! We have to go out and release over deep water!"

The engine coughed again while Scarlatti moved them lower still. "No time for that!" he shouted back. "It's a shot from midcourt . . . clock running out. . . . We have to make it count!"

"But we're too close to the island! If our eggs hit rocks before they reach the boat, they could blow us out of the sky!"

"I'll make sure they clear the edge, then we'll have about ten seconds to get away!"

"That's enough time!" Wong added.

Desperate to forestall the inevitable, Harper came up with yet another hypothetical calamity. "If our fuel runs out right after we release, we could land in front of our own torpedoes!"

Scarlatti had heard enough. "Casey—shut the fuck up!"

The engine sputtered again . . . resumed . . . but their time aloft was obviously ending. Then the edge of the island passed beneath, and Scarlatti knew the moment had come. "Releasing!"

He hit the levers and two Little Macs dropped free to begin their short, sharply angled descent. He jammed the throttle and yanked back on the stick to lift them up and away from the twin fireballs that would erupt in ten seconds.

Then all hell broke loose.

The blast came beneath and slightly behind them, and only two seconds after release instead of the ten they expected. The concussion sheared off their main rotor blades and tail, followed by a peppering of basalt rubble that bored through the remainder of their craft like magnesium tracers.

Bobby Wong's head was crushed inside his helmet as a big fragment smashed into his face. Then his right thigh was struck, splattering blood, bone, and muscle up where his face used to be.

A piece the size of a shotput tore through Casey Harper's lower back and shattered the Plexiglas canopy of their mortally crippled machine. His torso sagged forward in his safety harness as what was left of his intestines spilled out onto his lap.

His constant dread of disaster had finally paid off.

Only Scarlatti was left coherent enough to understand that their torpedoes had hit a submerged shoal and exploded on impact. Such obstacles were common around islands, and Harper had been justified in his concern about the possibility of hitting one. But the fuel situation had given them no chance to circle around to approach from the deep side.

It was then or never, and their luck hadn't held.

Or maybe the Russians' had.

Vito Scarlatti's biggest regret at that moment wasn't his realization that the only thing that could have saved the *Potkin* had actually happened. It was spending the final seconds of his life knowing he'd blown his last-second shot from midcourt.

□ XCIX □

Lubov rolled his Porsche to a halt in the parking area of Marsh's cabin. He could scarcely believe his arduous journey was finally over. He turned the ignition off in blessed relief because even his car's quiet idle pounded in his ravaged brain.

The country silence washed over him like cool breath.

He was sorely tempted to just lean forward across the steering wheel so he could rest and gather strength for the final push. But he knew even a moment's relaxation might slip him into the unconsciousness he longed for so desperately, but from which he was certain he'd never awake.

This is it . . . he realized. *Only a little longer . . . and then sleep . . . forever. . . .*

He opened the door and lifted his feet out onto the gravel driveway. At his first attempt to stand, his head spun so badly he had to sag back into the seat to collect himself for a second try. Then a sudden wave of nausea left him with no choice.

He poured himself out of the car, down onto his knees, where he endured several heaves that produced a small puddle of dark, bitter stomach bile. He stayed on his knees, head hanging down, until his short, gasping breaths pumped enough oxygen through his body to defeat all the little rebellions surging within it.

When he was finally able to rise to his feet, and then stand unaided, he removed the black Stetson covering the broken crown of his head. During the past couple of hours, it had started weighing more and more heavily on him; and now, despite its support for his wound, removing it was another blessed relief.

He tossed it on the sloping nose of his car, and it slid to the ground. He didn't notice. He was looking at the cabin, looming like a huge dark blot in the watery, shrouded distance.

His vision was so bad by then, he'd driven the last hundred miles at less than forty miles per hour. Anything more and he couldn't distinguish outlines of other vehicles soon enough to react to them. Even so, he was still more or less on schedule, and thoroughly elated now that the worst was past.

Time to get on with it . . . time to make an end.

As he took his first step forward, something flashed in the corner of his right eye—something coming from a dim, shadowy area beneath a large tree. He turned toward it and was hit full in the face by a bright glare of some kind.

Unable to imagine what it might be, he went to investigate.

Ten yards from the tree he figured it out. The late-afternoon sun was shining into the left corner of a dark car's rear fender, casting the glare that had caught his attention.

A car! Someone's here!

He quelled his rising panic with the thought that he could easily be hallucinating. He *had* to be hallucinating! He'd come too far at too much expense to lose it all at the last moment.

Fate couldn't be so twisted!

He stepped to where he thought the car was and reached out a palsied hand. He touched the hard, cool metal of its roofline. With a burst of internal anguish, his knees buckled and he had to lean against the car to keep himself upright.

It's real! Then he had another, more hopeful thought: *Maybe it's just a friend! Someone who doesn't know about the basement!*

Charged with the adrenaline rush that possibility generated, Lubov pushed off the Corvette and staggered toward the flagstone walkway leading up to the cabin. It *had* to be a friend, his stupefied brain reasoned . . . someone who'd heard about Marsh's difficulties and dropped by to offer sympathy or assistance.

Better yet: *A friend will be easy to eliminate!*

He started to reach into his jacket to pull out Gretchko's pistol, but then thought better of it. What if the visitor was watching him approach from inside the cabin? He couldn't let whoever it was see he had a weapon. He had to catch him or her completely by surprise so it could be over in an instant.

Smile! he told himself. *Smile and seem happy!*

☐ c ☐

When the cabin basement's trapdoor was first opened, its heated, fouled air drifted up and out, while cool, clean outside air rolled down and in. So by the time Nat and Karen started making their way down the stairwell, they dismissed and then forgot about the faint odor of death they'd noticed emanating from inside it.

Nat led, with Karen following closely at his back as they crept down. After only a few cautious steps they began hearing the high-pitched, powerful humming of Marsh's primed machines.

"Hear that?" Nat whispered as the sound registered with him.

He stopped moving so Karen could hear it too. She listened for a moment, nodded, then returned his whisper. "What is it?"

He shrugged. "Beats me. . . ." Then he took another step down.

"This gives me the willies!" she couldn't help muttering. "What if he comes back while we're down here?"

"I hope he does," Nat countered. "I'd give anything to see the look on his face when he realizes he's been had."

By then they were nearing the bottom two steps, the ones that turned right and faced out at the horseshoe of equipment.

Nat was first to get a glimpse of its winking, glowing mass, so he stopped moving. Karen was looking down at the spaces between the steps, trying to focus on the blanket-covered bundle shoved under them, so she continued moving and bumped into him.

That slight impact knocked him out of his awestruck reverie.

"Holy shit!" he exclaimed, pointing at all the machinery. "Would you look at *that*?"

Then the stupendous, overwhelming magnitude of it hit him with such force that, as he stepped down onto the floor to move closer to it, he started shouting like a kid at a carnival.

"I don't believe it! It's a monster! And it's alive!"

He whipped around to face Karen, who'd stepped beside him and was looking at it with the same awestruck expression he'd exhibited only moments before. He was pulsing with excitement, literally jumping up and down.

"We've got the bastard now! We've got him! He's all ours!"

"Oh, my God . . ." she finally managed to croak. "It's huge!"

"Huge?" he repeated, laughing. *"Huge?* This is the goddamn Titanic! The Great Pyramid! The Grand Canyon! Godzilla!"

She stayed pragmatic. "Which is the phreaking part?"

That brought him down from the clouds of exultation to begin his first attempts at rationally analyzing what they'd stumbled onto. He stood there for several long seconds, trying to make sense out of what he was looking at. It was impossible.

"I can't tell," he admitted. "Maybe that blue part there in the middle; but it's ten times bigger than the biggest rig I've ever seen." He paused to consider. "If that *is* it, though, he can probably phreak Venus and Mars on it. It reeks capacity!"

He moved into the horseshoe itself, listening to the whine, analyzing the winking, glowing display of lights all around him.

He couldn't get over it. *Incredible . . . just incredible . . .*

Karen gave him several seconds like that, then said, "What's going on with it? Is it doing something, or what?"

He shook his head. "No, I think it's just primed."

"Primed?"

"*Ready* to do something. But don't ask me what."

She swallowed her next question.

About that time his eyes found the two yellow legal tablets stuck off to one side, on the waist-high metal flange circling the horseshoe's inner perimeter as a continuous desk all around it. With the steady hum ringing in his ears and Karen sticking close to his back, he moved over to examine those tablets.

Mismatch, he wondered. *What the hell could that mean?*

"What's that stuff?" she asked. "Looks like hen scratch."

"A flow chart," he replied. "The kind of thing you draw up to organize a computer program. This one's called Mismatch."

He pulled up the rolling chair, sat at the flange-desk, and thumbed through sheet after sheet of Marsh's brainchild.

"Can it tell us what's going on?" she finally asked.

"I sure hope so," he said, grinning wickedly as he glanced around. "That would be a giant red cherry on top of all this!"

Then she had another thought. "Why would he leave it alone and unguarded if he was planning to do something with it?"

Nat shrugged again. "Maybe he leaves it partially primed all the time. Maybe this is its natural state. Hell, it doesn't matter! What matters is that it's here, we've found it, it's running, and we have a golden opportunity to figure out what's going on with it. So what do you say we get busy and make the most of whatever time we have before he gets back, okay?"

Karen glanced worriedly over her shoulder, again subliminally noting the blanket-covered bundle shoved up under the stairwell. "Okay. But if he does get back before we leave, you do all the talking. I'm just along for the ride."

He grinned with absolute delight, then reassuringly patted her bottom. "Don't worry your pretty little head."

She glanced archly at where he was patting. "Looks like you need an anatomy lesson."

This time he laughed out loud. "Sign me up!"

☐ CI ☐

When the *Potkin*'s sail broke the surface, Captain Barzlin's hands were on the periscope's control handles, while his face was pressed tightly against its eyepiece.

Across the control room, Chief Popov activated his powerful sail transmitter to begin the process of contacting Moscow via a communication satellite hovering in space.

The moment the periscope's viewpiece stabbed into air, Barzlin started looking for the trouble he didn't believe would come. He just felt in his bones he was going to win this battle of wits and wills, the same way he'd win chess matches whenever he forced his opponent into making all the wrong moves.

His first view was of an empty sky all around, so his heart and spirit soared. *I was right! We're safe!* But then—like an apparition in a daydreamed nightmare—an SH-3H cleared Traynor Island's central ridge, bearing down hard on their position.

Without considering its effect on his crewmen, he emitted a startled cry as he thought, *Impossible!* All heads in the control room twisted around to see their leader stiffen and press harder against the periscope's eyepiece. *Only one! Why only one?*

"Dive! Dive!" he shouted reflexively, though it was far too late for escape. They were lying broadside to an ASW helicopter hurtling toward them at 200 mph. It would be on top of them in a few seconds, probably after dropping torpedoes at their flank.

Suddenly, an endgame thought flashed through his mind, as if he'd just found himself checkmated. *We're finished!*

As that thought formed in his brain, he saw the two MK-46s drop from the SH-3H's undercarriage, nosing down side by side, measure for measure, putting his vessel only seconds away from destruction. *But how? Why? I did everything right!*

Then, like a message straight from The-Powers-That-Be, he saw the torpedoes impact the water, disappear inside the white foam of their splashes, and explode with a pair of thunderous blasts that seemed to lift the ocean one full meter.

Before he could form another thought in response to that miraculous stroke of luck, the explosions' shock wave slammed into the *Potkin* and bowled it over onto its side. The captain himself was ripped away from the periscope. *Wha—!*

Those twin blasts' tremendous force uprooted everyone who wasn't anchored in chairs or bunks. Barzlin flew across the control room until he slammed against a bulkhead, which created sharp pains and loud, cracking noises in his left side.

Numb with shock, struggling to draw a breath, he slumped to a sitting position on the deck. In seconds his gathering senses had him trying to feel his chest injury. He lifted his left hand and saw it dangle limply, broken just behind the wrist.

Inside the *Potkin*, sailors were just beginning to deal with the severe agitation that followed the explosions. Then, as soon their boat had righted itself from that, it was hit by a small tidal wave thrown up by the blasts, which sent it pitching and tossing like a square-rigger in a storm. Men were shouting to be heard above the screams of the injured, and their panic only increased as the boat struggled to right itself a second time.

The control room was particularly disrupted, though there was less physical panic in Barzlin's presence. Each man had a specific job to do, so they fought their fears in order to help save all their lives. But it was hard to hear themselves think through the relentless din of alarm bells warning of hull ruptures, buzzers indicating systems breakdowns, and klaxon horns notifying everyone of the impending dive.

Suddenly, Barzlin realized what those warning buzzers and bells meant. "No dive!" he gasped. But his ragged whisper was drowned out by the cacophony throughout the control room.

"No dive!" he tried again, again to no avail.

Out of nowhere, Damovitch stepped forward and took charge. "No dive!" he shouted above the din. "No dive! We have punctures! We can't go under!"

Sitting on the deck, Barzlin felt the pumps turn on to start clearing the flooding ballast tanks. He closed his eyes with relief. Now if only Popov would continue sending the message, they could still complete their mission despite this disaster.

Do it, Josef! Do it!

Unfortunately, at that point relaying the message was the least of Popov's concerns. Despite being in his chair when the shock wave hit, he'd been upended by it and tossed to the floor, where he slid almost to the forward hatchway before being stopped by the legs of the chart table. That rough trip and abrupt stop left him stunned for several seconds, but essentially unhurt.

When he gathered his addled senses, the first thing he noticed was his captain and friend crumpled in a heap across the room. He lurched to his feet to go be of help if he could.

Damovitch, meanwhile, had arrived at Barzlin's conclusion regarding the message, so he was looking for Popov as the radioman came staggering forward. Damovitch grabbed the lapels of his jumpsuit and shoved him back toward the radio consoles, where Rykoff was already trying to resume their connection.

"Continue transmitting! Now! I'll see to the Captain!"

Popov stole a worried glance at his injured friend, gave his would-be replacement a hard look, and said, "Don't fail. . . ." Then he grudgingly returned to his chair.

Damovitch turned to go aid Barzlin. The first thing he noticed was the broken left arm. "Ach!" he muttered.

Barzlin opened his eyes to see a deep gash in the center of his first officer's forehead. It was streaming blood down the bridge of his nose—blood he paid no more attention to than if it had been sweat. The old warrior knew these moments were the truest measure of the man, because only in a crisis does a basic nature reveal itself.

Damovitch was proving to be a worthy successor.

"My ribs . . ." the captain managed to gasp.

Damovitch felt his right side, then the left. He grimaced. "Several are broken. Sit still while I get a medical team."

He stood and went to get help, while Barzlin again closed his eyes. *What had happened?* It had all been so sudden . . . so unexpected. He barely knew where to begin analyzing it. But in another moment he realized the cause no longer mattered.

What mattered now was that they'd been delivered from the jaws of doom: him, his men, and his vessel. They were disabled, surely, by flying debris hurled out with enough force to puncture the tough shell of their hull. But they had *not* been stopped. Bloodied, but not bowed. And since there'd been no follow-up attack, it

seemed safe to assume that—for whatever reason—the SH-3H that
hit them had acted alone and now was finished.

If that was indeed the case, they could complete their message
relay and simply wait for help to arrive. They were on the surface
and still floating, the sky was reasonably clear, and Moscow could
see their trouble at that very moment. Something would be done
for them as soon as was humanly possible.

He was as certain of that as anything he'd ever believed.

□ CII □

When Lubov reached the cabin porch's three plank steps, he
climbed them with rubbery legs and a powerful sense of purpose.
That feeling promptly changed to dizziness caused by the exertion
of climbing. He staggered across the porch and sagged against the
front door frame, hoping whoever was inside wasn't watching.

They'd think he was drunk or crazy—or both.

When he'd recovered his equilibrium, he reached out to knock
on the door. At his touch it moved, which meant it had been left
ajar. Also, the light had been left on; he could see it spilling
through the crack. So he opened the door a bit wider and said,
"Hello?" No response.

His next move was to push the door open all the way to completely reveal what lay beyond. But before he gave that final push,
a thought wormed into his mind. What if the person inside wasn't
actually a friend dropping by to offer help or sympathy?

What if . . . ? He hated to even think it. *What if it's someone
official? Someone like . . . the FBI . . . or . . . the Cowboy!*

With that as even a remote possibility, Lubov knew he had to be
extra cautious. He reached into his coat pocket and removed
Gretchko's Smith & Wesson. He steadied himself, then swung the
door open and jumped inside with the pistol extended.

That sudden movement started his head spinning again, and his
vision started to fade. But it was impossible for him to miss the
open trapdoor in the middle of the living-room floor.

No! Not that!

Desperately, frantically, he staggered over to the trapdoor, staring at the empty stairwell as if it were a direct passage to Hell. And for him, at that moment, it went beyond Hell because it meant the worst possible scenario had occurred. Someone was down there destroying what Marsh had wrought, which was also destroying his own dream of ultimate victory for his homeland.

He was as devastated as any man had ever been.

Suddenly, as quickly as they'd been crushed, his spirits revived. He realized he still had an option left, a way to even the score—at least partially—before he laid down and died.

He could kill whoever was ruining his great scheme!

Gripped with anger and frustration, driven beyond all sense of caution, he started lurching down the stairway. Despite his rage, however, he kept enough of a hold on himself to focus his attention on each step, making certain he didn't slip.

When he reached the bottom steps, he gazed under them to check on Marsh's blanket-covered corpse. As best his blurry vision could tell, nothing about the scene had changed.

It looks the same as I left it!

If it was, then whoever was down there couldn't possibly know Marsh was dead! And that meant they wouldn't be altering anything because, friend or not, nobody would dare to disturb Marsh's equipment without his permission. Not even the Cowboy would risk something like that without legal justification.

Suddenly, an entirely new scenario came to him, one he realized he should have considered at the beginning. And he might have, if not for his injury and his emotional agitation.

It's possible nobody's down here!

Why couldn't somebody have arrived hours ago, he asked himself, checked the cabin and basement, found the lights on and the machines primed, but missed discovering the body?

A person finding all that could logically conclude Marsh had been there and left, but probably wouldn't be gone too long. And if all that was the case, then the person involved might well be upstairs, resting or sleeping, in one of the bedrooms!

As quickly as he'd plunged to the depths of despair, Lubov soared to the heights of optimism. *Please, God!* he thought, pleading once again in a moment of crisis to the nonexistent deity of his mother's and his own remote past. *Let it be so!*

With that prayer in mind, he stepped onto the first of the final two steps that would put him on the floor of the basement and give him his first view of exactly what he was up against.

□ CIII □

As President Daniel Baxter, Chief of Staff Mike Gravelle, and Joint Chief Dale Weatherspoon watched the encounter at Traynor Island unfold, they felt the same helpless futility as every other American who saw it. Just when it looked as if their side would win . . . just when the SH-3H seemed in perfect position to blow the *Potkin* out of the water, something went wrong.

Something terribly, horribly, irrevocably wrong.

As the President watched the shattered SH-3H plummet into the ocean fifty yards beyond the *Potkin*'s bow, his first concern was not what Moscow would say about the attack on their vessel. They wouldn't respond until they knew exactly where they stood.

Now the question was how long they'd wait to find out if the message they were receiving was legitimate. And if it was . . . if American communication equipment did start to fail . . . would they initiate an attack when the shutdown was complete?

With a tightening knot in his stomach, Daniel Baxter realized that at the first sign of a shutdown America would find itself faced with an appallingly stark choice:

Launch a preemptive strike against Russia.

Or simply wait and pray for a miracle.

He gazed around the elevated enclosure that was his operation base in the Situation Room. The command bubble. Apt name. While providing perfect visual access to the Big Board monitoring screens, it insulated him from the controlled chaos that swirled on the floor below during a crisis. But even with two good men at his sides, he'd never experienced the bubble's isolating effects more profoundly. He felt utterly alone.

He turned to Mike Gravelle and said, "Get Harley on a line."

Vice President Harley Hudson was still upstairs, negotiating the embassy crisis. But he'd been discreetly informed of the immeasurably greater threat looming in the basement War Room.

Now he had to be appraised of this latest turn of events.

The President lifted his receiver, then began without preamble. "We didn't make it, Harley. Our bird's eggs hit the water and blew up on impact. It got knocked down by the blast."

Hudson was a short, corpulent man in his late fifties who'd made his political reputation sawing the legs off Mafia dons when he headed a task force against organized crime. He was also an efficient, even-handed, hard-nosed administrator whose round, undistinguished face had made him the perfect media mate for a battle-scarred old war-horse like Baxter.

And he didn't rattle easily.

"Any damage to the target?" he asked.

"It got shook up pretty badly . . . peppered with rocks from the blast . . . but nothing really serious."

Hudson sat at his desk upstairs, pensively gazing out at the top of the Washington Monument, searching for a glimmer of hope in the rapidly worsening morass. "Any chance to follow up?"

"None. . . . The Russians pulled a beautiful move on us. Matter of fact, we were damn lucky to get the shot we had."

There was a pause as Hudson absorbed that verdict. "So they're relaying right now, and we can't possibly stop it."

The President took a deep breath and let it squeeze out slowly. "That's about the size of it."

Hudson had never been one to waste time mourning his losses. "What happens next?"

"I'm not sure," the President answered truthfully. "Let's take a few minutes to kick it around."

There was another pause as each man grappled for a place to begin such a momentous discussion. Then Hudson simply took the bull by the horns. "If our communication systems go out, we'll be totally vulnerable to anything they throw at us."

After a hollow silence from the President's end of the line, Hudson added, "Especially a few well-aimed big ones."

The President finally said, "True enough. But then again, Moscow might decide it's not worth the damage to their quality of life to put that much radioactivity into the atmosphere. And they also have to consider our submarine forces launching counterattacks once they figure out what's happened onshore."

The President felt a tap on his right shoulder. "Just a second, Harley," he said as he put a hand over the receiver's mouthpiece to look at Weatherspoon.

"That's not exactly correct, sir," the general explained. "Their attack subs could knock off our whole ballistic fleet, one by one, and the others might never be the wiser."

The President's eyes glazed over as another door to safety slammed shut in his face. Then he resumed his conversation with Hudson. "Scratch that last point, Harley. I guess our best bet is to count on the other side's innate humanity."

An eloquent silence emanated from the upstairs end of the discussion, then Hudson spoke in a strained murmur. "Do you honestly think we can we afford to trust them, Mr. President? Hell, could they trust *us* if the shoe was on the other foot?"

The President sighed heavily, finally facing up to the inevitability of their position. "I guess not. . . ." Then his tone hardened. "But we can still hope like hell the message is bogus. We're treating it as if it's real because we got so caught up in trying to stop it; but we could easily be on a snipe hunt."

"I hope to God we are," Hudson replied, with all the sincerity a man in his position could muster. "But just in case, you might want to consider putting everyone on full alert before our systems start to fail."

"Good idea," the President said. "For what it's worth. . . ."

There was a chilling pause as both men wondered whether—if the time came—they'd be able to find the courage to initiate the beginning of the end for everyone.

"Thanks for calling," Hudson said.

The President lowered his receiver, then closed his eyes and squeezed his temples between his fingertips. The enormous strain on him was obvious to his two companions, who glanced at each other with deep concern before Gravelle spoke softly.

"Anything we can do, Mr. President?"

The President nodded disconsolately. "Pray like you've never prayed before that the message is a hoax."

☐ CIV ☐

Nat had spent several minutes studying the overall thrust of the Mismatch flow chart he'd found in Marsh's basement. Meanwhile, Karen hovered in silent frustration just behind his back.

When she could stand it no longer, she said, "Any idea yet?"

He was silent another long moment, then he lowered the pages he was looking at and leaned back in the chair to ruminate.

"I'm no expert, but there are lots of acronyms in here that I'm familiar with: ARVNCOM . . . DEFCOM . . . SEALANT . . . WMMCS. . . ." He pointed each out as he mentioned it. "They're all major parts of our computer-linked communication network."

"Is that so strange? I mean, wouldn't he have to be fooling around with those no matter what he's up to?"

Nat chewed on his lower lip. "Maybe, maybe not. Not all of them at once, anyway. That's the part that really doesn't make sense: Why would they *all* be here in the same chart?"

She shrugged. "Maybe it's a really *big* program."

That observation would have been exactly what Nat needed to begin solving the riddle of the flow-chart tablets. But he didn't get to absorb it because over Karen's words came the distracting sound of Lubov's first footfall on the steps leading down into the basement. The hum of the primed machines had prevented them from hearing his stumbling footsteps on the heavy floor overhead, but his first lurching step into the stairwell rang out unmistakably.

"Uh-oh!" Nat whispered as he quickly pushed up out of the rolling armchair. "Sounds like Daddy's home. . . ."

He quietly led Karen over against the opposite wall, up under the stairwell, between the three metal filing cabinets and the blanket-covered mound that was Marsh's corpse.

As they tiptoed across the basement, he whispered again: "Let me surprise him so I can see the look on his face!"

Karen felt that was rather childish, but she didn't have the heart to object to him getting the most from his moment of retribution. He was brimming with gleeful anticipation.

They watched as the descending legs and feet became visible through the spaces between the middle steps. They saw expensive-looking loafers worn under stylish gray slacks.

Karen cupped her hands against Nat's ear to whisper, "Those don't go with his bedroom mess!"

Nat knew that as well as she did, but he shrugged off his doubt and his eager expression returned. All he wanted to think about just then was the sweet revenge he was about to achieve.

The legs paused momentarily above the final two steps, then their owner stepped down into view, his face directed toward the humming array of machines. Not only had Nat or Karen never seen him before, they were shocked dumb by his physical appearance. The guy looked like a grisly death warmed over.

And even more shocking was the gun in his hand!

☐ CV ☐

The President, Mike Gravelle, and General Weatherspoon stood in the White House Situation Room's command bubble, watching the three backup SH-3Hs arrive over the wallowing *Potkin*. The one in the lead positioned itself directly above, while the other two broke away and headed toward Traynor Island.

"Those two are going to cover Scarlatti's wingmen until the rescue birds arrive," Weatherspoon muttered absently. "The other one will stay over the sub until we give it further orders."

"Let's get some more rescue choppers on the way out there," the President said. "We need to be going through the motions of helping that sub's crew until we know for sure where we stand."

As the general left to carry out that instruction, Gravelle shook his head in dismay. "I can't believe we're sitting here trying to put the best face on all this! It's *their* fault!"

Before the President could respond, a computer-toned trill erupted from a red console at the far left side of the bubble. The President and his chief adviser looked at each other with surprise and mild alarm. They hadn't expected the Soviets to react so quickly, especially now that they had their message and knew what the Americans were trying to prevent. Such a rapid response could only mean they were equally surprised and alarmed.

Both the President and Gravelle knew perfectly well that if this had been one of the Kremlin's planned maneuvers, it would have been handled with more subtlety and the shutdown engineered with no warning of any kind. So that had to be Premier Kolokov on the line, calling to try to prevent an American first strike if their communication systems did actually start to fail.

For a moment the President stood there wondering what he might say if he were in Kolokov's shoes. Would he try to offer assurances that his side had no intention of acting on the information they'd just received? Or would it be best to admit the impossibility of holding the military wolves at bay, and simply ask for outright surrender? But how could any assurances, no matter how heartfelt, actually be believed? And how could any degree of surrender be enforced without massive bloodshed?

By putting himself in his counterpart's shoes, the President came to a stunningly clear understanding of where everyone now stood. The bottom line was that it didn't matter in the least what either side said to try to convince the other. Such assurances were—and always had been—impossible to believe.

Suppose he accepted a promise of restraint and forswore a preemptive strike? The Soviets could then safely attack as soon as all the relevant communication systems were down.

But suppose he rejected their promise? That would be tantamount to an open declaration of war. Then it would only be a matter of who launched the first missile barrage.

With the worst in the long series of shocks he'd experienced that day, the President realized that regardless of whatever else might happen, nuclear annihilation would have to begin shortly after any American communication systems started going out!

He couldn't trust the Soviets, and the Soviets couldn't trust him. Both sides were trapped in a sticky web of duplicity spun out over fifty years of mutual distrust and antagonism.

Then the most devastating thought of all came to him: *It's what we both deserve!*

He debated whether to pick up the receiver attached to the red console, or just let the damn thing go on trilling. On one hand, answering would let both sides get things settled. Each could determine where the other stood, which would reduce the problem to a simple wait for American systems to begin failing.

On the other hand, not answering would spare the finality of such an exchange, thereby avoiding the possibility that Kremlin leaders might get nervous and launch a first strike of their own. It seemed better to wait until everyone knew for certain . . . until the systems started going out and there was no turning back.

In the end, the President split the difference. He lifted the red console's receiver and spoke to the translator he knew would be on the other end.

"This is President Baxter. Tell whoever's calling that I'm indisposed. I'll get back to them as soon as I'm able."

Without waiting for any kind of response, he lowered the receiver and recradled it. That action wasn't taken with anger or sadness or satisfaction of any kind—just an overwhelming sense that it was the wisest thing to do at the moment.

☐ CVI ☐

When Lubov arrived at the final step down into the basement, his sensitized hearing assured him Marsh's machines were still working as he'd left them. That meant that even though he couldn't see the switches from where he stood, he could safely assume they were ready to be lowered.

He could hardly believe his luck.

He stepped forward eagerly, anxious to drop the switches that would fulfill his life's great purpose. But then, unlike he'd originally planned, he wouldn't be able to leave things at that. The shutdown was going to require at least an hour to complete, and that process couldn't be interrupted in any way.

It had to play itself out in every detail, start to finish, just as Marsh planned, or the whole procedure would be at risk. That meant he had to sneak back upstairs and take care of the person or persons he'd convinced himself he'd find asleep there.

Because the switches were on the side of the array nearest the stairwell, he was standing before them after three unsteady, shuffling steps. He reached out his empty, trembling left hand and felt them. They were still in position!

This is it! he realized—the moment he'd been striving for all of his adult life. And then, for some reason he couldn't begin to understand, he started having second thoughts.

What if he was doing something intrinsically wrong? What if he wasn't making the proper Communist choice? Those doubts made him search for direction in the swirl of his addled senses. Then something came to him: an insight he felt answered all his questions about whether to take that final, fateful step.

If his mother's God did in fact exist, surely He wouldn't have allowed things to get to this point if He didn't want the mission carried through to its conclusion. And if He didn't exist, then humans were nothing more than animals, like dogs or cows; and the loss of several million would be little more than culling out the sick members of a diseased pack or herd.

With those thoughts firmly in mind, and with a powerful conviction he was doing the right thing, Lubov pressed the edge of his hand down and felt all three switches snap into place.

I did it! Then he remembered his role had only been one of secondary importance, so he gave proper credit where it was due. *We did it—the King and me—together!*

Despite the pain it caused, he couldn't help beaming with satisfaction and gratitude as he stepped over to the middle of the horseshoe to more fully experience the miracle he'd helped create. Storage discs started spinning, cranking up to stream out the many millions of data bits Marsh had put into them over the years. And he could distinguish that glowing lights were beginning to wink and winking lights were beginning to glow.

But it was the changes in sound that held his fullest attention—precious sound—the only physical reality left to him that he could be absolutely certain of. *Yes! It's happening!*

He could hear the steady *hummmm* of before being replaced by the powerful, throbbing *whirrrr* of a wire-and-silicon life-force of infinite complexity and destructive capacity.

Marsh had indeed done his work well, providing Lubov with what he regarded as the sweetest sound he'd ever heard. And because he was in such a euphoric mood, he couldn't help feeling the moment should be shared with the man who'd made it possible.

He glanced over his left shoulder at the blanket-covered corpse lying under the base of the stairwell. But his head didn't swing far enough to notice the two people huddled against the filing cabinets at the other side of the wall.

Even if his eyes had swung that far, though, his blurred vision wouldn't have identified them as people rather than cabinets. By then, vague shapes were all he could distinguish.

"You see, Percy? It works! You did a magnificent job. Not the job you intended, I admit." He turned back, smiling, to the array of furiously working machines. "But a job that needed to be done. In one hour America will be completely without communications, just as you planned. But now, just as *I* planned, it will become permanent instead of the five-minute warning you intended."

And then, from behind him and to his right, came the most unexpected, blood-chilling words he could ever have imagined.

"You maniac sonofabitch!"

For one brief moment he thought Percy Marsh had come back from the dead to rebuke him.

□ CVII □

What President Daniel Baxter would never have guessed was that the Hot Line call he refused to take wasn't from Soviet Premier Andrei Kolokov. It was from High Commissioner Yuri Medveyev, a portly, patchy-haired man of sixty-nine who'd survived countless purges by being constantly ready to do his superiors' shit work: Things like getting out of bed in the middle of the night to handle a crisis brewing in America.

Had the President decided to answer that call, alarm buzzers would have instantly sounded in his mind. Medveyev was only fifth-in-command in the Soviet power structure, and therefore was a grossly inappropriate choice to handle the critical circumstance both sides were facing. So the President would have been able to conclude—quite logically—that the opposition either didn't know what he knew; or they thought the situation was totally different from what it actually was.

In fact, the second alternative was indeed the case in the Soviet Union. Yuri Medveyev stood in the middle of the Kremlin Situation Room's equivalent of a command bubble, glaring at the nervous little translator holding their end of the Hot Line.

It was that poor fellow's first time to be on the translation detail when the Line was to be utilized, so he felt sweat trickling down between his shoulder blades as he repeated his American counterpart's explanation for the delay.

"The President says he is indisposed, High Commissioner. He promises to return your call as soon as he is able."

Flabbergasted, Medveyev lifted his own receiver to see if the American translator was still on the line. He heard nothing but the empty white noise that substituted for a dial tone on the most exclusive private telephone line in the world.

"Arrogant bastard!" he shouted into the silent receiver.

Then he turned to face a pair of Hot Line technicians standing several meters away. "Try once more to complete the call in this manner," he snapped. "If he avoids me a second time, call his private White House number—the bathroom number."

He gave that last instruction with an air of superiority, then turned to retire to a nearby easy chair to await the results. This affair was growing ever more puzzling to him, and he wanted a few moments alone to try to sort things out.

At that point all the Soviets knew for certain was that an American ASW team had stalked and attacked one of their looper submarines as it was attempting to relay an emergency message. That much had been visible from their observation satellites. And there could be no doubt the message was of vital importance because such vessels relayed only the most sensitive information. But all the sub had been able to transmit before being struck by the torpedo blast was twenty characters of code, which was barely enough to identify the sender as the SSN *Mikhail Potkin*.

Situation Room personnel had naturally assumed one or more pieces of the rubble that tore into the side of the *Potkin* had struck and disabled the radio transmitter in its sail. So there'd be no way to determine what the message was about until the vessel's sailors were returned to the USSR.

Depending on the sensitivity of the message, that could take days or even weeks. As he himself would do in a similar circumstance, the Americans would most certainly find excuses to hold the crew until it was strategically safe to release them.

All that was left for Medveyev to do, really, was to insist in the strongest possible terms that the Kremlin intended to hold America and its leaders up to the glare of public censure for this—already he was phrasing an appropriate protest in his mind—"unprincipled, barbarous, and wholly unprovoked attack!"

That was the kind of phrase the Politburo loved to shove down American throats. In fact, no matter what the unknown message turned out to say, Medveyev didn't think it could possibly be as valuable as the propaganda they'd gain from the clumsy American attempt to stop it from being sent.

Suddenly Medveyev's thoughts were intruded upon by a worried voice verging on alarm. It was the senior of the two Hot Line technicians. "High Commissioner, the Line has suffered a major technical breakdown. We can't be certain of the problem's exact nature—or even where it is—but our first indications put it somewhere on the other side."

Medveyev scowled. *This is unprecedented!*

The technician cleared his throat. "Uh, were you serious about calling the President's bathroom number?"

"Of course!" Medveyev roared. "What they've done is an outrage! They must be forced to account for it!"

"At once, High Commissioner!" the technician yelped.

That left Medveyev to wonder what in hell could possibly be going on those many thousands of miles away. And of even more importance to him at that moment was his concern that his foul-tempered sow of a wife might not believe the delay hadn't been caused by a side trip to the apartment of his mistress.

☐ CVIII ☐

President Baxter, Mike Gravelle, and General Weatherspoon were sitting in somber, bomb-ticking silence behind the flurry of activity going on beyond the Situation Room's command bubble.

Suddenly, one of the overhead intercoms crackled to life.

"Mr. President!" came the alarmed voice of the Marine colonel in charge of the floor. "We just lost two primary coding links and a third is going down! No such activity reported from anywhere else yet, so it looks like this room is ground zero!"

The President's fingers stiffened around his sending mike; his head drooped; the color drained from his liver-spotted scalp. He took a brief moment to collect himself, then he flicked his mike switch on and said, "Thank you, Colonel."

"What do we do now, sir?" the colonel said in a voice pleading for guidance and, if possible, reassurance.

"I'll be back to you in a moment," the President answered. He then switched his mike to the closed position so no one except the two men with him in the bubble could hear his next words.

"I never dreamed it would come to this. . . ."

And he hadn't. Anyone who aspired to ultimate leadership in either America *or* the Soviet Union had to have powerful means of convincing themselves the end of the line wouldn't be reached during their watch. Otherwise, none of them would accept the job, much less seek and endure what was necessary to obtain it.

"So what's the decision, Mr. President?" a sallow-faced Mike Gravelle asked his old friend and mentor. "Do we strike the first blow? Or wait to see if they decide to take us out?"

This was it, the most momentous decision any human would ever be required to make: Whether or not to initiate a nuclear holocaust over a large portion of the planet—if not all of it.

The President looked first at his chief of staff, then at his chief military adviser, then out toward the Situation Room personnel who were breaching etiquette by looking at him expectantly, waiting to execute the orders he was about to give.

He flicked his mike on and began speaking to each of them.

"I want you all to know how terribly sorry I am . . . sorry for
all of us on both sides . . . sorry that we've worked so hard to
create a world to live in where trust and coexistence is impossible
. . . a world where, even with the best of intentions, we find ourselves with no choice but to launch a first strike."

Everyone listening knew that awesome and horrible decision
represented their only viable recourse . . . the only solution that
would in any way work to their advantage. And when they got
right down to the bottom of their collective heart of hearts, that
was what every last one of them wanted to insure.

They wanted to know their turf would be protected and all their
wrongs avenged until the final, bitter end—and beyond.

The President lifted his eyes to gaze fixedly at the Big Board
graphic representing the world he was about to incinerate. Slowly,
and with somber, leaden tones, he spoke for all to hear: "Prepare
to launch everything we have . . . on my order."

The Marine colonel in charge of the Situation Room at that
moment was a handsome, well-proportioned fellow in his mid-for-
ties who looked to be a man's man if ever there was one. Yet there
was a distinct tremor in his voice as it came back through the
command bubble's overhead intercom. "Yes, sir. . . ."

☐ CIX ☐

"You maniac sonofabitch!"

Nat had impulsively shouted that when the man with the gun
explained what Marsh's activated machines were doing. Now he
had to suffer the potentially deadly consequences of that action.

The startled man whirled around with his weapon extended,
obviously ready for use. In an instinctive effort to protect Karen,
Nat shoved her to his left, up under the descending stairway, to
take her out of a direct line of fire.

Nat's unexpected shove caused Karen to lose her balance and
tumble rump-first onto the blanket-covered mound at the base of
the stairs. The uneven, hard, yet squishy surface of Marsh's rigor-
mortifying body caused her to give an involuntary gasp.

Nat cast a quick glance her way, made certain she was all right, then muttered in a desperate rasp, "Don't move!" He then turned his attention back to the threatening stranger, who seemed to be struggling to hold himself and his weapon steady.

The very last thing Karen wanted to do was move—if only so she could stay out of the wavering pistol's line of fire. But she simply *had* to get off the odd-feeling, foul-smelling blanket Nat had pushed her onto. It was an overpowering urge.

While she did that, Nat crouched down and went into a boxer's bob-and-weave, simultaneously pulling out the flashlight he'd put in his jacket pocket after checking under the cabin. He hadn't thought through what good a flashlight might be against a pistol, but it seemed a lot better than just standing there with only his bare hands for protection.

Meanwhile, Lubov stood in the center of the room trying to focus on the two fuzzy blurs lurking in the shadow beneath the stairwell. His sensitized hearing had already told him the one to his left—the one who'd whispered—was male, while the other—the one who'd squealed—was female. That meant half of his immediate problem had been solved: He knew who to shoot at. All that remained was getting control of his palsied hands long enough to take decent aim and fire.

Nat continued his bob-and-weave tactic, wondering if that movement was actually delaying the gunman's attack. Then it occurred to him that the guy might not be in full control of his faculties . . . maybe drunk or stoned—or crazed! If that was the case, then maybe a head-down forward lunge might be—

Nat's thoughts were cut off as the pistol was suddenly pointed and held in his direction. With a supreme effort of will, Lubov was gathering the last of his physical resources to attempt a decisive blow against his adversaries. He was intending to put a bullet through the heart of the man, then do whatever it took to finish off the woman. Or die trying.

Nat could see a shot was coming, but what could he do? All he had to protect himself was . . . *The flashlight!* Using a few more of the milliseconds he needed to think of it, he flicked the light on and pointed it at the gunman's face. Its beam bored out of the shadow under the stairs and into the man's eyes a split second before he squeezed the trigger.

That bright stab of light didn't really hurt Lubov as much as it surprised him. But the important thing was that it caused him to flinch, ever so slightly, just as he fired at Nat.

Each person in the room was rocked by the overwhelming sound of that shot. And instead of hitting the heart it had been aimed at, the hollow-nosed bullet smashed into Nat's left shoulder, shattering itself into tiny metal fragments. Those, in turn, shattered Nat's shoulder joint in an explosion of blood, bone, and flesh that erupted from the wound like a tiny volcano.

The strike angle twisted Nat backward and to his left, slamming him down where Karen was crouched, near Marsh's corpse. It all happened so suddenly, Karen didn't even have time to scream before Nat's body rammed into her.

Lubov, meanwhile, had also been wounded by that shot.

The cramped, metal-filled basement amplified the pistol's report to an excruciating degree, even for someone with normal hearing. Lubov's sensitive ears carried every magnified decibel straight to the core of his ravaged brain, which caused him pain that was the most intense, blinding agony he'd ever experienced.

As Nat fell against Karen and tumbled them both over onto Marsh's corpse, a howl of anguish came from the middle of the room as Lubov sagged to his knees. His howl was immediately followed by a deep, guttural moan as he dropped the pistol to the wooden floor, squeezed his eyes shut, and clasped both hands tightly over the pulsing screech in his ears.

Meanwhile, Karen gasped and threw both hands over her mouth at her first glimpse of Nat's wound. Around its gaping center was blood-soaked, shredded flesh, peppered with chips of bone and bullet and mingled with tatters of blazer and shirt cloth.

Despite the severity of his wound, Nat maintained enough presence of mind to release the flashlight and clamp his right hand over the bloody hole. Once Karen's horrified view had been blocked, her attention was caught by the tormented moans coming from the man on his knees in the center of the room.

Then she realized: *He wants to kill us!*

At that pivotal instant, her survival instinct and her feelings for Nat combined to thrust her into action. She scrambled out from underneath him, jumped to her feet, and tried desperately to take him with her. She quickly found she couldn't move him without jostling his shattered, dangling arm.

Once . . . twice . . . three times she tried. But at each heaving movement, Nat moaned as loudly as Lubov. Then, from the haze of her mounting panic, she heard him hiss through clenched teeth, "The gun, dammit! Get the gun!"

She looked across the ten feet separating her from Lubov. He was on all fours by then, feeling around for his lost weapon, his vision so eroded, he couldn't see more than a dark fog. She saw the gun immediately, however, down between his knees.

She froze with the realization that he might find it and shoot again. Which was exactly his intention. He'd recovered from the sound of one shot and knew he could recover from another—and more if necessary. He was determined to kill both intruders, whoever they were, whatever they wanted.

"Get it!" Nat rasped as he regained even more of his senses. "Get it before he does!"

He grabbed Karen's right wrist with his bloody right hand and tried to yank her the way she had to go. Her hand slipped through his slimy grasp, but the motion was enough to snap her out of her trance. A surge of adrenaline propelled her forward as Lubov's equally adrenalized fingers touched the gun.

She was halfway to him as he lifted it. It was at his waist as she dived, hands outstretched. She slammed into him and got a firm, double-handed grip on his right wrist, extending his arm out and away from Nat. The two of them ended up sprawled across the floor, thrashing about in a struggle for dominance.

Lubov's first tactic was to try to disable his opponent with a sudden, telling strike. He brought his knee up, hard, squarely into her crotch. She flinched at the unexpected blow, but didn't lose her wind as a man would have. She stayed on top.

Needing to regroup, Lubov twisted away and tried a rolling motion Karen also successfully countered. In desperation he pulled the pistol's trigger, hoping the sudden noise might loosen his opponent's grip. A shot rang out and another hollow-nosed bullet exploded in the ceiling, only inches away from the bright overhead light that was the room's only source of illumination.

Karen held fast.

The pain that shot caused Lubov was every bit as intense as before. But his tolerance threshold had been elevated by that first shot, so he was better able to withstand the second one. Nevertheless, he knew he was losing ground. His strength, his awareness, his will to complete his mission were all but gone.

With even more desperation he pulled the trigger again, which blew a fist-sized hole in the plaster wallboard below the central console. Twisting and turning to try to break free from the tenacious grip holding his wrist, he started punching his opponent's ribs with his free left hand.

As they thrashed about, Karen wanted nothing more than to keep the gun pointed away from herself and Nat. So she kept her arms stiff and extended from Lubov's body, paying no heed to his blows raining into her rib cage. Besides, they were only hard enough to sting slightly, and each seemed weaker than the last.

Another shot tore into the back of Marsh's empty rolling armchair. Another splintered against its heavy metal base. Then suddenly Nat's voice arrowed into her frantic awareness.

"Don't hit the machines! We have to stop what he started!"

Not only was that an important warning to Karen, it had a galvanizing effect on Lubov. He knew he was running out of time and bullets, but he also realized the man's instructions to the woman could work to his own advantage.

He made a last desperate surge to roll over on top of her, and this time she let him succeed. Which did get the gun aimed away from the horseshoe. But at a terrible tactical cost.

Once Lubov was on top of Karen, his pistol was aimed in the opposite direction, right at Nat and the blanket-covered mound beside him. And to her absolute horror, the first image she focused on was Nat's chest just beyond the wavering barrel.

Then she felt Lubov's wrist ligaments compressing!

Knowing that meant another shot was coming, she yanked with all her strength just as the gun fired. Instead of exploding upon impact with Nat's chest, the bullet grazed a corner of the blanket beside him. Its velocity lifted that corner up and back, which exposed Marsh's head to view.

Not only did the bullet lift the blanket as it went ripping past, it grazed along Marsh's hollow-eyed, split-lipped, black-tongued, blue-tinged face, slicing into his cheek at an oblique angle, gouging a furrow along it, then tearing off the soft tip of his pug nose before exploding against one of the bottom steps.

That final, ghastly disfigurement of Marsh accomplished what all of Lubov's struggling couldn't: It caused Karen to release her grip as she threw both hands over her gaping mouth.

Lubov wasted no time seizing the opportunity she presented.

He jammed the pistol into her ribs to make sure he'd hit vital organs, just as Nat saw the impending disaster and shouted from his sitting position near Marsh. "Nooo!"

At that point nothing on earth could have diverted Lubov from his deadly purpose. He pulled the trigger again!

A hollow *click* permeated the room's bristling stillness as the hammer hit on an empty chamber. *No!* he thought. *Nooo!*

Shocked by that sound almost as much as he would have been by the one he expected, he pulled the trigger two more times. Those same sharp, empty *clicks* reverberated to the farthest reaches of his spirit, shattering his depleted resolve the way high notes shatter crystal.

Meanwhile, at the sound of those *clicks* Nat sagged back in profound relief, while Karen was utterly unaware of the death she'd so narrowly escaped. She'd been looking from Marsh to Nat to Lubov, then back to Marsh, feeling her mind turn to jelly.

Suddenly, the absolute horror of it all registered on her with full impact. She let out a soul-searing scream directly into Lubov's right ear, the pain of which caused him to finally pass out.

He collapsed down onto her like a bag of wet cement.

Propelled solely by instinct, Karen kicked and shoved at the limp body pinning her to the floor until she was free and able to scramble to her feet.

She left Lubov lying there, his still functioning lungs pumping like bellows while the rest of his body lay unmoving . . . as spent as the empty gun lying near his head.

☐ CX ☐

The news relayed to the White House command bubble was both unexpected and potentially disastrous. It came from the Marine colonel on the Situation Room floor, the man charged with implementing the President's order to launch-prepare all of America's submarine and land-based nuclear missiles.

Again he breached etiquette by facing the President as he spoke into his mike. And this time his alarm wasn't concealed.

"Sir! We're not—repeat, *not*—able to establish or verify the proper arming or firing codes—land or sea! It looks like the first thing they disabled was our ability to do that!"

A chilling silence filled the bubble as the three men there came to grips with that news. It meant they were already too late—they couldn't initiate an attack because they couldn't properly send or verify the orders to do so.

Mike Gravelle summed up their combined feelings. "Goddamn Russkies never miss a fucking trick, do they?"

There was another pause as each man tried to figure out what to do next. Then General Weatherspoon snapped his fingers. "Alan Pinkley said shortwave wouldn't be affected by a shutdown. Why don't we try to establish a shortwave VLF audio link with our submarine forces?"

The President looked at Gravelle, who shrugged. "It's a mile-long shot, but what the hell? It beats sitting here with our thumbs up our butts."

The President flipped his mike switch on. "Colonel, can we beat the onshore tangle by using a shortwave VLF audio patch?"

The worried colonel was ready to grab at any straw. "I'm not sure, sir. This room seems to have been hit across the board—top to bottom. But we'll do everything we can to get you connected."

"Just do the best you can, Colonel," the President said.

At that he flipped his mike switch off and turned to face his two companions. The expressions of both men had swiftly changed from the utter despair of thinking they were going to be the first to launch an all-out nuclear strike, to angry frustration at apparently being prevented from doing so.

There was no clearer indictment of the competitive system that had brought America and its Soviet rival to this dreadful, unthinkable impasse. And the most damnable part of it to Daniel Baxter was that he was feeling exactly what his companions felt.

While his civilized veneer was utterly appalled at what he was trying to do, his nationalistic core was struggling every way it knew how to prevent an ultimate triumph by the enemy.

That realization made him sick to his stomach—sicker than he already was.

□ CXI □

Only Karen's overwhelming concern for Nat kept her from sinking into hysteria. Crying and gasping for breath, she clambered from underneath Lubov's wheezing, prostrate body and staggered over to her wounded partner. And this time her adrenalized brain and muscles ignored his groans of protest as she heaved him to his feet to move him toward the steps.

"No!" he snapped through a tight-jawed grimace as she tugged on his good elbow. "We have to try to stop this thing!"

"How?" she shouted in desperation. *"Why?* That guy killed Marsh! And he tried to kill us! Let's get out while we can!"

Nat shook his head while gazing down at Marsh's disfigured face. Incredibly, amazingly, he was feeling an emotion he never thought he'd be capable of in regard to his great, hated nemesis.

He felt genuinely sorry for him.

Using his foot to slide the edge of the blanket down to re-cover him, he said to Karen, *"That's* why we have to stay. Because what's going on here is important enough to kill for."

Though his wounded shoulder was still seeping blood at a steady rate, it had grown numb enough to disregard as he began concentrating on the vastly more serious problem they now faced.

Wiping the sticky, drying blood from his right hand on the front of his shirt and jacket, he lurched toward the pair of yellow legal tablets lying near the rolling armchair.

"But what can *you* do?" Karen demanded.

He was already so focused on trying to defeat Marsh's grand design, he didn't bother answering her. His single-mindedness also kept him from thinking to hog-tie the body sprawled on the floor. He simply led Karen around it, gingerly, and then hunched over the tablets to see what he could do to thwart their purpose.

"All you know is *what's* happening," she persisted. "You don't know *how* it's happening or how to stop it! Can't we just leave and send someone else back to take care of this mess?"

He whirled around to face her with fire in his eyes and blood soaking his left side. "He said it would be over in an hour! There's no time for someone else to come stop it!"

"But I say again, what can *you* do?" she countered. "Look at you! You can't even type!"

That stopped him for only a moment. "No, but *you* can! Sit down in front of that keyboard, and I'll tell you what to do!"

"Why don't we just pull the plug on all this and—?"

"Listen!" he shouted. "We have no way of knowing how much of the data stream is already on its way out, so pulling the plug now will eliminate only part of it. And if we do pull the plug, there's no way we can use what's here to undo the damage that's been done. What's already down will stay paralyzed for months— maybe years! So our only chance to prevent that is to figure out what he did, find a way to stop it, then backtrack every step he took and make everything the way it was. Okay?"

He paused to take a deep breath, then assumed a deadly serious expression. "Now, sit your ass down in that chair and do exactly *what* I tell you, *when* I tell you! There's no more time to waste arguing!"

Seeing no room for further debate, Karen did as instructed. But on her way to the armchair she glanced back at Lubov's body to make certain he wasn't recovering. He wasn't.

Once she was seated, Nat refocused on the first tablet.

"Now I see why all the military acronyms come up front," he muttered, riffling through the top pages. "He set up a domino chain that takes out the most complex, important systems first."

"Dominoes?" Karen said from the chair.

"When a chain of dominoes starts to fall," he replied absently, never taking his eyes from the flow chart, "each one has to fall onto the next one in the chain and take it down, cleanly and completely, or the whole process stops."

She nodded. "So . . . ?"

"That's what's going on here. He made a big string of electronic dominoes out of our entire communication network, starting with vital military systems and working his way down."

"For God's sake, Nat!" she protested. "You could bleed to death by the time you reprogram so much!"

"But don't you see?" he countered, his eyes desperately scanning page after page, looking for what he needed. "All we have to do is take out *one* domino—the correct domino—and the falling stops! We just find it, reprogram it, and we win!"

If there's one like that in there, she thought. *If you've got the smarts to find it. And if my typing is good enough!*

She simply couldn't help doubting their combined ability to tackle what seemed to her the most daunting task on earth.

□ CXII □

The command bubble was silent as the three men inside it looked down on the floor crew beyond, desperately searching for a way to comm-link the President to his fleet of missile-carrying submarines. They all knew it wasn't going to be easy, but they wouldn't know if it was impossible unless they tried.

For lack of a better focus for his attention, the President stared at the Marine colonel in charge of the Situation Room. It was the man's haircut that caught and held his interest: a brownish thatch trimmed skintight to the top of his scalp—the famous "jarhead" style he himself wore as a young Marine.

He wished the colonel would move close enough for someone in the bubble to read his name tag. He felt a strong urge to address the man by name, as a friend, the next time they communicated.

For reasons Baxter didn't understand, he couldn't keep his mind off the unknown, unnamed, but now vitally important colonel. And that made him wonder if it had been a mistake to never bother getting acquainted with the people who operated out on the Situation Room floor.

Maybe it was the seriousness of their jobs that made him tend to avoid them. Or maybe the fact that he preferred handling crisis situations in the comfortable familiarity of the upstairs offices, rather than those in the basement. Whatever the reason, however, he was sorry now he'd never taken the time.

Thinking about the upstairs offices reminded him of the embassy takeover. He wondered, *What must Harley be thinking now?* He had an urge to lift a nearby phone receiver to tell his Vice President he was sitting around waiting to hear if their people would manage to find a way to let him blow up the world.

What would he say to that? The thought was almost comical.

What he wanted to think about was his family: his wife and his children and their children—his beloved grandchildren. But in order to be evenhanded with those around him whose families he was also trying to destroy, he'd deliberately avoided making an attempt to save his own. And now he couldn't hold on to the simplest thoughts about any of them, no matter how hard he tried.

All he could focus on was that lone Marine colonel's back as he rushed around issuing orders and receiving information. And as he watched, he couldn't help asking himself, *What will that fellow's family look like after it happens?*

With great consternation and overwhelming sadness, the President realized that he couldn't even imagine a stranger's incinerated relatives. Everyone—including his own family—had become a distant abstraction to him: the abstract reality of untold millions he was ready, willing, and trying to kill.

Which he took to mean his soul was already dying.

Or dead.

☐ CXIII ☐

"Bingo!" Nat exclaimed, stabbing his right, blood-caked forefinger down on the twenty-fifth page of the first yellow tablet. "Here it is! Just what we need!"

"What? Where?" Karen asked, leaning over in the armchair.

"Right here: The shutdown process for the WMMCX system. See? Only one track in and one track out."

"What's the WMMCX system?" she asked as he found some clean sheets at the back of the second yellow tablet, picked up a pen, and started drafting a flow chart of his own.

"Early-warning radar . . . stretched along the U.S.-Canadian border . . . old array . . . low-priority . . . really basic technology. Looks like Marsh picked it to bridge the gap from military to private sector. See? It tracks into the flow behind the last government system, and it tracks out to one of Ma's biggest long-line trunks."

She nodded at where he pointed, but the letters and symbols made no sense to her. "Can you handle it?" she asked worriedly.

"With a hell of a lot of luck, maybe," he replied.

"You don't sound too confident."

"Let's not kid ourselves. I'm a decent programmer, not a great one. And the time crunch here is a colossal ball-buster."

"What do you mean?"

He kept working as he talked. "WMMCX could already be down right now . . . as we speak. If it is . . . I'll be reprogramming after the fact. But . . . in our favor is what that guy"—he jerked his thumb over his shoulder, in Lubov's direction—"said about the shutdown taking an hour. That's our edge."

She glanced back at Lubov's still, prone body. "Huh?"

"Figure it out. There's eighty pages of flow chart in both these tablets. If the whole program takes an hour to run, that means it averages forty-five seconds per page. The WMMCX shutdown is on page twenty-five. That means it shouldn't kick in for at least eighteen minutes, going at the average speed."

Karen checked her watch. "Will that be enough time?"

"If it strictly maintains the average . . . probably not." Then he gave her a hopeful wink. "But since the first programs were those big military suckers, they may go slower than some of the others that take up just as much space on the flow chart."

She forced a smile. "Can I do anything to help?"

By then he had the basic reprogramming steps down and was ready to start doing the detailed piecework off Marsh's tablet. So he nodded and said, "Give me about five minutes of silence, and as many prayers as you can jam into that much time."

Despite her fears and misgivings, she couldn't help smiling at his raw determination. "You got it, kid!" she muttered.

Then she focused herself on praying and watching him work.

□ CXIV □

What neither Nat nor Karen realized was that the gunman they'd forgotten about had returned. Though still lying facedown on the basement's plank floor, Lubov had regained consciousness. And just as when he'd regained his awareness after Marsh waylaid him, he'd been totally disoriented at first. But the exchanges between Nat and Karen soon reached his still sensitive ears.

No! was his logical reaction. *I have to stop them!*

As Nat frantically scribbled out the computer program he hoped would cancel the WMMCX part of the shutdown, and as Karen sat there absorbed with watching him work, Lubov began gathering his physical resources for one last attack on the intruders trying to foil his great scheme. *First, a weapon . . .*

He carefully turned his head and saw Gretchko's empty pistol lying not even a foot away. That would do. He could sneak up on the man, knock him senseless, then deal with the woman in any way he could manage. Whatever it took, he *would* prevail.

Slowly, stealthily, he reached out and picked the gun up, then clamped its butt between his teeth. That sent a blinding pain shooting through his head, so he was forced to take another tack. Struggling not to grunt with effort, he reached behind himself and shoved it under his belt at the small of his back.

Once his weapon was secure, his next task was getting to his feet. He quickly discovered there was a big difference between lifting the empty pistol and raising his body. On his first attempt to push his torso off the floor, he managed only a few inches before his trembling, energy-depleted arms told him he'd have to find another way to get up.

He considered for a moment, then remembered he was only a few feet from the edge of the horseshoe where the three toggle switches were located. He dug his palms and toes into the rough-hewn floorboards, then pushed. He wasn't sure after the first attempt, so he waited a few seconds and tried again.

That time he was certain—*I moved!*

Inch by painful inch he struggled forward, careful to make no sounds that wouldn't be drowned out by the steady whirring of the machines. After what seemed an eternity, his sweat-soaked forehead touched the cool metal base of the left-side consoles.

Using the console base as a prop, he inched forward until he attained a sitting position underneath the metal flange that was the desk part of the array. Struggling not to wheeze, he reached up and gripped the edge of the flange. It was a perfect support to help him rise, first to his knees and then to his feet.

Once upright, he was overcome by a severe but familiar bout of dizziness, which—as before—faded his already dim vision to total black. But he clung to the flange tenaciously, refusing to give in, and soon the dizziness passed—as it had before—and his vision returned to what it had been.

Tears of relief sprang into his widely dilated eyes as he realized he was going to succeed. But he quickly wiped them away as he reached behind his back and pulled out the pistol, shifting it in his hand as he'd done just before ending its owner's life.

Despite his impaired vision, he could tell the man was the upright figure at the other side of the horseshoe. The bright overhead light was providing more than enough illumination for him to be sure of that assessment.

He gathered the last of his courage and strength and will, and unsteadily pushed off on that long journey across those final few steps. And then, after his third step forward, something totally unexpected happened.

Because he no longer had the presence of mind to anticipate mistakes and avoid them, he let his torso move in between the overhead light and his victims. That shoved a long, dark shadow between the two of them, which he saw too late to prevent. *No!*

Nat was so absorbed in constructing his counterprogram, he was beyond noticing anything. But when Karen saw the arm-raised outline lurching their way, she cut loose with a yelping shout.

"Nat! Behind you!"

Some primal instinct caused Nat to duck down and to his right, away from the sweeping roundhouse aimed at the ear on that side of his head. He ended up leaning away from his attacker just enough to avoid the pistol butt, which grazed the hairs on the back of his neck as it went whistling past.

Meanwhile, Lubov's missed swing pulled him to his left, toppling him toward Karen's position in the rolling armchair. Before she had time to do more than shout her warning to Nat, Lubov was on top of her again, pressing down on her back.

She sat there for a stunned moment, with all Lubov's weight squashing her torso onto the metal flange and across the keyboard she'd be using to try to halt the shutdown in its tracks—*if* she got the chance. Then she gathered her own strength and pushed up with all her might, which forced Lubov back upright.

He was left standing unsteadily with his back to Nat, who promptly forgot about his injured arm and tried to take a swing with it. Searing, white-hot pain immediately stabbed into his shoulder, which forced him to try an alternate plan of attack.

Reaching out with his good right hand, he gripped Lubov's throat and squeezed. Lubov's eyes bulged and gurgles rasped up out of his windpipe. Gritting his teeth, Nat squeezed harder.

Lubov countered by jabbing an elbow into Nat's sternum, which freed him from Nat's tenacious grip. He stepped away and turned, so he could deal face-to-face with his one-armed foe.

Nat gave him no time to regroup, lunging forward in a determined effort to regain his throat-grip. Unfortunately, his dead arm threw his balance off enough to make him miss. But his momentum carried him into his opponent's chest.

That contact sent Lubov staggering backward, away from Nat's grasp and toward the center of the room. He tried desperately to regain his balance, but his ravaged brain finally rebelled and sent him reeling to his left.

As everything before his eyes began sweeping to his right, he windmilled his arms in a heroic effort to stay vertical. But he was lost to the grip of his own ruinous momentum—a resistible force seeking its immovable object.

His gyrations twisted his torso so that when he landed, the back of his head hit flush on the floor. It split open like an overripe tomato, splattering dark, coagulated blood and grayish-pink brain tissue out around his head in a symmetrical corona.

His once-handsome face was left wide-eyed and openmouthed, staring straight up at the Death that had come to claim him—the top of his head not three feet from the blanket covering Marsh.

There was a grim, grisly irony in that because both men lay done in by different aspects of the same technological Hydra—a Hydra whose powerful heads were still grinding U.S. communication systems to a halt at mind-boggling speed.

Though both were dead, their god lived on.

A wheezing Nat Perkins understood that as he stood gazing at the spectacle on the floor beneath him. Then Karen was at his side, gasping in shock as she got her own view of the carnage.

"Oh, my God, Nat! You killed him!"

"He killed himself," Nat countered. "After killing Marsh . . . after trying to kill us. Whoever he was . . . whatever he was . . . I'm damn sure he had this coming. Now . . . let's get back to what we were doing . . . so what *he* tried to do won't happen."

Without another word or a backward glance, both resumed their desperate attempt to stop Marsh's falling dominoes.

☐ CXV ☐

For twenty minutes, the scene in the White House Situation Room had been one of controlled frenzy as the floor crew tried to set up a shortwave VLF patch to connect the President with the commanders of America's ballistic-missile submarines.

It was a desperate race for them against the fading images appearing on the Big Boards, images being drastically affected by the ever-increasing, ever-expanding shutdown. Meanwhile, the flurry of activity on the floor was being quietly offset by tense, hopeless, yet hopeful waiting in the command bubble.

It was hopeless in that all three men inside knew what the Soviets would do soon after the shutdown was complete. Yet they couldn't help remaining hopeful because the floor crew was making good headway connecting the shortwave patch.

Overlaying everyone's hopes, however, was the tension caused by knowing that the commanders of America's warhead-carrying submarines were under strict orders to ignore verbal commands of any kind, in all circumstances. Especially if someone claiming to be the President tried to convince them to launch their missiles.

Consequently, even if the patch was connected, Daniel Baxter knew he faced one hell of an uphill climb to convince his sub commanders that America was facing imminent destruction.

Suddenly, as the President and his two key advisers stood within their glass bubble, the Marine colonel in charge of the floor lifted his desk mike and turned to face them. He spoke without emotion, as if numbed by what he'd been trying to do.

"We have an unusual development, Mr. President. It may or may not be significant . . . but for the past few minutes nothing in the Situation Room has shut down. Since there's a good chance we were targeted as ground zero . . ."

His words trailed off into pregnant silence.

"What does that mean, son?" the President finally asked.

"Two possibilities, sir. Downside, it's just a pause in the operation sequence. Upside, the whole thing's over. But neither case changes our position. If the Russians plan to attack us—if that's what this shutdown is all about—then they know we've already lost most of our military-response capacity. And that's all they needed to eliminate before doing whatever they want."

"Not necessarily!" Gravelle rasped from where he and General Weatherspoon were standing, behind the President's back.

The President flicked his mike switch off, then turned to face his shrewd old friend. "What do you mean, Mike?"

"They don't necessarily know what went out first! It's not anywhere in the message, and there's no indication this thing was planned! It's just fallen into their laps, the same way it's fallen into ours; so they can't know the shutdown sequence!"

"He's right, sir!" the general added with honest enthusiasm. "This might be a chance to run to daylight!"

The President thought it over for a moment, then showed his skill at quickly arrowing to the heart of a problem. "But can we afford to hold off to see what happens? I mean, they could be pushing their buttons right now—this minute!"

"I think it's worth a call to make sure," Gravelle insisted.

"How?" the President shot back. "Everything here is dead!"

"What about upstairs?" Weatherspoon suggested. "If the shut-down *is* stopping, and if it hasn't taken out the private sector yet, maybe you can call Kolokov on the bathroom line."

Daniel Baxter realized that if he left the security of the Situation Room at this critical juncture, he'd be taking a personal risk of the highest magnitude. On the other hand, the fate of the whole world was clearly at stake.

Knowing he had no choice, the President grabbed his mike.

"Colonel, continue trying to connect that shortwave patch for me. But hold off activating it until I get back. I'm going upstairs to try to call Moscow."

"Yes, sir!" the colonel snapped. "But if you'd permit a question?" he added.

The President was already turning away, but the colonel's quietly urgent words stopped him in his tracks. He turned back around, toward every other desperate face out on the floor.

"What will that accomplish, sir?" the colonel asked.

"If I get through, it should tell me two things: how much they actually know about what's going on over here; and what they're thinking about doing with whatever it is they know."

"What if something happens while you're upstairs, sir?"

It was a good question, with implications that couldn't be ignored. "I'll send the Vice President to take my place. If I don't get back, he talks to the sub commanders. Understood?"

"Yes, sir!"

☐ CXVI ☐

Due to sequencing quirks in Marsh's shutdown program, many regular telephone lines in the D.C. area were still functioning. So the President had only a little trouble connecting with Soviet Premier Andrei Kolokov's private number, a line both leaders used about half as frequently as the strictly business Hot Line.

That "bathroom" line was a connection known and utilized only by only those with the highest levels of access in each government. It was used when the President and Premier wanted or needed to talk to each other man-to-man, without translators or advisers, or any other hindrance to nonpolitical discussion.

"I'm sorry to disturb you like this, Andrei," the President began. "I know it's the middle of the night over there."

"I've already been disturbed tonight," Kolokov answered, in the excellent English he'd learned as a spy during World War II. "Yuri Medveyev tells me you wouldn't take his calls."

Shit! Baxter thought. *I blew it!*

Kolokov's last statement told the President everything he needed to know about the situation in Moscow. It meant the Soviets couldn't possibly have received the message, or Medveyev wouldn't have been the one calling. And Kolokov's tone would have been a far cry from the polite caution he'd expressed so far. Which meant the *Potkin*'s sail transmitter must have been disabled by flying rubble from the torpedo blasts.

It also meant the President's job now was to avoid giving away any portion of the truth about what was actually happening. If Kolokov got even a hint of what that was, he might feel compelled to fire his own missiles—out of the same sense of paranoia driving the Americans to excuse trying to fire theirs.

"Medveyev also told me one of your ASW helicopters attacked one of our submarines without provocation," Kolokov went on. "He said you then dispatched rescue helicopters to aid our vessel and its seamen. Now, while I applaud the nobility of the second gesture . . . I can't help but wonder about the reason for the first —especially since it was so foolhardy."

The President noted Kolokov's subtle but clear change of tone and knew the game was under way.

The Soviet Premier was an old political war-horse in the same mold as his American counterpart. But instead of appearing much less than he actually was, like Baxter, Kolokov looked exactly like what he'd been as a young man—a butcher. He was thick-bodied, square-headed, and blunt-featured, but with exquisite intelligence and verbal skills.

Behind his back it was said he could talk a saint into Hell.

"As far as we can determine, Andrei, it was an unfortunate accident of training. That's why I'm calling you like this, to personally assure you it was in no way a premeditated or coordinated aggression by our forces. And I want to further assure you that whoever was responsible will pay dearly for it."

"I'm sorry, Daniel," Kolokov replied, his austere tone hardening even further, "but I must seriously doubt the assurances of a man who waits nearly an hour after the incident to call me about it, and then fails to mention that the submarine in question was in the act of relaying an emergency message."

The President couldn't help admiring how well Kolokov played his cards—especially aces like the fact that the *Potkin* had managed to get off some of its message before Scarlatti put a stop to it. Admiration aside, however, all he could think of to counter that deft ploy was a weak "What do you mean?"

"Don't play me for a fool, Daniel! You know precisely what I mean! You also know what I mean when I tell you my technicians are trying to determine what's happened to your communication systems. Many have malfunctioned, not the least of which is our supposedly invulnerable Hot Line. Yet while that line is down, you and I are talking on a standard overseas connection.

"Please excuse my skepticism, but I can't help thinking that somehow there's a link between the attack on the submarine sending the emergency message, and the disruption in your communication systems. Now, am I wrong in that assumption?"

Baxter had to hand it to the treacherous old bastard: He was a damn smooth operator. But not quite smooth enough.

"Sorry, Andrei—I have no indication they're related in any way. Matter of fact, I'll let you in on a little secret if you promise it'll go no further than this conversation."

There was a pause on Kolokov's end. "Proceed. . . ."

"The breakdown is part of a top-secret exercise we've been planning for a long time. In case any of your people ever got the idea we might be vulnerable to that kind of sabotage."

The eruption the President expected wasn't long in coming.

"You expect me to believe you severed the Hot Line connection as part of an *exercise*? An exercise we weren't told about in advance? What if we misread that signal? What if we thought it was part of a preemptive attack?"

The President couldn't help grinning as he countered that one. "That's why we left these lines open, Andrei. So if your people did panic"—he came down hard on the word *panic*— "you could call the bathroom number to straighten it out."

"Medveyev tried! Why wouldn't you take his calls?"

The President sensed the wind going out of his opponent's sails. "The sub flap came up unexpectedly, so I had to drop everything to handle it. Besides, I never dreamed your side would get so upset over some communication systems going down."

Furious but stalemated, Kolokov could only retreat behind bluster. "This is a reprehensible attitude, Daniel! One I'm shocked and disappointed to see you display! Not only that, I assure you I'll be going public with my misgivings about such unilateral exercises! You haven't heard the last of this!"

I'm sure I haven't—but not in the way you think!

Kolokov slammed his receiver onto its cradle and turned to face a trio of advisers standing just inside the periphery of his voice. Their worried eyes searched for clues to how the encounter had played out beyond what they could hear.

The Premier merely shrugged.

Thousands of miles and a near eternity away, President Daniel Baxter let out a whoop of sheer delight.

The crisis was past and he knew it.

All that was left was mopping up. . . .

And finding a way to make sure it would never happen again.

EPILOGUE

In the weeks and months that followed what came to be known as the *Potkin* Affair, significant events occurred in the lives of those who played primary roles in it. But the first order of official business was to clear up the electronic logjam that Marsh and Lubov had created throughout America's government and military communication systems.

Using Marsh's two programming tablets, and with Nat Perkins's skilled advice, a legion of government and military computer and communication specialists was able to repair the damage. But it required seventy-two of the most technically sophisticated hours any of them had ever imagined.

FBI agents Brandt and Doppler, whose overaggressive zeal initiated the chain reaction that created the *Potkin* Affair, suffered no adverse consequences as a result of their actions. And though they no longer work as a team, they and others like them continue similar escapades whenever it suits their purposes.

For her diligent efforts during the crisis, Lieutenant (Junior Grade) Hanna Buckley received a Distinguished Service Medal and a well-deserved promotion to lieutenant. She delivered an eight-pound girl three weeks after earning those accolades. Her husband was delighted on all counts.

Junior Quinlan received a Special Commendation Award, along with promotion in grade to a top-level posit. He and Ode Samples wound up becoming great friends, with the old code wizard taking the backwoods phenom under his wing to pass on as much of his arcane knowledge as the youngster could absorb.

The U.S. government kept a lid on what really happened to the

SSN *Mikhail Potkin* by sticking to the President's claim that it was nothing more than an unfortunate training accident. And once the *Potkin*'s sailors were returned home to tell the truth, Moscow chose to remain silent about it in order to keep its deep-cover program from being exposed to close media scrutiny.

Lieutenant Vito Scarlatti and his dead crew were officially tagged as the *Potkin* Affair's scapegoats. They were depicted as three drunk rowdies buzzing the Soviet sub for laughs, when a pair of their torpedoes accidentally released. Publicly, little was made of the incident beyond the usual liberal breast-beating.

Admiral Lucius Horton escaped all blame and got his seat at the Joint Chiefs' table in Washington, right on schedule. He nominated Admiral Vince Tarnaby as a potential Fleet Admiral, but Tarnaby was passed over on his first chance at it.

Captain Nikolai Barzlin recovered from his injuries, but he was officially censured by the Soviet Naval Presidium for failing to relay the message as soon as possible. He retired in disgrace and died within a year, reportedly by suicide.

On the other hand, Valeri Damovitch was highly lauded for his heroic efforts after the attack. He was rewarded with his promised promotion to command of the *Potkin* as soon as it was seaworthy again. One of his first acts as captain was to have Communication Chief Josef Popov transferred to another vessel.

Captain Jim Stickles received no medals, promotions, or commendations, as it was felt he came close to negligence in handling his role in the *Potkin* Affair. He was allowed to retain his command of the *Gremlin,* however, because of the unquestioned excellence of his abilities as an instructor.

Lieutenant Norton Vent's coolness under fire was praised by several of his shipmates, the most prominent of whom was Captain Stickles. He'll be taking command of a nuclear sub of his own, as soon as the last of his training requirements are fulfilled.

To avoid the notoriety that would have been generated by a court-martial, the Navy let Lieutenant Commander Ken LeBlanc off the hook by allowing him to quietly resign his commission. He's become a successful real-estate developer in South Carolina.

As Ivan Gretchko expected, the CIA took charge of the investigation of his death—as it did with the deaths of Marsh and Lubov.

Also as he expected, they covered up all evidence of his role as a long-term Soviet agent. His death was attributed to murder by an intruder, and his family is none the wiser.

For local press consumption, Marsh and Lubov were depicted as a homosexual couple who'd suffered an ultimate lover's quarrel. Their bodies were autopsied and then cremated as soon as the initial press report of their deaths had been released.

No one looked beyond the surface of that pat cover story.

Karen Glass became Mrs. Nat Perkins six months after the incident at the cabin. Because the CIA clamped such a tight security lid on the *Potkin* Affair, she was unable to print any kind of story about it. Despite that professional setback, she remains one of the Bay Area's best investigative journalists.

Nat's shoulder will never function as well as it did before his wounding, but he remains the country's top expert on antiphreaking techniques. However, because the King's death was such a serious blow to the Network, it won't be much longer before his work in that area is finished.

In addition to Nat's antiphreaking efforts, the breakup of Ma Bell into various regional entities has brought him to the fore as an independent contractor leasing his services to the government.

At Washington's request he's played a major role in building enough inefficiency into the new phone system to insure that danger-level phreaking—along with thoroughly reliable connections—will soon be a thing of the past.

You're probably already aware of the results of his efforts.